The Crimson Trap

The Volkov Illusion
Book 2

The Crimson Trap

The Volkov Illusion
Book 2

OPHELIA WREN

Trigger Warnings

- Blood, gore, and graphic violence
- Child sexual abuse (referenced in dialogue, described in detail with Damiano's past)
- Coercion & threats of sexual violence
- Domestic violence
- Drugging/forced drug use
- Human trafficking
- Kidnapping/Abduction
- Murder
- Physical restraint (handcuffs, gags, whips, etc.)
- Power imbalance/captivity dynamics
- Pregnancy threats
- Psychological abuse and degradation
- Sexual assault/Rape (multiple, graphic scenes)
- Threats of harm to loved ones
- Torture

Content Warning

This story explores dark and heavy themes, and it is darker in tone than the first book. While books can provide an escape into another world for a brief moment in time, your mental health always comes first. If you are struggling right now, this may not be the best book to pick up. Please take care of yourself—you matter.

Chapter

ONE

Rainey

Cristiano sits across from us, one ankle resting casually over the other knee. He looks irritated by her presence, which is rich, considering he's the one who abducted us.

"How is it that you managed to be here? The deal was for her." He flicks a finger in my direction.

Niki stares blankly at him. "Is that so? And what deal would that be?"

He shrugs. "Can't say I'm at liberty to share, but now that you're here… I just might sweeten the pot."

When his attention shifts to me, he takes his time scanning me from head to toe. Leaning forward, he reaches out, brushing my hair aside, exposing the tattoo on my neck.

"Cute," he mutters, voice flat as he lets his arm drop, sinking back like I'm no longer of interest.

Niki sighs. "So what now? You planning to kill us?"

I gape at her, trying to figure out why she's deliberately poking the bear. The family knew him once, years ago, but a lot has changed since then, and I can only imagine how much his hatred has festered. Either she's confident he won't pop us off right here, or she doesn't care if he does.

He lazily shrugs, then jerks his chin in my direction. "Her? Yes."

My stomach sinks. No flare of panic—just that cold, suffocating drop.

I'm going to die.

This psycho is going to kill me.

"You?" He looks at Niki. "I hadn't planned for, but I'll find ways to keep myself entertained."

"My brother is going to kill you."

His expression doesn't change. "Maybe. But I'd bet he wants her bad enough to hand himself over."

No, no, no. I'm going to be used as bait. I send up a silent prayer, hoping Dom can somehow hear that I'd rather die than see him trade his life for mine.

The distant sound of tires rolling over gravel has him glancing back as a sedan enters the warehouse. He claps his hands to his thighs, slides them down and back up, then rises, motioning to the men.

"Take them."

Two guards move in. One grabs Niki, the other hauls me up by the arm. We both struggle, but it doesn't matter. We're dragged to the waiting vehicle and shoved into the backseat. I press against the door as far as I can, while she leans into me, trying to keep space between herself and the man sliding in beside her. He rests a gun on his knee, barrel pointed at us, making it clear he won't tolerate any funny business.

I flinch when Niki rears back and kicks Cristiano's seat, calling him a bitch and a coward who has to drug people just to kidnap them. I don't know where to look. At her? At him? Or at the gun in the man's hand? The barrel is pointed at me, and if it goes off, whether by accident or on purpose, I'll be the recipient of the bullet.

Cristiano turns in his seat, saying nothing, though the message is received. The guard grabs Niki's face. She tries to jerk away, but he forces the gag back into her mouth. When he turns to me, I don't bother fighting. He's rough anyway, stuffing the cloth between my teeth intentionally making it hurt.

When we begin to move, I try to catch a glimpse of anything that might tell me where we are. Nothing is familiar. It was still light when we walked into the boutique. Now it's dark outside, and I have no idea how long I was out.

Damiano has to know I'm gone. He has to be searching for me by now.

Out of my periphery, I see the man's hand move to Niki's thigh. She jerks her leg, trying to shake him off, and his lips curl into a sinister grin. He slides higher under her dress, and she starts thrashing, screaming into the gag, fighting against his touch.

Not a chance.

Now it's my turn to do something reckless. My hands are useless, cuffed behind my back, but my foot to his face will hurt, or at least I hope it will. I drive my heel into his jaw as hard as I can, knocking his head into the window.

Shock flashes across his features before it twists into rage. He roars as his fist collides with my temple.

Agony explodes from the point of impact, radiating outward.

The last thing I hear is Niki's muffled scream before everything fades to black.

Consciousness returns slowly, pulling me up from the dark. My head is throbbing, confirming I really was kidnapped, and I was most definitely punched in the face. I test my jaw, parting my teeth while keeping my lips closed. The gag is gone.

Carefully, I shift, expecting to bump into a car door or Niki's body. Instead, I'm lying flat on something soft. My fingers twitch, stiff but free. I'm no longer handcuffed either. I splay them out, brushing against fabric that sinks under the slightest pressure.

I'm on a couch. This is definitely a couch.

I blink my eyes open, vision slowly sharpening as I take in my surroundings. It's a large living room with ceilings so high I can't see where they end without moving my head. How would you even change a lightbulb up there?

Everything about the room feels curated. Not a single thing is out of place. It's so spotless that even dust seems too afraid to settle.

I doubt this is even his primary residence. Dom hasn't been able to find him for all these years, and I'd bet we're still within a couple of hours radius of him.

I blink a few more times, hoping this is all just some awful dream. Maybe Damiano has already found me. Maybe I'm still dreaming and I'm about to wake up to him sitting in front of me, smiling. But as I take in the room, nothing about this place is familiar. Even the air feels suffocating. Every part of me is on high alert, and my spidey senses tell me I'm definitely in danger.

A piercing screech echoes through the house, and it takes me a second to register that I know the person that voice belongs to. It's my best friend. It's Niki.

My pulse spikes as I scramble to my feet. I stand too fast and sway, trying to regain my balance, but I don't make it far. I grab the arm of the couch to steady myself as my head spins.

I'm ready to move in the direction of the screams but freeze when I see Cristiano is already standing in the doorway, hands buried in his pockets like he's been waiting.

"She's a little upset." His voice is unnervingly calm. "She didn't like our conversation. But she can sleep it off."

Any chance of hiding my fear vanishes with the heavy, shallow rhythm of my chest rising and falling.

"Is she hurt?"

He tilts his head side to side. "I don't believe so. She's always been quite... dramatic."

"*She's* dramatic? You don't think what *you* did was incredibly dramatic."

He remains impassive, like I'm not worth a response.

"Where is she being taken?"

He straightens with a sigh. "To her own room. A guard will be stationed outside the door. Don't worry, she'll be alone." He nods toward the hallway. "Come."

I don't move, looking from him to the spot he indicated, then back. "Where?"

I'm well aware I don't have a choice. I'll be going wherever he wants me to. But I cling to the naïve hope that stalling might give me time to come up with a plan and find a way out of here. Of course, it could just as easily backfire and piss him off, which is the last thing I need.

"We're going to have dinner."

By the serious expression on his face, he's not joking. I couldn't eat even if I wanted to. I don't believe a word he says, so claiming she's alone and insinuating that she's not being harmed doesn't mean anything.

"How do I know she's safe?"

"You don't."

We stare at each other, and I chew on the inside of my cheek. He straightens, pulls his phone from his pocket, messes with it for a moment, then turns the screen toward me. It shows Niki in a massive bedroom, lying on the bed. She's curled in on herself, and I can't tell if she's asleep, but then she stretches a foot out and I realize she is. There's a tray of food next to the bed, and from what I can barely see, she didn't touch it.

He locks the screen and tucks it away. "Let's go." Then turns and walks out through the back patio door.

I scan the room again. There's a guard at every exit, each one watching me like a hawk. Any attempt to run would be shut down instantly by someone armed and ready to beat the shit out of me. With a sigh, I follow.

A table is already set for two, a chair pulled out as he waits. He watches me, expecting me to move, and when I don't, he gestures toward it.

Is this where I'm ambushed?

He follows each step I take, and my pace slows the closer I get. I stop a few feet away, gaze shifting from him to the chair.

"You will sit," he says calmly. "It's just a question of whether you do it willingly… or with my help."

I grit my teeth, glaring at him, then move wide so I don't touch him—not even a little. I lower myself into the seat, making myself as small as possible, not even wanting his aura to touch me.

He sits on the opposite side, unfolding a napkin and placing it over his lap. It's quite impressive how nonchalant he is about everything, knowing the woman at the table with him is someone being held against her will.

I remain as still as possible. Maybe he's actually really stupid and will forget I'm out here with him.

He leans back in his chair, brows lifting slightly as he draws in a breath and slowly exhales.

A man and woman arrive quietly. He fills our glasses with wine, and she places dinner plates on the table.

I take in the food and want to barf. Fish, seasoned with what looks like dirt, and vegetables pushed off to the side.

I'm hungry, but not *that* hungry, and I certainly don't want to eat anything he's providing.

The servers vanish as quickly as they came. I watch, willing them to acknowledge me so I can try to tell them with my eyes that I need help. But neither of them does.

He takes a bite, chews, wipes his mouth, then sips his wine as he gazes at my untouched plate. "Something wrong with the meal?"

I say nothing.

"Eat." He gestures to my plate with his fork, then takes another bite.

I keep staring at him, trying to figure out why I'm here, why he's eating dinner with me. I would think, out of me and Niki, he would want to have dinner with her. They know each other. Maybe she could calm him down and get him to think this over instead of just offing me. This feels an awful lot like a predator playing with its prey. He's toying with me, and I don't like it.

"Are you not hungry?"

"I don't want anything from you."

He lifts his brows, waiting for me to elaborate, but I stay silent.

"You refusing to eat when there's food in front of you is only hurting yourself."

"Why would you care whether I eat or not?"

"I don't." He stabs another bite. "But I don't appreciate you wasting a meal that was prepared for you."

While chewing, he studies me closely, then lets out a low scoff. "You think it's poisoned?"

"I don't really care if it is. I'd probably prefer that over the alternative..."

"And what's the alternative?"

"I don't know. Why don't you tell me? I'm assuming you plan to torture me." I keep my tone steady, trying to seem unbothered, though I'm scared shitless and hoping he'll tell me I'm wrong.

"You're probably right. But I'm not going to do it with poisoned food. I just wanted to make sure you had energy."

Silence stretches between us. I don't know where to begin processing the ways he plans to hurt me. I dread the thought of him mutilating my body and sending it to Damiano. My heart aches at the thought.

I turn my attention to the massive pool across the manicured lawn. He doesn't strike me as someone who would step foot in a swimming pool, so why have one at all? Especially one that size. I'd bet nobody has ever used it. It's probably just here for the aesthetic appeal.

He finishes eating, sets his napkin on the table, and leans back. I can feel his gaze on me, and I want to flip him off. Now isn't the time to dig myself into a deeper hole than I'm already in. The longer he focuses on me, the more my patience wears thin.

My eyes start to sting and dry out from how long I've gone without blinking. I force a few slow blinks, trying to look casual, though I'm sure he sees the twitch under my eye and the way it starts to well up from the strain. So much for looking unbothered.

He follows my line of sight, then returns to me. "Would you like to go swimming?"

"Is that how you plan to kill me?" I face him with all the emotion of a brick wall, unimpressed and done.

"Is that how you'd like me to kill you?"

I scoff. "I get a choice? Wow."

Don't roll your eyes... don't roll your eyes.

"Do you know how to swim?"

I want to laugh at the question, because the truth is both sad and reminds me that I'm sitting here from the domino effect of my worthless mother. The only reason I know how to swim is because I used to sneak into the local rec center for the pool and use their showers whenever our water got shut off. I was too young to get a job, too broke to do anything else. But am I about to tell the enemy any of that? Hell no. I want him to believe I can't swim so when he inevitably tries to drown me or pull something, I'll be the one dragging his ass under instead.

"No," I lie.

The wheels in his brain turn. He doesn't know shit about me, so he has to take my word for it, though it's obvious he's questioning the validity of my answer.

"Are you planning on wasting your dinner?"

"I just want to go to bed."

He inhales, annoyed. "As you wish." His palm turns up, fingers curling in a silent summon as he beckons someone over, then looks at me again. "Come."

Chapter

TWO

Rainey

He leads me through the house in silence. I try to track every hallway and opening, making mental notes of which ones have guards posted nearby. But it's no use. He has men everywhere.

We walk down a long corridor until he stops, pushes open a door, and gestures for me to go in. I pause, watching him for a moment before edging past, keeping as much distance between us as possible. I expect a cold, empty cell, but it's not.

The bedroom is something out of a magazine, like the Volkovs', except Cristiano's taste isn't to my liking. Actually, out of all the Volkov bedrooms, Damiano's is my favorite. His taste is exactly mine.

In here, a bed sits to the left, while dark furniture is dotted around the rest of the space. This room is so large, it makes even the bed look small.

I stop in the center of the room, scanning for anything that could double as a weapon or hint at a way out. The options are endless. This place is filled with things I could use to fight. The door shuts behind me, and I assume he's gone. But when I turn around, he's standing there, watching... from *this side* of the closed door.

"What?"

He shrugs. "I didn't say anything."

"Then why are you still here?"

He already showed me that Niki's alone in her room with a guard posted outside. If he plans to linger in here, I'll immediately promise to be good just to get him to leave faster.

"You'll be staying here… with me."

I blink, thrown off. "Why? You don't have an extra bedroom?"

Niki has her own room. Why would I have to share? I nearly laugh. In a house this size, there's no shortage of empty rooms.

He steps closer, eyes fixed on mine. "Because Damiano Volkov took what was mine. So now I'll take what's his."

He moves to the buttons of his shirt.

It takes a second for his words to sink in. I stand frozen, watching his hands move slowly, one button at a time. Panic begins to rise in my chest. Of all the scenarios I imagined when being kidnapped, why did this one never cross my mind? I never even entertained the idea that I'd have to worry about… *this*.

It's been well known how much Damiano and Cristiano hate each other, so I assumed he'd be just as repulsed by me. That he wouldn't want to be anywhere near me, let alone touch me. Torture? Sure. I fully expect him to drag that out until I'm dead. But arousal? From Damiano's girlfriend? No. I should make his skin crawl. I should make him sick.

He undresses without breaking eye contact until he's fully naked… and very much ready.

He steps toward me, and my entire body locks up. I should run. I think I'd prefer to get shot than for him to touch me.

I glance at the door, trying to see if it's locked from the inside. Maybe he didn't lock it.

"I deal in drugs," he says calmly. "If you try anything, I'll have a needle in your arm before you can blink."

I don't doubt him. Not for a second.

"Remove your clothes or I will."

My eyes sting. I don't want to do this again. I am so tired of men forcing me into sex. Every first time I've ever had has been taken. And now it's happening again. Another moment I'll never be able to forget. Only this is worse. It's Damiano's enemy. The man he hates more than anything. I don't want to hurt Dom like that. He would never touch me again if he knew Cristiano put his dick inside me. That thought alone has bile rising in my throat.

"No," I whisper, shaking my head. "Please don't do this." My voice wavers.

His expression doesn't shift. "You can drag this out, but it ends the same way no matter what scenario you play out in your head."

"Please." A tear slides down my cheek.

He walks around me to the nightstand. I don't lift my head. My breath catches when I hear him return, only this time, he steps close enough I feel his body heat on my back.

A blade slips beneath the strap of my dress, cutting clean through. The other one follows. The fabric slides down my body and lands at my feet. He moves in even closer as his chest presses into my back, and I can feel his exhale on my shoulder. I squeeze my eyes closed and when he pulls my underwear out, I look down just in time to watch the blade glide through the material there too.

I stand there, exposed, my arms wrapped tightly around my-self. I've never felt so naked in my life. I feel like he's stripped even my skin away, and my soul is laid bare.

He moves around me like a shark, inhaling through his teeth as he takes me in.

"Drop your hands."

I stay frozen.

He moves in until there's no space left between us, his erec-tion firm against my butt. His fingers slide down, locking around my wrists. The touch is careful—too careful for what his inten-tions are.

As he tries to pull my arms from my chest, I tense, locking them in place.

"You're going to make this worse." His grip tightens just enough to force them down. I resist, but it's no use.

He circles back in front of me, eyes dragging over every inch. It's obvious he likes what he sees, and it pisses me off. He's ogling someone else's girlfriend. He literally cut the clothes off of another man's girlfriend.

When he reaches for me, I squeeze my eyes shut.

Just being watched by him felt gross—but that's nothing com-pared to the way it feels when his thumb grazes my nipple.

Silent tears slip down my cheeks.

"Get on the bed."

I don't move. My entire body shakes. Breathing feels impossi-ble. *I can't let this happen.*

He repeats the command, more firmly this time, and all I can do is open my eyes and look up at him.

He takes a step forward.

I step back.

Each time he advances, I retreat, until I hit the edge of the bed. There's nowhere else to go.

"Can we… can we get under the blankets?"

He nods once. "Yes."

I turn, reaching for the covers. As I climb onto the mattress, I glance over my shoulder. He's staring at my ass, completely distracted.

I make my move.

I donkey kick as hard as I can, my heel slamming into his jaw. He stumbles back, clutching his face in shock, and I scramble across the bed to get away.

He lets out an angry grunt and lunges for me but misses.

I tumble off the far side, hit the floor hard, and run to the other side of the room. My chest heaves with adrenaline as I spin back, expecting him to be right behind me.

He's not.

He stands near the bed, wiping the back of his hand across his mouth. Blood smears across his skin. I guess my kick was really spot on, because I made the fucker bleed.

His eyes lift to mine, blank and cold.

Then he moves, coming toward me, and I bolt for the door. It feels like being a kid playing tag, racing for base, that brief moment when you're almost safe. I'm right there, just about to reach it.

A sudden, slicing pain wraps around my ankle, yanking me backward. I crash to the floor, my body twisting as I scream. When I turn my head, I see he used a whip, coiled around my leg like a lasso. It's excruciating, but there's no time to process it.

He's already over me, dropping to his knees, grabbing my legs. He tears them apart as I attempt to fight him off.

"No!"

I thrash, kicking and scratching, but it only enrages him.

His hand cracks across my face. The pain is instant and blinding. My vision blurs, and before I can recover, my wrists are pinned above my head, his body wedging between my thighs as he lines his penis up, then forces himself inside me.

He lets out a pleasured groan at the same time I wail out Damiano's name, wishing somehow he could hear me, find me, and make this stop. The violation is unbearable, each sharp, unwanted stretch tearing through me. My body wasn't prepared for him, and every thrust drives a fresh wave of pain.

I fight. Every second. I push against him with everything I have, but it only fuels him. He becomes rougher.

He sits up on his knees, gripping my hips so hard it feels like he's going to pull the flesh from my bones. He leans back and slams into me repeatedly, so violently a cry is ripped out of me.

Even as I try to push my feet against the floor, just to gain leverage while pressing on his chest, he doesn't stop. He's too strong. He spears me on his cock so many times and so forcefully I feel like I can't breathe.

Scratch that. His hand closes around my neck. *Now* I can't breathe. I claw at his arms, dragging my nails across his skin, writhing beneath him in a desperate attempt to escape.

I viciously try kicking him off. He slips his arm under one knee, hikes my ankle onto his shoulder, then collapses his weight back over me, driving in even deeper. The pain is blinding, but I can't cry out—his hold around my throat strangles every sound.

My limbs go heavy. Darkness crawls in, closing around my sight.

I'm still trying to hold on when my body decides it's done.

A rough thrust jars me fully to consciousness. His body slumps on top of mine, nose pressing into the crook of my neck as he continues moving, and with the last bit of strength I can summon, I grab a fistful of his hair and yank hard. He growls and grabs mine in return, pulling until my scalp burns.

He groans something I can't understand. I don't want to know what he's saying. I don't want to hear anything from him, because he sounds like he's having the time of his life, each moan confirming how much he's enjoying this.

He presses in as deep as he can and begins to pump again, shallow and fast. It's so painful I feel like I might puke.

When his body stiffens, I know he's finishing. I can feel his release and want to vomit just knowing he's leaving his nasty semen inside me. I dig my heels into the floor and try to push away.

What I get is a fist to my stomach, so hard my head lifts off the floor and my mouth hangs open, all the air knocked from my lungs. When I'm finally able to suck in a breath, a sob slips out and my body aches everywhere.

He relaxes, his body going limp on top of mine, and he lets out a long, contented sigh, just lying there. Every once in a while, his body jerks, and I wonder how much semen he's putting in me. When was the last time he got laid? This orgasm feels like it's going on forever.

He sits up, watching as he slowly drags his cock out, then stares between my legs. He doesn't say anything; just looks. Then, as if snapping himself out of a trance, he stands and walks away.

I stay where I am, broken and shaking, curled in on myself.

The shower turns on, and I hate that he's getting clean while I have his nasty shit seeping out of me.

My tears streak to the bridge of my nose, pooling there before dripping to the floor. One after another. All I want is Damiano. I want to go home. I want to hold him.

I picture him lying next to me, eyes soft and full of love, leaning in to kiss me. I keep my eyes shut, wishing that's what I'll see when I open them.

When footsteps approach, I don't move. I can't. My body aches in places I didn't know could hurt, mostly my heart.

He stands over me. "Get on the bed."

I want to tell him to fuck off, but I'm sure I'd end up with another fist to my gut, and that didn't feel good at all. "Can I shower?"

"No."

"Your disgusting sperm is leaking out of me."

"We're going to add to it eventually."

Those words make me so mad. He assaulted me. He screwed Damiano's girlfriend. He fucked my life up. He fucked my relationship and future up. He succeeded. *Congratulations.* Why would he need to do it again? It only took one time to destroy everything. He hates Damiano. Why would he intentionally fuck me again?

"Get on the bed."

No. Because fuck him.

He nudges me with his foot. When I still don't move, he does it again, harder this time. I snap, swinging my fist and striking his leg.

Big mistake.

His kick lands fast and hard, connecting with my mouth and nose. Pain erupts instantly. I gasp and turn my face to the floor as blood pours from my nose, running past my lips and dripping onto the ground.

Rough hands clamp around my arms, yanking me to my feet and dragging me across the room. I stumble alongside him, my legs barely keeping me upright. In the bathroom, he lowers me onto the edge of the tub, then turns and starts rummaging through nearby cabinets. I keep my eyes on the floor, watching as blood continues to trickle in thin, dark lines down my chest and legs.

With a cold pack, gauze pads, and a sealed bottle of antiseptic, he returns and kneels beside me. After activating the pack, he presses it to the bridge of my nose. I flinch but don't pull away.

"Lean your head forward."

I obey, letting it drain freely as he hands me a thick wad of gauze to hold under my nose.

He grabs a cloth and wets it under the tub faucet. Kneeling in front of me, he wipes my mouth and chin, then moves to my chest, working his way down to my thighs, where streaks of red are still sliding across my skin.

He says nothing, and I just sit there, empty, letting him clean the mess he made.

Once the bleeding stops, he tells me to stand. I do it without thinking. When he gestures for me to follow, I go.

I lick my lip, feeling how swollen it is, and wonder how bad I must look. I probably don't even want to know the full extent of the damage he's caused.

He points to the far side of the bed, then begins untucking his side. "Lie down."

I walk around to where he indicated, pull back the blankets, and climb in, staying on the very edge.

The mattress shifts as he settles beside me, and the room goes dark when he flicks his lamp off.

Chapter

THREE

Damiano

The man tied to the metal chair is barely conscious. His head lolls forward, blood dripping from his chin and pooling in his lap. One of his eyes is swollen shut, the other fixed on me with the dull sheen of a man who thought he was untouchable. Until now.

"Tell me her name," I growl, gripping the handle of the blowtorch as I inch it closer to the exposed skin of his thigh. His pants were cut away an hour ago, and I've already seared through parts of his legs and chest.

He groans, shaking his head. "I don't know. I don't—I swear to God—"

I click the torch on, letting the fire roar just inches from his skin. "Wrong answer."

"Please," he whimpers. "I'm just the contact. I just move the girls, I don't pick 'em. I didn't know she was fifteen."

"You followed her from her high school. You followed her when her mom drove her to softball practice, and you followed them back home when her dad picked her up. How do you not know she's underage?"

People like him irritate me. He actually thinks his lies are believable, that I'll just nod along and accept the story that he thought she was of age. He took videos of her. She looked fifteen. Not like Rainey, who looks younger than she is but still passes for legal. This girl looked like a child. Undeniably.

"She was screwing a nineteen-year-old."

"And? Do you believe you're in her age range? That if you were, it would make your actions justifiable?"

He shakes his head. "No."

"Do you think a bunch of shriveled-up, sixty-year-old drug addicts having sex with her was equivalent to her willingly sleeping with her boyfriend?"

More sobs.

"She's dead because of you. Her family wants to bury their child, and you can't even give them that. You can't even produce a body for them to bury. Tell me how you disposed of her remains."

He sobs harder, curling in on himself.

I run the torch along the side of his abdomen, the heat searing his flesh. Skin bubbles and blisters almost instantly, then splits open in jagged lines. Fat glistens beneath the surface, yellow and sizzling.

The smell of scorched flesh doesn't bother me. I keep the door sealed tight when I'm using fire. The others can't handle it. They'd be puking their guts out if they could smell what I'm breathing in right now.

When I shut the torch off, he's still screaming. Strings of spit stretch from his clenched teeth to his trembling lips and drip down his chest. His entire body quivers from the pain, but this is nothing compared to what that girl endured at the hands of this sick bastard.

"How did you dispose of her body?"

He's unable to form words.

"Are there remains I can uncover?"

More hysterics, followed by a slow shake of his head.

"How did you dispose of her body?" I repeat.

His shoulders tremble as he weeps. I flip the torch back on. The hiss of gas igniting pulls his head up. His eye widens as much as the swelling will allow.

"Vital organs were sold," he finally chokes out, "and I cut what was left into pieces. Fed it to wild boars."

I inhale slowly and exhale even slower. "Stupid."

I turn the torch on him again. I'm going to burn every inch of flesh off his body.

I glance over my shoulder at the banging on the wall. I flick off the blowtorch when I see Marko standing there, eyes wide, panic written all over his face, his phone pressed against the glass.

I'm out the door in seconds, sprinting across the basement to the stairs. I take them three at a time, flying through the library and down hallway after hallway until I reach the main living room. My brothers are already there, strung tight and radiating panic.

"Track the fucking phone!" Dante bellows, his voice raw.

When I enter, every face turns toward me.

My chest constricts.

Dante's hand drops to his side as he stares at me, pain etched into his features.

"Is she still alive?"

"I believe so," he answers.

"Cristiano?" I grind out.

Dante covers his mouth, his jaw clenched tight. After a beat, he gives a slow nod.

"Taken from here?"

"No," Gio says. "She went to pick something up for Ma. She was ambushed."

"How long ago?"

I didn't realize how much time had passed since I went into the basement. Rainey usually comes to get me when she's ready to go home. It's 8 a.m., and somehow it feels like only an hour has slipped by. I hadn't even registered that she never came for me.

Dante ends a call and looks at me like he's carrying my rage in his own chest.

"We're going to get her back, Dom. If it's the last thing I do, I'll get her back."

"Where was she?"

"In the city, picking up Ma's dress," Gio answers.

"How was she picking up Ma's dress? YOU said she can't leave the property. Who authorized that?" I bellow at Dante.

"I didn't know, Dom. I wouldn't have ever let her leave."

"My girlfriend is in the hands of Cristiano! Let that sink in!" I smack my palms against my head, then throw my arms wide in disbelief.

I can feel my anger rising fast. My fingers twitch, then curl into fists. This is rage like I've never felt. It's so intense and demanding to be let out. I force in a breath and let it out slowly, staying still, because I know the second I let it slip, there won't be any coming back. If I explode, it will be a detonation no one has ever seen before.

"We are, Dom. We know how bad this is. We're doing everything we can," Gio says sympathetically.

I rub my hands up and down the scruff on my face. I know the kind of vermin he is. I know the things he's going to do to my sweet, innocent, perfect girl. She's strong, she will survive, but mentally, knowing he's assaulting her… No. I can't think like that. I won't break down. I won't fail her.

Andrei has his laptop open on the kitchen counter, fast-forwarding through security footage. When the feed stops, he waves us over. I stand directly behind him, leaning in to watch. It's from the boutique.

"Fuuuuck," Nikolai mutters when the video shows not just Rainey, but Niki walking in first. "She said she wasn't coming home until next week."

We lean in closer as the girls head to the back. The camera angle changes. Four men are already waiting. Rainey walks in first, and as she turns, one of the men is already lowering Niki to the floor. Then a man steps up behind her, pushing a needle into her neck. She freezes for a second, face contorting with horror, before collapsing. The man lifts her easily, draping her over his shoulder and slapping her butt while smiling at the others.

Both girls are carried outside to a waiting van with the doors already pulled wide open. They're laid just inside, hands cuffed in front. A gag is shoved into each of their mouths, followed by a burlap sack pulled down over their heads. Then they're dragged deeper into the van, the doors slammed shut behind them, and the vehicle pulls away.

I hate Cristiano. I've imagined every possible way I'll torture him when I finally get to him.

But the man who took her, the one who spanked her butt and kidnapped her, dragging her away from me, I hate him more. I didn't think that was possible, but it is. And when I find him, I'll make him wish he'd never been born.

Andrei tracks the van across the city, jumping between security feeds. It weaves through streets, slipping past cameras, until it finally pulls into the same warehouse where we were ambushed. Then nothing. Hours pass and nothing happens.

Eventually, an SUV arrives. Ten minutes later, it pulls away.

Cristiano isn't stupid. He knows how to disappear. The SUV enters a parking garage, and minutes later, seven identical vehicles exit, each one scattering in a different direction.

We track them all. Every single one leads to nothing. Each trail ends in silence.

Andrei rewinds the footage, replays it, freezes the screen each time a car exits, searching for a clue we missed.

More hours pass.

We still don't know which car she was in. We're still no closer to finding her.

Ma strides in with urgency, her face filled with worry. She scans my brothers before locking onto me, and the second she does, her expression twists with pain. She walks straight toward me, reaching out.

I don't move. My arms stay crossed over my chest. I don't like being touched. Not by anyone except Rainey.

Someone must have told her already, but we just found out. How could she possibly know Niki was taken too?

She hugs me tight, then pulls back and grips my biceps, staring up at me.

"I'm so sorry, my boy. Anything you need, just let us know. We'll help you through your loss the best we can."

I'm trying to figure out how she's staying so calm. Then it hits me. She doesn't know Niki has been taken. She thinks it was only Rainey.

"I'll get her back."

She slowly shakes her head. "It's probably already too late, sweetheart. You know who he is." Her eyes become glassy as she looks at me with sympathy.

"You're saying you don't want us to go after her?"

"You can't. It would be a death sentence for you too."

"She's my girlfriend."

Her lips press into a thin line, and her eyebrows draw together. "I know, son. And that's exactly why he will punish her for the past."

She's not wrong. Rainey will bear the retaliation for my actions. But Rainey isn't sick like Carmella. Rainey would never hurt a child. Carmella deserved what happened to her.

Nobody stopped her, so I had to. I had no choice once she dragged Dante into her sickness. His life was in danger because she was pregnant with his child. That baby would have looked like a Volkov. Dante would have been killed for getting her pregnant.

But the truth behind that pregnancy never would have come out. The baby would have been murdered the second it was born and someone pieced together who the father was.

"I wasn't asking for your permission. I was telling you what we're doing."

"You don't get to do whatever you want! I'm calling Papa. He'll be heading home. You won't be leaving this property. None of you will." Her tone rises as she scans the room, daring anyone to challenge her.

"We're going after her," Dante says.

"No! We can't risk this family. Damiano, son, I know how much she means to you, but she's likely already dead. I know that's harsh. I know it's not what you want to hear, but it's the truth."

I scoff and move to step around her.

"No," she shouts, grabbing my arm.

I bristle at her touch. "Remove your hand."

She lets go immediately. She knows this tone. She knows it never ends well for whoever I'm talking to.

"Maybe she's not dead." She backpedals. "Maybe we just need to wait. Let him reach out. Let him tell us what he wants." She opens her palms in a show of false reassurance.

"We're going after her," Dante repeats.

Her posture stiffens, lips curling with disdain. "I'm sure he's railing her. She seems to have a magical pussy."

The room goes completely still. My jaw clenches so tight I can feel the pressure in my molars. Why she needed to add that is lost on me.

"I forbid you to leave this house!"

My brothers shift uncomfortably, glancing around stuck in the middle of a standoff.

"Fine," I concede calmly.

Dante gapes at me like he can't believe what he's hearing.

I lock eyes with her. "Let's just hope Niki has the same magical pussy."

Her chin jerks back. "Leave your sister out of this!"

"Niki came home a week early. She was with Rainey. He has them both."

Her gaze bounces from me to Dante, then to Andrei. He turns his laptop toward her and hits play. On screen, Niki is shoved into the same van, her body just as motionless as Rainey's.

All the color drains from Ma's face.

"Let me know when the first body parts show up. And whether it's Rainey's or Niki's."

Her sobs erupt behind me as I walk off. Nikolai stays to comfort her while the others follow me to the meeting room.

"He's going to send something," Silvano says, pacing. "A video or a photo. Some kind of taunt."

"He's going to want to trade her for you," Gio adds.

"I'm not trading anything with him. I'm going to take back what's mine."

Chapter

FOUR

Rainey

I wake to hands on me. Groggy and dazed, I barely have time to process what's happening before he's gripping my hip, pulling me back against him as he presses into me from behind.

My eyes shoot open. "Stop!" I struggle, desperately reaching for the edge of the mattress to scoot away. When that doesn't work and he only yanks me closer, I dig my nails into his hands, trying to tear his skin apart.

All it does is make him angry. He shoves me onto my stomach and climbs over me, straddling my legs, pushing down on my back as he thrusts into me again. I try to yell, but every time I make a sound, he slaps the side of my face hard while the other tightens painfully in my hair.

A broken sob escapes. The deeper he goes, the more unbearable it becomes.

When his hold finally loosens, I think it's over. Instead, he lifts me enough to shove a pillow beneath me, forcing my butt higher. The new angle lets him slam in even harder and a choked cry escapes.

My body protests violently, every nerve raw and burning. My face is swollen from the repeated slaps, right over the same spot he kicked last night, the same area already bruised and tender. Now he's adding to the damage.

He's cruel. So unbelievably cruel.

When he starts groaning, muttering that I'm wet just for him and calling me his dirty whore, I lash out, swinging my fist back in a desperate attempt to get him to shut up.

He shifts, forcing my legs apart as he settles back on his heels. Grabbing my waist, he drags me onto him. My thighs stretch wide around his lap as he sinks back in. I claw at the bedding, trying to pull away, but he keeps a firm hold and pistons his hips into me with ruthless rhythm.

The scream that bursts from my throat doesn't sound human. I don't even believe it came from me. But it drives him on, his palm landing over and over against my skin until his fingers hook into my cheek and pull, splitting the corner of my dry lip.

He doesn't stop until he's releasing inside me. And when he stills, I don't move. I don't dare. Not when he's holding me like a fish on a hook. Not when I know what he's capable of. He could easily rip the side of my mouth straight up my face.

As soon as it's done, he withdraws and gets up, heading for the bathroom. The shower starts almost immediately.

I remain folded over the pillow, staring straight ahead at the crumpled bedding, numb, as if I'm no longer part of this body.

When I finally roll onto my side, everything aches. The disgusting wetness seeps out, and the urge to vomit climbs higher. I stay facing the bathroom door, needing to see when he returns. A cramp twists through my stomach, sharp enough to make me sick, and my body trembles.

My mind drifts to Damiano. Surely he knows I'm gone by now. Is he as upset as I am? He knows what kind of man Cristiano is. He must know what's happening to me.

I flatten my palm against the sheets, wishing I could touch his skin. Just once. One last time. Even if it's only to say goodbye.

A single tear escapes, sliding down and soaking into the bedding. Another quickly follows.

Moments later, the bathroom door opens and light spills into the darkened room. He strides toward the bed with a towel wrapped around his waist and something draped over his arm. He doesn't even look at me as he tosses the garment onto the mattress.

"Get dressed," he says flatly, turning away and disappearing into the closet.

It takes everything I have just to sit up. My limbs are heavy, like I'm wading through water. I brush at my face, trying to clear the tears, but wince from the injuries.

When I dab at the corner of my mouth, something wet clings to my skin. I pull back and stare at the blood.

I rub it between my fingers before reaching for the dress. Using the soft fabric, I wipe my hand clean, watching crimson stain the pale pink material. I lift it to my lip and blot gently. Another bloom of red spreads through the delicate threads. I have no business wearing something so pretty when I'm in the state I'm in. But I put it on anyway.

It's thin and exposing, and I want to take it off immediately, but I'm sure that would only end in me being assaulted again.

I take in the stained sheets and the blood-marked pillow. Despite the sting, I lower myself onto the edge of the bed, gripping my knees and fidgeting in place, as if the movement might distract me from the ache radiating through my body.

When he reappears, he's dressed in attire similar to what he wore yesterday. That stupid flat cap is on his head, and he's wearing tailored slacks and a button-up, the sleeves rolled neatly to his forearms, with a dark waistcoat over top. The same pocket watch chain hangs at his side. He looks polished and powerful. Not like a piece of shit who just raped me. Twice.

"Come," he orders.

I stand on trembling legs, each step reminding me what he did to me last night and again this morning.

But I follow because I have no choice.

He points toward the bathroom, and a fresh wave of panic crashes through me just thinking about what might happen next. As I move in the direction he indicates, he tells me to relieve myself and meet him back here when I'm finished.

I do as he says, but when I try to flush, nothing happens. I mess with it a moment longer, but still nothing. Peering closer at the toilet, I see that my pee is held and collected in a clear plastic pan.

What the fuck?

The door behind me is pulled open, and I jump, turning around quickly.

"Out." He points.

I hurry past him and rush to the sink, scrubbing my hands as if I can wash away the whole morning.

We step onto the patio, returning to the same table as before. He pulls out the chair like he did last night, only this time he doesn't need to threaten me to sit. I move to it on my own, keeping my gaze fixed on my lap as he sits catty-corner to me.

When he leans over and drags his knuckle along my arm, I turn my face away.

"Tell me what you like for breakfast so I can have it made."

I say nothing.

"You will eat."

My silence only seems to irritate him further. He yanks my chair closer, then grabs my jaw and forces me to face him.

"Listen to me very carefully. You're mine now. I'll do whatever I want with you. If you want me to be an asshole, I will be. But let me make one thing clear. I've got a short temper, and you are the only one in line at the receiving end of it. Act up, and you will be punished."

"Get the fuck off me!" Niki yells from inside, sparing me from having to respond to him.

She's dragged out, still fighting. The guards force her into the chair across from Cristiano and cuff her wrists to the arms. She scowls at them until her eyes land on me.

"Are you okay, Rain—" her voice falters.

She stares at me. At the dress. My face. My silence.

I keep my head bowed. Unable to let her see the full extent of what he did to me, what he's done to Damiano, and what he's done to my relationship.

"You fucking bastard!" She struggles to stand, but one of the guards holds her down. "How could you do this? How could you rape her? You honestly couldn't have found someone willing?"

He scoffs. "Like you? I'll pass."

"Fuck you!" she sneers.

"We had a nice night and morning, didn't we, Rainey?" he drawls.

I try to blink away the tears, willing them not to fall, but they do anyway.

"I hope my brother cuts your dick off and shoves it up your ass!"

He smirks. "Now there's an idea. Maybe I'll cut his off and shove it up yours."

Niki spits at him from across the table, and it lands true, sliding down his cheek.

He wipes it with his napkin, nose wrinkling. "How many diseases did you just put on my face?"

"Like you care. You purposely slept with your enemies girlfriend. Putting your dick in the same places he's getting off in. You're nasty."

I know she's just trying to get under his skin, but talking about Damiano or even me like that is hurtful. I already feel gross without anyone making comments.

"I thought I might puke, but that passed once I saw that body naked."

His eyes drop to my chest, then drag back up. "And that pussy…" He sucks in a sharp breath through his teeth.

"Just let her go," Niki pleads.

My head lifts fast, lips trembling. "Go where? Damiano will never touch me again now. My relationship died the second *he* fucked me."

She shakes her head. "Damiano will always love you, Rainey. Always. No matter what."

Her words are meant to comfort me, but they fall flat. I turn away, trying to hold it in, but the sobs keep coming. I miss Dom more than I can take.

"Fuck," he groans. "What is this, a joint menstrual meltdown? You're both a hormonal wreck."

"Fuck you. Let us go."

He leans forward. "You don't get it, Nikita. You're not fucking understanding this. I didn't just wake up and decide to take your brother's sloppy seconds. I'm a businessman. I deal in transactions."

"And what transaction would that be? You want Damiano. You took his girlfriend to get him to trade himself. You're so predictable."

He remains serious, then smiles, showing his overly white teeth. "Some things never change, I see. Your family is a bunch of snakes. At least they stay consistent in that aspect."

"Are you high? Or do you purposely talk in riddles? Because it's really annoying."

"I'm not high. Are you looking to get high? I remember you used to enjoy a little nose candy back in the day." He flicks the side of his nostril.

"Gee, and who supplied it?" she retorts. "I'm done talking to you. Let us go."

"You're in no position to be trying to call the shots. Unfortunately for her, even if I had considered all of this not worth the headache, that changed the second I got a taste of that." He jerks his chin toward me. "That's a pussy unlike any I've ever had. And your brother? He's probably losing his goddamn mind knowing I'm the one buried in it. I'm the one enjoying that plump little cunt."

I know it's absolutely impossible, but Niki hearing what he's saying feels as if the words are being spoken directly into Damiano's ear, and I feel like total scum.

He places a hand on the table in front of me, just close enough to make it clear his words are meant for me.

"We enjoyed getting acquainted with each other, didn't we, Rainey? Although, I thought it'd take longer for your body to respond to me. Guess we've both been waiting for the right sexual partner."

"Fuck you." I glare at him.

He grins and gestures as if backing off. "You're the one who came within a minute of me sticking my penis inside you."

"You think this is funny? You think I wanted that to happen?" My voice cracks, humiliated that he said it out loud. I prayed he couldn't tell he got me off. I could feel it building, and when I clenched my walls, trying to hold the orgasm back, he started panting even louder, whispering, *just like that*. When I relaxed, it was already too late. I hadn't made a sound, hadn't moved when it happened, and he came right after, so I hoped he didn't notice.

"I don't find any of this funny. In fact, I was on vacation when this little offer was brought to me. And now I get to spend the rest of it here, figuring out what to do with you." He turns his attention to Niki.

"I have an idea," she deadpans. "Let us go. Maybe I'll put in a good word with my brother. Instead of him torturing you, he can put a knife through your heart. Oh wait, he already did that." She smirks.

"Niki," I chastise. I'm not about to watch him put one through hers.

"What!" she snaps. "We were fucking kidnapped, Rainey. I had just talked to Nikolai. He was with Dom. Dom literally said he was going to hurry so he could go home and cuddle you. Cuddle you, Rainey. All my brother wanted was to finish working fast so he could wrap his arms around you. And he never got to. This piece of shit is hurting everyone. Especially you." She motions her finger up and down, as if my appearance says it all.

"I'm well aware of what I look like," I hiss. "My face feels swollen like a balloon. I felt every hit. I'm the one who had his naked body pressed against mine—"

My words cut off as he lets out a loud, exaggerated sigh.

"You two together are insufferable."

Our food arrives, quietly placed in front of us. I want to believe that ends the exchange, but of course, he has more to say.

"Are you wet?" he asks, locked in on me.

I hold his gaze, the message in mine unmistakable: *over my dead body.*

"I don't mean horny. I doubt you've managed to release all of my semen yet. Hopefully, my seed is making its way to your egg right now."

He glances at Niki. "She's ovulating. As you know, I've always wanted to be a father."

At his words, my stomach twists so violently I double over the side of my chair and dry heave. A hand clamps down on my arm, but I hear Cristiano tell them to release me, and it falls away.

I can never have his baby. Not ever. I only want Damiano's children.

I pray there is something wrong with me, something that makes it impossible to get pregnant. I would rather die than give this monster a child that is half me.

Niki leans as far as the cuffs let her, whispering that it's okay, that Dom will find us. I want to believe it. But I don't.

I'm ordered to sit up and eat. When I stay down, he jabs my side. I recoil, pulling away to make it clear just how repulsed I am.

He shrugs and reaches for his fork. "You should eat." His eyes remain vacant as they meet mine. "I won't have to be so rough with you if you'd just do as I ask."

"How about you don't touch me at all, and I won't resist so hard."

A slow, predatory smile stretches across his face. "Oh, I'm going to do a lot more than touch you. I'm going to fuck you again. And again. And again. I'll keep filling you morning, day, and night. I'll do it until my child is growing inside you. And you? You'll learn to crave my penis as much as I crave your pussy."

Rage clouds my vision. I spot a knife sitting on the plate beside the butter dish and swipe it up, lunging as I scream like a mad-woman, driving it toward him.

He catches my wrist easily. Before I can register what's happening, I'm folded over the table, chest pressing into his plate of food. I beg for him to stop as he grabs my dress and hikes it up over my hips. My face grinds painfully against the iron table, but I can't get up.

"Do you want to show Nikita how much you enjoy me?"

His hand begins to slide over my skin, around my thigh and up my leg.

I shake my head as much as I can, and his movements immediately halt.

He leans down, his teeth clenched as he snarls into my ear, "Eat your fucking breakfast, or I'll let every one of my men come out here and fuck her while you watch."

I was ready to tell him to go to hell. I was ready to let him do whatever else he had planned. But the second he mentions Niki, my defiance shatters.

I will do anything to keep her safe. And I mean anything.

"Do you understand?" he demands, pressing my head harder against the table.

I nod, the motion slight but enough for him to know he's won.

Finally, he steps back, slapping my bare buttcheek, then yanking me upright. His breakfast is smeared across the front of me, but he doesn't seem to care. He just stands there, looming, victorious.

With no regard for how rough he's being, I'm shoved back into my chair. He smooths down the front of his shirt before taking his seat again. A woman rushes over to clear the ruined plate, and another swiftly replaces it with a fresh one.

He picks up a napkin, places it neatly in his lap, then signals to one of the guards. The man approaches, leans in, and Cristiano mutters something in a language I don't recognize. The guard nods once and disappears into the house.

When our eyes lock, even for the briefest moment, he smirks. When his attention shifts to Niki, the smugness fades. His face contorts with disgust. He hates the Volkovs so much he can hardly look at her. Maybe that's a good thing. Maybe it means he won't do to her what he did to me.

"I don't want anything from you. The deal was never for you. If an arrangement can be made for your release, I'll allow it. If not..." He shrugs. "Then I'll kill you."

He gestures between himself and me. "We leave soon. I won't wait. And quite honestly, I don't want you or anyone with your bloodline in my house."

He stares at her like a man studying an insect he's about to crush.

"Well, that's mutual. We don't want to be anywhere near you either. Yet here we are."

"Yes, here you are," he says with a sigh.

"You must have been so stressed, knowing you're going to die. Look how gray your hair's turning," she mocks.

His hair actually isn't very gray, but anger still flashes across his face. Apparently, he's vain, doesn't like being reminded he's aging. One subtle lift of his finger, and a man steps up behind Niki, jabbing a needle into her arm.

"No!" I shout, bolting upright so fast the chair crashes behind me as I hurl myself toward him.

Pain rips through my scalp as I'm yanked backward. I scream, flailing, as I'm shoved down again. I brace for the ground, but the chair is already upright.

"Look at me," he grinds out.

I don't. I stay turned away, breathing hard.

"I said look at me."

He grabs my chin, forcing me to face him. The second his skin touches mine, I lash out and slap him.

His lip splits on impact. Blood beads instantly.

For a second, he doesn't move. Just keeps his head turned. Then he stands. The backhand comes fast and hard.

Pain explodes across my face. My vision narrows, the chair rocks beneath me, and I blink through the ringing in my ears. My slap didn't do a fraction of the damage his did to me. That's for sure.

He adjusts the collar of his shirt, then sits again, snatching a cloth napkin to dab at the blood.

"Don't mistake my calmness for letting your disrespect go. I'm going to fuck you until you can't walk. You want to act like a wild animal, I'll treat you like one."

A man approaches with a tray of supplies. He heads toward Cristiano but is waved off.

"Her," is all he says.

The man pivots toward me and starts opening sterile packages. He begins with my lip, gently cleaning the split, then moves to the fresh cut near my eye.

Cristiano appears to disassociate, his attention fixed on the wedding band he keeps twisting back and forth on his finger.

Back and forth. Back and forth.

Where is his wife?

Does she know who he is? What he does?

What kind of woman marries a man like this? Maybe someone just as rotten. Just as cruel. Or maybe someone who never had a choice, just like me.

The antiseptic stings, but I don't show it. I'm convinced he gets off on knowing I'm hurting.

I hope someone makes him bleed the same way he makes everyone else bleed. And I hope I get to watch.

Chapter

FIVE

Nikita

I know my family is already searching for Rainey. Technically, I'm not supposed to be home for another couple of days, but the footage from the boutique would've been pulled by now. They'll know I'm with her. And Ma hasn't heard from me in a while. We talk constantly, even if it's just a quick call. Since I left with Pa, we've been checking in at least five times daily.

Nikolai and I usually FaceTime for hours, just leaving the phones up while we work or move through our routines. We've always been inseparable. I hate thinking about how he's doing in all of this. He has it bad for Rainey, so that alone would throw him off. But now I'm gone too.

I keep replaying our last conversation with Cristiano. *He's a businessman. He wouldn't have ended his vacation early without a reason.*

Someone orchestrated Rainey's abduction. Accepting that truth is the hardest betrayal I've ever had to face.

I know it wasn't Damiano. Obviously it wasn't Damiano. It wasn't Nikolai. I've gone over every single person in the house, every guard, every girl, trying to find something that doesn't make sense. But nothing sticks out. And no one would risk crossing Damiano. They're all terrified of him.

I've been confined to my room ever since the breakfast fiasco. Three meals are delivered throughout the day, just inside the door. But other than that, I have no contact with the outside world.

The first day, I tried not to eat, holding onto some small thread of control. By the end of the second day, hunger won out, and I practically scarfed it down.

The space I'm locked in is huge, nice enough to pass for the main suite of the house. But I know it's not. That room belongs to Cristiano. My heart clenches, realizing Rainey is also sharing that room with him.

I've found six cameras hidden in various locations, high enough that I can't cover them, so I make sure to flip them off every time I spot one. I know I'm being watched. I'm sure they find it funny how mad I get anytime I acknowledge one. But fuck them. Fuck all of them.

There's a TV in the room with access to every movie and show imaginable, but even that can't hold my attention. Every second that ticks by reminds me of what's happening to Rainey. While I sit here locked up, she's being assaulted by a man driven purely by his hatred for her boyfriend.

The helplessness is unbearable. I have never felt so powerless. Trapped and useless, knowing she's suffering and I can't do a damn thing to stop it.

I know Damiano is losing his mind.

I remember when he came to me and asked for help. I agreed before he even finished because my brother never asks for anything. After he laid out his plan, I asked if he was sure she was worth all of this.

He said she makes his heart beat. That he couldn't explain it, only that he'd always felt empty until he saw her. That just being near her makes him feel whole.

Over time, it became clear he has it bad for her. At first, we worried it might fade. That he'd move on and she'd be left with a broken heart. But it never faded. It only got stronger. He watches her constantly, like she's the most precious thing he's ever beheld.

He can contain his rage when he needs to, but I wouldn't be surprised if his killings have escalated, if his tortures have become more gruesome. He will destroy anyone who stands between him and Rainey.

And he will find her.

But what's left of her won't be the same girl he fought so hard to have.

If I could take her place, I would. A million times over.

The door opens and two guards step inside. I push myself upright, watching as a woman rushes in, clutching a black dress and a pair of heels.

"Put this on, please." She sets the shoes on the mattress and holds the dress out, waiting for me to rise.

I study her face, then glance past her to the men.

"Please," she repeats, her voice trembling. That's when I realize she'll be punished if I don't cooperate.

I stand and slip out of the pajamas that were provided. She lifts the dress in front of me, shielding my body enough to give me a shred of privacy from those leering bastards.

Once I've changed, she kneels to help me into the heels. After slipping them on, she rises and glances at the guards. One of them jerks his head toward the door, and she rushes out just as quickly as she came.

I'm ordered to turn around and put my hands behind my back. My first instinct is to curse him out. I don't get far. Within seconds, I'm slammed to the floor, one of them grinding my face into the carpet while the other snaps the cuffs around my wrists. They grab me by the arms, drag me upright, and force me out of the room.

One of the last times Rainey and I hung out at her and Dom's house, she told me something Anya had once confessed. She said that during Cristiano's meetings, Anya was the entertainment, and the men would rape her throughout.

Hearing about it was one thing. Being here is something else entirely.

As I'm led into a room, the first thing I notice is the arrangement of the chairs. They're circled around what, at first glance, looks like a table.

But it's not a table.

It's a bed, elevated and padded, with handcuffs anchored into polished steel at its center.

Cristiano is already seated, with men occupying every other spot.

I hate that my body still reacts to him the way it did when I was younger. I had a crush so big I used to flirt with him every chance I got, just hoping he would give me the time of day. He never did. He was always loyal to his disgusting wife, but that never stopped me from trying.

I used to daydream about us falling madly in love. I imagined my parents celebrating when we announced we were together. I never pictured this. Never thought the man I once fantasized about having sex with would be raping my best friend under the same roof.

And I hate to admit, even to myself, that part of the reason I would trade places with Rainey is because I never fully got over that crush.

I'm sick.

I'm fucking sick.

Next to him, what looks like a simple drink stand proves otherwise when he slides open the drawer.

No glasses. No liquor. Just rows of toys. Metal. Silicone. Leather. All neatly lined up.

I'm the only woman in the room.

I don't need anyone to explain it. I already know what I'm here for.

Entertainment.

Cristiano made his disgust for me clear days ago at breakfast, so he certainly won't be the one touching me.

I keep my eyes forward, refusing to let anyone see my fear as I'm dragged toward one of the tall marble pillars near the edge of the room. My wrists are chained above my head, causing the short black dress to ride up almost enough to expose me to the room. I wasn't given panties to wear, so I guess it will make it easier for them to do whatever they plan on doing.

From here, I have a clear view of everything: Cristiano, the bed, and every face at the table.

I realize the handcuffs in the center are designed so the person can be shifted around without being freed. That way, each man in the room can… participate.

The meeting picks up from where it left off when I was dragged in, but tension builds fast. Voices rise. The men argue over territory, money, betrayal. All of it blends together, and I barely process their words.

Cristiano doesn't speak right away. I know this demeanor. He's trying not to explode.

He's never had Dom's composure, and his fury is rising fast. He runs both hands through his hair and snaps his fingers once.

A man steps forward. Cristiano says something I can't hear, but I don't need to. I already know.

Carmella used to tell Ma she would purposely push his buttons because she loved their angry sex. She said it was the only thing that ever seemed to calm him down once he was worked up.

Only no. I don't. I wasn't expecting the needle when it pierces my neck.

Everything shifts at once. My muscles go slack. My knees buckle, but the chains hold me upright.

I'm temporarily paralyzed. Not unconscious. Just frozen inside my own body. Once again. I can still see, still hear, still feel. I just can't move. I fight back in the only way I can. I memorize faces, one by one, cataloging every man at the table.

I will remember them. I will make sure they pay.

The door slams open and Rainey is dragged in, completely nude, kicking and screaming, thrashing between two guards as she fights like hell to break free.

Her body is covered in whip marks. They aren't deep enough to break the skin, but they're welted so badly I can feel the sting just looking at her.

Her wrists and ankles are raw, rubbed down to angry flesh, and my stomach knots at the sight.

She's bent over the bed, right in front of Cristiano, giving him a perfect view of her backside.

Her arms are yanked above her head and locked into the waiting cuffs. He doesn't try to draw out what comes next. He doesn't try to build anticipation. He's so angry, I don't think he can help himself.

He stands and unzips his pants. This isn't the first time I've seen him naked. I once saw Carmella give him head. All the adults were drunk, and he was sprawled out on the couch with his shirt open. I remember wanting to trace my tongue over every ridge of his defined abdomen. And when she pulled out his cock… I thought about that cock for years. It's just as I remember—thick and veiny.

I bought a dildo close to his size and fucked myself with it until I bled. I was terrified afterward, but I didn't say anything. In my mind, it was Cristiano who had hurt me like that, and somehow it felt good.

The room falls silent. A complete and unnatural stillness. He slams into her in one brutal thrust, burying himself deep, then grips her hips and pounds into her so hard she cries out.

Only her voice is hoarse now. Probably from all the screaming she's done since the last time I saw her.

No one stops him. In fact, they're enjoying the show. The tension that filled the room moments ago is gone, replaced by their sick fascination with watching someone be raped.

Cristiano drives into her like she's nothing more than a body to punish, a vessel for his rage. Like she isn't even human.

I want to look away, because what he's doing now is everything I used to want from him for years, back when I imagined myself as someone willing. But Rainey isn't. She's not consenting. He is hurting her in front of all these men.

When he finishes, he tucks himself back into his pants and calmly takes his seat again.

Then he opens the drawer and keeps going.

For the next two hours, he runs the meeting while sexually torturing her in front of everyone. He reaches down between commands to grab new objects, inserting them, adjusting the angle, drawing orgasms from her that she doesn't want to give.

He smirks every time she comes.

He talks about supply routes and executions with the same mouth he uses to whisper vile things to her. If something sets him off, the entire room knows it by the sound of her agonizing wails.

His fingers push inside her. His tongue tastes what isn't his to take, all while she cries.

And I watch it all.

Frozen.

Trapped.

Helpless.

But not forever. One day, he will pay for everything he has done.

The meeting drags on until the arguments die down. The shouting fades into quieter voices. And now, it's just silence.

Cristiano stands from his seat, sliding his hands over Rainey's red, welted butt. He squeezes, his eyes rolling dramatically as he does, then bends over her, taking a fistful of her hair and yanking her head back, forcing her face toward me.

"Look," he snarls, making sure she sees me, making sure I see her.

My arms are still bound. My dress clings to me, soaked with sweat and fear.

My eyes lock onto hers.

I wish I could speak. I wish I could tell her how much I love her. How much Damiano loves her. That this is not her burden to carry.

But I can't move.

I can't speak.

All I can do is look at her and hope somehow, some way, she knows.

"Everyone here is fucking horny," Cristiano says, sweeping his hand lazily across the room. "And to celebrate a successful negotiation, I want them to have some fun." He turns and points at me. "So tell me, Rainey. Do you want them to have their fun with her… or with you?"

Tears run freely down her bruised face. Her voice is barely a whisper when she says, "Me."

My eyes go wide, pleading silently. *No. No, not you. Let them take it from me. I haven't been touched. You're already broken and bleeding.*

But she won't look at me now. She stares down, trembling, her lips quivering.

Cristiano tightens his grip in her hair and growls, "Again."

And again, she says, "Me."

She's flipped onto her back, her legs yanked apart, as he places her feet on the edge of the bed.

"One time," he warns. "One fucking time you fight back, and I'll take her right to the edge of death." He points at me.

He acts like she's betraying him, like she should be ashamed for choosing herself over me, when he's the one who forced her to choose in the first place.

He must have been confident she would sacrifice me instead. Now that she didn't do what he expected, he can't take it back.

Rainey nods. Her whole body shakes as she squeezes her eyes shut.

Then the men approach, one by one. They aren't allowed to climb between her legs. In fact, when one man begins to unbutton his pants, Cristiano tells him to get out. He says they aren't allowed to fuck her, only to touch.

The rest of them seem satisfied just to get their hands on someone as beautiful and flawless as Rainey, and they take full advantage.

They grope and suck on her breasts and shove various toys inside her.

And she doesn't move.

Not even when one man clamps his mouth on her nipple and sucks hard enough to bruise.

Cristiano looks beyond furious the entire time. At one point, when the men keep coming, more hands touching her, he shifts repeatedly in his seat, his breathing turning shallow as he struggles to maintain his composure.

His façade snaps when one of the men makes her come. Her legs shake, and her back arches. Cristiano stands abruptly.

"Get the fuck out," he bellows.

The man pulls his fingers from her and immediately sucks on them.

"Delicious," he says, winking at her as he adjusts his pants and saunters toward the door.

For an hour, she endured their hands on her. And for that hour, Cristiano sat painfully close, only a foot away, while they violated her. He looked like he wanted to kill every single one of them.

And then, just like that, it ends.

The others leave. The room empties.

Cristiano leans forward and roughly pulls the toys from her body, tossing them aside, then unlocks the cuffs around her wrists.

"Sit up," he orders.

She obeys.

The slap comes so fast, so brutal, it sends her flying off the bed. She lands hard on her hands and knees, swaying from the impact.

"You fucking whore!" he roars.

She doesn't even get the chance to lift her head or let the spinning stop. He grabs a fistful of her hair, pulls her up, and flings her back onto the bed.

"You like being a slut? You liked letting them touch you, huh? You filthy piece of trash."

Another blow strikes her other cheek, now red and swelling. Then his fist slams into her stomach. She folds instantly, a strangled gasp parting her lips, but no sound follows. The breath has been stolen from her lungs.

She reaches out, searching for something—anything to grasp.

He kicks her arm away. Literally kicks it, and I can see the way it swells. He broke it.

"You don't touch me. You're fucking disgusting."

Then comes another hit across her cheek, and this time she drops face-first onto the floor, unmoving.

He stands over her, panting, rage radiating off him. Then spits on her.

"Cunt."

Then he kicks her hard in the ribs. The pain must have brought her back to consciousness, because she screams out.

"Get this fucking whore out of my sight," he snaps.

As the men approach, she sobs and tries to push herself up on her good arm. He kicks it out from under her, and she lets out a strangled yell. I know she's lying there now with both arms broken. He grabs her by the hair, sits her upright, and stares at her, his face venomous. Then he hits her one last time, knocking her unconscious before walking away.

Blood smears behind her as she's dragged out.

I can't see where they take her. All I know is she's gone.

Then a guard steps up to me. He unfastens the chains from the pillar and tosses me over his shoulder.

I'm carried through the house, silent and paralyzed, dropped onto my bed, then the cuffs are removed, and the door locks behind him. And I'm alone again.

It starts to sink in. Not just what I witnessed, but what I've done.

I helped Damiano get her. I practically helped deliver Rainey into this hell.

No matter what I told myself at the time, no matter what reasons I clung to then, I'm complicit.

Her screams echo in my head. Every time I close my eyes, I see a replay of what happened to her. And it was my hands that opened the door. My hands that unlocked the path that led her here.

This is on me. Every bruise. Every tear she cries. Every single bit of fear or sadness she feels here, it's my fault.

I should've fought harder. I should've done something. And now she's paying.

Chapter

SIX

Rainey

I fucking hurt.

But I welcome the pain.

The unbearable physical ache is the only thing holding me together after everything that's happened. It distracts me from thoughts of Damiano, the abuse, the unwanted hands that touched me.

It all feels so violently illegal, like the fact that it is illegal should somehow make it stop. But it doesn't. None of this has stopped, and no one is coming to save me.

The X-rays confirm what I already knew. Both arms are broken. The bones are aligned, stabilized, and wrapped in compression bandages. My left collarbone is fractured, and that arm is placed in a sling.

When the nurse offers pain medication, I shake my head. When she insists, I tell her I don't want anything they're offering.

I need to hurt.

I want to feel every ounce of it.

It's the only thing I can process right now.

Because if I let my mind even brush against the emotional wreckage, I won't survive it.

The woman adjusting my sling looks horrified just at the sight of my injuries.

"Pretty bad, huh?" I mutter.

"I've never seen him do this to someone he was having sex with."

I want to ask how many women he kidnaps and beats, but I have a feeling *I'm the only one.*

"Lucky me."

Cristiano enters the room, stopping near the bed, his hands shoved in his pockets as he assesses me, then addresses the nurse.

"Have you administered pain meds?"

She glances over her shoulder at him, then finishes adjusting the sling.

"No. She won't take them," the woman says as she rises.

"Then do it through the IV."

She looks at him head-on. "She doesn't want them."

"I don't care what she wants. Sedate her."

She glares, then lets out a sigh and goes to the cabinets, gathering supplies before returning to the bed.

"I'm sorry," she whispers as she puts a concoction directly into the IV.

When I feel woozy, he's there, grabbing me by the shoulders and laying me down.

The physical pain dulls just enough for the rest to seep in. The memories flood my mind: the wet tongues, rough fingers, and toys that were shoved inside me.

I lie on the stiff hospital-style bed, no longer able to hold my tears back. I cry because I want Damiano. I cry because too many men have touched me in ways I never wanted. I cry because Dom has only ever been with me, and yet my number keeps rising.

He will think I'm disgusting.

The man he despises most has had sex with me all day, every day since I arrived, and there's nothing I can do to change that.

My eyes flutter shut, but when they open again, I'm still in the same bed. I hoped I had died, but nope—I'm still here.

"Welcome back to the land of the living," says the same nurse as before, coming over to remove the IV.

"You were out for fourteen hours," she informs me. "I'm gonna help you up, just let me know if you feel woozy at all. I'll help you back to your room."

I could protest, but I'm sure she's under strict orders to bring me back when I wake. And since Cristiano's such a piece of shit, no one dares disobey him.

As we walk, an older woman steps up behind us and follows. Once inside the bedroom, we're left alone, and the woman goes to the bathroom and fills the tub. Her presence is warm, but her face looks aged with years of stress and fear.

She points, and I understand—she wants me to get in. I do, hesitantly. The wooden board laid across the rim is tapped next, a silent signal to rest my arms there and keep them dry. Then the bathing begins.

Each stroke of the cloth is careful. I wince when she brushes over my ribs. They're broken. I know there's nothing that can be done. They just have to heal on their own. But the skin is so blackened and tender that, for a moment, I think I might pass out from the pain.

She pauses at my shoulder and leans in.

"Anya. She is safe?"

I blink up at her, wanting to deny knowing anyone by that name.

She quietly murmurs her name—Fedora—and in that instant, I understand. This is the woman who helped Anya escape.

Tears sting my eyes as I nod. "She's safe."

She speaks in a soft rush, her eyes lifting to the ceiling. A prayer, maybe.

"She is treated well?"

"She's with Silvano Volkov. They took a liking to each other. He's taking good care of her… at least I think so. Last I knew."

She nods slowly, her eyes searching mine. "Which one is he?"

"The third oldest."

She places her palm to her chest. "Will your Damiano come for you?"

My Damiano.

I pause, my throat tightening at hearing someone else say his name—referring to him as *mine.*

"I don't know." The words crack as they leave my mouth.

The door opens with an alarming thud, and Cristiano storms in.

"Get her out. Now."

Fedora scrambles to obey, quickly wrapping a towel around me. I trap it with my elbows to keep it from falling, and she carefully helps me out, doing her best to steady me.

He's radiating fury, and I already know I'm about to be the recipient of it.

He snaps his fingers, and she begins to guide me toward him.

When we're only a foot away, he angrily tells her to step back. She does immediately.

The towel is yanked from my body and tossed aside. I'm lifted and set on the counter, and with a forceful grip, my thighs are ripped apart, his focus locking between them.

My skin burns with shame.

Fedora bows her head, face turned away. She can't save me. No one can.

He assaults me right there. With her still in the room.

He calls me names for letting other men touch me. He spits on me, saying I'm filth. I'm slapped for sleeping with Damiano… my boyfriend. My hair is yanked so hard I think he's quite literally going to scalp me, all while he asks if that's how I like it when Damiano fucks me.

His name quickly becomes tainted. Each time it's said aloud, I get hit. It doesn't take long before I start to associate his name with pain.

When he's finished, he pulls me off the counter and drags me from the bathroom. I'm shoved onto the bed, but it doesn't come with sleep.

Only him.

And it lasts all night.

I'M REWARDED, IF YOU CAN EVEN CALL IT THAT. I'M GIVEN THE DAY TO rest. He doesn't touch me. Doesn't talk to me. Just silence.

When he finally comes in, he sits on the edge of the bed, staring down at me. I pretend to be asleep, but I give myself away when he trails lightly down the curve of my back and I flinch.

"Do you feel better, darling?" he murmurs.

Darling? I want to vomit at him calling me that. Who the fuck calls somebody something endearing like that after they just did the unspeakable things he was doing to me?

"You had a busy day yesterday. Slept all day today. You must've been exhausted."

I don't respond. I want to tell him: *of course I had a busy day. You raped me all morning and afternoon, only stopping when you left, just for guards to storm in, rip me out of bed, and drag me into a room full of people where you continued to assault me. Then you allowed everyone to participate.*

Afterward, for no reason other than the fact that you're a monster, you beat the shit out of me. But yeah, why could I possibly be tired.

He brushes a strand of hair from my face.

"Come on. Let's get you changed. We don't want to be late."

Late? Either I've slept myself stupid, or there's a huge piece of this conversation I've missed.

As I sit up, I catch sight of my wrists, both in full casts now.

Perfect.

Fucking asshole.

There's a pink bandage in the bend of my arm, the kind they use after drawing blood. My head's swimming. I'm dazed. The only reason I'm not writhing in pain is because they must have drugged me heavily, especially since I had entire casts put on without even being aware it was happening.

He helps me to my feet, then pulls a dress over my head, sliding it down my body with slow, hungry fingers. My stomach knots, bracing for what he might try. But he doesn't. He smooths the fabric, adjusts my hair, and rests his palm against my spine again.

Outside, it's night. My feet carry me numbly across the front driveway in the direction of one of the waiting sedans.

"RAINEY!"

I turn just as Niki comes sprinting toward me. She crashes into me, sobbing uncontrollably.

I hold her as tightly as I can, desperate to melt into her, to become one person so we can never be separated again.

Then we're torn apart.

We both scream, kicking and reaching for the other as guards drag us backward, our fingers straining to brush for one last second before they slip away.

"Put a bullet between her eyes," Cristiano says callously as he walks past. "And ship her back to her family."

My mind stutters, trying to catch up to what he just said.

He can't mean...

He can't.

A sharp sting bites into the side of my neck. I gasp and instinctively cover the spot, already knowing what just happened, but it's too late. Everything starts to slow. My legs stop kicking, and my vision blurs.

No. No.

A heavy fog drags me down. My thoughts get slower. I try to speak, but nothing comes out.

Then I hear a single gunshot.

And the darkness swallows me whole.

Chapter

SEVEN

Nikita

"Nikita."

My name is being called over and over, and a soft tap-ping lands against my cheek repeatedly.

"Nikita, wake up."

More taps.

My eyes crack open, blinking against the too-bright light. My head is foggy, my mind racing to catch up. I reach out, confused, brushing against a face.

"Am I in heaven?" I whisper, as I stroke Nikolai's cheek.

I'm pulled into his chest and hugged so hard it steals the air from my lungs. I turn my head, dazed, and see Dante. Gio. Silvano. Andrei. All of them here, watching me.

When he pulls back, his eyes rake over me. "Are you injured?"

And I break.

My body shudders because I already know—Rainey's not here with me. She's still with *him*.

When Damiano bursts through the doorway, I collapse onto the couch, hugging my knees to my chest as violent, uncontrollable sobs take over.

He kneels in front of me, his forehead pressed against my shins, arms wrapping around my calves. "Tell me she's alive," he whispers.

My cries deepen, and after a second, I let go of my legs and fall forward, holding onto him.

I haven't hugged my brother in—actually, I don't think he's ever let me hug him.

"Is she alive?" he asks again, his voice breaking.

This is the first time in my entire life that I've heard real emotion from him. Real fear. And it makes all of this that much worse.

I nod, clinging to him. "Yes."

"Is she physically still intact?"

I know what he means. Not about bruises or broken bones. And though Cristiano is torturing her, that's not what he's asking. He's asking if anything on her body has been removed.

"Yes. She is."

He pulls back, his eyes flicking between mine. "Where's he taking her?"

I shake my head. "I don't know. I'm useless. I'm so fucking useless. She was raped and beat, and raped and beat, and I was fucking useless." I thread my fingers through my hair and pull as hard as I can, trying to yank the memories from my brain.

The couch sinks beside me, followed by an arm sliding around my shoulders, rubbing back and forth. I know it's Dante, just by his scent.

"Niki, we're gonna give you something to help you relax, okay?"

"Give me something to kill me."

Damiano must be furious that I'm the one sitting here instead of Rainey. I'm so mentally wrecked. I just want it to end. I just want to die.

The moment the medication hits, I feel it. My limbs grow heavy, and my chest loosens. My thoughts settle and everything goes quiet. The pain doesn't leave; it just stops screaming. Dante gives my shoulder another reassuring squeeze, asking if I'm ready to proceed.

When I finally begin to speak, they all listen.

"I flew home early to surprise everyone. When I was pulling up, Rainey was leaving, and said she was picking up Ma's dress, so I went along. At the boutique, the owner seemed caught off guard to see me. When she told us the dress was in the back, I knew something was wrong, especially since she had us go first.

"I don't remember anything after that until we woke tied up in a warehouse, and Cristiano was there.

"When we left, a man in the backseat tried touching me, and Rainey kicked him in the face. He punched her so hard it knocked her out.

"I was brought to a room and left alone. Cristiano came in and talked to me, said I look more and more like Ma every day. Commented on how I'm a woman now, and how he wants me out of his house. Before he left, he said he put earplugs on the nightstand so I wouldn't hear my friend screaming while he… while he…" I can't finish it.

"It was the longest night of my life. Every second, I feared someone would come in and hurt me. But nobody did. I could hear men outside the door. I couldn't make out their words, just that they were talking.

"In the morning, I was brought to breakfast. I assumed Rainey must have been put in one of the rooms nearby with a guard watching her door.

"Cristiano and Rainey were already on the patio."

My lip starts to quiver as I try to avoid Dom. He's probably already pieced together what I'm about to say, so I just say it.

"He had beaten her so badly. The dress he put her in already had blood on the front. She could barely sit up."

I pause, the images flooding in. Her head was hanging. She wouldn't even look at me. She felt shame for what had happened to her, like she could somehow control it or prevent it. But she put up a good fight. I could tell by the way she was injured that she fought back. The only reason she was that hurt was because he didn't like her resisting.

"He talked about how he planned on cutting Rainey into pieces and sending them back to Dom, but after he had sex with her, he decided he was keeping her.

"One of the housekeepers said he assaults her constantly, day and night. And when a guard asked when he could have a turn, he was killed."

I look up.

"I was chained up in one of his meetings. The chairs were all circled around a bed. A bed, not a table. I thought for sure I was going to be the entertainment. But then Rainey was dragged in and bent over the bed in front of him, her arms cuffed above her. He raped her in front of everyone. Then he used toys on her for the rest of the meeting."

A sick silence hangs in the air.

"And when the meeting ended, he made her choose whether she wanted the men to take turns on me or on her. She chose herself.

"He was so mad she chose herself. He let the men use their fingers and toys. He told her if she made a single noise he would let them all rape me. I've never seen her so quiet. Then, when it was done, he beat her again and said she's a whore for letting other men touch her, even though she was cuffed and unable to move.

"He blamed her for it.

"Her face—it's unrecognizable. She has broken bones and so many bruises and cuts. It's sickening what she looks like… what she's enduring. I don't know where he was taking her, but from the looks of it, wherever we were, he didn't plan on returning. Not any time soon, anyway."

Dante drags his hands down his jaw, silent and tense. The rest of my brothers are in different states of emotional turmoil.

"Does it seem… Cristiano likes her?" Damiano asks softly.

I nod. "A lot."

A memory flickers in my mind, something strange from when I was younger. I remember Carmella once told Ma that Cristiano was so selfish, he wouldn't *"eat her cat."* I didn't understand then. But when I got older, I understood what she meant.

I overheard Cristiano telling someone Rainey's pussy tastes so good, the only way he'll die is with it in his mouth. So he couldn't bother to do it for his wife, but he will for someone else's woman. A woman who doesn't want that from him.

"But he lets others have sex with her?" Dante presses.

I shake my head. "No. Never. Only him. He makes her share his room, and if he's somewhere else, she's with him."

"But he lets others touch her?"

My eyes sting as I nod again. "Yeah," I whisper. "Just the once—that I know of."

I hadn't realized Dr. Winn was here until she speaks from the edge of the room.

"He was testing himself. Trying to see if he could share her and realized he couldn't. So he punished her to mask his feelings. Pinned the blame on her. I don't think he will allow anyone else to touch her again. Not after that. I believe his feelings for her are stronger than he expected. And even though he won't let anyone else near her, every time he feels overwhelmed by his emotions for her, knowing she's in a relationship with Damiano, he will hurt her as a punishment."

My elbows drop to my knees, and I cover my face wishing I could block the world out.

I can hear them talking around me—low voices, anger laced with sorrow. But it all blurs.

Nikolai slips his arm around my shoulder and pulls me to him, one hand cradling the back of my head while the other presses gently against my spine. I fold into him, sobbing into his chest, and he just holds me.

I don't know what to do from here. I don't know how to save Rainey. I think I could relay the layout of the house and the landscape from my bedroom, but I know they won't be there. As I was being taken out of the room, I noticed covers were being placed over the furniture, and I realized everyone was leaving.

Maybe they can track him through private flight logs to figure out where he went. But Cristiano is smart. He would make sure anything he did couldn't be traced.

I rest my chin on my arms and stare at Dom. He's completely shattered, and it breaks my heart.

"He's trying to get her pregnant," I whisper after a long silence.

Dom's eyes lock with mine, but he doesn't say anything. The look on his face is enough.

This is all my fault.

The pain on everyone's face, it started with me.

If she ends up pregnant with Cristiano's child, Dom won't recover. I know he'll find her, but if she's carrying that monster's spawn, I don't know what will happen. I don't think he'll let that child live.

My chest tightens as I close my eyes, knowing I need to get this next part out if Rainey has a chance of getting justice.

"She was assaulted, and I was paralyzed, trapped in my own useless skin. I couldn't move. But I memorized every face. I remember everything each of them did to her."

Dante stands and Andrei takes his place, settling beside me. He opens his laptop and begins clicking through different programs and tabs.

"Start from the beginning. Anything you remember. I'll ask questions as we go."

I close my eyes again, and the white, round bed from that night surges into my mind. I can see her dragged in, her wrists pulled tight against the cuffs. The tears spill from my closed lids, burning tracks down my cheeks.

I recount every vile detail. I describe the way they watched as Cristiano raped her while she screamed. I describe the way he held Rainey's face toward me as he made her choose whether the men in the room raped me or her.

When she was repositioned on the bed, her feet on the edge and her legs spread, she just allowed it. Let them put her how they wanted.

I speak of the toys pulled away bloodied, of the way she lay there afterward, her eyes vacant as they remained fixed on the ceiling, as if she had mentally transported somewhere far from that room.

I describe the way everyone cleared out, leaving just us and a couple of guards. I thought it was over, that he might let her crawl away to some corner of the room to recover.

But then he called her disgusting. He spat the words at her, telling her she was filthy for letting other men touch her.

I describe the way his fists smashed into her, one after another. I tell them how I heard her wrist snap when he wrenched her arm back and threw her to the floor, how her body crumpled in a heap.

I describe the way he kicked her, and the way she tried to push herself up on her good wrist, only for him to kick it right out from under her. The crack of bone is burned into my memory.

I focus on the coffee table as I shake my head, remembering how she lay there unmoving. I watched in horror, thinking he had killed her, thinking my best friend's lifeless body was mere feet away from me—dead—and I couldn't do anything about it.

I couldn't save her. I was right there, and I couldn't save her.

Dom climbs to his feet, staring hard at Andrei, who hasn't stopped typing. His eyes scan the screen rapidly, then he turns the laptop toward me.

Names, along with the faces of every single man who touched her, gaze back at me, triggering immediate flashbacks. My vision swims with a revolting slideshow of hands, grins, and whispered praises of her body. The images blur together, moving fast, each frame another stab of guilt and rage, until it feels like my heart might seize completely.

Then my stomach heaves, and I double over, retching onto the floor. Bile scorches my throat with every memory I just relived.

Chapter

EIGHT

Rainey

My arms are strapped to the sides of the chair on a private plane, then I'm buckled into the leather seat. Cristiano stands in front of me, watching closely.

"If you're good, I won't gag or drug you."

My throat tightens, but I manage a quiet, "Okay."

He studies me for a moment, maybe waiting to see if I'll stay composed. I lower my gaze to the floor and leave it there.

He takes the seat beside me just as the engines begin to hum, and the plane starts to taxi.

"Ever flown before?"

I shake my head. "No."

There's a pause. Then his fingers slide over mine, curling around them, his palm pressing against my cast. I stiffen, but he only grips tighter, unaffected by my discomfort.

I squeeze my eyes shut as we gain speed, half wishing the plane would explode and half praying it doesn't.

Only once we're fully in the air does he finally let go. He adjusts his shirt cuffs, then walks down the aisle to join a group of his men seated around a table. They're already laughing, passing around drinks, and speaking in another language. I'm relieved I can't understand what they're saying, especially when one of them jerks his chin toward me and mutters something that makes the others glance my way. Cristiano turns his head too, then returns his attention to the conversation.

A flight attendant with boobs bigger than her head approaches, leaning flirtatiously on the back of Cristiano's chair as she smiles down at him. He doesn't seem to acknowledge her, but two of the other men do. After a few exchanged words, they both rise, and she leads them to the back of the plane. She winks at me as she passes.

My brows draw together. I don't know how she can smile, let alone look happy about what she's about to do with them. Then again, she probably gets paid well for it.

When I turn back, Cristiano is staring at me again. I'd like to stick my tongue out at him but settle for turning to the window instead, focusing on the darkened sky and the blinking light on the plane's fin.

I'm cargo. Or the flesh Cristiano screws. But I'd rather be the cargo.

Hours pass, and the need to pee becomes unbearable. I try to ignore it for as long as I can, but eventually it's too much. I'm going to make a mess if I don't say something.

"Cristiano?" I manage, but it comes out too soft, the first part of his name barely audible. I clear my throat and try again. "Cristiano."

He doesn't hear me, but one of the guards does. He points in my direction, and Cristiano finally looks up. He finishes the drink he's holding, sets the glass on the table, and stands. His stare doesn't waver as he walks toward me, his brows lifting slightly like he's surprised I'd intentionally call for him.

I clear my throat again. Part of me wants to back out, but the pressure in my bladder says I have maybe two minutes before disaster.

"I need to use the bathroom."

He must realize how badly I have to go, because he doesn't give me a hard time or tell me no. He undoes my restraints and guides me to the back.

By the time I'm hiking my dress up, I don't even realize he didn't bother to close the door. I should care. I don't.

I lower my panties and sit, nearly sighing from the relief. He stays planted in the doorway, like he's preventing me from leaving—yet I have nowhere to escape to, so it seems pointless.

As I reach for the toilet paper, he steps in and knocks my hand aside.

I blink up at him, annoyed.

Seriously? Am I not allowed to wipe myself now?

He tears off a clean stretch of paper, folds it neatly, then touches my knees, nudging them apart.

My body stiffens. Is *he* going to wipe me?

I start to protest but he cuts me off. "Open your legs."

I do. He's made himself very acquainted with my vagina, so there's no need to be shy now.

When he finishes, he pulls me up, adjusts my panties, and points toward the doorway.

I step aside as he moves to the sink. Once he's done, he walks past me, and I follow on autopilot.

I'm buckled back into my seat, arms positioned on the armrests, expecting him to secure them too. He doesn't. He just sits down beside me.

After a moment, I lower them into my lap, fixating on my casts and how I'm literally being broken limb by limb.

He will eventually kill me.

Whether he means to or not. I am living on borrowed time.

I stay locked in a dazed trance, only snapping out of it when he clicks his seatbelt into place and reaches across, clasping his hand over mine.

No one ever mentioned where we're going, but with how long we've been flying, I know we've left the country.

The plane begins to descend. Even though I try not to, my other hand tightens over his. My stomach turns with every dip and shake. I don't know how the pilot plans to see in the dark to land this thing.

Maybe this is it. Maybe this is where I die. And honestly, I'm okay with that.

I mentally slip away to Damiano. I envision him walking toward me in slow motion, his smile so breathtaking. His hands remain in his pockets until we're close enough to touch, then he pulls them free just as I throw myself into his arms.

He catches me, and we cling to each other, laughing as he twirls me in a circle. When we finally ease apart, we lock into that deep-rooted connection where every fiber of my being molds to his, and we're no longer two separate people but one: one soul, connected in two bodies.

Then he kisses me.

It's hot and urgent. His mouth claims mine like he's starving for it, and I kiss him back like I've been waiting for this forever. I love this man so deeply it scares me.

A sudden jolt rips me back to reality. The plane slams against the tarmac, the tires screeching as we race down the runway.

Eventually, we slow, the engines humming lower as we roll to a stop inside a hangar.

I glance out the window and take in two blacked-out SUVs already waiting.

The door opens, and Cristiano rises, tossing a quick "Let's go" over his shoulder as he heads for the exit.

I rush after him. As much as I hate to admit it, I'd rather stay close to him than be left alone with any of the other creeps on this plane.

When we reach the SUV, he retrieves something from his pocket and passes it to me.

"Put this on."

It takes me a second to realize what I'm holding. A blindfold. I don't budge, hoping he'll change his mind. But the way he raises his brows tells me he's ready for a fight if I refuse.

Reluctantly, I slide it on. It's not fully covering the way it should, but it's on. He reaches out and tugs it down the rest of the way, and I'm surrounded by total darkness.

My sling is slipped back over my head, and my arm is secured in place. Then he guides me into the vehicle and buckles me in. A moment later, we're moving.

The drive feels endless.

Being blindfolded heightens everything else. Every sound, every shift in the air, every breath. I know Cristiano is on my left, but I can sense someone else on my right too. I don't want to touch either of them, so I try to make myself as small as possible. Still, they're both broad, and no matter how much I shrink into myself, our shoulders keep brushing.

No one speaks. The entire ride is silent.

Eventually, the vehicle slows, then comes to a stop. I hear muffled voices outside, distant at first, then growing louder as they approach.

The door opens, and Cristiano pulls me out from his side. A second later, he slips the blindfold off, and my mouth hangs open as I stare around, trying to make sense of where he's brought me.

Chapter

NINE

Rainey

We're in a warehouse, but not like any I've seen before. This one is alive with activity, workers moving in every direction.

Tables stretch across the floor, cluttered with equipment and clear plastic bags in various stages of preparation. People measure, cut, and seal in an entirely streamlined process.

They're making drugs. Right here. Right in front of me.

I swallow hard, feeling like an unwilling accessory to something criminal. I don't want to be involved. I shouldn't be here. But that doesn't matter. I am. And if anyone finds me here, it won't matter that I was forced into this. I'll still be held accountable.

As I scan the room, a few heads lift. I came in with Cristiano. They probably assume I'm here by choice.

He stays beside me, his hand on the small of my back, guiding me through the room. Everyone steps aside to let him p—

Whether it's fear or respect, I don't know. Maybe it's both, but my guess is fear.

At the far end, we reach a set of metal doors that swing open into a dark, wide-open office space. The floor is bare concrete, stained and cracked. The furniture looks like a garage sale graveyard, each piece mismatched and overly worn. Twelve men sit around a long table, all of them waiting. It reeks of B.O. and sweat, and I don't know how long we'll be stuck in here, but the thought of marinating in this stench makes my stomach churn.

One leans back in his chair with a scowl. "You kept us waiting a long time." His thick Russian accent and his sneer makes my skin crawl.

Cristiano shrugs, completely unbothered. "You shouldn't have minded. You had someone to keep you occupied."

All at once, their gazes crawl over me. There's a foulness clinging to them. Half of them look like they don't even know what a shower is, which makes the smell all the worse.

He walks to the far end of the table and takes the chair at the head. I remain in place, unsure what I'm supposed to be doing. A gun nudges my spine, and it's all the encouragement I need to start walking.

Once I reach him, I stop just behind and to the side of his chair. He doesn't say anything, so I take that as permission to stay here.

The men begin talking again, the conversation immediately sounding heated, something about shipments, territories, percentages, and cuts.

I hear movement, a soft, faint sound coming from the corner of the room. I turn my head and feel the color drain from my face. There, in the shadows, chained to a metal-framed bed, is a girl.

She looks no older than twenty-two. Her dark hair is matted to her scalp with sweat and days without a shower. The dress she's wearing looks like it was once pink, maybe, but now, after being worn so long, it's torn and discolored. She's curled against the wall, arms wrapped tightly around her legs. Her eyes are hollow, like whatever life once lived behind them was ripped away long ago.

Cristiano must sense what I'm planning to do. Before I can even take a single step toward her, he clamps a hand around my elbow.

"No."

I freeze mid-motion and glance back at the girl.

She's staring at me. I want to reach for her, to offer even the smallest touch of comfort. Her gaze drags down my body, likely cataloging all of my injuries too, recognizing the truth: *we are both prisoners.*

The meeting seems to take a turn abruptly, the conversation overlapping with growing intensity as a couple of men start yelling over each other.

One of them slams his hand on the table and surges to his feet, pointing at another man. He yells at him, spit flying from his mouth, then turns to Cristiano, shouting something as he points at *me.*

I had been tuning out the meeting until I was suddenly acknowledged. Now I'm hyper-aware of everything.

I don't know what he said, but I get the feeling he's trying to have sex with me. I might become the next girl chained to that bed.

Cristiano responds coolly, without emotion. It's the first time I feel a flicker of gratitude toward him, because even though I don't understand the words, I know he told the guy no.

Behind us, the guards step forward, rifles held tight across their chests.

The man snarls something, then storms around the table, unfastening his belt as he marches toward the girl, and my stomach plummets.

I freeze as the sound of his pants zipper fills my ears. The girl presses tighter against the wall, but she doesn't make a sound as her ankles are grabbed and she's yanked down onto the mattress.

I can't breathe. My knees wobble, and I sway, struggling to stay upright. I fight the urge to collapse. I force myself not to scream. I try to tune it all out, to disappear into the quiet corners of my mind, because there's nothing I can do to help her.

Cristiano speaks to his men in his unfamiliar language. A moment later, a chair is brought over. One of the guards sets it beside him, and Cristiano pulls it closer.

He gestures for me to sit, but my brain and body are disconnected. It's almost as if I've physically forgotten how to move.

Then the first grunt, accompanied by a soft whimper from the corner, reaches me, and the room seems to tilt.

I don't know who guides me to the chair, but I sit willingly. Another man hands Cristiano a water bottle. The cap cracks open, and he holds it out to me.

I take it with shaking hands and drink. Water runs down my chin, but I don't care.

Cristiano leans in, his voice low enough that only I can hear.

"Don't you dare break. Not here."

I stare straight ahead. I try to look composed. I try to breathe evenly. I try to pretend I don't hear what's happening just a few feet away.

I blink fast, trying to keep the tears from falling. If I start crying now, I won't be able to stop.

The creak of the bed has my hands trembling, and the way the men watch what's being done to her makes me imagine all the ways I want to kill them.

I stare at the surface of the table, forcing myself to focus on the grain in the wood, as if that will drown out everything else.

The meeting continues, filled with words I don't understand. But what I do understand, without needing a translation, is that every single man in this room is a monster.

When they finally rise at the end of the meeting, the mood shifts. Everyone appears to be in better spirits, having come to an agreement with product numbers and supply.

I feel like I might pass out from how badly I want to get out of here.

As we begin to move toward the door, I realize the girl on the bed is just being left there. Who knows how long she's already been here. I reach out and grab Cristiano's arm.

"I want her coming with us."

He turns his head, looking at her, then at me.

"Please," I add.

He exhales slowly, like even entertaining the idea is an inconvenience.

"She can come. But you will service me tonight."

This is not a request. This is a transaction.

I glance back at the girl, and there is no question in my mind. I will sleep with this piece of shit to save her.

"Fine," I say firmly.

He nods once to a nearby guard, who moves across the room, unlocking the handcuffs and pulling the girl to her bare feet.

Cristiano places a hand on my back and begins to guide me out.

We go back the way we came until we reach his vehicle again. He opens the back door and nods for me to get in.

The man with the girl says something to Cristiano, and he scans her.

"What?" I ask. When he says nothing, I ask again.

He looks at her a moment longer, then down at me. "She's… filthy."

"And?" I bite out.

"Do you want her sitting next to you looking and smelling like that?"

My mouth hangs open at their audacity. She didn't choose for this to happen to her. It's not her fault she hasn't gotten to shower in days.

"Of course."

He nods to the guard, signaling that it's fine for her to get in with us.

On the other side, he forces her into the vehicle and slams the door.

I climb in and slide toward the middle, choosing to sit closer to her than to Cristiano.

Her eyes stay fixed out the window, and her hands remain clasped tightly in her lap. Deep, raw marks circle her wrists where the cuffs had been. She doesn't look afraid—just empty.

I shift slightly, reaching over and quietly taking her hand.

She blinks, startled at first, then slowly looks at me.

We hold each other's gaze for a long moment. No words. Just two girls caught in the same nightmare.

Then she gives my hand the faintest squeeze. Even without the cast, the pressure is so light it wouldn't have hurt my broken bones.

But it's enough to break something open inside me.

I turn my face toward the front before the tears can slip free. I keep my grip on her, holding on to the one thing in this moment that still feels human.

Cristiano glances over, landing on our joined hands, and a smirk tugs at his mouth. He turns back to the window, amused by two abused girls trying to comfort each other. It feels like he's already decided how to twist it into something he can use against us—against me.

We wind along a narrow road, climbing steadily higher until we reach the top of a hill and come to a stop in front of a massive estate. The house rises at the edge of a cliff, overlooking the ocean far below. It looks like a fortress. Guards are positioned all over, something that should be terrifying to see, that was terrifying to see the first time I was at the Volkovs. But now, this is normal, I suppose.

Cristiano probably has more than a couple handfuls of people who want to bash his head in, so it makes sense he has a bunch of guards to protect his bitch ass.

The girl is pulled from the vehicle and guided toward the entrance. I'm relieved when I see Fedora. She steps forward and takes her, saying something about getting her cleaned up. Then they vanish inside.

His hand settles on the small of my back, and I tense under the touch.

"Dinner," is all he says.

We move through the house and out onto a wraparound patio, where the table is already set. Plates. Wine. Candles. Everything arranged as if this were meant to be a romantic evening for two.

He pulls a chair out for me, motions for me to sit, then takes the seat across from me.

He's radiating anger. I can see it in the way he chews each bite. The muscles in his jaw tense like he's really having to work to keep his mouth shut.

We make it halfway through the meal before he studies me.

"How are you this weak?" He gestures vaguely in my direction. "You came from the Volkovs."

The name alone sends a lance through my chest.

"You break in front of one of my clients, and I'll personally break you."

I know he means it. He would beat me within an inch of my life and never lose a wink of sleep over it. I don't respond. There's no point. I have nothing to say that would matter. So I keep my mouth shut and let him ramble.

He goes on about how soft I am. How Damiano is a coward. I stop listening. I can't bear to hear him speak about Dom like that. Not when he's the only man who's ever truly loved me. The only one who's ever cared.

I'm not sure when Cristiano stops talking. Maybe he finally realized I wasn't going to respond and decided not to waste his breath. When he stands, I know what comes next. Bed. And I know exactly what that means after what I agreed to.

"Get up."

I stay seated.

"I didn't finish eating," I say, stalling.

"Too bad," he snaps, yanking me from the chair.

I'm dragged toward the back door, and I tug my arm, trying to get free. "I'll walk. You don't need to squeeze so hard."

He exhales sharply, annoyed, but releases me.

"We had an agreement," he reminds me.

I want to deny it, to say I don't know what he's talking about. But I know that lie would cost me. He'd probably beat me anyway.

When he opens the bedroom door, a wave of discomfort hits me. For a second, I contemplate shitting myself just so he'd be too disgusted to touch me.

But every thought vanishes the moment I see the girl from the warehouse waiting at the edge of the bed. She's clean now, her hair damp, a thin white nightgown clinging to her frame. She glances at me, then quickly looks away.

I step inside, and Cristiano shuts the door behind us. I linger just past the threshold, not wanting to go in any farther. I didn't realize he was going to traumatize her more by making her watch. Maybe that's his way of reminding me what I agreed to.

He doesn't waste any time. He starts unbuttoning his shirt, then moves to his pants.

She and I both remain unmoving. It's like watching a train wreck. You want to look away, but you can't. I know she doesn't want to see any of this. Her chin dips toward her chest, yet her eyes still lift, drawn to the unfolding scene.

"You wanted to play savior. And you made a deal. Take off your clothes."

My mouth opens to protest. I want to tell him we should wait until tomorrow, that it's been a long day and we both need sleep. But the words don't make it out.

He steps forward and slaps me so hard across the face my ears start to ring.

I gasp, cupping my cheek. The burn spreads instantly, and rage courses through me.

"You fucking prick!"

Another slap. Even harder.

"Stop fucking hitting me!" I scream, shoving him with both fists, hoping my casts might hurt him.

He doesn't budge.

"You're not in Damiano's bed anymore, darling," he growls. "You will listen the first time I tell you to do something, or you will be punished. Now. Take off your clothes."

"Fuck you!"

His hand comes down again. Then again. Again and again.

The blows keep coming until my legs go weak. My face is burning. My head is spinning.

He drags me across the room, then rips my sling off, throwing it to the floor, and shoves me onto the bed. I fight with everything I have. I kick, I scream, but it only seems to fuel him on.

I thrash, legs flying as he starts tearing the clothes from my body.

I agreed to this.

I did it for her.

And now our roles have flipped.

Now she's the one watching, listening to the same thing that was done to her. Only the men at the warehouse just wanted sex, and none of them lasted very long.

Cristiano can go for so long.

He's rough. He chokes me. He calls me names. He slaps me, spanks me, bites me. He doesn't just fuck me to reach an orgasm. He does it to cause pain. He comes over and over, his erection never going down.

Each time he moans out his release, I pray he's done. But he starts again, sometimes giving me a couple of minutes before going right back in.

When he truly finishes, my entire body aches. My skin burns from the slaps. My scalp throbs from where he yanked my hair. And when he gets up, he looks perfectly composed. Not a hair out of place.

But I lay here just wishing for death to claim me.

"While you're here, mourning what was taken, I want you to know I offered the Volkovs a trade. Damiano for you." He straightens his spine. "Damiano himself refused it."

The words cut deeper than anything else could.

"The man you cry for doesn't want you. If he did, he would have come for you. Be thankful your pussy is as good as it is. That's the only reason you're still alive. You disgust me for spreading your legs for him. And you have an atrocious attitude. You belong to me now, Rainey. The sooner you accept this, the better off you'll be.

"I want to make myself very clear. From this day forward, your refusals to sleep with me will result in *her* punishment."

Then he strides away.

He disappears into the bathroom, the door slamming shut behind him.

And I break.

I sit at the edge of the bed, head hanging forward, crushed beneath his words. My chest caves around the ache, and the silence feels unbearable.

Damiano doesn't want me? He's truly not coming for me?

He's untouchable. He's invincible. There's nothing he can't do, nobody who doesn't fear him. And yet, it's a mirage, right? Because Cristiano took his girlfriend. He turned down a trade. He didn't even want to discuss one. He fed me to the wolves and didn't even care. And now, I'm Cristiano's sex doll.

Trembling hands reach up toward my face. She kneels on the floor in front of me, holding tissues. One presses gently against my bleeding lip, the other rests beneath my nose.

"Why did you agree to that?" she whispers. "You don't even know me."

I meet her gaze. "Did you like what was happening to you?"

Her lips part, then her eyes soften. "No."

"Then say thank you."

"Thank you." After a pause, she adds, "I'm Giulia."

I glance up at her. "Rainey."

She grabs more tissue, replacing the soiled ones with clean ones. She's doing her best to patch what's broken on the outside, but my insides hurt in ways I don't think are survivable.

When he returns, he walks straight to the bed.

"You can sleep on the floor," he says, tossing a pillow beside where she's still kneeling.

He climbs in, adjusting his pillows behind him, then reaches over and flicks the light off while saying, "Lie down."

She and I both stay put. When the light flips back on, her entire body tenses. I'm not about to have us both get in trouble for him being a piece of crap, so I turn. "You just beat the shit out of me. She's trying to clean me up."

He sighs, then pushes the covers back off as he marches around the bed.

"Move," he bites out.

She immediately does, and he steps into her place, grabbing my chin and tilting it back. He lets out a scoff as he reaches for more tissue.

I push his hand away, moving my head back. "Go to bed if you can't be bothered to clean up a mess that you created."

He reaches for me again and I pull back. He inhales deeply before taking my chin as he wipes at the blood.

His eyes rake over my face, and I don't know why he's looking at me like this.

"What?" I snap, feeling self-conscious.

He shakes his head and keeps blotting at the blood. "You're absolutely breathtaking, you have no idea."

His words have me ready to spit out a retort, but then my mind catches up with what he said.

He thinks I'm breathtaking? And yet, he beats the shit out of me daily? What a scumbag.

Once he's finished, he tells me to lie down. I do so, curling onto the edge as he makes his way back to his side.

Giulia picks up the pillow he threw down to her, and curls into a ball on the floor.

I stare down at her, hating that she's not in a proper bed. He didn't even give her anything to cover up with, and this room is really cold. I peer to the end of the mattress, then reach for the throw blanket at the foot and gently lay it over her—the only comfort I can offer.

He clears his throat, and I freeze.

"If you want her to keep that blanket, you'll kiss me."

I don't move. I stay completely still, praying he won't actually force that.

Suddenly, the blanket is flung back onto the bed. Apparently, even she would rather go without one than force me to kiss him.

He laughs, the sound low and cruel, then leans over and tosses it back down.

I'm rolled onto my back as he props himself up on one elbow beside me, gently brushing my hair away from my face.

"You're so beautiful," he whispers.

His lips brush against mine, and I close my eyes.

Damiano.

When his tongue slides into my mouth, I respond. Not for him, but for the memory of Damiano's smile—the way it lights up his entire face, the way he only ever smiled like that for me.

When he finally pulls away, he gazes down at me. "Quit making me hurt you. I want to see this beautiful face without bruises."

Then he turns his back, settles into his pillow, and lets out a contented sigh.

I lie there, staring at the ceiling, my chest aching with a hollow kind of longing. For just a moment, I wish I could hold Damiano.

Chapter

TEN

Rainey

I'm groggy, half-asleep and disoriented when I'm rolled onto my stomach. My mouth moves. I think I'm asking what's happening, but whatever comes out is slurred and unintelligible.

There's no warning. No permission. Just the weight of a body on top of my back, then he's guiding himself to my entrance, and I feel the pressure of his invasion.

It's quieter this time. Slower. Not gentle. Never gentle. But not as violent as usual. Maybe because he just woke up too. Maybe because it's morning and he somehow thinks that makes a difference.

How could he see an unconscious woman, and think it gives him the right to just shove his dick inside her?

He drives into me with long, deep strokes, each one making me wince. I grip the edge of the bed, trying to hold on as he moves

Giulia's fingers lace between mine and squeeze. I squeeze back, focusing on her touch in a desperate attempt to mentally escape.

The whole time, she holds on. Her thumb moves in soft circles, trying to soothe me. I know she's helpless in all this, and it's the only comfort she can offer, which I appreciate.

I remember how powerless I felt in the warehouse, how I couldn't even reach her. Maybe that's why she's doing it now. We all try to comfort others the way we wish someone would comfort us. Maybe that's what would have helped her.

He's getting more aggravated by the second. Each time he grunts in frustration, I tense. He starts jerking himself off to get hard again, but nothing happens. This only fuels his rage. My hair is gripped, and I'm rolled onto my back. My legs are spread on either side of his thighs as he sits back on his heels, one hand tightening around my throat, the other forcing its way between my legs.

He fingers me roughly. I can't process what's happening, but my face is burning and a sickening orgasm builds. I fight my body, not wanting to give him that, but it betrays me. He keeps hitting precisely the right spot. I claw at his arms, trying to get him to loosen his grip. He holds tight until my hips shoot off the bed and I try to gasp as my climax rips through me, my body convulsing.

He lets go of my throat, yanking my hips onto his lap as he spears me with his cock. I'm fucked so fast and hard I scream out from the pain… and unfortunately, the pleasure. The fullness of him, while I'm still coming down from my orgasm, makes another one build and release without warning. My walls constrict around him so tight, his head falls back, eyes closing with a grin.

Two more pumps and he buries himself deep. His body falls limp over mine as he groans and gives a few small, shallow thrusts.

I lay there, still as a statue. He got his erection back, and I don't want to give him any more of a reason to keep going. I even try to keep my vagina from clenching around him, but it's useless.

Apparently, she's a whore and likes fat cock, even when it's not her boyfriend's.

Fuck you, vagina.

He sits up and smirks down at me, proud he stole an orgasm from me—two actually.

My ankles are lifted into the air, and my eyes widen in confusion. Then I realize he's trying to make sure his sperm makes it to the egg.

With no thought whatsoever, I blurt out, "I have STDs. A lot of them. That would hurt a baby."

His grin stretches wider as he places my ankles onto his shoulders, pushing them toward my face while leaning in.

"Yeah? Were those from your virgin, psychotic, killer boyfriend?" he mocks.

Pretty much everything he just said offends me and pisses me off.

"No, I just assumed I got them from your slimy ass."

"And what gave you the impression you have an STD?"

"My vagina itches, and burns, and has lumps all over it."

He releases my ankles, pressing on the insides of my thighs, spreading them wide. Leaning down, he drags his tongue from my asshole to the top of my vagina, then pulls back with a wide, self-satisfied grin.

"Tastes just fine."

I gape in disbelief, stunned that he actually licked his own semen. Somehow, it's revolting coming from him, but when Dom does it, it's hot.

He climbs off the bed and stretches, yawning as he says, "Let's go."

I stare, dreading the idea of going anywhere with him. He'll probably make me get tested for STDs, and no matter the results, I know he'll find a reason to punish me.

"You want to spend more time in bed with me?"

Nope. I throw the covers off and swing my legs over the side. "Where are we going?"

He doesn't answer. Instead, he heads into the bathroom. Seconds later, I hear the water running.

"Come here." He calls out.

I sigh but walk to him, letting him help me into the shower.

He glides his fingers from my sides up to my armpits and pushes until my arms are straight up. I wince from the pain. My left collarbone doesn't want to go that high.

"Keep them raised. These can't get wet," he says, tapping my casts.

"Maybe you shouldn't have broken my bones."

He ignores my comment, pumping body wash into his palm. He lathers my skin thoroughly, gliding over every curve. He rubs my breasts, slow and intentional, then gives the same treatment to my ass before shifting between my thighs. He strokes over my folds, never entering, just teasing the outside with unbearable precision.

When he takes the handheld spray and begins rinsing me, he moves back between my legs and circles my clit. I don't want to like it. I try to think of anything else to keep my mind busy, but my body is already hypersensitive from him getting me off earlier, and it doesn't take long before he steals yet another orgasm from me.

He smirks triumphantly. "You're so responsive."

"Good for you. You're ninety-four and know where a clit is."

He steps toward me, and I step back, pressing against the wall. I'm out of space to retreat.

He leans in, and I glare up at him. He smiles and bites my lip, pulling away until it pops free.

"Gross." I wrinkle my nose as I wipe my mouth with my bicep.

It earns me a low chuckle as he points for me to sit on the bench. I do as he says, wondering if he's gonna make me suck his dick now as repayment for him getting me off.

He gets on his knees in front of me, pours more soap into his hands, then lifts my foot. He doesn't just wash them. He massages them with deep, intentional rubs that make my guard slip. My head falls back, eyes rolling as I give in to the feel of it. They're so sore, it feels incredible. I almost think I might be drooling. But when he sets my other foot down, I'm back to reality. All drool still contained in my mouth, and I'm angry again.

I don't want him making me feel good. Never again. I'll never give in to anything he does that makes me feel good. Do you hear me, vagina? Never again. This will only work if you're on board.

After the shower, he gives me a towel and tells me to wait by the sink. He leaves and returns with a dress.

I stare at it as he holds it out. "Where are my bra and underwear?"

"You won't need them."

I cross my arms and lift my brows.

"This isn't a negotiation. You will put this dress on."

I roll my eyes and take it. It hugs me tightly at the top. The straps are thin, and my boobs are pushed together. I actually hate how good they look in this dress, because I don't want any of the freaks in this house ogling them.

My fear is immediately confirmed when he turns toward the mirror and halts, locking onto my chest.

"What?" I demand.

He snaps out of whatever that was. His gaze darkens, and he picks up a toothbrush still in its packaging, slamming it on the counter by the other sink. "Brush your teeth."

I do. We both do. I can feel him watching me, but I look at the wall behind me through the mirror.

When he finishes, he goes to walk out.

"Giulia needs a toothbrush."

He glances back, then sighs when I turn toward him, not backing down. He walks to a closet, pulls out another one, extends it toward me, and walks away.

"Can I get her?"

"Yes."

Before he fully leaves, I ask what she is supposed to wear. I'm not sure if he heard me. If he did, he didn't acknowledge it.

I hurry out and peek into the bedroom. "Psst, Giulia."

Her head pops up from the side of the bed. I give a small wave, motioning for her to come. She does. I offer her the toothbrush, not sure how I expected her to react, but she just stares at my casts before finally taking it.

"What?"

"Nothing."

"Obviously not nothing. You're judging me for something, and I want to know what."

"I'm not judging you. I'm making an observation. Your hair is wet, and your casts are dry." She states, not elaborating, but it feels like an accusation.

She obviously heard what happened in the shower, and it probably sounded consensual. But nothing he does is consensual. Even if it feels good, I don't want him doing it.

"And that's supposed to mean what? My arms are broken. I'm fucking helpless."

She finishes, then turns to me. "I didn't mean anything by it. I didn't mean to upset you. I don't like that he washed you. I'll do it. I don't want him doing it."

My chin jerks back. "And you think I do?"

She holds her hands up defensively. "Rainey, I'm sorry. I didn't mean to upset you."

"You didn't mean to upset me?" I huff out a laugh. "Every day I'm being fucked by someone who isn't my boyfriend. I'm in hell, and I can't use my hands. But you want to pass judgment because my hair was washed by my captor? Maybe you haven't noticed, but I'm a prisoner here. I don't get to make decisions. Exhibit A and Exhibit B." I hold my casts up one at a time.

"I didn't mean that. It came out wrong."

Cristiano appears, standing in the doorway. He's dressed in his usual attire, another dress slung over his arm.

"Drama?" he drawls, sounding amused.

"Eavesdrop much?" I bite out, yanking the dress away from him.

"You have two minutes," he calls over his shoulder as he walks out.

The dress he gives her is like mine, tight on top and flowy at the bottom. Her boobs almost spill out of the neckline, and she keeps trying to hold the fabric together, but it's no use.

"You're perfect," I whisper.

"I've always hated having boobs."

I shrug. "I like boobs."

"Tell me how much you like them after every man who uses your body goes straight for them, when you're reduced to a pussy to fuck and tits to suck."

"Well, that escalated quickly. I just think yours are nice. I wasn't meaning any disrespect toward past trauma. Sorry."

"Well, I think yours are really nice too."

Chapter
ELEVEN

Rainey

Breakfast is on the patio, same as yesterday, the day before that, and so on.

Cristiano doesn't say what Giulia should be doing. Usually, he leaves her inside, but he didn't today, so when he pulls out my chair, I ask if she's eating with us. His expression shifts, like he's taken aback to see her here, but I shut down any chance of a response by pointing to a seat and telling her to sit.

After we finish eating, a housekeeper rushes over and starts to kneel in front of me. Cristiano smacks her arm and motions for her to go to Giulia, simultaneously jerking a pair of wedges from her hands. Apparently, he intends to put mine on himself.

I try to pull my ankle back, annoyed he thinks he needs to put my shoes on. He tightens his grip, staring up at me, daring me to resist again. Reluctantly, I let him take my foot.

I assume we have plans, considering we're all dressed, but I have no idea what they might be. At the Volkov property, I wasn't allowed to leave. So when we actually pass through the gates, it catches me off guard.

The drive into town is breathtaking. Everything is so vivid: vibrant blooms spill over stone walls, trees line the pristine streets, and the sky looks almost too blue to be real. Massive estates dot the cliffside, with views nearly as stunning as Cristiano's. The architecture is mostly old but updated to meet luxury standards. This must be where the rich come.

We stop at several stores, where he speaks to specific people, then we're back in the vehicle, heading down the coast until we reach the water. The docks are lined with yachts of all sizes. The largest one at the very end is being loaded with boxes and pallets, and we head straight toward it. I pray we aren't getting on, but I realize we are when Cristiano stops to speak with someone, then boards.

Giulia starts to step forward, and I remain in place, not wanting to go. It's massive, incredibly intimidating, and the thought of leaving land is terrifying. At least here, it feels like I have a sliver of a chance at escaping. But on the water? I'm screwed.

I peer behind me to gauge my odds of running, but at least ten men are heading down the dock toward us. I stand zero chance of getting away.

My arm is yanked painfully, and I already know whose cowardly hand is jerking me around like that. As I'm dragged toward the yacht, I try to pull away.

"Don't fucking touch me," I murmur quietly, not wanting to cause a scene. But we already are, just from him having to come retrieve me.

Once we're on board, he releases me and turns to shake hands with a man already on deck.

"Do you understand what he's saying?" I whisper to Giulia.

She nods. "He's asking if the product was loaded, if the chef is here, how his kids are…"

Cristiano jerks his chin toward me, and the man glances over, smiling as he claps him on the shoulder.

"What did he say?" I ask.

"That you're… going to be his wife."

My body goes cold. He's delusional.

"I literally have a boyfriend."

"He doesn't seem to care."

I wonder how shocked both men would be if I hauled off and punched Cristiano in the side of the head. I'd get beat for sure, but it would be worth it. It would make a statement that I'm not his anything… especially not his future wife.

They talk for a while longer before he begins giving us a tour, casually chatting as they catch up. We're shown to our bedroom, and he grins, waggling his eyebrows.

"This is where you and the missus can make the boat rock," Giulia whispers.

I wrinkle my nose, and she nods in agreement.

The bed has shopping bags on it, and I wonder if they're meant for us. I assume they are, since they're in the room Cristiano and I are supposed to be staying in.

While the men stare out the window, I peek into one of them and feel sick when I see lingerie inside. I open it wider, nudging her foot to get her attention. She has the same reaction.

I let go of the bag and pretend to be fascinated by the ceiling when they turn around.

Cristiano drags a finger down my arm as he passes, and it's Giulia's grip tightening that keeps my expression in check.

We walk down the hall to another room, and the man gestures toward Giulia.

Cristiano glances at me, then shrugs. "My woman will decide where she wants her to sleep," Giulia translates.

The man starts speaking again, and she quietly adds, "Two beautiful women all to yourself. You're a lucky man, Mr. Fierro. If you want to loan out the other one, I'd like to have her for the night."

My mouth drops open. "She's not a fucking whore," I bite out.

His eyes widen. "I'm sorry, miss. It was a joke in poor taste. My apologies."

I look to Cristiano, somehow believing he'll act like a man, acknowledge how inappropriate that comment was, and address it, but of course, he doesn't.

As we set sail, I start to panic. I've never been on a boat, and it's overwhelming. Maybe he senses it, or maybe he just sees that I'm ready to hurl myself into the water, because he wraps his arm around my waist and holds me to his side. Even when I try to discreetly move away, he only grips tighter.

Yep. He definitely knows I'm thinking of a way off.

I'm not in any sort of ideal situation, but I can't seem to wrap my head around how I keep ending up surrounded by wealthy people. I can't comprehend this kind of money, or why rich people would want anything to do with me. Damiano doesn't seem to care about money at all, yet all the Volkovs are loaded.

This would be the kind of yacht that, if I were with Dom, I'd have sex with him in every single room. I'd excitedly explore it, knowing that no matter who he brought with us, I'd be safe from harm. But here, every corner could hide danger. Everyone with a penis is a situation where I could be raped. Or Giulia. And I'm not willing to risk her safety.

When the tour ends, Cristiano says he has business to take care of and tells us to relax on the back deck and get some sun. We do as we're told, settling onto a cushioned couch in the shade beneath the awning. It's warm and sunny, and I wish I had a pair of sunglasses. Without them, the glittering ocean trails behind us are almost too bright.

"Where are you from?" I ask, glancing over at her.

She tucks her legs under herself and leans back. "Naples. I haven't been back in years."

I try to imagine what her life was like before all this.

"How did you end up at the warehouse?"

She pauses, scanning the water. "Sometimes they bring me to meetings or parties. Other times, they put me in brothels. I was taken when I was sixteen. There were three of us. We were on a school trip when our bus was stopped by a van blocking the road. Men with guns stormed on and pulled my best friend, another girl, and me off. We were brought to a house where we were all stripped of our virginities within minutes of arriving. It was horrifying. That was the last night I saw either of them. We were all sent to different places. After a while, you stop asking questions."

I stare at her, knowing I can't comprehend how terrifying that must have been. What I've dealt with has been shitty, but nowhere near her level of trauma. "I'm so sorry, Giulia."

"For a long time, I wondered how my mamma and Papà handled it—me being taken. Or how my younger sisters did. But I realized blocking those memories was the only way to survive." She turns to me. "What about you? How did you end up there?"

"My boyfriend is Damiano Volkov. His mom sent me to pick up her dress for a party or something. I was attacked at the dress shop."

Her eyes widen. "He kidnapped you from Damiano Volkov?"

"Yeah. You've heard his name before?"

"Uh, yeah. I think everyone has. I actually thought he was gay."

I blink at her, caught off guard. "People say that?"

"Not at all."

"Then why would you think that?"

She shrugs. "One of the houses I was in had girls coming in and out constantly. Not all of them were workers, but they would still talk to some of the girls. One of them said she was at a party with the entire family, and his name was thrown around because he always looks like he's about to kill someone. She said he was super hot, so she tried to take him to bed, thinking he probably just needed to get laid, and he told her if she ever tried talking to him again, he'd put a bullet through her brain."

I laugh out loud, because that's just like something he'd say.

She looks confused. "What?"

"Nothing. That just sounds exactly like him."

Her eyes go wide. "And you're not scared he'll kill you if you make him mad?"

I shrug. "There's no one else I'd rather be killed by."

The horror on her face only makes me laugh harder. "He's truly the best. He just doesn't like being touched."

"…then how do you guys have sex?"

"We touch each other. We have wild, filthy sex."

"But I thought he hates being touched?"

"I'm his girlfriend. We like to touch each other." I shrug again. "But no, he's definitely not gay."

I sigh as I lean back on the bench. I fucking miss him so much.

Her head rests on my shoulder, and she laces her fingers with mine. "Thank you for saving me."

I scoff. "Is that sarcasm?"

"No."

"I saved you from being raped just for you to have to watch me get raped."

She squeezes my fingers. "I'm sorry."

"Don't be. I'd rather it be me stuck with his dumbass than you with those pigs at the warehouse. My fate was already decided. He was going to have sex with me regardless. But at least we changed yours."

"Yeah, they were gross." She pretends to vomit, pointing her finger in her mouth.

I smile and nudge her cheek with my shoulder.

"How old are you?" she asks.

"Twenty-seven. You?"

"Twenty-five. How old is Cristiano?"

I shrug. "I'd guess around forty-five."

"He looks young."

"Yeah," I agree. "He's such a piece of shit, but everyone here is dazzled by him."

"I noticed that too. They wouldn't be like that if they knew how he treated you. They see a good-looking guy with money and power and don't care about anything else."

"Yep."

She glances around behind us. In a quieter voice, she asks, "He has a wedding ring on. Where is his wife?"

I shrug. "Who knows. Probably raping boys or something. I'd imagine to be married to someone like him, you'd have to have similar taste."

"What do you think she'll do when she finds out about you?"

I swipe my finger across my neck.

Her eyes widen. "For reals?"

"I mean, I'm sure she would see it as consensual sex. Especially since—"

I don't want to admit out loud that he managed to get me off. I'm still mad at my body for feeling good with what he does when I don't want him touching me.

We fall into silence, just staring out at the water.

"What are you thinking about?" she asks.

"Dom."

"What about?"

"I don't know. A lot. How he's doing. If he misses me or thinks about me. We lost our virginity to each other. It was something we shared with only the other. But, at one of their parties, I was raped. While Dom tortured them for what they did, I slept with his brother… for days. My body count went from a special one to seven in less than a week.

"Then I end up here, and Cristiano constantly sleeps with me. During one of his deals, he let ten or fifteen different men assault me. I actually don't know how many touched me. I zoned out, tracing patterns on the ceiling the whole time.

"What used to be something special turned into double digits in the blink of an eye. And now I can't stop thinking about how Dom could ever want me again—especially when he's only ever been with me. And I don't even know the exact number of men I've been with anymore."

Then it dawns on me—he won't be mine forever. I try to accept the reality of it, but the thought of him with someone else hurts.

I begin to picture him married, holding his child, and my eyes sting. I wipe the tear away and force the thought out of my mind. I can't let myself go there.

We remain put for the rest of the day.

Periodically, Cristiano comes and checks on us. He never comes outside—just stands in the window. The first couple of times, we would look, but now, every time I feel him watching, I ignore him. Each time, Giulia whispers, "Your stalker is back," and I respond, "Yep… fuckin' loser."

When the sun begins to go down, I know we'll have to go in soon, but I don't want to. I don't like nighttime because it's a sure thing he'll have sex with me.

As it gets darker, I'm honestly shocked he hasn't called us in. I'll stay out here as long as he lets me. I'd sleep here if I could, even with the temperature dipping the way it is.

"Do you see that?" Giulia sits up, squinting at the open water.

I follow her gaze and spot another yacht moving steadily in our direction. At first, I think it's just passing by, but it doesn't veer off. It keeps coming straight toward us.

We both straighten, unsure of what we're looking at.

"Are they going to hit us?"

I take her hand, ready to bolt inside, just as it finally starts to slow. It pulls right up to the back of ours, bumping gently against the platform.

Panic claws at my throat as the first man climbs aboard, but then Cristiano appears with three other men, walking out like they've been expecting this.

It's not just men. There are women, more women than men, and they're all dressed in scant attire. Laughter spills from the group as they are guided inside.

As one of the girls passes, she looks Giulia and me up and down with open disgust. We do the same right back when we see her dress is completely see-through and her underwear is wedged between her butt cheeks.

More walk by, giggling. Some glance at us sporadically, their expressions letting us know they think we're beneath them.

"What was that?" Giulia asks once the last of them makes it inside.

"No clue."

We watch until the entire group disappears from sight, but their yacht stays tethered to ours.

When it's time for dinner, a woman tells us we need to come in.

She brings us straight to a dining room where all the extra visitors are loud and boisterous. The table is long, and both seats next to Cristiano are occupied by women. Thank you, Jesus.

We take two available seats at the end of the table, and nobody seems to notice us. In fact, everyone is drunk.

Even Cristiano's eyes are glazed over.

I eat quietly, suffering through the most annoying flirting I've ever heard. When I can no longer take that nails-on-a-chalkboard giggling, I decide I'm done.

"I'm gonna sneak out," I whisper. "I'm tired."

"No." She grabs my arm, shaking her head subtly.

"He's drunk. I'm not staying here listening to this. Plus, he's too wrapped up in them to see anything else."

"He will punish you."

"Doubt it. He probably can't get it up."

As I stand, she grabs my arm again, silently pleading.

"I'm not staying. Come if you want, or don't."

Her eyebrows knit with concern as she peers down the table to where one girl is now shirtless, unbuttoning Cristiano's pants while he leans back, watching her with hooded eyes. It's enough for her. She follows me out and we sneak the entire way to our room.

We both sigh with relief as soon as the door closes, thankful we made it back safely.

"I think he was going to sleep with those girls," she says.

"Good. It will give me a night off."

Her face falls as she stares at me sympathetically. "I'd have sex with him if he would agree. I'd do anything to make you suffer less. I know I can't help, but I would if I could. And I'm willing to have that conversation if you're up for it."

I shake my head. "Absolutely not. I'm not going to subject you to his abuse."

"Rainey, this has been my life for nine years."

"No."

I'm not even going to entertain the idea if she's doing it for me. Especially not if she thinks sex is the only way she can help. I remember when Anya told me that, after a while, she started craving it. I don't know if it's like that for everyone, but I'm not going to ask. I want Giulia to have sex that's consensual.

A couple nights ago, Cristiano managed to draw orgasm after orgasm from me, even when I cried out in frustration each time. When he made me go down on him, warning he'd shoot me if I bit him, I tried to disassociate as he fucked my face. That's when I accidentally saw Giulia pleasuring herself as she watched us. For someone so used to sex, maybe the break from it wasn't as good as

I thought it would be. Maybe she's still wanting it, no matter how it comes.

Apparently, the firmness of my no killed any conversation we might have had. We fall into silence as hours pass in a fragile calm.

The door slams open unexpectedly, and we both jump as Cristiano storms in, his steps unsteady. He's drunk, and I mean big drunk. His eyes are bloodshot, and the second they meet mine, I know I'm fucked.

He starts yelling something about betrayal and control, but the words slur together as he marches toward the bed. His hand flies out and strikes me across the face so hard I gasp. My head whips to the side, the sting blooming instantly.

The stench of another woman clings to him, and now it's on me. He slapped me, and her smell is what he left behind.

He yanks at my clothes, tearing them off with a violent strength. But he doesn't take his off. He always undresses first.

I watch him scan the room, and I follow, desperate to figure out what he's looking for.

When his gaze lands on a bottle of body spray on the dresser, I wonder if he thinks I'm what smells, but that scent is the pussy *he* brought in here with him.

He's gone long enough to retrieve it, and then he's stalking toward the bed. I try to scoot away, but he grabs my leg and yanks me back. A struggle follows. I kick, twist, and beg him to stop. He slaps me, then again, harder. The more I fight, the harder he hits.

There's a strength in him tonight that comes from alcohol and fury. It terrifies me. When he digs around in a bag I watch as he pulls open a bottle of something and starts pouring it on me. He's so wasted I don't even know what he's intending with it. It's slick and oily—lube maybe?

He rubs it over my vagina, then pours a handful into his non-dominant hand. It becomes horrifyingly obvious what he's planning when he grabs the body spray bottle and lathers the end with the lube.

I start screaming. Pleading. Telling him I'll do anything he wants me to. I'll go down on him without complaint or let him go down on me. I beg for him to stop.

He doesn't.

He uses that same drunken strength to assault me with the bottle. I've felt physical pain. I've felt humiliation at the hands of this monster. But this… this is on a whole new level.

When it's over, there's blood everywhere—on the sheets, on his hands, on my thighs. My body trembles uncontrollably, a violent mix of adrenaline and rage, and I sob from the unbearable cramping.

He's still seething afterward. He paces the room, muttering under his breath, then lets out a roar and sweeps everything off the dresser. Even that doesn't ease his fury. He just starts looking for the next thing to destroy.

Giulia watches me, then rises abruptly. "She needs a doctor."

He whirls around on her. "Then go find one."

She sniffles as she rushes for the door, yanking it open, fleeing from the room.

I curl into the fetal position. I can feel it everywhere, inside and out.

"Shut up," he snaps. "Stop crying!"

I try to quiet myself, but it hurts too much.

He grabs me by the waist and spanks me hard. I scream out. Each slap is excruciating, until I can no longer tell whether the numbing pain is from the repeated hits or if my skin is cold from blood. It feels like my ass is raw, but I know realistically, spanking alone wouldn't do that.

Giulia returns with a man carrying a black medical bag. His expression changes the moment he sees me.

He says nothing as he kneels beside me and attempts to pull my legs apart.

"No," I wail.

Giulia climbs on the bed and wraps herself around my head, locking me in a tight embrace.

"I'm so sorry. I'm so sorry," she repeats.

My sobs turn to full-body shivers as I hold on to her for dear life.

"She has a second-degree perineal tear. It starts at the lower vaginal opening and runs toward the rectum. She'll need stitches."

"Hurry the fuck up and get out!" Cristiano bellows.

I don't hear anything else. He goes to the bathroom, slamming the door.

Giulia runs her fingers through my hair, subtly rocking me back and forth.

"The first time you saw Damiano, what did you notice? His eyes? His smile? Facial hair?"

She practically describes him, and with each word she says, that part of him comes to mind. His beautiful dark eyes, his perfect teeth, the stubble on his face, the gauges in his ears. When she mentions his height, I remember running across our bed into his waiting arms, wrapping myself tightly around him as we laughed and he spun me in circles.

He's so tall. My big, tall man.

She mentions his hair, and the memory of his soft, wavy locks makes my fingers ache with longing. I asked him to get a eurohawk once, and he did. We didn't even make it home before I rode him in his truck because he looked irresistible.

I relax into her as he fills my mind completely, distracting me through every second I'm being stitched up.

"The numbing injection I gave should last you through the night. You're gonna be sore tomorrow," the man says as he cleans up the bloodied and soiled dressings.

Cristiano comes out of the bathroom, freshly showered, and is informed that I have three stitches and can't have sex for two weeks. He scoffs and tells him to get out so he can fuck me.

He tries to explain that it will cause permanent damage, and Cristiano says that's exactly what he's trying to do—cause permanent damage.

The man goes on to explain that he only has limited medical resources here and I could end up needing emergency surgery if my vaginal trauma gets any worse.

Cristiano stomps toward him and slams the door in his face.

When he turns around, I grip Giulia tighter. He sits on the edge of the bed, then flops back, the knot in his towel holding strong.

And then he's snoring.

Chapter

TWELVE

Rainey

When I wake, the room is filled with soft morning light. I feel a gentle tug at my scalp and turn my head slightly. It's Giulia. She's sitting next to me, one arm around my shoulders, her fingers weaving through the strands as she stares out the window at the ocean.

I peer around the room, and Cristiano is gone.

Relief washes over me. For once, I wasn't woken up for the morning sex he demands.

"He's in the bathroom," she whispers.

A moment later, the door opens. He walks out put together, not a single trace of last night's intoxication in sight.

He goes to a suitcase, unzips it, and pulls out clothes for me, laying them neatly on the bed.

"Get dressed," is all he says, turning and walking out.

Giulia helps me up and into the outfit. I'm relieved I was provided with underwear today, which is a good sign he won't try anything. I wasn't sure he'd remember what he did, but he either does or someone told him. I notice she's already changed, but I don't ask where her clothes came from. She and Cristiano were both up before me, so he must have given them to her.

When we open the door, he's waiting just outside, speaking with one of the men from the other boat. Their conversation cuts off as both of them look at me. Cristiano's gaze drags down my body, and if I'm not mistaken, there's lust in his eyes. Then, without a word, they turn and start walking.

They lead us to the same dining room, though this time we enter through the doors directly behind the chair Cristiano sat in yesterday. As he approaches it, the same two women from before are already seated beside him, each in the exact spot they occupied yesterday, smirking up at him.

"Move." He jerks his chin at the one who was undressing him.

She looks genuinely shocked, like she expected him to be happy to see her.

"Get the fuck out of that chair," he snaps when she makes no attempt to get up.

Her mouth falls open, gaze flicking around the table, searching for someone who might be just as baffled by this interaction as she is. Especially after they slept together. Nobody reacts, except Cristiano, who grabs a fistful of her hair and yanks her to her feet. "When I say move, do it."

He releases her, and she stumbles back, holding her head.

"We had sex last night," she says, like it should mean something.

His nostrils flare, and the muscles in his jaw tick. "You've announced it to the room—now why don't you tell that to my girlfriend."

Girlfriend?

The woman turns toward *me* confidently. "I fucked your boyfriend's big cock last night."

I have no idea what's happening. Why he would tell her to say that. Why he'd call me his girlfriend. Why he pulled her out of the chair in the first place. I don't care what he does with someone else. Perhaps I should, if he's not using protection, but that's where I draw the line when it comes to caring about his extracurricular activities.

The backhand he lands across her face comes so fast and hard, I flinch. It's powerful enough to knock her straight to the floor. Her face twists in confusion, as if she doesn't understand what just happened.

I'm guessing he absolutely didn't want her to actually tell me that. He was most likely expecting her to keep her mouth shut.

"Your blown-out cunt couldn't satisfy the biggest penis in the world. Get the fuck off my boat."

I'm stunned frozen. Even when he takes me by the arm and guides me to the now-empty chair, I don't resist.

When I try to ease into a sitting position, pain lances through me. I don't even put all my weight down before I'm right back on my feet.

"I'll stand, please." I face him, not wanting the room to know where I'm injured.

He grits out something under his breath, and the man by the door hurries out.

When he moves closer, I tense. I wouldn't put it past him to do something crazy right here at the table. What he does is unexpected for him, though it might seem ordinary coming from someone else. He wraps an arm around my waist, pulling me in close, then cradles my chin, tilting it toward him. His thumb glides gently over my cheek as his gaze traces every feature.

The man returns quickly with a pillow and passes it to Cristiano, who sets it on the chair. He holds the edge steady as I ease down onto it. It still hurts, but not as badly.

I subtly shift to one side, trying to take the pressure off my stitches. That helps. A little.

The room isn't as crowded as it was last night, but enough familiar faces remain that I know their boat is still docked out back.

I expected breakfast to be awkward after he kicked that woman out, but everyone acts like nothing happened. Even the second woman sitting in the other chair, doesn't seem the least bit bothered by how he treated her friend.

She keeps staring at me, and after the fifth time we make eye contact, she clears her throat. "I'd like to apologize to you… both of you," she says, glancing between me and Cristiano. "For my behavior last night. I didn't mean to cause any hurt by my actions."

I shake my head, wanting to stop her right there. "We aren't together—"

He squeezes my thigh under the table, and I turn to look at him.

His expression says to shut the fuck up. I'm too exhausted to argue about it, so I just stop talking—then listen as he starts going on about us being in a relationship.

Honestly, I think it makes him look like a scumbag. He cheated on his *girlfriend* while she's on the same boat. I'm so glad I'm not truly anything to him other than his prisoner. If he were Damiano, I would have started a cat fight. I probably would have tried to grab any sort of weapon to kill anyone who touched what was mine. But Cristiano, he isn't mine, and I'm not his.

His hand remains on my thigh, and I push it off, giving him a dirty look.

At this point, I'm just picking a fight, but who cares. My vagina hurts, and I'm cramping so badly it's painful to sit upright. All of it because he got blackout drunk and mad for no reason.

I still don't know why these people are here. It felt random, the way they just showed up, got wasted, and are now eating with us.

After breakfast, the rest of the guests leave. Giulia and I return to the same couch at the back of the boat, the only place that doesn't feel so suffocating.

When Cristiano heads in our direction after seeing them off, I purposely avoid acknowledging him. Hopefully, he's not in the mood to deal with me and just keeps walking.

But I'm not that lucky. He sits beside me, his arm resting along the back of the couch, fingers lightly tracing my shoulder. Fear rushes through me. *He's going to have sex with me, and he's going to tear my stitches.*

"I apologize for last night. I hope you can forgive me."

I scoff. "Well, I don't."

"I shouldn't have had that much to drink. I am sorry."

I assume we're talking about the same thing, that he's apologizing for sodomizing me with a perfume bottle.

"I will make amends in any way I need to for having sex with those two women. I never wanted to cause you emotional turmoil, truly."

I gape at him. "You're apologizing for screwing random chicks, even though I couldn't care less who you stick your disgusting dick in, and not for literally kneeing a body spray bottle into my vagina, ripping me almost to my asshole?"

His chin jerks back. "That's what you're upset about?"

"Yes!"

His confusion shifts into pure anger as the realization sinks in. He thought I cared, thought sleeping with someone else would hurt me, maybe even make me jealous. But I don't care who he touches, and now he knows it.

He sits there, staring straight ahead. I can only imagine the whirlwind of thoughts he's trying to sort through. I hope he's realized he will never be Damiano. He will never be as good as Damiano, and I will never care about him.

I subtly glance at Giulia, giving her a *why the hell is he still sitting here* look, and she shrugs, just as confused.

Then he turns to me.

"Lie down."

I glare at him, appalled by his audacity. "Are you kidding me?"

"No. Now lie down."

He's actually going to do this. He's going to try to put his dick in me while I still have stitches.

He flicks his gaze to Giulia, and she immediately scoots down the couch. I keep my focus forward, fully aware he's watching me. After a moment, I sigh and roll my eyes, turning and lying back in her lap.

My thighs are spread, and he leans in, sliding my underwear aside to get a closer look at the damage.

He stares for a long time before lowering his head and placing a soft kiss against me. Maybe he's hoping for some kind of reaction, but I give him nothing.

His tongue slips between the folds, moving slowly over my clit with a flicking rhythm. I stay silent. Even when he traces slow, focused circles that might have felt incredible under different circumstances, I keep my expression flat.

He tries again, even slower this time, more precise. Still nothing.

With a frustrated breath, he sits back. "I'm trying to make you feel good."

I lift my head and gape at him. "Why the fuck would I want you making me feel good? Do you want me to nail that perfume bottle into your ass with my knee like you did to me?"

He shoves his fingers into his hair like he's trying to push the stress out of his skull, then flops back against the couch.

"My penis is bigger than the bottle I used."

"Your penis has never split me open like that. You used a cylindrical object and jammed it inside me. You knew it wasn't fitting, and you used your fucking knee to force it in. You're disgusting!"

We glare at each other, both breathing heavy.

"What do you need from me then?" He grits out.

"Am I allowed to sit back up?"

He lets out a sigh and waves his hand, giving me permission.

I do, scooting closer to Giulia. "I want to go home," I say, answering his question. "You want to know what I need from you? I want you to send me home."

"We will be on shore soon."

"That's not what I mean, and you know it."

He stares at me flatly.

I'm tired of him thinking this is all normal, that I could possibly forget the life I was stolen from. I may not know all the nefarious things the Volkovs were up to, but I was happy. Blissfully happy in my own little bubble with Damiano.

We sit here in silence, and I'm annoyed he's still next to me.

"What were those people even doing here? We're in the middle of nowhere. How did they know where we were?"

"They were given our coordinates."

My head snaps toward him. "Why?"

"It was a drop," he says casually.

"You mean a drug deal?" I retort.

He shrugs. "That is what I do for business."

"And they met us in the middle of the ocean because…?"

"You don't need to know about the business aspect of our lives."

Our lives? I want to laugh and tell him I don't want my life mingled with his in any capacity, but I'm still injured and sore and don't want to make him mad enough that he forces his stupid cock inside me.

"What was the point of that many of them coming?"

"It's just how some clients like to live. Surrounded by women."

"And you don't?"

He shakes his head once. "No."

"Why?"

He seems to think about it. "I've never been interested in that. My interests are limited. My business, money, and the person I'm with." He looks at me. "You."

I blink. *That's unfortunate.* Not sure how I could be of interest to him when he's such an asshole to me.

"So what happens if we get caught?"

"We won't," he says, and it's not a guess. It's a promise, like he's already decided that reality has to obey him.

"Why live like this? It's dangerous."

He rests his elbow on the back of the couch, facing me, and props his temple on his fist.

"Look around. Every luxury you're surrounded by is because of the work I do. You'll never want for anything because of it."

"Why would you want to raise a family in this kind of life?"

"I won't."

I lift a brow. "And you believe that because…?"

"I own everything I have. When we're expecting, I'm done with the business."

And conversation over. I'm not making a family with him. I cross my arms and turn my head away so he knows I'm finished talking.

After a couple minutes of him still sitting here, I huff. "You can go." Then I turn away again.

Still, he doesn't move.

"Do you not have something better to do than sit here?"

I know it's rude, but I don't care. I don't like being around him.

He rests his forearms on his knees and presses his fingertips together. "It's taking everything in me not to pull your panties down and bury myself inside you, so don't fucking test my patience right now."

"Screwing two different women last night wasn't enough for you? They are probably still nearby, call them back."

His hand snaps up to my face, squeezing my cheeks as he turns my head toward him.

"The only pussy that I'm interested in is the one you're sitting on. The only cock that belongs to you is the one I'm trying not to shove inside you. Keep testing my patience, and I will fuck you."

When I stay quiet, he pulls my face closer.

"Do you understand?"

I glare at him, but as he squeezes harder, I respond, "Yes."

He leans in and kisses me, then shoves my face away.

"Good chat," he says sarcastically, striding back inside.

Chapter

THIRTEEN

Rainey

I'm not entirely sure how long we've been on this yacht, but between Giulia and me, we agree we've each counted ten sunrises and ten sunsets.

I'm craving land. The ocean stretches endlessly, and somehow, it feels worse now than it did the first time I stepped on this boat. It's suffocating. Being stuck out here is starting to wear me down.

Cristiano hasn't had sex with me, but he's made me give him head every night. I try to make it as bland as possible, hoping that if it's boring, he'll stop asking. But he never does. He forces me to look at him while I do it, and I've noticed that when I do, he finishes faster.

It's strange, considering he's a complete asshole when anyone else looks him in the eyes. But if staring this motherfucker down gets it over with sooner, I'll do it.

Tonight, though, he doesn't make me. I wait, expecting the usual command, but it doesn't come.

Giulia is lying on the long cushioned window bench a couple of feet from my side of the bed. From where I am, she looks like she might be sleeping, though she could just be pretending.

The bed shifts behind me as he moves closer, his arm wrapping around my waist, and I feel his erection press against me. His hand trails beneath my silk nightshirt, squeezing my breast as his nose presses into my neck. He kisses along my skin, his breathing already heavy.

He was sleeping. I could hear his soft snoring. When it stopped, I assumed he was just shifting positions. But boy, was I wrong. He's half asleep and horny.

He slowly rubs my nipples while his hips begin to move, sliding his erection against the back of my silk shorts. Quiet moans escape under his breath as his tongue trails over my neck.

I don't let him know I'm awake until his hand moves lower, grabbing the back of my shorts. He pulls them down just enough to expose my ass, and I know what's coming next.

"I have stitches," I remind him.

He freezes for a moment, then pulls away.

Relief washes over me until I hear the soft pop of a cap, followed by the sound of something being squeezed into his hand.

Damn it.

When he comes back, I can hear the slick, wet sound of lube as he strokes himself.

He scoots closer, sliding the length of himself down my ass crack, coating me in it.

"Please," my voice quivers.

"I'll go slow," he murmurs as he eases in.

As soon as he breaches the rim, he exhales a shaky breath of arousal.

"Ow. Owww," I cry out. "It hurts so bad."

He immediately withdraws. "Okay, okay."

I continue sobbing as he goes into the bathroom and closes the door behind him.

The moment he's gone, my sobs stop, and I grab some tissue off the nightstand.

Giulia sits up, her mouth hanging open. "Did that even hurt?"

I lean over as I wipe the line of lube from my butt and roll my eyes when I meet her gaze. "No. I don't want him touching me."

"That was amazing," she says.

"Yeah, except if he ever finds out, he'll never let me get away with it again."

We can hear the unmistakable sound of him jerking off in the bathroom only he grunts with annoyance as he does it. I sigh, adjust my shorts, and lie back down.

This man has a permanent erection.

Chapter

FOURTEEN

Rainey

The first thing I see when I open my eyes is Giulia. She's already awake, staring at me. I give her a small smile and a subtle wave. She smiles back, lifting her fingers slightly from the pillow.

We stay like that for a while, just watching each other. She always looks so soft in the morning, fresh and innocent. She's so naturally beautiful. There's something comforting about it. About her. I'm lucky to have her with me through all of this.

Cristiano yawns behind me, and I startle at the sound. The bed shifts as he pushes the covers back and climbs out.

"Rainey. In the bathroom. Now."

I wrinkle my nose at Giulia and throw the covers off.

Apparently, we're showering.

He positions me to face the wall with my arms raised to keep my casts dry while he washes my hair, then my body.

Just like last night, he has an erection. And just like last night, he keeps rubbing it against my ass.

"Ugh," I huff. "Why are you always fucking horny?"

"I'm ready to stitch your fucking mouth shut. Just don't even talk unless I ask you to."

"Don't fucking touch me and I'd gladly never talk to you again," I retort.

"You'd be the perfect woman if your attitude was as good as your body and face."

"Funny. My boyfriend thinks I'm perfect just as I am."

I can tell he's trying not to freak out on me as he pushes away from the wall. But then he steps back in, wrapping his arms around my body. His hands come up to cup my breasts, and he leans in, biting my ear.

"No, I think you're nearly perfect."

Insinuating that he's my boyfriend.

"What would your wife think?"

He doesn't even miss a beat. "She doesn't."

She doesn't. Is he saying she doesn't think? Is she stupid?

Ha.

Of course she's stupid. She married him.

He keeps rubbing his cock up my butt crack, and with every pass, my irritation builds.

"Hurry up."

I feel him smile against my neck. One arm wraps tightly around my waist, and he jerks my hips back. His other hand grabs his cock, and he pushes into my ass. I whimper at the sudden stretch.

I want to pretend it hurts. I want to stay angry. But my brain short-circuits the second his fingers find my clit, rubbing in slow circles as he works himself deeper.

He starts with long, steady thrusts, easing in and out. But it doesn't take long before his pace changes. He moves faster, harder, until he's slamming into me, and the heat in my body snaps.

We come fast. My moan tears from my throat, loud and shameless, but I can't stop it. I can't think. The pleasure is too much. It crashes through me so suddenly my legs shake, and he has to hold me up.

Fuck.

Fuck.

Fuck!

I press my forehead against the wall, the orgasm ebbing away as we both pant. I swallow, trying to calm my breathing, and shrug my shoulder to get his head off me.

"I fucking hate when you do that," I bite out.

"Do what? Make you come?"

"Yes."

"Why? It's a human need. We're very sexually compatible."

"Me and my boyfriend are."

He slaps my butt. "That's what I just said. *We* are compatible."

"Get your come out of my butthole," I say, turning to look at him.

He rolls his eyes and pulls the shower sprayer off the wall. As he rubs over my butt with one hand and sprays it with the other, he suddenly pushes a finger inside. It catches me so off guard I rise onto my toes.

"What the fuck? Ow!"

He pulls out, rubbing over my butt crack again. "You said get it out of your butthole."

"Okay, you didn't have to penetrate it."

His response is turning away and shutting off the water.

He holds out a towel, and I snatch it from him.

His eyes darken at the disrespect. "You won't do that again." I know I absolutely won't be doing it again, because I will be punished.

As we get dressed, a wave of nausea rolls through me. I've already taken something for motion sickness, but it seems this morning my stomach didn't get the memo.

After breakfast, Cristiano gives me more medicine and allows me to go back to bed. Giulia lays with me, rubbing my back until I fall asleep.

When I wake, I'm alone.

"Giulia?"

Nothing.

"Giulia?" I say louder as I climb out of bed and walk to the bathroom.

It's empty too.

Panic starts to set in as I rush out. I check her designated room first, but it hasn't been touched. I go down hallway after hallway, climbing stairs and searching every door I come by. For twenty minutes, I'm in full-blown panic mode. My brain starts to come up with wild scenarios. Maybe she fell overboard. Or worse, maybe she was killed and dumped in the water.

I'm going to vomit.

I clutch the wall and gag, my stomach squeezing as I bend over, but nothing comes up.

"Miss, you are okay?" A woman in a housekeeping uniform rushes down the hall carrying sheets.

"There's a girl that was with me. Where is she?"

"Come. I show you." She waves for me to follow her. She leads me to a room and points to the door. "Inside."

"Thanks."

I walk in and freeze.

There are a few leather chairs facing a large glass window. On the other side is a room. And in that room, three men are having sex with someone.

That someone is Giulia.

I bolt forward, slamming my casts against the glass.

"Giulia!" I scream, frantically banging as hard as I can. "Giulia!"

"She can't hear you."

I whirl around to find Cristiano standing calmly in the doorway.

"You stupid bastard!" I lunge at him, my hands flying wildly, but he blocks every hit.

He grabs me, locking my arms behind my back, and moves me forward.

He flips a switch. Suddenly, the room fills with the sounds coming from the other side—her moans. Loud. Unrestrained. And they don't sound forced.

"She has needs too. Said she was horny and tired of watching you have all the fun, so I provided her with some."

I jerk in his grip, struggling to get free. "I don't believe you."

He shrugs.

I watch, helpless, as one man fucks her from behind while another lies beneath her. She's riding them, her hips moving against their thrusts. And the third? She's blowing him.

Not just blowing him—deep-throating him.

If I put in even a fraction of the effort she's giving that guy, I'd have Cristiano wrapped around my finger.

He makes me watch for ten full minutes. Ten minutes of moaning, thrusting, and sounds I've only ever made with Dom. I stare until my eyes burn, until I can't take another second. My legs go numb from standing. My head hangs in defeat, and my body slackens.

Cristiano turns us toward the door and guides me away.

He leads me through the yacht. We pass a lounge with velvet seating and a grand piano, and a bar stocked with every bottle of liquor known to man.

We reach the far end of the corridor, and he nods for me to go in.

The room is quiet. Shelves line the walls, filled with books. Real books. Hundreds of them. There's a large window looking out at the endless stretch of ocean, and in the center of the room, an oversized chair with a throw blanket draped across it.

"Stay here. Do something useful with your time," he says, then shuts the door behind him.

I keep staring long after he's gone. I want to leave and go save Giulia, but deep down, I know she was willing in that. I just don't understand why.

I run my fingers along the spines of the books beside me, try-ing to remember what book I was reading back home, but I can't. I could start a new one, but if it's good, it will forever be tainted by the memories of what's happening to me. So instead, I'll sit here and let time pass, if only for a little while.

She's gone the entire day. I cry for hours in this chair. I don't want to be away from her. I hate being away from her.

I hate it here.

I hate being away from Dom.

I. Just. Hate.

I startle awake when a touch brushes along my cheek.

The room is dark, cloaked in shadow from the moonlight out-side, and for a moment I can't breathe. A figure stands above me, his outline barely visible. My heart stutters as I stare up at him.

"Dom," I whisper. The name slips out on a shaky breath.

The lamp beside me clicks on. I wince, shielding my face from the sudden brightness. When I finally lower my hand and my eyes adjust to the light, the hope drains from me.

It's not Dom.

It's Cristiano.

And the helplessness that settles over me is deep and paralyzing. The tears don't stop, but now they fall for a very different reason.

When we get back to the bedroom, I hope Giulia is there. But when she's not, my heart sinks again. There's no way she's still with those men. It's been at least nine hours. Is she wondering where I am?

As Cristiano heads to the door, I just want to know where she is.

"Where's Giulia?"

He doesn't even turn back. All he says is, "Mind your own business."

"Dickhead."

When she finally comes into the bedroom, she's showered and in pajamas. I think it's Cristiano at first, but when I see it's her, I fly off the bed and hurry toward her, wrapping my arms around her.

"Are you okay?"

She smiles, but it seems like she feels guilty. "Of course. Why wouldn't I be?"

I gape at her, confused. "Because we've been apart all day?"

"We don't have to be together every second." Her tone is playful, but she walks off toward her bed, ending the conversation.

I gape at her. "Are you joking?"

She turns, but before she can say anything, I add, "I searched this entire boat until I found you. I saw you getting fucked."

"Okay? And?"

My jaw practically hits the floor. "And? I was trying to save you."

"I didn't need saving."

"What?! You were being raped."

Her brows pinch together. "No. I wasn't."

"You—"

What am I even trying to say?

"I have needs too, Rainey. I've been having sex for over half my life. I have to finger myself every night just to get by because I want to be there for you. But I want sex sometimes too."

I'm utterly speechless.

"Don't look at me like that. I didn't do anything wrong. You are so miserable because you aren't with Damiano that you make everyone else miserable. Everyone watches you get treated like royalty and get good sex. I'm tired of being jealous. I want sex too. I want good cock too."

My sadness turns to burning hot anger. "Fuck. You. I *am* fucking miserable without Dom. Every second of the day, all I want is him. I want my own bed, my own house, my own clothes, and my boyfriend. I'm glad it comes off that way because that's the truth. I want to go home. And that *'good cock'* you sit there and talk about? I'm raped with it. So while you fantasize about the size of Cristiano's dick, just know I hate every single second it's inside me."

She scoffs. "Yeah, you sounded like you hated it in your shower this morning."

Don't freak out, Rainey.

I take a calming breath, and then my rage flares right back up. "You know what? If I make you so miserable, then go back to your own room."

"Gladly," she bites out.

The door opens and Cristiano walks in. He lets out a long sigh as he looks between us, then shakes his head.

"What? You obviously have a fucking comment!"

"Go to bed, Rainey." He starts undressing.

"You go to bed!" I bite back.

"Did you enjoy yourself?" he asks, looking past me to Giulia.

"Don't fucking answer that," I snap, pointing at her.

"I did. Thank you again."

"Of course. They thoroughly enjoyed you too."

I go full-blown crazy. I grab his pillow off the bed and start swinging it wildly at him. "I fucking hate you!" I scream.

He grabs me and picks me up, carrying me to the bed. Then he lays me down, pinning my hands above my head as he straddles me.

I keep screaming and kicking, telling him to get off me.

"Giulia, you can go," he tells her.

"Thank you," she says as she leaves.

"No!" I scream after her, still struggling beneath him. "Get off me!"

Chapter

FIFTEEN

Dante

Rainey has been gone for seven weeks.

Seven excruciating, soul-crushing weeks.

We check on Dom constantly, but we get nothing.

He doesn't sleep. He eats everything in sight, and in those seven weeks, his muscles have noticeably grown. He spends every waking hour in the gym. His fists smash into the heavy bag until his knuckles split open. He pumps weights until he can't lift anymore. And he kills.

He says nothing. He's never been one to talk much, and I wouldn't even know how to start a conversation about how he's holding up.

But the love of his life is somewhere out there, enduring the unimaginable, and he's keeping it all bottled up.

I don't know how.

I'm losing my mind and I'm not even the one who lost her.

I've been talking to Gio about it nonstop.

He said everyone is upset she's gone but asked me why I care as much as I do. After a long silence, I told him the truth.

Everything.

He was stunned. But now he gets it. Now he understands why I can't function. Why I'm unraveling from the inside out.

He checks on me every day.

Always the same questions.

Always the same answers.

No, I didn't sleep. No, I haven't eaten. And no, I can't explain what it feels like to know that when we finally get her back, I won't be able to touch her. I won't be able to hold her the way I want. I won't get to pull her into my bed and worship every inch of what's been broken.

That kills me more than anything.

Gio walks into my office and drops into the chair across from me.

"You get any sleep?"

I shake my head.

"Eat something?"

Another shake.

He leans forward, elbows on his knees. "You need to stay focused. When we find her, she's going to need you whole. I know food is the last thing you want, but you gotta keep up your energy."

I nod, but the movement feels hollow.

"I reached out to some of my contacts," he says. "Put the word out across Hungary, Portugal, Slovakia, and Turkey. If someone sees anything, we'll hear about it."

I finally lift my eyes to him.

"We had people search his main house in Qatar. Looks like no one's been there in a while."

The pit in my stomach deepens.

"We're going to find her. One way or another."

I want to believe him. I try. But hope feels like a dying thing inside me.

A ping on my computer has me looking at the screen. An encrypted file appears. No sender. No message. I lift my hands in the air not wanting to accidentally touch something I shouldn't.

"What's up?" Gio walks around the desk to see. "What the fuck is that?"

"I don't know. It just popped up."

But I do know. I feel it in my gut.

"It's her," I whisper. "It's Rainey."

Gio grabs his phone. "Get to Dante's office now," he tells Andrei.

He claps a hand on my shoulder. "Don't jump to conclusions. We don't know what it is yet."

"It's her," I say again, dragging my hands over my face. "I know it is."

The office door swings open, and Andrei walks in.

Gio points to my computer. "Someone is trying to send something. Dante suspects it's Cristiano."

I stand as Andrei moves straight to my chair and begins typing.

"I can't trace where it came from," he mutters. "But I've isolated it. If it's a virus or spyware, it won't get through."

Gio and I stand behind him, no one speaking.

Andrei double-clicks it, and a video pops up across the entire screen.

For a moment, I think maybe it was sent by mistake. Maybe someone hit the wrong contact.

But that thought doesn't last long.

The camera jostles, then steadies.

Cristiano's face comes into view—or part of it.

He moves subtly, the camera shifting as it's handed off to someone else. Then it settles back on him.

"Here," a man off camera says.

There's a shuffle, then Cristiano looks down. A wet sound follows, like something being rubbed or spread.

"Put extra. For the stitches," the voice says again.

"I did," Cristiano replies.

He smiles as he looks down, and the camera tilts to follow his gaze. Smooth legs rest over his lap. And the vagina that goes with those beautiful legs, the one I know intimately well, is slick with oil.

His cock glides along her folds, slick and glistening, then more oil is dripped between her thighs.

"Careful with her stitches," the voice repeats as Cristiano adjusts, guiding himself to her entrance.

The camera lifts back to Cristiano's face. He begins to push inside, not even trying to hold back a moan. His eyes close, head tilting back just slightly, mouth falling open.

Then he moves again. His eyes flutter open. A faint, satisfied grin forming.

I feel every muscle in my body lock tight. My throat burns and the screen becomes blurry. Until I realize the screen didn't go blurry, my eyes are glazed over with moisture.

Gio and Andrei remain motionless.

He pushes into her slowly, and when he sinks fully inside, he stays still for a moment. His chest rises and falls with shallow breaths.

"Pull out," a voice says off-camera.

He does. All the way. Then his fingers spread her open, and the camera zooms in.

"Okay, stay gentle like that. The stitches are still intact."

The pressure in my chest becomes unbearable. I grip the back of my chair with one hand, the other flying to my mouth as bile creeps up my throat. I think I might vomit.

He hurt her perfect vagina. The damage was so severe, she needed stitches.

He pushes back in, painfully slow, then presses his thumb between her folds, rubbing her clit.

There's no way she's awake for this. She must be sedated. She would never lie there willingly. They're on what looks like a workout bench, angled upright. He grips her hips and begins pulling her down onto him.

The only sound is his breath. She doesn't make a noise. When the camera crawls slowly up her body, I see every bruise, every mark on her skin. Both arms are in casts, tied above her. Her head hangs limp to the side, resting against her left arm.

She's completely unconscious.

She's completely unaware of what's happening to her. I wonder if she's been kept like this the entire time, but I already know she hasn't. The type of abuser Cristiano is, he will want to make sure she suffers as much as possible, knowing how much it will hurt Dom.

He slides up her body, squeezing her breasts, then leans down and draws one into his mouth. He bites onto her nipple, and when he pulls away, it stretches with him until he lets it pop free. Still, she doesn't respond.

Whatever he gave her, it's strong enough to take everything from her. Awareness. Will. The ability to fight.

Gio's voice cuts through my mental agony. "Fuck. Should I get Dom?"

I shake my head without looking away from the screen. He can't see this.

"Is this in real time?"

Andrei points to the timestamp. "It was an hour ago."

Andrei shifts in my peripheral. "Should I cut the video?"

A tear slips down my cheek. I don't bother wiping it away. More will inevitably follow.

Andrei starts working again, quiet and focused. Tabs multiply across my second monitor as he digs through the data, trying to trace where the file came from.

Cristiano deals in drugs. He could have given her anything. She doesn't respond when he touches her. She doesn't even flinch when he strikes her. He does it repeatedly.

He bites his lip and jerks his chin for the camera to tilt down. When it does, it focuses between her legs, her core visibly pulsing around his shaft. He's drawn an orgasm from her, one she doesn't even realize she's having, and he looks victorious over it.

And as horrifying as it is, there's a small, sick part of me that's relieved she isn't present for it. At least she doesn't have to live through the knowledge of this part.

The rage is consuming.

My jaw clenches so hard it feels like I might actually break my teeth. I look forward to the day Damiano gets his hands on this piece of shit.

As soon as the video ends, I grab the trash can beside my desk and throw up.

Gio is at my side instantly, one hand clapping my back while he murmurs that it's okay, that we're going to find her and bring her home.

But it's not okay.

I can't believe what she's enduring.

If Rainey comes back even remotely the same woman she was, it'll be a miracle.

The office door opens, and Ma walks in.

I wipe my mouth and straighten, but the second she sees my face, her expression falls.

"Son. What is it?"

I don't answer.

She turns to Andrei, then Gio.

"What happened?"

Gio glances at me before answering. "Dante got a video."

She waits, eyes shifting between us, expecting more.

"What kind of video?"

Gio doesn't sugarcoat it. "Of Cristiano assaulting Rainey."

Ma's hand flies to her mouth. Her eyes shine, but she doesn't cry. "Has Damiano seen it?"

"No," Gio says, shaking his head.

"Don't tell him. Don't show him anything."

That makes something snap in me.

"Don't you want to ask how she looked?" I wonder how she could dismiss what was just told to her and go right into protecting Dom. "Or if she was okay?"

Ma's eyes settle on me. "No. I already know how he works."

"Both her arms are broken. Her entire body is covered in bruises."

"Dante, enough!" She slashes her hands through the air to drive her point home.

"Her vagina has been stitched up, from being torn open—"

"You're done!" she shouts.

"He's not! He's not done! He will continue to rape her! He's torturing her!" I bellow, so loud her features go slack with shock.

She gulps, like she's trying to collect herself.

"Your daughter is traumatized. She cries nonstop. She watched the horrors of a snippet of what's being done to her best friend. Your son eats, exercises, and kills. If she dies, he will put a bullet in his own brain."

"Enough!" Her voice wobbles, and tears fall down her cheeks.

I know the thought of her losing Dom is too much for her to bear. The thought of losing him is too much for all of us to bear. But Rainey is his lifeline. He will lose any humanity he has left if something happens to her.

"This is the reality. If anything happens to Rainey, our entire empire will fall. It's already crumbling."

"She's one person!" she bites back.

"Get out!" I yell, pointing to the door. "Get the fuck out!"

We stare each other down, and then she straightens and looks to Andrei. "Do you still have the video?"

"No," I say, clipped, just as Andrei starts to answer yes.

His elbow rests on the desk, and he casually wipes at his upper lip while raising a brow. He glances at me, then back at Ma.

She narrows her eyes, catching the lie.

But I don't care. No one else is going to see that footage. Not if I can help it. I won't let anyone else look at her like that. If hiding the truth is the only way I can protect her, then I'll lie through my teeth.

"Dante—"

"I said we don't have it."

Her nostrils flare.

The silence stretches until I finally say, "If you don't need anything else, we're handling business."

Her neck flushes, and her chest heaves with anger.

"I don't have the capacity for niceties right now. Leave my office."

She stares a beat longer, then turns and walks out.

Andrei slowly turns in the chair, his eyebrows raised in a silent question.

"Nobody sees that video," I say, looking first at him, then at Gio.

Gio gives a firm nod.

Andrei studies me, then says quietly, "Yeah. Of course."

Pa arrived home hours after we received the video. Ma's doing, I'm sure. She is desperate to get her hands on that footage.

As I head toward my office, Pa stops me with a quiet, "Can we talk?"

I agree and lead him inside.

The door shuts behind us, and I immediately know it's about Rainey.

I stop in the middle of the room, giving him the space to speak first. But when his brows lift and he releases a long, heavy sigh, my stomach drops. If he says she's dead…

"I don't want to ask this, but I need to know… how good was she?"

I'm stunned into silence.

He brushes past me to sink onto the couch. Another sigh escapes him.

"He's fucking her," he says flatly. "We knew he would be. If only to hurt Dom. But I thought we'd be getting body parts by now, and instead—nothing. I need to know if it's because she's that good. Good enough to make him put his hatred and vendetta on hold. Good enough to make him keep her." His eyes meet mine. "I need to know Dom is going to be okay… if she dies…"

"She won't," I say. "He won't kill her."

Because he won't.

She *is that good*. Not just in bed, though he'll never feel the full depth of what Rainey gives when she wants to. He won't feel what Dom felt. What I felt. That fire, that pull, that ache to possess her and protect her at the same time.

He'll crave her to want him. Because Rainey? She's electric. You don't just notice her. You get pulled in.

And her beauty… it hurts to look at. It hurts when she belongs to someone else.

Pa nods, like he's trying to convince himself of something, but it doesn't quite settle.

"I still don't get it," he says. "Why take them both and let Niki go?"

"Rainey must've been the target."

It's a truth I've been trying to accept. I will find who did this to her. And they will be turned over to Dom.

Chapter

SIXTEEN

Rainey

I wake, and I'm in a bedroom. My vagina feels… used. Sore, even. But it's not painful.

I blink, and then I hear my name. It happens a couple more times before I can focus on Giulia standing above me.

She starts crying, then leans over me, hugging me.

"I'm so sorry. I hate what I said to you. I was so desperate for sex, and Cristiano said he would get me some. I thought it was him. I thought he was going to have me sleep with him, and then you would get a break. And maybe if he liked having sex with me, I could sleep with him so you didn't have to. But then he brought me to one of his friends, and then two more joined. And I'm sorry I liked it. I hate how you looked at me."

She stares down at me, her eyes pleading for me to say something.

I sit up, but I feel strange. Groggy, like how I feel after I'm injected with a sedative.

"Where am I?" I hold my head and squint against the light.

"We're at one of Cristiano's houses."

"We're not on the boat?"

She shakes her head.

"How did I get here?"

"You were trying to beat Cristiano with a pillow, and he gave you something to calm down."

"How long have I been out?"

She looks like maybe she's mentally counting, and then she says, "Maybe four days."

"Four days?"

How was I out for four days?

"He had sex with me, didn't he?"

She looks confused.

"Did Cristiano have sex with me?"

She shakes her head. "I don't know? I just got here."

I shove the covers back, pull off my underwear, and lay back on the bed, spreading my legs open.

"Look!" I practically yell. "Does it look like he had sex with me?"

She's quiet, and I lift my head. "Well?"

"I can't tell. It looks maybe a little red around the hole, but your stitches almost look healed. Why?"

"Because something has been inside me, and I don't remember anything that happened the last four days."

"Can I touch you?" she asks, moving in closer.

"Yes," I say, leaning up on my elbows and spreading my legs wider.

She gently parts my lips and looks closer, her face remaining neutral as she examines me.

"I think maybe. But the stitches seem fine."

I hold my hand out to her, and she helps me up. Cristiano has been having sex with me since he took me. I mean within hours of him taking me, he started, and it hasn't stopped. But I'm most mad that I was drugged and kept unconscious for days. I don't know what he did, or what anybody did to me, during that time.

I'm dressed in a nightgown, and I peel it off, discarding it onto the floor. I look down at my body, then turn and glance at her over my shoulder.

"How do I look? Do I have any marks or anything?"

She scans me up and down. "No?"

I turn and hold my arms out, showing her the front.

"Still no, Rainey. What are you worrying about?"

"I don't know. Maybe he sold my kidney or something. Where's a bathroom?"

I move toward the door I think it probably is, and thankfully I'm right.

I stare into the mirror, making sure I don't have anything different on my body. Maybe he inserted a tracker or something.

"Take me to him."

She nods once and turns to lead the way. I follow her out of the room, not even trying to remember the way back. This is just another mansion he bought with his illegal drug money.

She stops at a heavy wooden door and pushes it open. Smoke curls out into the hallway before I even step inside.

Cristiano is at a circular table, shirt unbuttoned at the collar, a thick cigar tucked between his fingers. Three men are seated with him, cards in hand, drinks half-full beside their chips. Laughter dies down the second I walk in.

I march straight to him.

"Did you have sex with me?"

He leans back in his chair, eyes dragging slowly down my body. He taps the ash from his cigar before finally meeting my gaze again.

"I've had sex with you many times."

"You know what I'm asking," I retort.

"How'd you sleep?"

"Let me rephrase. You kept me drugged and unconscious for four days. Since I can tell someone has had sex with me, are you the only man who stuck their penis inside me?" I bite out.

The smug expression on his face immediately disappears.

"Nobody else will have sex with you. You are mine and only mine."

"Why did you drug me to sleep with me?"

"For once, I didn't have you fighting me."

"You're fucking disgusting. You know that."

He stands and grabs my arm, squeezing it tightly as he drags me from the room.

After a short drive, we pull into the parking lot of a small medical office. There's no wait when we walk in, which is a relief, since all he put me in was yoga pants and a sports bra. The receptionist barely glances at us before motioning to someone down the hall. A nurse steps forward almost immediately and guides us through a door.

They must have been expecting us.

We're brought into a private exam room. I sit on the padded table while Cristiano scoots a chair next to it and rests his elbow on the table, his hand on my lap.

When the doctor comes in, he doesn't acknowledge me at all. He shakes Cristiano's hand and speaks in Russian. The two of them continue their conversation, and I catch a few repeated sounds, but I have no idea what any of it means.

A few minutes later, a nurse comes in with a cast saw. After even more time, my casts are removed, my arms and wrists finally free again. My arms look pale, thin, and dirty. Dead skin flakes off in patches.

She leads me to a sink where I'm told to wash. I scrub until my hands and arms are red, sloughing off as much dead skin as I can. The nurse watches, then hands me a towel and points to another door.

They take X-rays next. Both arms. My collarbone. My ribs.

Cristiano stays nearby the whole time. He doesn't speak to me, but he watches every single thing I do.

Eventually, the doctor returns with a stack of prints in hand. More Russian and nodding.

Cristiano shakes the doctor's hand firmly, says something that sounds almost like gratitude.

I don't understand, but from the way he's smiling and the way they both seem satisfied, I figure I must be healed.

When we arrive back to Cristiano's he leads me down the hall. When he opens a door and steps aside, I glance at him warily before walking in. It's a living room.

"Sit," he says.

I do.

He pulls a second chair close beside me.

A woman walks in a moment later, her dark hair pulled into a tight bun. She sets a canvas bag on the table, then holds her hand out to Cristiano, who shakes it. She offers the same to me.

"I'm here to do some light physical therapy with you," she explains.

She pulls out a clipboard and sets a sheet of paper in front of me, along with a pen. "Just write a few lines. Whatever you want."

I grip the pen and begin scribbling. My wrist feels stiff, but not terrible. She watches carefully, then nods.

I draw a compass encircled by rope.

"Good." She turns the paper slightly to fully see it, then pushes it away. "Now let's do a few stretches."

She guides me through some simple movements. Flexing, extending, rotating. Then she has me write again. It's a little easier the second time.

She pulls out a few hand therapy tools and shows me how to use them. Grip balls. Resistance bands. A plastic putty that I'm supposed to knead between my fingers. It's all fine, manageable, and normal.

And then she reaches into her bag again.

I watch in confusion as she pulls out a large, flesh-toned dildo and suctions it to the table. I freeze, my mouth slightly open as I blink at it, then at her. She opens a small bottle and squirts lube right onto the tip.

I slowly turn to Cristiano, wide-eyed. "You've got to fucking be kidding me. I'm not riding that."

He smiles still relaxed in his seat. "As sexy as that would be, you're not riding it. But you will give it a hand job."

My mouth falls open.

The woman chimes in with a professional calm. "Would you like me to demonstrate?"

Fury flashes through me. I stand, grip the stupid thing with both hands, and slide the lube from the tip down the shaft, swirling my fingers around it with practiced ease.

"Like this?" I say sweetly. "I got really fucking good at doing this to my boyfriend's massive cock when I was desperate to make him feel good."

Then I flick my fingers toward Cristiano, sending a smear of lubricant right at his face before turning on my heel and storming out of the room.

I stay in the bedroom the rest of the day. Giulia must know I'm upset because she doesn't even try to talk.

When he comes to bed, I stiffen, bracing myself for whatever I'll be expected to endure tonight. But he climbs in, rolls toward me, kisses my cheek, then turns away and switches off the light.

Chapter

SEVENTEEN

Rainey

Cristiano's been in an odd mood all day. He's typically alert, but today he seems dazed. He zones out for long stretches, then suddenly snaps out of it and resumes working. I should try to figure out what's bothering him, since I'm the one person here who will suffer if anyone messes up while he's like this.

When I dress for dinner, I decide to approach the evening with a better attitude. Nothing came of me disrespecting him by flicking lube in his face, which means one of two things: either my punishment is still coming, or he's going to let it slide. I'd rather not risk it, so I paint on a smile for the devil and head out.

The patio is quiet, just like always. I'm escorted to my seat, and he's already there, scrolling through his phone.

He's never distracted during dinner, and the fact that he doesn't acknowledge me makes it obvious something's definitely bothering him. Even when I stopped putting up a fight when it came to sitting, he still pulled my chair out for me. He might be an asshole, but he was clearly raised to be a gentleman. Somewhere along the way, his wires got twisted when he became a heartless monster.

I pause with every bite, unable to look away from him.

He's reading whatever's on the screen, absently twisting his wedding band.

"You're married?" I ask, lifting the wine glass to my lips. I've briefly brought his wife up before, but the longer I'm here, the more it sinks in. I won't be leaving, and unfortunately, I'd assume sooner or later, she'll be coming around. He can't really keep me a secret forever, and I'd rather not be blindsided by a scorned woman attacking me for "sleeping" with her husband.

His eyes lift slowly, like he's trying to figure out if I really just asked a personal question. After a moment longer, he exhales. "Was. She was murdered."

That's not the answer I expected. I thought I'd catch him in some pathetic lie, something I could use to talk shit to him for being a cheater. Or maybe he'd say they're in an open relationship and she wouldn't care about his involvement with me. But not that.

His gaze burns with pure hatred.

"She was three months pregnant with our first child."

I study him, trying to decide if he's being honest, but the grief in his expression makes it clear he's telling the truth.

"I'm sorry."

He lets out a bitter scoff. "Funny. You've now apologized more than the man who killed her."

"I didn't mean to—"

"It's in the past."

Chapter

SEVENTEEN

Cristiano's been in an odd mood all day. He's typically alert, but today he seems dazed. He zones out for long stretches, then suddenly snaps out of it and resumes working. I should try to figure out what's bothering him, since I'm the one person here who will suffer if anyone messes up while he's like this.

When I dress for dinner, I decide to approach the evening with a better attitude. Nothing came of me disrespecting him by flicking lube in his face, which means one of two things: either my punishment is still coming, or he's going to let it slide. I'd rather not risk it, so I paint on a smile for the devil and head out.

The patio is quiet, just like always. I'm escorted to my seat, and he's already there, scrolling through his phone.

He's never distracted during dinner, and the fact that he doesn't acknowledge me makes it obvious something's definitely bothering him. Even when I stopped putting up a fight when it came to sitting, he still pulled my chair out for me. He might be an asshole, but he was clearly raised to be a gentleman. Somewhere along the way, his wires got twisted when he became a heartless monster.

I pause with every bite, unable to look away from him.

He's reading whatever's on the screen, absently twisting his wedding band.

"You're married?" I ask, lifting the wine glass to my lips. I've briefly brought his wife up before, but the longer I'm here, the more it sinks in. I won't be leaving, and unfortunately, I'd assume sooner or later, she'll be coming around. He can't really keep me a secret forever, and I'd rather not be blindsided by a scorned woman attacking me for "sleeping" with her husband.

His eyes lift slowly, like he's trying to figure out if I really just asked a personal question. After a moment longer, he exhales. "Was. She was murdered."

That's not the answer I expected. I thought I'd catch him in some pathetic lie, something I could use to talk shit to him for being a cheater. Or maybe he'd say they're in an open relationship and she wouldn't care about his involvement with me. But not that.

His gaze burns with pure hatred.

"She was three months pregnant with our first child."

I study him, trying to decide if he's being honest, but the grief in his expression makes it clear he's telling the truth.

"I'm sorry."

He lets out a bitter scoff. "Funny. You've now apologized more than the man who killed her."

"I didn't mean to—"

"It's in the past."

I watch the way he twists the band. He always does that when he's concentrating, and I wonder if it's in those small movements that he remembers her.

"How long ago did she die?"

"She was brutally murdered eleven years ago." His voice is lethal. "It's our anniversary."

Well, that explains the dazed look all day.

"Do you always spend your anniversary moping around?"

I don't mean for it to sound as terrible as it comes out. I was trying to bridge a gap, trying to find a solution so he doesn't spend one day a year being a Debbie Downer.

He glares at me, then lets out a dry laugh and takes a drink of his wine.

"Do you think she would want you spending your time like this?" I gesture to him. He's been depressed all day, and it's… odd.

"I think she'd want me to get justice for her and our child."

"Have you ever tried to forgive the person who killed her?"

"Would you?" he demands. "Would you forgive someone who gutted Damiano like a fish and sat there watching him gasp for air until he finally took his last breath? Maybe it would be easier for you since he wouldn't be able to carry your innocent child in his womb. But for me? It's not that easy."

I meet his gaze, stunned I never noticed the depth of his pain. His anger isn't just anger; it's grief. It's love that never got to finish.

"So you plan on holding onto all this resentment for what?" I ask, trying, but failing to understand.

"No. I plan on killing the man responsible."

"And then what? It won't bring her back. Is that what you think will finally ease your pain?"

"I'm not looking to ease my pain. I'm looking for payback."

There's nothing I'll be able to say that will make him feel better. I should stop while I'm ahead. But I have so many questions.

"Does the person know you're planning to kill them?"

He studies me for a long moment.

"I don't know. Does he?"

My brows lift.

He lets out a bitter scoff, rolling his eyes. "I suppose that wouldn't be a bedtime story you'd tell the woman you're courting, would it?"

"Courting?" I blink, even more lost now.

He smiles, but there's nothing kind in it.

"He's always been mental. Of course he wouldn't do anything romantic."

"What?" I pinch my eyebrows together not understanding.

"Damiano."

"What about Damiano?"

He watches me, his features hard. "I'm sure even when he's fucking you or going about his day, you've seen it—snippets of how dangerous he is, how mentally unstable he is. He slit my wife's throat without a second thought."

My lips part in horror. "Damiano would never—" I start, but he cuts me off.

"To prevent yourself from feeling foolish later, just don't," he snaps.

I want to argue. I want to scream that Damiano would never kill a pregnant woman. And if, by some crazy chance, he did, there would have to be more to it than him just murdering her in cold blood. But pushing him right now, when he's barely holding back his fury, would probably end in an explosion I haven't witnessed yet.

It would make sense, though. His cruelty toward me is easier to understand if he truly believes Dom is the one who killed his wife. Of course he would want to punish me. It would also explain why the Volkovs are so protective of him and wouldn't let him leave the property.

We sit in brittle silence.

"You do realize, even if Dom is the one who killed your wife, treating me like fucking worms won't bring her back, right? And if this is truly the kind of man you were, especially as a partner and husband, I can assure you she's much happier where she's at now."

I knew my words would get a reaction out of him, and I confidently said them anyway. He stands abruptly.

"Come."

I remain stiff, wanting to refuse, but I get up as requested.

He takes a step toward the house, and I move to follow. I don't expect the blow that lands across my face. All I know is one minute I'm standing, and the next I'm on the ground.

He towers above me, glaring as if I'm the most atrocious thing he's ever been around. "You ever disrespect me as a husband or my late wife like that again, and I'll knock your teeth down your throat."

He turns back toward the house. "Get up."

I can already feel my cheekbone swelling. I can even see it out of my periphery. Guess I found what makes him tick—and detonate.

As we step inside, dread presses down on me. I know he's going to be rough. Not only did I force him to talk about his wife, but I also told him that her being dead was better for her than being alive and having him for a husband.

My nerves twist, and I slow my pace, wanting to drag out the inevitable.

He grips my arm roughly and drags me through the house to his office. Somewhere along the way, Giulia falls into step behind us, though I don't notice until he's shoving me into his desk chair and she's standing just a few feet away. He clicks angrily across the keyboard, entering passwords and opening folders. When he double-clicks on a video file, he waits for it to begin, then sits on the edge of the desk, facing away from the screen while I'm left staring straight at it.

At first, it's just a beautiful woman in a form-fitting dress and high heels, walking toward someone just out of frame. She looks happy as she holds her arms out for a hug. But then her smile falters, and her arms stay outstretched until the open invitation for a hug turns into her hands coming up, almost as if telling him to calm down or just listen.

Then Damiano steps into view. He's young, but I recognize him instantly.

He's visibly angry about something. I can't hear the conversation, but I can see it unfold. The way her body stiffens, the way she starts yelling at him. Their argument escalates quickly. She looks like she's pleading now, hands clasped in front of her as she begs for something. When he turns to walk away, she grabs his arm. He shakes her off without effort, says something, and she slaps him hard across the face.

He doesn't react right away, just stands there, motionless. Then he slowly straightens and looks back at her. Her eyes go wide, and she takes a step closer, pressing herself to him. One hand slides down his pants as she squeezes. Her lips are moving, and then she's twisted around. The blade is already at her throat, then on the other side so fast I don't even know what happened. Her eyes widen, horror and betrayal written across her face. Blood pours through her fingers as she clutches her neck. Damiano shoves her away, letting her crumple to the floor.

Shes trembling as she reaches for him. He crouches in front of her, just watching. It looks like maybe he's talking, but I can't really tell. Then she goes still. He waits a second longer, then walks away.

I cover my mouth and nose, trying to hold it all in, but it's useless.

I grab the trash can beside the desk and violently puke into it, my body heaving with the force.

I feel his hand on my back, surprisingly tender as he rubs slowly up and down.

He was right to cut me off. I was going to defend Dom, and now I feel foolish for even thinking it, even though I never actually got the chance to say the words.

I hear the soft pull of tissue being yanked from the box, and he holds them out to me. I wipe my eyes and blow my nose.

This hurts.

This hurts really fucking bad.

And the realization that I'm here, enduring all this abuse because of Cristiano's hatred for Damiano, sends a surge of fury through me.

I stand abruptly, frantically ripping open the desk drawers.

"Rainey, stop," he orders.

I ignore him, digging faster until I find a paper cutter knife and a gun tucked deep inside. I grab them both and shove them toward him.

"Do it. Kill me. Take your revenge. Kill me and send me back to Damiano. Do whatever you want. You deserve to get closure, and I'm the only thing that will hurt him!" I shout through sobs. "Kill me!"

He takes them, sets them on the desk, then wraps his arms around me. I push against him, hitting at his chest, but he only locks me in tighter.

"This isn't your fault," he says against my hair.

"You punish me daily like it is!"

"Stop fighting me and I won't get so angry with you."

"Why did you seek me out? Why did I deserve this?"

He rubs my back in slow strokes. "Valentina set it up."

My body goes rigid as my mind starts piecing together what he said. Valentina was the first word. She was best friends with his wife. That same woman was murdered by her own son. I pull back and look at him. "What?" I whisper, needing confirmation that I heard him right.

He holds my gaze. "She wanted the feud to stop. Said she would offer up Damiano's girlfriend. An eye for an eye, if you will."

I shake my head, trying to understand. Why? Why would she do that?

"So you're waiting to kill me?"

"It took a single look at you to know I wasn't going to kill you."

"Why would Valentina do that to her own daughter?" I ask, unable to comprehend how she could set up her own child to be kidnapped.

"Nikita wasn't part of the plan. I don't know how she got mixed up in it."

I think back to the day Valentina asked me to pick up her dress, how she told me not to tell anyone. I remember how Niki showed up at the last second as I was leaving, saying she wanted to surprise her family. I remember the way the shop owner seemed caught off guard to see her, mentioning that Valentina had said I would be the one picking up the dress.

"Are you planning on using me as a bargaining chip to get Damiano instead?"

He shrugs. "I would have, but you're better than having him dead. I did offer the trade. He refused it."

I gape at him, a flood of emotions crashing through me all at once. I would have been furious if Damiano had tried to trade himself for me. But knowing he flat refused makes a different emotion flare up: hurt, rejection, desertion.

"You weren't lying about this? He really did refuse to get me back?"

"Yes."

That one word, that single confirmation that Damiano abandoned me to this bastard, has a scream ripping from my throat. I can barely breathe as I thread my fingers through my hair, pulling at it, then shove everything off the desk, sending papers and objects crashing to the floor.

"Fuck!"

The door to the office bursts open. Guards rush in with their weapons drawn, and Cristiano holds up a hand, stopping them. Then he's wrapping his arms around me, locking me against his chest.

"Calm down, Darling."

I sob harder, thrashing against him, trying to fight him off. My chest tightens, squeezing painfully, and the air refuses to fill my lungs. I claw at him in panic, gasping as my vision starts to tunnel.

"I can't," I manage to choke out before the panic completely takes over.

Cristiano is yelling for medical, his voice sounding muffled.

Everything blurs. I hear rushing footsteps and frantic voices shouting. The room tilts around me. I feel a quick, sharp poke in my arm, and then everything goes black.

Chapter

EIGHTEEN

Rainey

I don't know what time it is when I drift back to awareness. I feel pressure inside me. Somewhere in the distance, I think I hear grunting, but it's muffled. Before I can process it, the darkness drags me under.

I wake again to the same feeling. Pressure. Movement. The weight of a body on top of me.

Through the grogginess, my heavy eyelids blink open enough to see Cristiano, his face tense, body undulating over mine. I'm overly hot, he's overly hot, and we're wet. We must be sweating.

Relief flashes through me at the sight of him, relief that it's him and not someone else, and whether it's the drugs they gave me or the exhaustion still pulling at me, I slip back into unconsciousness.

When I finally wake for real, and my brain isn't foggy, the room is quiet.

Giulia sits on the bed next to me, gazing out the window, our hands loosely clasped together.

I blink, confused. My body feels heavy and sore. I shift to sit up and immediately freeze.

The sheets are soaked.

I stare down at them in stunned confusion. The fabric sticks to my skin, and I poke the sheet as I lift my thigh, trying to peel it free.

Giulia turns her head and offers a soft, sympathetic smile. "I'll pull them off once you get up."

"What is that?"

Her eyes drop to the bed before meeting mine again. "You had a panic attack."

"And it made the bed sticky?"

She shakes her head. "Cristiano went all night long."

My stomach twists. I remember the feeling of something thick inside me, my walls feeling like they were being stretched apart… and the grunting. And I realize she's right. He never stopped, not even while I was slipping in and out of consciousness.

I gape at her, horrified. "How the hell did he go that long?"

"They gave him something. After he finished the first time, he called someone in here, told them his intentions, and whatever they provided worked."

I wrinkle my nose in disgust, finally taking in the amount of semen coating the sheets, the overwhelming mess of it. "Did I participate?"

She shakes her head. "You were out cold."

I crawl out of bed, defiled and used, and stumble into the bathroom. The moment I step beneath the scalding spray, I sink to the floor, letting the water burn across my skin as if it could wash away the filth and shame clinging to me.

Memories of Damiano fill my mind. Him walking toward me after getting my purse back. The way he held my chin as he looked at the damage Ricardo left. How he saved me in the bathroom, told me to go back to the bus while he took care of the two men. The way he stared up at me when I pounded on the window for him and then came to my room. That first kiss.

My stomach fills with the same butterflies I felt that night as he held me.

I didn't even realize at the time that one day I would give anything just to go back to that moment. I was a prisoner and felt utterly trapped, and now I'm truly a prisoner. I want to laugh at how free I actually was back then.

I lean back against the tile as beads of water fall from above. I used to look up the same way, eyes half-closed in bliss, when Dom and I would shower and he'd take me from behind. I'd brace myself against the wall, gaze fixed on the cascading stream. Back then, I was in heaven. Now, I want to go down the drain right along with the droplets.

I knew Dom killed. I saw him kill with my own eyes. And maybe it's the trauma that is my life, but I didn't care. The people he killed deserved to die. I'd stand behind him 100 percent for that. But killing a pregnant woman? An innocent, married, pregnant woman who was carrying her and her husband's first child? I can't stand beside him on that. It's sick and cruel. He's sick and cruel.

And he wants to kill Cristiano? The Volkovs want to kill Cristiano, all because he dares to make it known that he wants to kill the man who murdered his wife and unborn child?

How do they even justify that?

I am so angry. I can't believe this is the bullshit I have to deal with. My life has never been easy, and apparently it never will be. I must have been a really shitty person in a past life to be dealt this hand.

I remain in the same spot until the water runs cold, then finally drag myself out.

I slip on one of the long dresses he always makes me wear and look at my reflection in the mirror. I don't recognize her. I don't know who that woman is, watching me from the other side.

Focusing on the tattoo on my neck used to remind me I was loved unconditionally by someone. Even if I forgot, Dom would remind me. He would show me that I'm his. That he's mine. But now, all I see is the bite mark of a man who killed an innocent woman, permanently etched into my skin.

"Are you okay?" Giulia asks.

I shake my head.

She walks over pulling me into her arms. "I'm so sorry, Rainey."

I think most of us are conditioned to say 'it's okay' without thinking, even when it couldn't be further from the truth. I want to say it, but nothing about this feels remotely okay.

"I didn't have a choice. Damiano chose himself for me. I was taken from my home by the Volkovs… by Damiano. I was led to believe I'd been trafficked, that I was going to be a sex worker, all while Dom already knew he wanted to be in a relationship with me. I should have hated him. He's done horrible things to me. And still… I fell so completely in love with him. I knew who he was. I knew what he did. But seeing the real reason I'm being tortured like this just hurts so much worse. I feel so betrayed. Like I was the scapegoat for the Volkovs. They get to move on, and I'm the one left to survive hell. And I hate that I want to go home. That I just want him."

"It's not fair," she agrees, "but had you not been at that warehouse at that exact time, I'd still be a sex slave."

I meet her gaze and realize she's right. If nothing else positive comes out of this, I got her out of a bad place, even if only for the time being.

I grab her neck and pull her into a tight hug. "I love you, Giulia," I whisper.

"I love you too, Rainey."

When we pull away, she offers her best smile.

"We have to go. There's a guard waiting outside the door." She points to where he's stationed just beyond it.

I almost ask where we're going, but she would know as much as I do. Zilch.

As we pass one of the large sitting rooms, laughter drifts toward us. I glance out the massive windows to the back patio, where Cristiano and four other men are sitting around a table.

I briefly consider rushing past, hoping to go unnoticed. But one of the men looks up and sees us, and the others follow his gaze. Cristiano gestures for me to come to him. Giulia gives my hand a gentle squeeze, and we walk outside together.

"Hello, darling," he greets, holding his cheek out, expecting a kiss. When I lean in, he turns his face and captures my mouth with his. His hand comes up, gripping the back of my head as he deepens the kiss, pushing his tongue into my mouth possessively.

He tastes like the cigar he's smoking, and I want to gag. But I keep my face neutral as I pull away.

I know if I embarrass him, he won't hesitate to beat the shit out of me in front of these men. He's so unhinged, he might even force me to sleep with them or take it out on Giulia instead.

I want so badly to wipe my mouth, but I know even that would shame him, so I force myself to stand still.

"How'd you sleep?" he asks, lacing his fingers through mine, lifting my knuckles to his lips.

"Fine."

"I hope you're not too exhausted from last night. Or too sore." He slides his hand down my hip and around to my butt, giving it a light spank.

I shake my head slowly. "I'm fine."

"Good."

He turns his chair and pats his lap for me to sit, so I do, making sure to put all my weight on him, hoping that after a prolonged period of time, his legs will go numb and he'll get uncomfortable. But after hours of being here, listening to men speak in a language I don't understand, he doesn't seem bothered in the least.

It's odd seeing him like this. He's so laid back. He seems almost normal. And had this been a different set of circumstances, and this was how I was meeting him, I'd probably be enamored by him.

Even the way he wraps his arm around me, resting his hand on my thigh, eventually lulls me. I've sat here for so long I relax and zone out.

When laughter draws me out of my trance, I realize our fingers are interlocked, and I'm actually clutching his hand back the way I do with Giulia. I loosen my grip and he doesn't seem to notice; he holds on just as tight.

I visually trace the outline of his perfectly groomed nails. I'm so messed up in the head, because his hands are so soft it makes me uneasy. Damiano's are calloused, his knuckles practically permanently split open because they're never given a chance to fully heal before being ripped open again from working or fighting. I want him to rub his rough hands over every inch of my body. His nails are always short from his habit of biting them. Sometimes his fingers would bleed, and I told him it grossed me out that he did that and then would finger me. He quit biting them that day. I'd give anything to be staring down at his bloody fingernails right now.

We sit in the stifling heat so long it feels like I'm on the edge of heat exhaustion. I'm so tired I can barely keep my eyes open, and I can tell Giulia is just as drained.

I know asking for anything comes with a price, so when I ask if we can lie down for a nap, he agrees but only in exchange for a blowjob. There's no point in asking if I can do it later because he thrives on humiliation.

I hate myself as I whisper, "Fine."

His lips curl into a wicked grin, and he leans forward, scooping an ice cube out of his drink. He traces it between my cleavage, up my chest and neck, to my lips. "Open your mouth."

I do, and he puts it in.

"Eat it."

The cold is incredible. As I lower myself to my knees in front of him, I try to save the cube for as long as possible, but it melts quickly. He lets out a groan when the coldness wraps around him. I hold it together while I follow through with my end of the deal, getting him off and salvaging what little power I still have.

AFTER DINNER, I LEAN BACK AND GAZE OUT AT THE EXPANSIVE LAWN, wondering how far I'd have to walk to truly see the stars. I slowly twist the chair side to side, resting my head against the back. When I turn, I catch him watching me, his cheek resting on his fist.

"Can I ask you something?"

He nods. "Sure."

"How did you know the Volkovs?"

He shifts back in his chair, lacing his fingers over his abdomen. "My wife was best friends with Valentina."

"Was your wife older than you? Valentina and Lorenzo seem a lot older."

"Yes. Sixteen years my senior."

"So you were around the Volkovs because of your wife's friendship with Valentina?"

He smirks. "There's more to it than that, darling. Lorenzo and I are both businessmen. We met through mutual clients and attended gatherings at their house to bring in potential business for both of us."

I bite the inside of my cheek. I want to ask the next question, but I don't want him losing his temper.

"I'm sure you're wondering if that's how Damiano and Carmella met. It is."

"How old was Dom?"

His eyes widen like my question is an accusation, and it clearly offends him.

"What does that matter? An affair is an affair."

That makes me bristle. "It matters because if he was under-age, he's not the one to blame."

"Excuse me?" His chin jerks back. "Whether she started it or he started it doesn't matter. He slit her throat and watched her die. That's the fucking problem."

"And I understand that, but she's a predator if she had relations with a minor. He wouldn't have been able to consent, even if he wanted her."

"Oh, he wanted her!" he bellows. "He was a mute psycho, and he went after a married woman!"

"Oh, and she had so little respect for your marriage that she stepped out for a child? And she's also a pervert for getting aroused by—as you say—a mute psychopath? Again, reiterating: child!"

He shoots up from his chair so fast it topples backward, then stomps toward me, grabbing my arm and yanking me out of my seat. He drags me through the house to his office and shoves me into a chair across from his desk.

He strides to a painting on the wall, swings it open like a door, and punches a code into a safe.

He pulls out several leather-bound books and throws them down in front of me.

"Read for yourself! He's a fucking lunatic! And you dare defend him in my house?"

His face is red with rage as he storms out, slamming the door behind him.

I turn to the books without hesitation and pick up the first one. It's a diary. Carmella's diary. The handwriting is pretty—girlish, definitely feminine.

She writes about Cristiano at first. Wanting a family. Baby names. Struggling to get pregnant. Most of it feels ordinary, the kind of hopeful ramblings you'd expect from a woman trying to settle down. I skim through page after page of symptom tracking, name combinations, and little notes about her mood.

Then I find the first mention of Dom.

She comments on how strong he is for someone so young, saying that if she didn't know his age, she would have guessed he was at least twenty-five. A few entries later, she talks about a dinner with the Volkovs. She says there was an empty seat next to him, and she took it because she could tell he wanted her there. But then she writes that he ignored her the entire evening.

More pages follow. Ramblings. Small talk. Nonsense. The longer I read, the more her handwriting changes. What started out neat and careful becomes shaky and messy, almost frantic. Her thoughts lose structure. She doesn't sound like a woman with a harmless crush anymore. She sounds obsessed.

She writes about the first time they kissed, saying he accidentally knocked her to the floor. Then she describes the first time she went down on him, claiming he couldn't get hard because he had never been with anyone before. Her entries grow more disturbing, more detached from reality. She insists he wanted her, that he was all over her. But I know Dom. This version of him doesn't exist. Not in any reality I've ever known.

Then comes the entry about the pregnancy.

She writes about how excited she is. How it finally feels like everything is falling into place.

But the dates don't lie. The timeline in her earlier entries is clear If there's any truth to what she wrote, the child she was carrying wouldn't have been Cristiano's, it would have been Dom's.

My hands tremble as I flip through the pages, tears slipping down my cheeks while I scan the dates. I keep going back and forth between entries, trying to make sense of what I'm seeing.

I keep reading. Her descent is impossible to miss now. She's spiraling, and it's all right there in ink. She rambles about being tired of having to tie him up just to get through foreplay. One of the last entries is filled with rage. She writes that she's wasted too many years loving him, and still, he refuses to have sex with her. She signs the entry with a string of insults—calling him broken, saying his dick is broken, calling him a limp dick who has never had an orgasm.

I freeze.

My eyes flick back across the earlier pages. Cristiano had been out of town for three weeks when she conceived. She insinuates the baby is hers and Dom's, but she also admits they never had sex.

She had sex with someone… but it wasn't Dom.

Holy shit.

I grab the books and hurry from the room. I want to show Cristiano that all of this is a big mistake. Yes, Dom killed his wife, but that baby wasn't his. It wasn't Cristiano's either. They need to figure out who the baby actually belonged to. Then maybe they can get some real answers and give their anger to someone who deserves it.

As I pass a sitting area, I stop. Cristiano's hand is being wrapped, and the entire room looks like a war zone.

I'm so convinced my news is important that I move toward him without thinking.

He looks up as I approach, glancing from my face to the books and back again.

"Damiano never slept with her. He wasn't having an affair—"

The first hit knocks me out cold.

The kick to my stomach brings me back.

I gasp, curling into the fetal position.

Then he's on top of me, swinging without control. When his hands close around my throat, I let my arms fall to the floor and watch the chandelier above me begin to blur.

I'm so ready to meet my maker.

Chapter

NINETEEN

Rainey

I've lost track of how long I've been away from Dom. If I had to guess, I'd say about four months. If I went by how it feels, I'd say it's been an eternity. Then again, I don't know how long I was in the hospital. I had a serious concussion and was so out of it I don't remember anything. What I do recall is waking up in pain from head to toe, and Giulia crying as she helped me get dressed to leave.

If I look anything like I feel, I'd probably cry too.

My time with Cristiano has blurred together. We've moved from one house to a yacht, sailed to another place, returned to land, and then been taken to a different house in the middle of the night. Sometimes we stay for a week or two, other times just a couple of days, before we're back on another yacht, heading somewhere new.

I don't think we've stayed in one place for more than two weeks. Sometimes we don't even stay for two days. Maybe this is just Cristiano's way of living, but it makes me wish I were back at the Volkov estate, even if I wasn't allowed to leave the property.

I heard the doctor tell Cristiano I shouldn't be discharged yet, but he didn't care. He said we were leaving tonight. I don't know where we're going, but I know he isn't just talking about the hospital.

We stop at a restaurant, and the driver goes inside, returning with bags of food. We eat in the car, and when Giulia and I both start to nod off, I know it's been laced with something. I also know that when I wake up, we'll be somewhere new. Again.

Just as I suspected, we didn't go back to Cristiano's. Judging by the rocking, we're on another yacht.

Giulia is still asleep, and I wonder if someone placed her here while I was out or if she woke up at some point and crawled into bed next to me.

I peer out the window, hoping to see a landmark or some part of the landscape that might tell me where we are. But there's nothing. Just water, stretching out in every direction. We've been sailing long enough that land is nowhere in sight.

When I turn around, she's starting to wake.

"Hey," I whisper, hurrying over to the bed and brushing her hair from her face. "Our food was drugged last night. We're back on a boat, and I don't see land anywhere." I'm not sure if she wants to know all the details, but if it were me, I'd rather wake disoriented with all the facts.

As she starts to sit up, I gently grasp her elbow and ease my other arm behind her back.

"Do we have any water?" she asks, opening and closing her mouth like she's testing the dryness.

"I don't think so. We can go find some though."

I climb off the bed and help her to her feet. "You good to walk?"

She nods and threads her fingers through mine as we head for the door. When I pull it open, I jump. Cristiano is there, pushing it from the other side.

"Where do you think you're going?"

"We need water." I step forward, and he moves in, blocking my way. "Are we not allowed to leave the room?" I snap.

"You can," he says, stopping inches from me, "but you haven't made me come yet."

"You've never seemed to have a problem getting yourself off with my drugged body. Not sure why you didn't do that hours ago." I fire back.

His jaw tightens. Without warning, he yanks us apart, shoving Giulia out the door before slamming it shut.

"Hurry up and rape me, you sick fuck, so I can get something to drink."

An hour later, I step into the hall. Giulia's eyes widen, and she presses her lips together.

I already know what she sees. My lip is split, and my jaw is swollen on the same side. He didn't like it when I clawed his face, but the bloody scratches down his cheek were worth every knuckle he slammed into mine.

He wouldn't have those marks if he hadn't made that disgusting comment. He said he was glad they added an extra stitch because my already tight cunt is now so tight he could die from the ecstasy of being inside me.

Just hearing that he would request something so disgusting makes my stomach turn. If it's true, if I really am tighter now, I hate that he's enjoying it. My body isn't his to enjoy—it's Damiano's.

Tonight, we have dinner with a small group of people. The conversation flows easily, laughter echoing through the room. Everyone seems to be enjoying themselves.

Cristiano has a glass of whiskey, something dark that smells as aggressive as he is. I notice when his eyes start to redden, blood-shot and glassy, and I do my best not to draw attention to myself.

He keeps touching my leg under the table. Every time, I shift slightly to the side, trying to escape his hand without making it obvious.

But eventually, I'm pulled into his lap. I sit stiffly with my back straight. The more he touches me, the more I push him away, hoping he'll take the hint. He doesn't.

Instead, he threads his fingers into the back of my hair and yanks my head back so hard my neck pops. For a moment, I genuinely wonder if he's paralyzed me.

His free hand slides up my dress and into my panties. He starts fingering me right there at the table.

"The sooner you come, the sooner I let you go," he murmurs.

I clamp my jaw shut and stare at the ceiling. I won't give him the satisfaction. I focus on anything and everything that might keep me from responding to his touch.

It works. But not in the way I hoped.

He leans in again. "You've got five minutes to come, or I'll fuck you instead."

So I give in. I let the rising tension twist through me. I let his skilled hand drag me there. And just as I start to come, my body arching, he bends me over the table and fucks me anyway.

He lied. He's a fucking liar.

When he finishes, the men around the table clap. They applaud him for assaulting me. Cristiano smirks as he zips his pants.

"Miserable bitch. Only thing good on her is her cunt."

"And yet you keep coming back, guess that makes you an idiot."

The slap comes fast and hard. Then he roars for me to get out.

Gladly.

I storm out, the sting on my cheek burning so badly it fuels my steps as Giulia hurries after me. I head straight to the back of the boat.

I'm so angry I can barely see straight. I hate him. I fucking hate him. I hate him so much I can't breathe. And somewhere in that rage, something inside me snaps.

I can't do this anymore. I can't keep living like this. I'm never going back to Dom, and I would rather die than spend another second near Cristiano.

I think Giulia sees it in my face before my plan is even fully formed. Just as I start to run toward the edge of the boat, her arms wrap around my waist and hold tight.

"Let me go!" I scream, thrashing against her. "I can't live like this!"

I claw at her arms, desperate and wild, shocked by how strong she is.

"No," her voice trembles. "I can't do this without you."

"Please," I sob, struggling harder.

"No," she says again, squeezing tighter as we inch closer to the railing. "You'll drown, or be eaten by a shark."

"I don't care!"

We keep fighting, locked in a desperate tug-of-war, until I notice flashing lights in the distance. At first, they're barely visible, just faint bursts of red and blue slicing through the dark. But they approach fast.

The glow grows stronger, reflecting off the water and casting streaks of color across the deck. Soon, uniformed officers come into view, standing at the front.

It takes a moment for my brain to process what I'm seeing. *Help is here.*

My body goes still as the realization settles. My adrenaline kicks in so hard it nearly knocks the wind out of me. After everything, after all the nights I thought no one was coming, someone finally did. We're being rescued.

Giulia stays wrapped around me as we freeze in place, both of us staring at the flashing lights.

Then an accented voice calls out, "Coast guard patrol! Is everything alright?"

Four officers board, and my knees nearly buckle with relief.

"Miss, are you okay?" one of them asks.

My voice shakes as I grab the front of his shirt, clutching it like a lifeline. "We've been kidnapped by Cristiano Fierro. My name is Rainey Lane, and my boyfriend is Damiano Volkov. Maybe you know his father, Lorenzo Volkov. Please, you have to get us off this boat now."

Behind him, the other officers reach for their weapons. I already know why.

Cristiano's voice cuts through the tension. "What can I do for you, gentlemen?"

My heart sinks, and I cling tighter to the officer.

"This woman was trying to jump off the back of the boat into shark-infested water. This one was trying to stop her," one officer explains, gesturing between me and Giulia.

"Trying to jump off the boat?" Cristiano repeats, glaring at me as he says it. Then he smiles. "Come here, darling. You're tired. Let's get you to bed." He extends his hand.

"She's claiming she's been kidnapped and that she's the girlfriend of Lorenzo Volkov's son."

Cristiano's eye twitches, but he keeps his composure.

"She gets upset when I drink," he says, trying to explain it away.

"Call Lorenzo. Please," I beg, looking around at each of them. "He will confirm. Or call Dante Volkov. Please."

The officers glance between me and Cristiano, weighing the situation.

I just know he's about to be arrested and I feel freedom just at the tips of my fingers.

Cristiano steps forward, splaying his arms wide. "No need. She's telling the truth. She *was* the girlfriend of Lorenzo Volkov's son, but the wife of Lorenzo reached out to me personally. She wanted the girl away from her son and off their property. So here she is."

My mouth falls open. He just openly admitted to kidnapping me while simultaneously making me seem like a burden that he was kind enough to deal with.

"This is all just a big misunderstanding. She's been emotional. As for her trying to jump overboard, I'll handle it. It won't happen again."

He flashes them a dazzling smile.

"We have some leftover lobster risotto if you gentlemen are hungry. And a good bottle of bourbon. I'd hate for it to go to waste."

The officers glance at one another, then agree. The men behind Cristiano step forward, welcoming them with easy conversation and leading them away.

He squeezes the back of my neck so hard as he pulls me to him. I'm too stunned to fight. All I can do is stare as they disappear inside.

Cristiano has them in his pocket.

And just like that, my freedom is gone.

"You ever try that again, I'll remove your tongue."

It's not a threat.

It's a promise.

Once we reach the bedroom, he hurls me forward, and I stumble into the edge of the bed.

He spins around just as Giulia steps in behind us.

"Wait in the hall."

"No!" I shout. "She's staying with me." I lunge toward the doorway.

"She's going to be rewarded for saving you from that suicide attempt. I'll be back to deal with you shortly."

He shoves me back and slams the door, locking it from the other side.

I lose it. I kick the door until my feet ache, throw anything within reach, and scream until my voice gives out. My throat burns from the effort. My hands throb from pounding the walls. I don't stop until I collapse to the floor, gasping through broken sobs that eventually fall into shallow, stuttered breaths.

If Giulia hadn't grabbed me, I'd be soaring with the stars right now. Maybe my soul would already be at home with Damiano.

When the door finally opens again, Cristiano steps into the mess I've made. He looks around, then walks toward me.

And I don't make a sound.

Not when he has sex with me right there on the floor.

Not when he moves me to the bed and does it again.

I'm done. I give up. The walls in my mind lock into place, sealing me off from the world, trapping me in one where only Damiano and I exist.

Because there, I can live.

When Giulia returns, her cheeks are flushed. Only she doesn't look broken like me. She looks relaxed.

I turn away, pull the blanket over my face, and close my eyes.

The bed dips behind me, and she wraps her arm around my waist. She presses her nose into my back and breathes in. A soft sniffle escapes her, and she clings tighter.

We sit in silence for a long time.

Then her voice breaks through, quiet and shaky.

"I'm sorry you're hurting so badly. And that I've been such a bad friend. I'm selfish. I can't stand the thought of losing you. Not just because I love you, but because without you, I'm nothing. I'm disposable. I'll be sold off or used by everyone around me. And I know he's awful to you. I really do. I'm sorry. But this is the best I've been treated since I was taken, which isn't saying much, because I've always been treated like I don't matter.

"But you make me feel like I do. You treat me with a kindness I haven't known since my parents. Even the other victims never showed me what you have.

"I couldn't stand the thought of you drowning, or your body being torn apart. I know it's your soul that's breaking now, but you're the strongest, most resilient person I've ever met. You're going to survive this. Not for any man, but because you are better than all these men."

She presses her forehead against my back and rubs it back and forth like a cat seeking comfort, her quiet sobs still audible. I roll over and pull her into my arms, resting my head against her chest. *She is my new home.*

I WAKE TO SOFT VOICES. MOONLIGHT SPILLS THROUGH THE WINDOWS as I glance around. Giulia is gone, and Cristiano sleeps beside me. The space where she lay is still warm. The door is slightly ajar, so I slip out of bed and quietly make my way toward it.

Down the hall, I catch the faintest sounds. I move silently in the direction of the noise until I come across a bedroom door left partially open. Through the narrow gap, I see Giulia straddling someone.

I just watch: not out of curiosity or judgment, but because I need to be certain this is her decision. That it isn't happening to her like it so often was. Like it still is to me. That she is choosing to be intimate with whoever that is. Because if she isn't, I'm going to kill him.

The man sits up, wrapping his arms around her. They kiss, slow and deep, and it's then I realize who he is. The chef. The one who travels with us anywhere we go. I remember wondering if she had a crush on him. He was the first man she'd smiled at since we were taken.

His name is Niko.

From what I've heard, he's a good man. One of the few decent ones here.

Apparently, he's a world-renowned chef. Cristiano had dined at a restaurant where Niko was working, and by the end of the night, he was no longer free. Cristiano threatened his life and forced him to become his personal chef. The rest is history.

I zone out, only coming back to myself as they finish. Stepping away as quietly as I can, I retreat down the hall and slip back into bed. Cristiano doesn't move—he's still out cold.

Some time later, the door clicks shut, and Giulia returns to her place by the window. She exhales a gentle sigh, then turns over and drifts off to sleep as if she never snuck out.

And I smile as I too, fall asleep.

Chapter

TWENTY

Rainey

I've been awful today. I know it.

I'm tired. Tired of being here. Tired of him.

We've been back on land for two days, and I've completely given up. I don't care about being hit anymore. The pain he inflicts is the only thing that reminds me I'm still alive.

Everything inside me feels empty, like I've been running on fumes for months. And those fumes finally ran out. Every beating feels like it gets me closer to the end. Sooner or later, one of us is going to die. It might be him, by my hands. It might be me, by his. Or maybe I'll beat us both to it and end it myself.

So I push him. I test his patience. I say things I know will set him off, hoping one of these times he snaps badly enough he goes too far and kills me.

At dinner tonight, I don't eat. He pushes my plate closer, a silent gesture for me to start. I lock eyes with him and shove it roughly back across the table to make my point.

He sighs and glances over my shoulder. A moment later, someone brings me a drink. Usually, I get a glass of wine with dinner, but tonight it's hard liquor.

The second it's in my hands, I down the entire glass in one go. Then I flash him a wide, mocking smile and stand, knocking my chair over as I leave the room.

I sit on the bed, blinking hard as the walls start to curve and bend around me.

It feels too warm, like the room is breathing. Shadows stretch, then curl, then pull back again. The blankets move when I'm not touching them. My skin feels like it's vibrating.

Giulia's voice breaks through the haze.

"Are you okay?" she asks, kneeling infront of me. Her features blur and pulse slightly, like I'm looking at her through water.

I nod, and the motion sends a ripple through the air. I blink again. The room looks deeper than it should, the corners bending in ways that don't make sense.

The door opens and Cristiano steps in, but he moves slowly, deliberately. His figure trails behind him like a smear of color. I know it's him, but something shifts. His image blurs, stretches, and changes.

It's not Cristiano anymore.

It's Damiano.

My Damiano.

The man I ache for.

My breath hitches. I stand on shaky legs, swaying slightly. "Dom?" My voice quivers.

He smiles.

"That's not Dom, Rainey. That's Cristiano."

I ignore her words, rounding the bed. One step, then another. The closer I get, the clearer he becomes. The tilt of his mouth. The way his eyes crease when he smiles. It's him.

I trace down his jaw, and it's smooth. That's wrong. He's never had a smooth face. He always had stubble, soft but rough enough to scrape against my skin when we kissed.

My mind fills it in anyway. I blink, and now the stubble is there. I can see it. I swear I can feel it. But under my fingertips, it's still smooth.

His eyes are the wrong color. They're too light. They were never blue. They were dark, almost black in certain lighting. My mind knows that, and slowly the blue turns dark. It settles into the color I remember.

He's not tall enough. Cristiano's height, not his. He should tower over me. He always did. I used to have to tip my head back just to meet his gaze. But my brain pulls the memory into the present, and when I look up, he's taller now. Just like I remember.

A tear slips down my cheek, and my lip quivers. He reaches up and wipes it away with his thumb, and I press my cheek into his hand.

"I missed you so much," I whisper.

His forehead rests against mine, and he whispers back, "I love you."

"I love you too. So much." I smile, wrapping my arms around his neck and pulling him close.

When I pull back, I trail down the front of his shirt. The fabric feels strange, like paper one second and silk the next. I work down each button and peel it off him, then do the same with his pants. Everything feels soft and fluid, like I'm gliding through a dream.

His tattoos are gone one moment, then fill themselves back in, as if my mind is redrawing them.

I guide him to the bed. He sits at the edge, watching me with hooded eyes while I peel away my clothes. He wants me still, just as bad as I want him.

His features glow in the light, and if I didn't crave him so badly, I'd gladly just stand here and admire his beauty.

I climb into his lap, settling against him, taking in his features, tracing the edges of him like I'm rediscovering something I thought I'd lost.

I look at his lips. Then his eyes. Then back to his lips again. I kiss him, slow and deep, wrapping my arms around his neck and holding him there.

It's different. Not as good as it used to be, but that's okay. It's been a while since we kissed. He must have forgotten how to. We'll learn again. Together.

I pull back, grasp his shaft, stroke it twice, then line him up exactly where I ache for him.

I sink down, letting out a soft moan. "I missed you."

I start to move, each roll of my hips sending heat curling through my body. His hands hold my waist firmly, moving with me as I ride him, chasing every wave of pleasure. And he gives it to me. Again and again.

"Fuck. That's so fucking good, darling."

I pause for a second, dazed, trying to hold onto the words. That's not right. Dom doesn't talk like that. He's never once called me darling. He doesn't even cuss.

Maybe I misheard him. My brain feels like it's coated in syrup, thoughts slipping out of reach as fast as they come.

When his mouth closes around my nipple, I sigh and hold him there, one hand gripping his knee, the other pressing his head tighter to my chest as I keep grinding on him.

He lets me ride him the way I want, in all the ways I've been deprived. Every time I shift, change angles, or move into a new position, he groans like it's the best thing he's ever felt.

And we go at it for hours.

I shoot upright, panic clamping down on my chest.

Cristiano's bedroom.

No. I had sex with Dom last night. Didn't I?

I wince when I touch my vagina. Yep. Definitely used and raw.

I scan the bed, then the room. It's empty. The sound of running water comes from the bathroom.

"Rainey? Rainey, hey." Giulia rushes over and sits beside me.

"Where's Damiano?" My voice trembles. "Where is Dom? I had sex with him last night."

Giulia breathes in deep, then slowly exhales. "Rainey… you had sex with Cristiano. Lots of it. Hot, steamy, wild sex with Cristiano."

I shake my head. "No. Dom was here. I saw him."

Cristiano steps out of the bathroom, fastening his belt.

"It was a hallucinogen. It made you see what you wanted most. I just can't fathom why that psycho has you in such a chokehold."

My head snaps toward him. "You fucking bastard."

He shrugs. "I'll be honest, I wasn't sure it would work. But it was better than I expected. You fuck like a pro. And now that I know you're truly good in bed, my expectations of you have changed, and you will keep fucking me like… that."

"You're disgusting!"

"Me?" he says, feigning offense as he places a hand over his chest like I've wounded him. "Darling, you were the banshee putting me in positions I didn't even know were possible.

"And I'm not sure what kind of kinky behavior you two were into, but I wasn't the one asking for your fingers in my ass. That was all you. And judging by how smoothly you pulled it off, it's obvious it wasn't your first time."

He steps closer, voice dropping like he's letting me in on a secret.

"In fact, you knew exactly where a male G-spot is. Had me coming so fast I barely knew what hit me. That's not something you stumble into by accident. That's the kind of knowledge you only have if someone taught you."

He pauses, just long enough for the punch to land.

"And after doing a little digging, it seems you were a virgin when you met your beloved. So I can only conclude that everything you did to me last night… you learned with him."

I want to claw the smug look off his face.

But I don't move. I won't give him the satisfaction of knowing he's struck a chord. Because if I open my mouth, I might say too much.

Like the fact that one of my favorite things to do is lick Dom's ass while I finger it. That 69 in the morning is my favorite position. That I'm so madly in love with Dom, I'd willingly and happily suck the shit right out of his ass.

ALL DAY, HE SMIRKS AT ME.

Apparently, whatever wild shit I did last night has his full attention, and everything to me feels like a blurry haze.

I know how real it felt, being with Dom, but I can't remember the details. I have no idea what "weird" positions I supposedly put him in.

When we go into town, he makes us stay in the car while he meets with someone.

As soon as the driver steps out to smoke and the door shuts, I clap my hand onto Giulia's thigh.

"Was I a freak?" My eyes stay fixed on the front window, wide with dread.

She doesn't answer.

I slowly turn my head to look at her. Her lips are pinched between her teeth, trying to hold back a smile.

"Just tell me," I whine, dragging the words out.

"You were so hot. I didn't even know you could move like that. If you ever wanted him to get bored of you, you ruined that last night. He had full heart eyes when you told him you loved him."

"Shut the fuck up. I did not."

"You called him Dom the whole time, so he knew it was Damiano you were talking about. But yes, you did."

I let out a groan and fold over.

"If it makes you feel better, you hit him."

My eyes widen as I gape at her. I mouth the words, "I hit him?"

She nods. "You had him in the Amazon position, holding his ankles in the air. Then you just slapped him. He looked stunned like he didn't know how to process it. And then you leaned down, started making out with him, and choked him. He looked like he died from the ecstasy."

"Yuck. I made out with him?"

She lifts her brows, almost looking apologetic. "Yeah. A lot. But hey, at least his mouth is clean. I've never seen someone brush their teeth so much in my life."

Well, that's something. Mouths are disgusting. But at least he has really good oral hygiene.

"It was that position, after you choked him, that you sat up, spit on your fingers, then reached back and slid them right up in him. He wasn't expecting it. Made this little startled noise and tensed up, but you just kept going. Then the next second, he was gripping your hips and pulling you down on him, groaning like he was possessed."

I wrinkle my nose. "Ew."

She pulls her lips tight and gives me *that* look.

"What?" I ask, instantly regretting it.

She zips her lips like she's sealing away a secret.

"We're already here. It can't get worse."

She raises her brows like, *Wanna bet?*

"Oh God. Just tell me."

She winces. "You… sucked on your fingers afterward."

I clutch my stomach. "Fucking barf! Are you lying."

She shakes her head. "I swear."

"Ew! And he let me? *You* let me?"

"There was a lot happening. I think we were all in shock. After the usual sexual encounters with you two… compared to that? It was like… whiplash."

I grimace. "Had I known I was fingering his ass and then licking my fingers, I would've rinsed my mouth out with bleach."

"I'm sorry," she murmurs softly.

"It's fine. It's not like saying something would've gone over well."

She shakes her head. "Not for that. I'm sorry you were taken from Damiano. I knew you loved him… but I don't think I understood the weight of it until last night. The second you said his name, I saw it all over you. You weren't just high, Rainey. You were in pain and heaven all at once. You thought you were making love to him. And if what I saw was just a glimpse of that love… I can't imagine what it's really like between you two."

I inhale slowly, staring ahead as my throat tightens. "Thank you. It's really hard."

She leans over and wraps an arm around me, pulling me in until our heads rest together. We don't say anything else. Just hold each other. And it's enough.

IT's light out when Cristiano says we're going to bed.

I blink at him. "It's still early."

"And?"

"And I don't want to go to bed. Go alone."

He turns, fixing me with a look. "We aren't sleeping. You're going to do what you did last night. Again."

"No the fuck I won't."

He sighs, rolling his eyes as he flicks his wrist. "Go outside then."

I scoff and rise from my seat. "Gladly."

Giulia and I sit on the back patio for an hour, maybe longer. Long enough for the heat to settle into our skin and leave us sweating.

One of the house staff brings out iced water, and we accept immediately.

"Thank you," I say before downing the entire glass.

It cools me off momentarily, but the heat is so exhausting.

For fifteen minutes, we sit in silence. And then it starts.

The glass on the table shimmers. I lean forward and tap it, and it ripples like water.

"Rainey?"

I flatten my palm on the surface, and it dips.

"Rainey, are you okay?" she asks.

When I look up, the trees look like they're dancing, each limb moving even with no wind.

"Rainey."

His voice reaches me.

I freeze.

It's not real. I know it isn't. Somewhere deep in my brain, I know I've been drugged. But when I turn, it's Dom standing there. Not an illusion. Him. My Dom. My beautiful, handsome man.

I try to blink it away, but he doesn't vanish. He stands just at the threshold, waiting for me.

I'm sprinting across the patio and throwing myself into his arms. He catches me effortlessly, lifting me like I weigh nothing at all.

"Hi, baby," I smile.

"Hi, darling," he answers.

For a split second, Cristiano's face flickers through, just for a flash, like a wrong frame in a movie reel. But I ignore it. I don't let it take root.

I lean in, sucking on his neck.

"Stay here," he says, but I don't understand what he means.

I start undressing him, desperate to feel his skin. By the time we reach the bed, I'm on him, frantically grinding on his cock. I ride him with everything I have, chasing the high already building.

I climb off and lift my ass in the air, resting my arms straight above me, cheek pressed to the mattress.

"Fuck me," I demand, and he does. I bounce up and down on him, rough and eager, making him groan louder. I glance back and smile. His head is thrown back, fingers digging into my flesh as he pants how good it is.

"Spank me," I say, breathless.

He does.

"Harder."

I'm so close. I roll my hips faster, begging him to spank me harder until I'm screaming out with my orgasm, pulsating on his shaft as I move back and forth on his length, letting the release consume me.

I sit back on his lap and begin moving again. He wraps his arms around my waist and licks my shoulder while I reach around his neck and hold on.

"Choke me." I grab his hand and guide it to my throat. "Yes," I praise as he squeezes.

He tightens, and my hips grind faster. Pressure and pleasure swirl in my head, and he grunts loudly as he pulses inside me.

I wake to the room still partially darkened, but morning light is starting to stream through the slits in the curtain, and the alarm clock is being shut off.

I'm rolled onto my back as a warm body climbs between my legs. I smile when he pushes in, wrapping my arms around his neck and biting at his jaw as I moan.

"Do you like that?"

I nod, panting, "Yes."

I press the balls of my feet into the backs of his calves and lift my ass, wanting him even deeper.

"That's it, darling," he groans.

Everything grinds to a stop. Reality crashes into me like a freight train and I gasp, shoving at him. "What the fuck are you doing? Get off me!"

He shifts instantly, his expression turning to anger. Whatever moment we were in vanishes. I keep pushing at him, trying to get free.

"Don't make this harder than it needs to be," he bites out, grabbing my wrists and pinning them above my head as I kick and scream.

When he flips me onto my stomach and pulls my arms behind my back, straddling me, I cry out as he fucks me hard, using my own arms as leverage to drive in deeper.

When he's finished, I lie there, furious that the wetness between my thighs isn't just his semen. I was soaked—letting him have sex with me.

What was I even thinking?

"That's the last time you fuck with me!" I yell as I climb out of bed.

He smirks. "You're so kinky, though. You truly are a freak by nature."

"So are you," I bite back.

But it's not the last time I let him fuck with me. In the days that follow—and the weeks that come—I keep letting him drug me, because those moments with Dom are worth it. Once he realizes how much I've come to crave them, he stops offering anything at all unless I have sex with him like that without the drugs. So I do.

Because I need to see Dom. And I'm a nobody whore he's never coming for anyway. I might as well use my pussy to get what I want, even if it's through drug-induced hallucinations.

Chapter

TWENTY-ONE

Nikita

My best friend has been gone for five months.

I'm lying in bed, staring at the ceiling, replaying every haunting detail from that night when my bedroom door opens and Damiano steps inside. I instantly feel nervous, like maybe he's here to blame me for what happened, to yell at me and make me feel even worse. He doesn't talk to anyone. He hasn't said a word to me since the night I came home.

I want to talk to him, to tell him how sorry I am, but he doesn't give anyone a chance.

"Get dressed."

I push up onto my elbows, blinking at him. "For what?"

It's the first time he's talked to me in months, and that's all he says? No explanation to go along with it. And in his state of mind, I need an explanation to go anywhere with him.

He leans against the doorframe. "Want to confront Darius Benedetti?"

The name hits me like a jolt of electricity. He's one of the men who touched Rainey. I sit up so fast, scrambling out of bed, rushing to my closet, yanking hangers aside until I find something suitable.

"Is he here?" I call out, pulling a shirt over my head.

"Dinner tonight at La Cittadella," he replies, following my frantic movements. "We'll be waiting outside."

An hour later Silvano pulls into the narrow, dimly lit alley behind the restaurant. Nikolai is in the front seat, while I sit beside Dom in the back, my knee bouncing with a nervous energy I can't contain.

Dom pushes the door open, then mutters, "I'll be back."

He slips out, his shadow stretching long against the brick wall as he disappears around the corner. The alley is creepy. I trace the plume of steam billowing from a vent on the side of the building, lit in a ghostly glow by the single light above a side door.

A few tense minutes pass before he reemerges from a side exit, his figure cutting a dark, foreboding silhouette against the pale light.

When he reaches my side, he pulls the car door open, leaning down. "He'll come out this way." He jerks his head in the direction he just came.

We all get out, moving to wait nearby. Silvano leans back against the brick wall, arms crossed over his chest. Nikolai stands beside him, his posture deceptively relaxed, one foot braced against the wall as he taps his thumb and pinky rhythmically on his thigh.

The hinges groan a moment later, and a man pokes his head out, glancing between us.

"He's coming. He's with two others," he whispers before dipping back inside.

My stomach tightens. Maybe this was a mistake. Maybe I'm not ready for this. Confronting him won't erase what he did to Rainey. It won't make the memories fade. My palms are damp, my heart racing as the door opens again.

A man I don't recognize steps out first, his head down as he tucks something into his jacket pocket. Another man follows, and when the third man steps out, my skin prickles with unease. The same anger and hatred I felt that night comes roaring back to life, burning through every ounce of fear. I was trapped and helpless when he roughly touched my best friend. But I'm not now.

I approach him as he lifts his head. "Not interested, darlin'." He moves to brush past me.

I step into his path, my chin lifting. "No, you wouldn't be, would you? You prefer your girls chained and helpless."

The men with him go still, their confusion evident as they look from him to me.

He scoffs, waving me off. "Go back to the gutters you crawled out of."

But he knows. He knows exactly what he participated in.

I take a slow step closer, letting the anger in my chest bleed into my voice. "My name is Nikita Volkov, and you sexually assaulted my best friend at Cristiano's. I'm sure you remember."

He's completely thrown off by this confrontation, his attention darting to his companions as if to check whether they believe what I'm accusing him of.

I hold his gaze. "Yeah, I was the one chained to the pillar, watching you put your disgusting fingers inside her."

He huffs a laugh, his bravado slipping. "Cristiano let us touch his bitch."

"She's not his," I snap, closing the distance between us. "She's Damiano Volkov's girlfriend."

The color drains from his face, his expression tightening as Dom's shadow stretches up behind me. His chin lifts, taking in the full measure of Dom.

"I—I don't want any issues," he stammers, taking a step back.

"You touched what's mine," Dom says flatly.

"Cristiano—"

"Isn't here," Dom interrupts.

The man's hands come up in a desperate, trembling gesture. "Do you want money? Tell me what you want."

"To fight."

The man blinks, brows pulling together as if he can't quite process the demand.

"I'm not fighting you," he says, his voice lacking conviction.

Dom steps closer. "Then don't." A fist drives into the man's gut before the words even register. The blow forces a choked, breathless wheeze from his lungs as he folds over.

"See, I can do this all night," Dom says, voice calm, almost conversational, as the man is shoved back against the wall. "Because my girlfriend is still gone, and men like you keep taking what isn't being given."

His next punch sends the man stumbling back, head snapping to the side, blood already trickling from the corner of his mouth. Catching himself against the cold brick wall, shaky hands press for balance while he blinks through the daze.

He wobbles as he struggles to stay upright, still swaying when Dom's fist slams into his ribs. He crumples, gasping, one hand clutching his side before spitting blood onto the concrete.

Dom steps back, watching him flounder, knees scraping against the ground as he fights to stand.

"Let me know when you're done." He drives a sidekick into his knee with enough force to shatter the joint. The scream pierces the air as he collapses, leg folding beneath him at a grotesque angle.

"I'm done. I'm done," he whimpers, one hand raised in a pitiful attempt at surrender, the other trembling as he tries to hold himself up.

Dom turns his attention to the men who haven't moved, their faces ashen, eyes blown wide.

"You're free to go," he tells them.

They trade a nervous look and inch backward, but the man on the ground shouts after them, his voice a frantic, desperate rasp, begging for help.

Dom steps forward, his shadow spilling over the man like a death sentence. He stares at the outstretched fingers curling in a silent plea, before driving his fist into the man's nose, cartilage shattering on impact.

He crumples, back hitting the pavement as blood streams from his face, chest rising in shallow, wet gasps.

Dropping to his knees, Dom straddles him and unleashes a brutal, unrelenting barrage. His knuckles split, blood mixing with blood as he pounds the ruined face, over and over, long after the lifeless form goes still.

It isn't until Silvano and Nikolai each seize an arm that Dom is forced to stop. They drag him back, but he breaks free just enough to stomp on the unrecognizable mess of flesh and bone that once passed for a cruel face.

The door to the restaurant creaks open, and a man in a chef's coat steps out holding a bag of ice, bandages, and a stack of towels.

"Go on, get out of here," he says, shoving the supplies into my hands. "Cops are on their way. We've got this from here."

Dom gives a curt nod, then looks down at the body one last time. "For Rainey," he says, stomping on his dick, grinding his boot down.

Nikolai climbs into the back beside Dom, taking the towels from me to wipe the blood from his knuckles before wrapping them and pressing the bag of ice over the bandages.

The ride home is silent. No apology could ever ease his pain, so none of us even bother trying.

Darius Benedetti was one of three men still alive, but he's dead now. Two men who assaulted Rainey remain at large.

Each one of those sick pigs met the same fate—they fought Damiano. Two still remain, their names hanging over us like ghosts, taunting us with their absence. It's like they've vanished into thin air.

Nikolai said the last group they found had been four men, holed up in an abandoned warehouse on the outskirts of the city. Damiano took them all on at once. By the time it was over, they lay in a twisted, bloody heap, and Damiano barely had a scratch on him.

But the last two are nowhere to be found.

As the days drag on without progress, I start to unravel.

The only solid piece of intel on Rainey says he's moving her constantly to keep her hidden, and unfortunately, he's doing a good job.

My mind clings to the horrors I refuse to let fade, because I don't want to forget Rainey. The images replay behind my eyes like a movie each time I close them. I see her broken and bleeding. I imagine those last two men doing even worse to her, their hands on her, their laughter echoing through whatever hellhole they've taken her to.

I quit eating. I can't stomach the thought of putting anything in my mouth while Rainey might be starving. For all I know, she's already dead.

I stop getting out of bed. The days blend together, the lines between night and day blurring until I can't tell one from the other.

I stare at the ceiling for hours, my mind a constant loop of all the things I should have done, all the ways I could have saved her. Each imagined scenario is more desperate and frantic than the last. I imagine her whispering my name, calling for me, and I hate myself for not being there, for not being strong enough to protect her.

At some point, the grief shifts. It doesn't lessen. It just sinks deeper, like stone settling in my chest.

I'm curled in the corner of my bed, the sheets twisted around my legs, my head pounding from days of crying and sleepless nights. My skin feels like it's burning from the inside out, my mind a relentless, churning storm of Rainey's screams.

I hear a soft knock on my door, followed by the hall light spilling into the darkened room as it slowly swings open. I don't bother looking up because I don't care who's here.

A small bottle hits the mattress beside me, the pills inside rattling against the plastic. I blink, my blurred vision slowly focusing on the orange prescription bottle.

I don't have to look up to know it's Em.

"I thought you might need something to help you sleep," she says, but I can hear the strain and worry in her voice. Perhaps she should take half for herself.

I remain unmoving long enough that she finally walks away, quietly pulling the door shut behind her.

As soon as she's gone, I grab the bottle, shake two pills into my hand, and swallow them dry. I don't care what they are, hell, I don't even care if they kill me.

I lean back against my headboard, waiting for them to do something. Anything.

When the warmth finally starts to creep into my veins, I let out a slow, shuddering breath, my eyelids growing heavy as the edges of my thoughts lose focus, the suffocating memories softening into a dull, distant ache.

The tension slowly drains from my body, the pain and fear slipping just out of reach, like a nightmare retreating with the first hint of morning.

Silence.

My mind is nothing but silence.

THE PILLS BECOME A LIFELINE, A WAY TO EASE THE MENTAL TORMENT, to drown out the endless loop of Rainey's suffering. I start taking more. One to get through breakfast. Another to make it to lunch. Two before bed, just to keep the nightmares at bay.

But it's never enough.

The calm I used to feel, that numbness starts slipping through my fingers, like sand in a clenched fist. My tolerance grows, my moods spiraling out of control. I snap at anyone who so much as looks at me, my patience fraying until it feels like every sound, every concerned glance is an accusation, a reminder that I failed her.

I raid the medical room one night, yanking open drawers and cupboards, bottles clattering to the floor as I search for anything to quiet my mind. Behind a stack of bandages, I find another bottle of oxy. I dump three pills into my mouth and shove the rest into my pocket.

But then the supply runs out.

I return days later, heading straight for the spot where I found the last ones. It's empty. Gauze scatter as I dig faster, but the pills are gone. Every last one.

I storm back to the main house and find Dante in the kitchen, his broad back turned to me.

"Where are they?" I demand.

He turns slowly, his brows pulling together, his jaw tight. "You're done," he says with finality.

"What do you mean I'm done?" I shout. "You don't get to decide that!"

He steps around the counter toward me. "You're done," he repeats, more resolute.

Rage erupts out of me. I sweep my arm across the counter, sending glass shattering against the wall. I grab a vase and hurl it against the cabinets, the shards exploding in a burst of white and green.

Ma rushes in, eyes wide, reaching for me. "Nikita, stop," she pleads, trying to catch my arm.

"Don't touch me!" I scream, wrenching free of her grasp. I shove a chair over, then another, my vision clouding with hot, furious tears.

Dante grabs me around the waist from behind, dragging me back as I kick and thrash.

"Calm down," Nikolai says, stepping in front of me, hands up, eyes pleading. "Nikita, please, calm down."

"It should have been me! I want Rainey! He's hurting her." I fight to get away, but Dante easily lifts me off the ground.

The sound of my own screams mix with Rainey's until I can't tell where mine end and hers begin.

I feel the sting of a needle piercing my skin, and my entire body stiffens, a cold, bitter hatred flooding my veins as I realize what they've done.

They drugged me. My own family. Just like Cristiano's men did.

My vision wavers, the world tilting and spinning as my limbs go limp, my head lolling back against Dante's shoulder as he lays me on the couch.

I try to curse them, to hit them, but my arms won't move, my legs won't respond, my body a useless, sagging weight as the darkness pulls me under.

When I wake, my head is foggy, my arms wrapped tightly against my chest, the thick, suffocating embrace of a straight jacket pressing against my ribs. I blink, slowly focusing on the windowless room at the white padded walls of betrayal. I've been committed to a psych ward.

Chapter
TWENTY-TWO

Rainey

The thing about abusers is that they feed off the suffering they cause. It's not just the control they crave, it's the reaction. The tears, the fear, the panic—those are what sustain them. But once you stop giving them that satisfaction, they escalate. They adapt, shift tactics, find new ways to slice deeper and drag you lower, because your silence threatens their power.

I stop reacting when Cristiano hits me. I stop fighting him when he forces himself on me, only engaging when I'm high or bribed with drugs.

It works for a while, until he realizes he has to drug me to get even the smallest show of affection. When that doesn't change, he shifts tactics. He becomes unpredictable, cruel in new ways, clawing for any kind of reaction. Some days I fake fear or offense, just enough to keep him from going further. Other days, I'm not pretending. Some days I am genuinely horrified by the man he is. Tonight is one of those nights.

It started earlier, with something so small it almost felt absurd. We were walking toward his office with two potential business partners when he told me to tie his shoe. I refused. His eyes flashed with quiet rage, and in that moment, I knew the rest of my night would be hell. He kept his mask on in front of them, smiling, cordial, composed. But the second the front door shut behind them and he turned toward me, I knew I was in deep shit.

What throws me off is what doesn't happen next. When we enter the bedroom, he doesn't start undressing. I remember what happened the last time this exact thing took place.

He walks toward me and begins tearing at my clothes, shredding the fabric without urgency, just irritation. I let him. I stand there still, expression blank, trying to seem bored, like none of this affects me anymore. But the second he forces me down and binds me, arms and legs pulled tight behind my back with a ball gag shoved in my mouth, I know I've entered a new level of hell.

I've never been so helpless. Hogtied and exposed, I lie there trembling while he sits lazily on the edge of the bed, still fully clothed, eyes gleaming with cruel satisfaction as I cry.

When he begins to speak, I know the words aren't meant for me. They're meant for the only other person in the room. Giulia.

"You will follow directions the first time I give them," he says, his voice smooth and unbothered. "Or you will be punished. Do you understand?"

There's a pause, and then I hear her voice, barely audible and quivering.

"Yes."

Even she notices the shift in him tonight. I'm guessing it's from whatever "new product" he decided to test. When he snorted it, I found myself wishing it would kill him. But it didn't.

He rises and walks to the side of the bed, opening a drawer and pulling out three dildos, tossing them carelessly onto the mattress beside my face.

My eyes squeeze shut as panic creeps up my spine.

"Choose one."

Silence falls between them, long enough I wonder if there's some sort of exchange happening behind me that I don't know of. Finally, Giulia says, "The purple one."

When I open my eyes, he's handing it to her. Thankfully, it's the smallest one.

I can't see much from my position, but I can feel the weight of his stare on her.

He grabs my knee and yanks it toward him while using his foot to push my other leg away, spreading me wide. I'm completely exposed and vulnerable.

"Have you ever played with another woman before?"

I don't hear anything, but she must have responded because he lets out a quiet laugh. "First time. Exciting." He leans casually against the bedpost and gestures toward me. "Insert it. Either hole is fine."

Giulia begins crying harder, and nothing touches me.

This is the first time he's ever tied me up like this, and it's the worst feeling. He's unhinged, and it's also the first time he's forcing Giulia to participate in his sickness.

He sighs and stands, walking across the room like he expected this outcome. He pulls the door open and waves two men inside.

I try to remain stoic while bracing myself for what they're going to do to me.

But they don't come for me. They're here for her.

The sounds that follow are hard to describe. Struggling. Whimpering. Skin-to-skin slapping. My heart twists, and I want to beg her to just do it, to do whatever he wants her to do to me if it will make them stop, but I can't speak over this gag.

When the noise finally fades and she's placed back down, I see blood smeared along the inside of her thigh.

The men leave with smug smiles. Cristiano turns his attention to her. "Are you ready to listen now?"

Through broken sobs she nods and answers a quiet "yes."

"Good."

I can't see what she's doing, but I hear his next command. "You had your chance with that. You'll use your fingers now."

There's a long silence.

Then I feel her hesitantly brushing the outside of me.

Cristiano leans forward again, doing something I can't see. Then she penetrates me. The movement is shallow, barely there, but it's enough to make my stomach tighten.

Apparently whatever she's doing must not be good enough for him, because he places his hand over hers, sliding two fingers in beside her one, and suddenly he's taking control, driving them in with ruthless speed. I gasp, my body twisting as I try to lift my hips away from them. I just want it to stop.

He's enjoying this. Every sound of discomfort only fuels him on.

When he finally pulls away, he sinks back into place, fully content to just watch.

He points at her again. "Start over."

She obeys.

She follows every one of his detailed, dehumanizing instructions. And I can do nothing but lie here and endure it.

When he tells her to use her tongue and not stop until I finish, she does. Her touch is desperate to please, but my body refuses to respond.

I realize the more stiff I am, the more hesitant she becomes. And I don't want this to go on all night. So I shift tactics. I force myself to relax, to let out a soft moan that sounds convincing enough. It works. Her movements grow more confident, and eventually, she gets me off.

But it doesn't end there.

He escalates again, pulling her deeper into it. The toys he laid out earlier are now in her hands, and he guides her through each cruel step.

When he finally decides to take me himself, he orders her behind him, forcing her to lick his ass while he fucks me.

When it's over, he tells her to take the dildos to the bathroom and clean them.

He unties the knots at my wrists and ankles, then removes the ball gag. My jaw throbs from being stretched open so long, and when I drag my tongue across the corner of my lips, it's raw.

I glance down and see the damage there too. My wrists and ankles are bleeding, the flesh torn from the tight bindings. The purple skin is trying to regain color.

He doesn't realize his strength when he's high, and his cruelty has no limits. Tonight proved that.

Whatever he took, it turns him into a complete monster.

He brings in a medic to clean and dress my injuries, then orders him away.

He points for me to lie down, and I do, not wanting to give him any reason to hurt me again tonight. Then he goes to the balcony and smokes a cigar before coming back inside. He crawls in bed, and within minutes, soft snores fill the room.

I wait until I'm sure he's asleep before I quietly slide off the bed and lower myself to the floor, where Giulia is curled up tightly.

I wrap my arms around her and kiss her temple. She tenses at first, then relaxes when she realizes it's me. She muffles her cries into my shoulder as best she can, holding me tightly.

"I'm sorry," I whisper, wanting to stop the guilt she's feeling.

We fall asleep clinging to each other. Two broken girls, worn down and emptied.

I don't know how long we're asleep before Cristiano's voice rips through the fog.

"Both of you. Get on the bed!"

We scramble to our feet, moving as quickly as our tired bodies will allow.

His eyes are ice when he looks at us… at me. "If you want to sneak off and sleep together so badly, then you can fuck instead."

For the next two hours, he forces us to use the toys on each other. He barks orders, commands us into degrading positions, until it satisfies whatever sick fantasy he's chasing.

It's supposed to be punishment. But the joke's on him. Because given the choice, I would rather fuck her any day over him.

WHATEVER INSANE DRUG HE WAS ON LAST NIGHT HAS WORN OFF. Thank God. He was a monster.

My wrists and ankles still burn. So does my cheek, where he punched me for "being good at eating pussy."

He forced me to go down on Giulia, and not only did I have no idea what I was doing, but I found out I'm apparently amazing at it. Worse, I didn't even mind. Her body reacted easily, and it was effortless getting her off.

But that made him furious.

He stormed off after and came back with a rag, shoving it into my face and telling me to scrub the scent off. Said I reeked of her.

This morning he acted like none of it happened. Now, he's forcing us to go with him to a meeting at a warehouse. He makes sure we're dressed how he wants. The usual dresses, hair curled, makeup perfect. He says his "partner" should make him look good, not embarrass him.

The fact our situationship is as dysfunctional as it is and he still refers to me as his partner is nuts. How delusional I find him in this scenario is how delusional I'm being over me still being in a relationship with Dom.

Eventually I'll have to give it up. But for now, I enjoy living in my fantasy.

At one point, he flips the fabric of my dress aside and rests his hand high on my thigh. All I want to do is punch him in the side of the head.

When we arrive, Cristiano and the driver step out. From behind the tinted windows, we watch the driver take position by the door, while Cristiano strolls across the lot toward a group of men. He starts talking, his gestures calm and controlled, like he doesn't have two hostages waiting in the back seat.

I turn to Giulia and speak softly.

"In the future, if he tells you to do something to me, just do it," I murmur. "You don't need to make things harder on yourself."

She looks at me, appearing shocked. "He made me rape you."

"And you got raped for refusing and still had to do it. So that didn't really do anything but, again, hurt you."

She glares at me.

I nudge her lightly. "Plus, you fuck a million times better than he ever could."

She blinks, startled. Then somehow, we both start laughing.

"Can I tell you something?" she asks, not waiting for a reply. "I told myself I'd never admit how good you felt, but you were incredible."

I smile and shrug.

"I'm still debating whether we should act like we hate it so he keeps making us do it for his own twisted enjoyment, or show how much we like it just to confuse the loser."

"I'll do whatever you think will get him to let us do it again."

Cristiano is still deep in conversation. I shake my head as I watch him.

"Sick motherfucker."

We spend the rest of the day being dragged from warehouse to warehouse, trailing behind him while he handles his business.

Most of it is waiting. Sitting in the car for hours with nothing to do but watch the sun move across the sky.

By the time night falls and we're finally headed back, exhaustion settles deep in my bones. I rest my head on the seat rest and close my eyes, just wanting sleep.

Then I hear a zipper.

I glance down and he's pulling out his penis, staring at me expectantly.

"What?" I ask flatly, knowing exactly what he wants.

"You two seemed to be having a great time in here while I was out busting my ass making deals so you can continue living like a queen. Show some appreciation."

"You think I'm living like a queen?" I ask, not bothering to hide the amusement in my voice.

He grabs the back of my neck and shoves my head down.

I inhale through my mouth as he thrusts upward, letting out a groan as I envelop him.

When I finally sit back up, I wipe my mouth with the back of my hand and stare out the front window, reminding myself the punishment for attempting to push him out of the moving vehicle wouldn't be worth it.

I can feel the driver's eyes on me. When I glance his way, he smirks, and I glare in return. He loves watching women get assaulted. He's the most disgusting man Cristiano has working for him.

His cocky grin feels like he's mocking me, and I know he enjoyed watching me be forced to do that. So I decide to be a dick to him too.

"You glaring like that because your puny little dick isn't even an eighth of his size?" I give him a smug grin right back.

I figure if I compliment Dumbass while insulting the even bigger Dumbass up front, Cristiano might not get so mad.

Cristiano's head snaps toward me, then turns to the front. His driver meets his gaze in the rearview mirror before turning back to the road.

"What?" I ask, draping my arm around Cristiano's neck. "He was smirking, and I couldn't tell if it's because he wishes someone other than his daddy would suck his dick, or if he's just never seen a dick as big as yours."

I lean in and nip at his ear, knowing it'll throw him off and maybe get his driver in trouble.

The best part is watching the driver's face fall. He thrives on women being powerless, and I'm shattering that image.

"Get your beady fucking eyes off the mirror," I snap.

He glares before returning his attention to the road.

I bite down lightly on Cristiano's bottom lip, tug it into my mouth, and casually raise my hand behind my head, flipping the driver off.

Whether he does it on purpose or not, he swerves and mutters something before correcting the wheel. He quickly says sorry, claiming an animal ran into the road, but both mine and Cristiano's heads slam together hard.

"Fuck," Cristiano shouts, shoving me back as he grabs his forehead.

I catch the smirk on the driver's face and know he did it intentionally.

Good one.

When we pull up to the house, Cristiano is still holding his head. He's so angry I don't even think about going near him. I turn toward Giulia's door, ready to climb out.

Suddenly, my hair is yanked backward, and I find myself staring up at the ceiling. He hovers over my face. "I got the door for you, darling."

I sit up slowly, my scalp tingling, and try to slide past him, but he catches my jaw and leans in. He kisses me possessively, his thumb grazing my cheek as he pulls back.

Then, with a smile, he takes my hand and guides me toward the house.

Chapter

TWENTY-THREE

Damiano

I come up from the basement for water. I usually find myself staring out the back door into the darkness, sometimes for hours each night around the same time. It's two in the morning, and I don't even make it to the kitchen. The light in Dante's office is still glowing beneath the door. When I open it, he's slouched on the couch, wiping at his eyes.

He looks worse than I feel.

"Hey," his voice is rough. "What's up?"

I cross the room and sit near him. After a long moment, I place my hand on his shoulder. I didn't think it would be me comforting him about my girlfriend being taken. But here we are.

"We're going to find her."

"Yeah." He nods, dragging his palms down his face. "How are you holding up?"

"As good as your hand held up in the *Round Room*."

His head jerks upright, his eyes wide as he stares at me.

"I knew," I admit. "Andrei found your *Reach Me* profiles. I knew who she was to you, and I didn't care. I knew she was the woman you told Ma and Pa you were going to marry and they rejected her. I didn't know who she was when I met her, but I figured it out. And I still didn't care that it would hurt you—that I was taking the woman you wanted.

"I had sex with her at the auction just to make a point that she was mine now. But after she was raped, I knew she would be suffering, and I didn't want to deal with it. You're better equipped to handle that kind of stuff. I knew you'd be gentle enough with her, that if she were scared of intimacy after what happened to her, you'd be patient enough and take your time to show her sex can still be safe with someone who cares about her… who loves her. So I pawned that burden off on you."

I swallow hard. "I know that was messed up. And I'm sorry for that. I could never care about you enough that I would have given her up to protect your heart. I'll never give her up."

He doesn't say anything. Just stares.

"When we get her back," I go on, "she might not be okay. And I'm not sure I'll know how to deal with what's been done to her. I'll take care of whatever needs to be done when it comes to Cristiano. I just know Rainey's going to need… you."

His eyes stay locked on mine, stunned.

He blinks and clears his throat. "I'll do anything for Rainey. Anything." He pauses, as if knowing he needs to take the conversation in a different direction. "I know I messed up, Dom—"

"Don't," I cut in. "It was going to happen eventually. Rainey chose to sleep with you. She never acted hurt or bothered by it, so I'm not bothered by it."

He breathes in deep and holds it. "What do you plan on doing?"

"How long have you been worried I'd kill you?"

He holds up his hand to show me the one he broke.

I smirk, leaning back against the couch. I shake my head, then glance over at him.

"You saved me from years of abuse. And I dragged you into it. Rainey choosing to sleep with you? That's not even on the radar of what I should be worried about."

He frowns. "Why are you so calm?"

I shrug. "I should probably talk to Dr. Winn," I joke, though it lands flat. "I went to the *Round Room*. Saw all the blood. Asked who was chained up. When they said Rainey, I knew. I watched the video."

I pause. "I remember how you looked when Carmella had sex with you. How broken you were. But this time, watching you with Rainey—it was different. You weren't ashamed. You weren't in pain. You looked blissful. Like something in you was finally being repaired.

"When she stayed with you after her rape, I hoped she'd sleep with you again. And when she let me touch her once I got back, I knew she had. I knew you'd gotten through to her."

I look over at him again.

"Watching her heal you started to heal me too. That part of my brain that's still scarred from what Carmella did to you—it didn't ache as much. And I craved continuing to watch you keep healing."

"You deserve her," he says after a beat. "I'm glad you're the one who got her."

I sigh. "Neither of us have her now."

He flops back against the couch, his arm crossing over his eyes as he shakes his head side to side. "Fuuuck," he groans.

Chapter
TWENTY-FOUR

Rainey

I've been hanging on to the hope that Dom was coming for me, but it's abundantly clear he's not going to.

I never let myself dwell on that. I'd probably have a total meltdown if I did. Instead, I tuck what Damiano and I had into my heart and hold onto it for dear life, not wanting to think about him, but not wanting to forget him either.

This morning, I woke up sad. Heartachingly sad.

I think it's sinking in that I'm never going home. That he truly did abandon me. That I'm stuck here with Cristiano until my stupid mouth gets me killed. And the realization feels like a breakup. One I never wanted to come.

Cristiano's been even more controlling the last couple weeks.

All day yesterday, Giulia was trailing after me with a large cup of water, as he pressed me to drink nonstop. And every time I went to the bathroom, he was there. Watching. Waiting. He checked the toilet before I was allowed to flush.

It's strange. Obsessive. And no matter how hard I try, I can't figure out what he's looking for.

Giulia once asked me if I might be pregnant with Damiano's baby. I hadn't even considered it until she said something, but then I remembered my first day here. Cristiano made me pee into a pan placed inside the toilet, and I was too disoriented to question it at the time.

Later, someone handed Cristiano something and said, "It was negative." I remember the flicker of relief that crossed his face before he looked back at me. He must have been testing my urine to see if I was pregnant.

Now, every time he hovers while I use the bathroom, I wonder if he's checking to see if I'm on my period, or if he's trying to collect another sample. Maybe he wants to know if I'm ovulating, or maybe he's trying to confirm that he's succeeded in getting me pregnant, like he swears he's going to do.

When he finishes having sex with me, he lets me use the bathroom. The day begins the same, with him checking it after I go.

Throughout the day, he does the same.

After this last trip, when he checks the toilet, he finally seems satisfied. His eyes linger in the bowl, and the corners of his mouth lift slightly.

"Let's go," he says, already striding away.

I glance at Giulia, confused. She shrugs, just as lost as I am.

We follow him through the house, keeping a good ten paces back.

When he reaches his office, he goes straight to his desk and sits. Giulia moves to the leather couch and sinks down, and I stop beside him like I've been trained to do.

He turns in his chair, facing me fully, eyes locked on mine. He waits expectantly.

I pause for a heartbeat, then lean down and offer my cheek.

His hand shoots up, gripping my jaw as he drags me in, his mouth crushing against mine.

I pinch my eyes shut and wait it out, forcing my body to stay compliant.

Finally, he releases me. I pull back quickly, turning to leave, but not fast enough to avoid the slap to my butt as he turns back to his computer.

I walk stiffly toward Giulia, scrunching my nose in disgust. She bites back a small smirk and reaches for me. We lace our fingers together and lean back against the couch, shoulders brushing.

Minutes drag by. Maybe hours. I've even learned not to doze off, because the one time I did, I woke up to my underwear being yanked away so fast, then him fucking me roughly, saying he works hard for us and that I'm unappreciative.

Eventually, without looking up from his computer, he speaks. "Giulia. Get Rainey water."

She stares, unsure what to do. When he turns and glares at her, her eyes widen in alarm.

"I'm not thirsty," I cut in quickly, trying to defuse it.

I don't even know why he randomly brings up me needing water. Do I look dehydrated?

His gaze snaps to me. "I didn't ask if you were thirsty, did I? I said you will drink the water."

Then, without looking away from me, he jerks his chin toward Giulia. "Go."

She gets up immediately. I sit perfectly still until she returns, handing me a tall cup filled to the brim.

I take it and murmur, "Thanks," under my breath, already moving to set it on the coffee table.

"Drink it."

His eyes flick up from the screen, pinning me in place.

Swallowing the lump in my throat, I lift the cup and take a small sip. When I start to set it down again, he stops me.

"Don't put it down until you finish it," he orders.

I blink at him, but one look tells me arguing isn't an option.

Later, during a meeting, he hands me a full 20 oz cup. "Finish it before I'm done."

I drink it, of course I do.

When I hand the cup back, empty, he immediately refills it. "Keep going."

My eyes widen. "Can I go pee first?"

All I get is a clipped "No."

"I will literally pee my pants," I say, trying to convey just how serious I am.

His head turns slowly toward me. "And you'll only drink even more."

I sigh, wondering why he's suddenly so concerned about my hydration.

By the end of the meeting, I'm bloated and desperate. "I really need to use the bathroom," I whisper.

He doesn't respond with words, just grabs my hand and leads me into a room I haven't seen before. Giulia steps in behind us, taking a seat in the chair next to the bed.

"Undress."

I do. It's instinct now, but so is the need to release my bladder. "I need to use the bathroom first."

"No," he replies flatly.

"Please," I practically beg. "I won't fight you if you let me go."

"I said no." He cuts me off and then stretches out across the bed, already naked, waiting.

I stare at him, crossing my legs, not even sure I can move at this point. I just about pee on the floor when he speaks his next command.

"Put your pussy on my mouth."

I glance back toward the bathroom, knowing I probably won't even make it.

"Do you want me to ask again?"

I shake my head and climb onto the bed, straddling his face.

"Sit," he demands, and I do.

His warm tongue moves against me, and I hate that my body responds. But the more pleasure he gives, the more aware I become of my need to pee. I actually start sweating with how badly I need to go, and I know if he gets me off, I won't be able to hold it.

When I try to move and get him off the spot that feels good, he wraps his arms tightly around my legs, holding me in place.

"Please," I beg, my voice breaking into a full-blown whimper, unable to hold it any longer.

He mumbles something I don't catch. When he repeats it, I finally understand.

"Relieve yourself," he says again.

I gape at him, our eyes locked, his mouth still latched to me. Then two fingers slide inside, moving with a brutal rhythm that rips a cry from my throat.

I try to hold it. With everything I have, I try to hold it. But I fail.

The release hits, shame flooding me even before the warmth escapes, but to my horror, he doesn't recoil.

He sucks harder.

He drinks every last drop like he's starved for it.

Relief crashes over me, so intense it feels like euphoria. My body trembles, no longer resisting as his mouth continues to work my clit, merciless and unrelenting. The orgasm takes me without warning, and I don't try to stop it, only muffle the sounds spilling from my mouth as it tears through me and my hips move against his tongue.

I collapse forward, pressing my forehead against the headboard as the intensity of what just happened settles over me.

I inhale a deep breath and hold it, then let it out. The embarrassment of what I just did wraps around me like a noose. I just peed in his fucking mouth. There's a small ounce of satisfaction at the thought that I used his face as a toilet, but just as fast, I realize he enjoyed it.

He drags his tongue from my ass to the top of my clit one final time before pulling back. A slap to my butt signals me to get off him, and I immediately do. Losing physical contact with him is something he doesn't have to ask twice about, I'll always comply in that regard.

I wrap my arms around my knees, and he sits up, grabbing my legs, spreading them over his lap, then proceeds to have sex with me fast and hard.

When he finishes, he stands and saunters to the bathroom.

I gape at Giulia, unsure if that entire thing actually happened or if I hallucinated it. When I see her brows lifted in shock too, I shake my head in disbelief. "Will that kill him?"

"I hope," she mutters back.

"Me too," I agree.

"Guess we know why he's having you drink so much water."

"That was so much pee." I say disbelieving.

We both startle when the bathroom door swings open, and he sticks his head out.

"Rainey." He motions for me to come.

I stare at him then glance at her as I scoot to the edge of the bed and walk to him.

He forces me to shower with him, but it's nothing like the ones I used to share with Dom, where his hands were always on me, touching, claiming. This shower is just that—a shower. And I send up a silent thank you to whoever might be listening.

It's a daily occurrence now. Cristiano makes me pee in his mouth.

The first few times were mortifying, my face burning with shame as I hovered over him, every nerve ending screaming that this was wrong. I'm fairly positive this is some sort of torture technique, because it feels like one.

He has me on a strict diet, each meal subtly tweaked over time, every change I'm pretty sure is meant to change the way I taste. I'm only allowed to relieve myself in the toilet first thing in the morning, and then once more after my first cup of water. Any time after that, I'm holding it until he's ready.

It started as humiliation, but now it's something else. Now, I'm practically running to the room when he calls for me, ripping my clothes off and clawing at his to make it faster. I end up shoving him onto the bed, straddling his face with a desperation that borders on madness, just to relieve myself. It's the only part of the day I even enjoy anymore, this twisted mix of pain and pleasure.

Worse, I'm starting to crave it. I barely want to go to the bathroom in the morning. I'd rather wait, rather let the pressure build until it's almost unbearable, until it collides with the pleasure of his tongue. I hate it. But I need it.

As we sit parked outside a building, waiting for him to come back out, I cross my legs, pressing my hand against my crotch, trying to hold it in. My leg bounces, every nerve on fire as the familiar desperation begins to claw its way free.

"Can you turn the air on?" I ask the driver.

He presses the button but angles the vents toward himself. I don't even care. It's better than it was a second ago.

When Cristiano steps out of the building, I sit up straighter, my pulse spiking. He pauses to speak with another man, and I groan, my leg shaking like it might somehow make him move faster.

"Come on," I whisper, practically vibrating with the need for release.

Less than thirty seconds pass before I'm leaning forward, slapping my palm against the horn and waving for him to hurry up. Both men turn, their heads snapping toward the car. The driver's mouth falls open, eyes flicking to me in disbelief before cutting back to Cristiano, who just looks amused.

When he finally climbs in, he's smiling.

"Hurry up," I say, grabbing his arm, tugging at him to get in faster.

He chuckles, leaning over to press a kiss to my cheek. "You're needy, darling."

"Can we do it here?" I whisper urgently.

That earns another deep, throaty laugh as he responds in Russian, his eyes sparkling with amusement.

"English," I snap, my body wound so tight I feel like I might explode.

"I said, be patient, my love."

The second we pull up to the house, I'm leaning over him shoving his door open, practically pushing him out. As we start up the steps, one of his guards approaches, his mouth opening to say something, but I cut him off.

"Shut the fuck up," I snap, grabbing Cristiano's hand and yanking him toward the door.

The guard's jaw drops, eyes wide as he stares at me, clearly stunned that I just spoke to him like that. But Cristiano does nothing, just lets me lead him inside without a word.

As soon as we near the bedroom, I strip my dress off, my panties following in a desperate flutter to the floor. I shove the door open, spinning back to him, fingers tearing at the buttons of his shirt. He chuckles, letting me claw at him, his gaze darkening with lust as he lays on the bed and I finally crawl over him to straddle his face.

Relief crashes over me, so intense I nearly black out, my body trembling as I let go, the euphoria so overwhelming it leaves me breathless.

Day after day, this is what I look forward to. I've become high on it. Dependent on it. Knowing he's the only one who can give me the relief and twisted pleasure that I crave.

Chapter
TWENTY-FIVE

Rainey

Cristiano is passed out. I know he's actually sleeping because he's snoring softly. I lay on the edge of the bed, my face partially hanging over as I stare down at Giulia, my fingers tracing hers gently as we talk.

"Tell me more about Damiano," she whispers.

I stare absentmindedly at our hands, the way our fingers slide softly against each other, and realize I haven't thought about him in weeks. I can't continue torturing myself with hope when it's pointless. But even her saying his name has his beautiful face coming to mind. Clear as if I was staring right at him and a small smile tugs at my lips.

"He's the most handsome man I've ever seen. He's serious but genuine. When he says something, you know it's the truth. He doesn't sugarcoat anything. He's intense, but he makes you feel safe. He took me to an underground fight once and kicked the shit out of three men. It was... incredibly sexy."

"I don't mean this disrespectfully," she says quietly, "but I've heard he's crazy. Is that not true?"

I smile again, a little wider this time.

"Sure, he is. He's passionate about the things he cares about. And if you're his enemy, he'll kill you without thinking twice."

"Do you ever worry he would kill you?"

I shake my head. "Not even a little bit."

"Why would his mom give you over? She had to have known what Cristiano would do to you."

I inhale slowly, then let it out. "I don't know. I thought she liked me. She always seemed to like me, anyway."

"Did anything happen between the two of you?"

This is the million-dollar question. I've asked myself countless times what could have upset her, but nothing stands out. I don't know why she hated me enough to send me away, or what she might have told Dom to make him not want to come for me. Whatever it was, I wish I could apologize.

I shake my head. "No. She was super supportive of me after I was raped. And then I thought Dom didn't want me anymore, and... well, I slept with his brother."

I smile when I think of Dante. He's always so wound up tight. Both of those two need to learn to let loose.

Then I think of Nikolai and how carefree he always was. He had the brightest smile. The exact same smile as Niki. *Niki.* The image of her slams into me. My beautiful best friend.

Tears slip down my cheek, and I realize now more than ever that Damiano and his entire family probably blame me for her being killed. The realization hits me so hard, I begin to quietly sob.

"Hey," Giulia says softly, her hand brushing up my arm.

"She was killed because of me," I whisper as I cry even harder, trying to stay quiet so I don't accidentally wake Cristiano. Especially since he's always horny.

"Who?"

"Dom's sister. She was taken with me. They killed her and sent her body back to the Volkovs. They lost their only daughter because of me."

"None of this is your fault."

I shake my head, knowing she's trying to be comforting, but this is my fault. Niki wasn't even supposed to be home yet.

Maybe they'll hunt me down to kill me for her death. There's a sort of poetic justice in that thought. I couldn't think of a better way to die than by the hands of the only man I've ever loved. And Damiano would do it, then never think of me again. But at that point, I wouldn't care, because I'd be six feet under dirt or whatever else he decided to do with me.

I've never even taken the time to think about how he and his family are holding up after finding out she's dead. I've been so selfishly wrapped up in my own situation, so mad they haven't saved me yet, that I didn't stop to consider they're probably devastated. And Nikolai. Oh, Nikolai. The sudden realization that he lost his other half makes me want to puke.

I keep my eyes shut, tears slipping down silently as Giulia leans in and clings to my arm, her head nestled close on the mattress beside me.

I SPEND DAYS SUNK IN THE DEPRESSION OF KNOWING NIKI IS DEAD. HE killed her. Nightmares plague me, and his idea of pulling me from them when I wake him is to have sex with me. I'm awoken from one nightmare to a physical nightmare of his big dick forcing its way into me while I'm still dry.

I don't feel right. More than just the depression, but physically. And today it's worse.

As I'm rolled onto my back he climbs between my legs, deviating from his usual routine of turning me onto my stomach. My mind is still foggy with sleep, but he pauses as he barely presses inside me, his brow furrowing.

"What's wrong?" His eyes narrow as he studies my face.

I blink, trying to clear the haze from my vision, my head throbbing as I struggle to focus.

"I'm fine," I say, the words coming out weak.

He presses the back of his hand to my forehead, his lips pulling into a tight line as his fingers linger there for a moment. Then he sits up, sliding free from me, his jaw tense as he reaches for his phone.

Moments later, the door opens and a woman enters.

"She's burning up with fever," he tells her, his gaze never leaving me.

The woman leans over, placing a cool hand against my forehead, her touch a contrast to my overheated skin. She frowns, then wraps a blood pressure cuff around my arm, squeezing the bulb until it tightens uncomfortably. I close my eyes, my head swimming.

She mutters something in Russian to Cristiano, then gently tilts my head, checking my pupils and pressing her fingers to my wrist to check my pulse. Her brow furrows as she continues her assessment, moving my arm to check for swelling, then pressing her fingers into my abdomen with a soft but firm touch.

When she straightens, she turns to Cristiano. "It's likely the flu or some other viral infection," she says in heavily accented English. "She'll need rest, fluids, and medication for the fever. It should pass in a few days."

What I wasn't expecting is for him to move me into a room by myself. Even Giulia isn't left behind to keep me company.

The same woman from before returns multiple times a day, bringing me medicine, checking my vitals, and urging me to sip on the soups and liquids she sets beside the bed. The first 48 hours are hell, my stomach churning as I vomit nonstop, my body wracked with shivers and sweats that leave me weak and trembling.

By the 72-hour mark, the body aches and chills finally start to fade, my fever breaking in slow, uneven waves.

After a week, I finally feel the strength returning to my limbs, my head clearer, the relentless nausea a distant memory.

Now that I'm showered, clean, and no longer contagious, I'm told I can finally leave the bedroom.

I step into the hallway, making my way through the house. My muscles ache from days spent confined to the same room, but the fresh air feels good.

As I near Cristiano's office, I hear the unmistakable sounds of pleasure. A soft, breathless moan followed by the low, guttural groan of a man.

I freeze, my pulse spiking.

The door is slightly ajar, and before I can stop myself, I take a small step closer, my heart racing in my chest.

Through the crack in the door, I see Cristiano has Giulia bent over his desk, his hips snapping against her as she clutches the edge, her head thrown back, mouth open in a silent moan.

At first, I'm furious because he's fucking her, but then she stands, wrapping her arms around his neck as he straightens, his mouth dragging along her throat, teeth grazing the sensitive skin there as she shudders, her fingers threading through his hair.

The sudden realization hits me like a ton of bricks. This is consensual.

My eyes widen, and I feel awkward and creepy for standing here, watching. I take a slow step back, then another, every instinct screaming at me to retreat, to disappear before they notice me. But with each step, a sickening dread settles in my stomach.

What if he wants her instead? He will kill me.

Panic claws at my throat. I'm going to die.

My chest tightens as I stumble back down the hall, the walls seeming to close in around me.

I barely make it to the far side of the house when I run into the woman who cared for me and one of the guards.

"Rainey?" she says, her brows knitting together in confusion.

"I'm actually not feeling very good all of a sudden," I blurt, my voice thin, my heart still hammering in my chest. "I was going to go back to my room."

"Nonsense," she replies, her tone brisk. "You're not contagious anymore. Come, I'll fill Cristiano in."

I hesitate, my feet refusing to move, but the guard beside her fixes me with a hard stare, the unspoken threat clear in his eyes. *Move, or I'll make you.*

Swallowing my panic, I force myself to follow her back down the hall, my pulse a deafening drumbeat in my ears.

When we reach Cristiano's office, she pushes the door open, her steps faltering as she takes in the scene.

"Oh, I'm so sorry," she stammers, stepping back and bumping into me. I try to retreat, but my back hits the solid wall of the guard behind me, trapping me in place.

Giulia scrambles to pull her clothes back on, her cheeks flushed, eyes wide with embarrassment. Cristiano tosses their used condom into the trash, wiping himself off before zipping his pants.

"Come in," he says, waving the woman forward.

Giulia's eyes meet mine, a flash of apology crossing her face before she looks away, her hands still shaking as she adjusts her dress. I quickly avert my gaze, focusing on the woman as she steps closer to Cristiano, murmuring something too quiet for me to hear.

Cristiano nods once, dismissing her with a curt, "Good. Thank you."

The woman turns to leave, her eyes flicking to me briefly, looking just as uncomfortable as I feel. Then she's gone. At least she gets to leave this awkward situation.

Cristiano steps toward me, scanning me from head to toe, his fingers brushing the ends of my hair, then drifting lower as his thumbs brush over the pebbled peaks of my nipples through my thin shirt.

"How are you feeling?" he asks, his thumbs tracing slow circles over my sensitive flesh.

Instead of coming in hot with an attitude, I force out, "I still feel sick."

He smiles softly. "Well, you're not contagious anymore, which is what we wanted."

"Can I go back to bed?"

He shakes his head. "I haven't seen you in a week. Come here."

When he tries to pull me in, I just remain stiff.

He doesn't seem to notice. As he pulls away, he smiles. He makes me sit at his desk across from him, and every time he looks at me, I want to flip him off.

I can also feel Giulia practically begging me to look at her. But I don't. There's nothing that needs to be said. If she enjoys sleeping with him, that's her business. And if she does enjoy it, I'd rather her continue to do it than me. I'd even gladly take her spot on the floor.

When we finally head to bed, the tension in the air is awkward. Giulia follows Cristiano into the bedroom, and I realize this must have become their routine while I was sick.

They both climb onto the mattress, and I stand awkwardly at the foot, unsure where to go. She slips under the covers, her head disappearing beneath the sheets, and a second later, I hear the soft, wet sounds of her mouth on him, the small, breathy noises she makes as she works him over.

I wonder if this is how uncomfortable Giulia has always felt being in the room when he and I have sex. I turn and make my way to the couch against the wall, deciding I'd rather take my chances with a stiff back and a crick in my neck than endure this.

"Rainey," Cristiano's voice halts me in place.

I glance back over my shoulder, meeting his expectant gaze as he holds out a hand to me. "Come, darling."

I huff a bitter laugh, turning back to the couch and flopping down onto it.

"That wasn't a suggestion," he snaps, sitting up, his attention fully on me now. Giulia pauses, her head popping up from beneath the covers, her eyes flicking between us.

"She has it under control," I say with a forced yawn, lying back and making a show of getting comfortable.

"Get over here. Now."

Just to really chap his asshole, I roll onto my side, making my declaration of defiance crystal clear.

I know I'll be punished for this.

I don't care.

I spent a week puking and shitting my brains out, locked away. This is the first night I feel fully better, and he's about to ruin it.

When I hear his heavy footsteps storming toward me, I force myself to stay relaxed, my head resting on the couch cushion like I'm too bored to care. But my muscles are tense, my pulse a rapid drumbeat, every nerve on high alert as I brace for whatever punishment he's about to dish out.

When his shadow falls over me, his hand reaching to grab me, I whip around and shout, "Boo!"

His entire body jolts, a violent shudder rippling through him, and for a split second, I see the shock in his eyes, his chest heaving. But then his expression twists, pure rage darkening his features as he lunges, his fingers twisting into my hair.

I barely have time to suck in a breath before I'm yanked off the couch, my scalp screaming as he drags me to my feet, the sharp burn radiating down my neck.

What happens next is a blur of pain and violence.

I lose track of time as he takes his fury out on me, a mix of toys and hands are used on me.

He tells Giulia to join and her voice shakes as she asks him if she can please just go to bed. A sharp slap silences her, the sound ringing out in the room as her hand cups her cheek.

Her hesitation evaporates, and she scoots in closer, taking the dildo from his hands as he holds it out to her.

"Use it and make it hurt."

Her eyes flick to mine for the briefest second, something like an apology flashing in them, but then she obeys, pushing it into me, the stretch painful. And she proceeds to do it exactly how he told her to.

When she pulls it free, my blood coats the toy, and she stares at it, her chest heaving, her eyes wide as if only now realizing what she's done.

"Good job," he says, his voice dripping with dark satisfaction.

Her eyes snap up to his, the concern that was there is now gone and a flicker of pride takes over at his rare, twisted praise.

Chapter

TWENTY-SIX

Rainey

We're jolted awake by the sudden crash of the bedroom door slamming open. Two guards burst in, shouting in rapid Russian, their eyes wide and urgent.

Cristiano is out of bed in an instant, voice cutting through their frantic words as he barks commands at them. He snatches a robe from the end of the bed, shoving his arms into it and barely tying it.

He then takes a throw blanket from a side chair and yanks me across the bed by the ankle, wrapping it around my naked body. One arm slips beneath my legs, the other behind my back, and then I'm airborne, pressed to his chest as we bolt from the room.

Guards rush past us, their weapons drawn, shouting back and forth as they secure the hallways. I hear the echoes of footsteps, racing through the corridors, and the tense, clipped orders being shouted in every direction.

I barely have time to process that we're no longer in bed before he shoves me into the back of a waiting vehicle, climbing in after me. Giulia stumbles in through the opposite door, wearing nothing but his discarded button-up shirt.

The tires screech against the gravel, the car fishtailing as the driver peels out, then speeds down the long driveway.

Giulia and I exchange panicked glances, neither of us understanding what the hell is happening.

Cristiano is on his phone, yelling in Russian, his free hand gripping the edge of the seat so tightly his knuckles turn white. I clutch the blanket tighter around me, my heart hammering in my chest, wondering if I should be fearing for my life right now. With the way everyone is acting, something bad is definitely going on. I didn't see police, so it couldn't have been a raid. I don't think.

We drive for hours, the dark countryside whipping past the windows, as we head toward nothingness.

At some point, we're shuffled onto a small plane hidden in the middle of nowhere. Cristiano buckles me into a seat, then takes the one in front of me and fastens his own belt. A guard secures Giulia near the front. The engine roars to life, the door shuts, the captain's voice crackles over the speaker, and moments later we're airborne.

Seven hours later, we touch down in yet another unfamiliar place.

I'm barely awake as we're hustled off the plane and into another waiting vehicle. The drive is long and silent, the tension suffocating, my body aching from the cramped, sleepless hours.

We eventually pull up to a small house, the headlights slicing through the early morning fog as Cristiano steps out, exchanging hurried words with a man on the porch.

A woman appears in the doorway, her expression wary as she motions for me to follow her inside. I look back at Cristiano, but he's still talking to the man before finally shaking his hand.

I'm led to a small, windowless room where a pile of clean clothes waits on the bed. She gestures for me to change before leaving me alone. I dress quickly, wondering where Giulia has been taken.

When I step out, Cristiano is dressed as well, giving the man a final, solemn shake.

He extends a hand to me, and I hurry to his side. Together we return to the vehicle, where Giulia is already dressed and waiting inside.

We wind through twisting roads, the scenery shifting from rolling hills to dense forest. Sleep tugs at me until I finally rest my head against Giulia's, who has been sleeping on my shoulder for the past couple of hours.

We both jolt awake at the sound of a car door closing. Cristiano approaches an older man and woman standing on the porch of a modest house.

He shakes the man's hand firmly, then leans in to kiss the woman's cheek.

When he turns toward the vehicle, he waves us over. As we near, every pair of eyes fixes on me.

The man says something, and they glance at the tree line before opening the front door and motioning us inside.

The lock clicks behind us, and we're led down a narrow hall to a small, cramped bedroom.

As soon as we're alone, I can't keep quiet any longer.

"What the fuck is going on?" I demand.

Cristiano turns toward me, threading his hands through his hair. "Don't worry about it. I have it under control."

I gape at him, adrenaline burning in my veins.

"Don't dismiss me," I snap, grabbing his arm as he turns away. "Are we in danger?"

He hesitates, his eyes flicking to the closed door then to me. "No."

"Then tell me what the hell is going on."

When he remains silent, I push harder. "You just dragged me out of the house completely naked, shoved me onto a plane, then into a car, then another house, then back into a car, and now this. Tell me what's happening."

A long, tense silence stretches between us, his jaw working as he considers his words. Finally, he lets out a heavy sigh, rubbing a hand over his face.

"Some cartel was planning to hit the house. Steal what they could, maybe send a message."

I blink, the words sinking in slowly, my mind trying to grasp the full weight of what he's just said. "What do you mean send a message. Are they going to try to kill us?"

His eyes harden, his expression shifting to that familiar, un-flinching confidence. "I will protect you. No matter what."

I stare at him, a bitter laugh bubbling up. Funny he would say that when he was assaulting me just last night, forcing Giulia to participate.

Annoyance flickers across his features, and he shakes his head in exasperation.

"I don't have time for your attitude. Lie down and get some sleep."

I huff, crossing my arms over my chest. "We haven't had breakfast, lunch, or dinner. It's late afternoon, which is a weird time to go to sleep, and my adrenaline is ramped up so high I'm surprised my heart hasn't burst from my chest yet, and I don't even have anything to sleep in."

Out of all of that, the only thing he responds to is my lack of pajamas.

"Then sleep naked," he retorts.

I scoff, unmoving, my arms still locked tight across my chest.

In an instant, he's grabbing my arms so hard, jerking me into him, his face just inches from mine.

"You being difficult might be cute when we're at home," he growls, "but right now, I'm not in the fucking mood. So either get in that bed with your clothes on, or take them off. I don't care. But you will shut the fuck up and get in bed either way."

I hold his gaze for a heartbeat longer, then rip my arms from his grasp. I walk to the bed, yank the covers back, and climb in, pulling the blanket up to my chin.

I don't even have the energy to care that the floor is hardwood, or that he'll probably make Giulia sleep on it.

He paces the room, phone pressed to his ear, his voice brusque as he barks into the receiver. Russian always sounds angry when it's spoken even in regular conversation. But when it's spoken and the person is actually pissed off, it sounds scary. The words are a harsh blend of orders and curses that echo off the walls fast and furious and I can't even understand what he's saying but it makes it impossible for me to even sleep.

Giulia lingers by the door, her eyes locked on him, her hands nervously twisting the hem of her shirt. She watches him with a mix of caution and concern.

When he finally pulls the phone away from his ear, staring down at the screen with a scowl, she takes a careful step forward.

"Are you okay?" she asks softly, her voice tentative. "Do you need anything?"

He doesn't even glance up, his eyes still fixed on the phone as he mutters, "No."

She hesitates, then approaches him as he moves to the chair and sinks down, elbows on his knees, phone dangling loosely in one hand.

She steps in behind him, kneading gently at the tension in his shoulders.

To my surprise, his eyes drift closed, head lowering slightly as if the weight of whatever is on his mind has finally caught up with him.

I watch in stunned silence, slightly impressed that she even tried to talk to him, let alone touch him when he's this mad, and a little shocked that he's letting her. He must really be stressed, especially since he's in, like, a permanent mood of *someone pissed in his Cheerios.*

When I wake, the room is empty. I sit up slowly, straining to hear any sign of life, but the house is silent.

I slip out of bed and make my way to the door. I pause, listening again, but still hear nothing.

As I creep down the stairs, I remain alert, my ears straining for the sound of voices, footsteps, anything. It isn't until I reach the last few steps that I hear the low murmur of conversation coming from outside.

I peer through the narrow window beside the front door and spot Cristiano with three other men. They stand in a tight circle, their body language tense, shoulders squared. Whatever they're talking about has them all on edge.

I'm so focused on them that I jolt when a voice speaks up behind me.

"Good morning."

I whirl around, knowing I've been caught spying.

It's the woman from yesterday, a kitchen apron tied around her waist with a smear of flour down the front.

"Are you hungry?" she asks.

I force myself to breathe, trying to calm my nerves. *I'm not in trouble,* I remind myself.

"Yeah," I manage.

She motions for me to follow. I trail behind her into the kitchen, sitting at the island, watching as she pulls out ingredients from the pantry and fridge. She hums quietly as she starts cracking eggs into a bowl.

She glances over her shoulder, her lips curling into a friendly smile. "You're really pretty. I heard Cristiano finally had a girlfriend but wouldn't believe it until I saw for myself."

I just blink. I don't know how to respond to any of that. Her calling me pretty or referring to me as his girlfriend. Because I'm definitely not his girlfriend and I don't care if anybody thinks I'm pretty. As far as I'm concerned anyone that associates with him on purpose is a piece of shit. So I just sit there, my hands clasped together in my lap.

She turns to the stove, the eggs sizzling as she adds a pat of butter to the pan. "How long have you and Cristiano been together?"

I stare at her, my mind scrambling for a believable answer. I don't even know how long I've been his prisoner. Months for sure. But how many, I don't know. Six. Maybe seven.

I clear my throat, forcing my expression to remain neutral. "We're not together."

She just smiles, unbothered. "Oh, I don't judge. I know it can get complicated, bringing another person into a relationship."

I lift a brow, caught off guard by her assumption.

She flips the eggs in the pan, her tone casual. "I mean, I know the three of you went to bed together last night."

"No," I say casually. "You're mistaken. I travel with them, but Cristiano and her are together. Not me."

She pauses, the spatula hovering over the pan as she turns to look at me, surprise flickering across her face.

"Oh. I'm sorry. I thought when he said one of you was his girlfriend, he meant you."

"Nope."

She nods, her expression apologetic. "I didn't mean to pry."

Giulia steps into the kitchen, her hair still damp from a shower.

Our host turns, her face brightening. "Would you like breakfast?"

Giulia offers a small smile and nods. "Yes, thank you."

"Where's Cristiano?" she asks me, and I shrug, taking a slow sip of my tea.

"He's just outside with my husband," the woman replies, moving back to the stove.

Giulia gives a small nod, lifting her own cup to her lips.

"How long have you and Cristiano been together?"

Giulia barely reacts, just lifts one shoulder in a shrug. "I'm not sure."

The woman's eyes flick between us, her gaze lingering on me for a second longer, scanning down me as far as she can, then back up, before shifting to Giulia. I can practically see the wheels turning in her head. She doesn't buy my earlier lie for a second, but I'd rather she believe anyone but me is intentionally involved with Cristiano.

A moment later, he strides into the kitchen. He lifts his brows, letting out a low sigh. "We leave after breakfast," he announces, walking up behind me. He leans over my chair, his face hovering close, waiting for a kiss.

The woman watches expectantly as if she is proud that she was right about not believing me. I turn my face toward him, and he captures my mouth in a brief but possessive kiss.

When he pulls back, he looks at Giulia, and for a split second, I think he might lean in to kiss her too, but instead, he just says, "Scoot."

That would have really confirmed her suspicions that we are a threesome or some shit.

Giulia quickly slides over one chair, and he drops into the seat beside me.

Our host pauses for a moment, then steps forward, placing the plate she had prepared for Giulia in front of him instead. She sets mine down a second later, then offers Giulia an apologetic smile. "I'll make yours now."

Chapter
TWENTY-SEVEN

Rainey

For the next week, we move from house to car to plane, the cycle repeating until my mind feels scrambled. I can't keep track of the days. Every time we land, it's in the middle of the night, leaving me disoriented and exhausted.

When we finally arrive at a sprawling mansion, I know immediately that it must be yet another one of his properties. The place looms ahead, with a massive stone façade. As soon as we step inside, I recognize some of the staff. The same guards. The same maids. The same chefs—specifically Niko, who immediately searches for Giulia, his eyes moving around until he spots her.

Cristiano turns to us as we begin to trail after him. "I have a meeting."

"It's the middle of the night," I tell him, wanting us to go to sleep.

"I'll be quick," he says, then motions to someone.

My confusion grows as a woman steps forward. She stops beside me, then gestures for me to follow.

I hesitate, glancing at Cristiano, but he's already walking away, his attention shifting to someone calling his name.

She waves for me to come with her, so I do. She opens a door to a small, softly lit room. In the center is a massage table covered in fresh white linens.

"Undress and lie down. I'll cover you with a blanket."

I hesitate, my mind racing as to why I'm getting a massage, but comply. Stripping down, I settle onto the table, my face pressing into the open hole in the bed. A blanket is draped over my lower half, leaving my back exposed.

She starts to knead my shoulders, working slowly down my spine. I exhale, letting my body unwind beneath her touch. It feels good. Better than I expected.

My eyes flutter closed, the tension draining away as she continues, her hands moving lower, palms pressing into the small of my back.

I start to fall asleep, only snapping back to reality when her touch shifts, drifting even lower, slipping beneath the blanket and sliding over the curve of my ass.

My stomach plummets when she trails directly between my cheeks.

I sit up onto my side so fast, about to ask what the fuck she's thinking, but she's already closing the door behind her. Cristiano is standing where she just was, his hands under the blanket, still on my backside, eyes locked on mine.

"Lay back down," he says, his voice low and sensual. "I want to make you feel good."

I stare at him, wanting to resist. But even the smallest touch feels good. I slowly return my face to the opening in the bed as his palms glide over my skin.

He starts gently, pressing into the tense muscles and coaxing my body to relax again.

His hands move lower, the blanket gradually sliding down as he works, past my hips, along my thighs, finally pooling around my calves. He kneads my muscles until the ache between my legs becomes impossible to ignore.

I silently praise him as he roams higher, until he's exactly where I need him.

He begins outside, stroking over my lips before slipping between them to circle my clit.

I bite my lip, trying to trap the sounds rising in my throat, but my body betrays me. My hips move on their own, chasing his fingers until they slide inside me.

I want to pretend I hate this. I want to cling to that lie. But the truth is undeniable. It feels good. I wait for him to lose the gentleness, to flip a switch and take, but he never does. Instead, he draws one orgasm after another from me.

The last one hits hard. My hands clutch the fabric beneath me, my ass lifting as I grind against his hand, chasing the release. My back arches, pleasure crashing through me and I don't even try to muffle my moans.

As my body trembles and I collapse down onto the table, he trails soft kisses up my spine.

And all I can think, as the final tremors fade, is how badly I want him to keep going.

THINGS HAVE BEEN TENSE BETWEEN GIULIA AND ME EVER SINCE I walked in on her and Cristiano having sex. Or maybe it's because of the unwanted threesome I was forced into. We never had a chance to talk about it because hours later we were jolted awake by men shouting and guns aimed in every direction. Now that we're settled here, I thought we'd finally have the chance. But it's been three days, and she's been gone most of each one. We're never usually apart, and it's making me nervous.

"Where's Giulia?"

Cristiano looks up from a stack of papers. "Busy."

"Busy doing what?"

He lets out a slow sigh. "Why, darling?"

My chin jerks back. "What do you mean why? Because I want her."

Now he looks genuinely confused. "You still want her around after—" He stops himself.

"After you spent the entire week I was sick sleeping with her? Yes, I still want her."

His brows lift, surprise flickering across his face. "I thought you'd want distance."

"Maybe ask next time."

"Fine," he says, then turns back to his stack of papers.

I stare at him, trying to let him work, but I can't sit still.

"So, where is she?"

He closes his eyes like I'm testing his patience, then looks across the desk at me again. This time, he seems like he's really trying to keep his cool.

"Darling, would you like to take a nap?" he asks, gesturing to the couch.

"No. I want Giulia."

His jaw tightens.

"I have a meeting tonight. A very important meeting with a very important client. I need to close this deal, but I've already heard he's planning to walk. Get me the deal, and you can have your charity case back."

"What do I have to do?"

"Right now? Shut the fuck up so I can finish this!" he shouts.

I roll my eyes, crossing my arms.

Later, I'm handed a tight red dress and a pair of red heels. I put them on and hold my arms out, turning slightly as if to say, *Well?*

His gaze travels over me, but he says nothing. Just gives a single nod of approval.

He acts as if I'm just barely presentable enough to be seen with him, but I catch the way his pants immediately tent.

On the drive to the meeting, his eyes keep finding me, and each time I meet his, he looks away.

When we arrive, he turns to me before we enter. "You'll do whatever it takes to make him agree. And whatever I tell you, you'll do it confidently and without question, or Giulia pays for your disobedience."

Super. That's not too much to put on my shoulders.

Five men sit around a long table, their voices low as they murmur to each other.

Cristiano strides forward and I follow. When he stops, I stop. He peers over his shoulder. "Wait there." He points, then turns away.

I do as he says, stepping to the side and leaning against the cool wall.

So far so good. I've complied without managing to get myself a silent tongue lashing from him. One point for me.

The men's eyes drag over me with varying levels of interest. I force myself to stare at my nails, picking at the skin around my thumb as I wait.

I can feel the weight of someone's gaze not leaving me.

When I glance up, I catch the eyes of the man at the far end of the table. He's been staring at me the entire time, his expression unreadable.

I should be uncomfortable. I should feel exposed.

But instead, a thrill sparks.

He's hot. Dangerous-looking in a way that makes my stomach twist. He has the same dark, commanding presence as Cristiano, if not more so.

The meeting takes a turn, voices growing louder as the conversation heats up.

I already know how my night will go if this meeting ends badly. He's gonna beat the shit out of me. And most likely Giulia too.

Suddenly, Cristiano looks over his shoulder, nodding his head to the side for me to come.

I push off the wall and saunter toward him.

"Take off your dress."

I do as he says, lowering it, knowing the man at the other end of the table is the one he's trying to make a deal with. I keep my eyes on him as I slowly let the fabric fall away from my body.

His eyes try not to drag down my figure, but they flick down briefly, and I see his Adam's apple bob.

I want to smirk, but I don't. I keep my face neutral, waiting for what Cristiano wants next.

He stands, his arms wrapping around my waist as one hand slides between my legs, his fingers pressing against my most sensitive flesh.

"I think we might be able to come to an agreement," he says smoothly as he meets the other man's cold stare.

The man leans back, his eyes trailing over me before his mouth twists into a mocking smirk.

"What makes you think I would want your leftovers?" His tone drips with disdain.

Cristiano shrugs. "Talk to her while I show the others the merchandise."

He calls for the men to follow, then turns to me, leaning in. "Use that smart mouth for some good for once."

I hold back my eye roll. "Meaning?"

"Meaning, suck his dick and get me the deal, or I will make this your most painful night."

There is no doubt he means it.

As soon as the door closes behind them, I saunter towards him, walking my fingers along the table until I stand a foot away, then sit on the edge, directly in front of him. He watches me, patient and amused.

"Don't take the deal," I whisper seductively.

"Oh yeah? Why is that?"

"Because I'm supposed to suck your dick to entice you that the deal is better, but my mouth can only do a fraction of what my pussy can, and that would only cause issues."

He looks to my lips and back up. "What kind of issues?"

I shrug. "I have an amazing pussy. Once you're finished, you'll want to keep me for yourself."

He grins. "That's awfully confident."

I shrug, scooting closer to the edge and spreading my thighs in front of him.

His eyes go exactly where I want them.

I see the want in his expression immediately.

"I should be. It's the truth. But I am good with my mouth and not just at sucking cock. I'm a great kisser." I lean forward and tug lightly on his tie, pulling him closer.

When my mouth hovers just over his, I murmur, "But don't kiss me, because if you do, you'll definitely want to keep me."

Our lips brush, barely a touch, before I give him a slow, teasing kiss. Just enough to leave a taste. When I go to pull back, his hand comes to rest on my thigh.

I smile as I lean back in, biting his lip and pulling it into my mouth, sucking gently before letting it go.

"You taste good," I say, pushing lightly against his chest. "It's a shame we won't get to sleep together. I can tell you have a big cock."

The way his ego inflates is almost comical.

"What makes you so sure we won't be sleeping together?" He slides his hands up my thighs.

"I wasn't given permission. I'm only allowed to give you oral." I push out a pouty lip. "And I already want more than just that."

"I have plenty of room for bargaining," he says.

I shrug, keeping my tone light. "Why would you want to?"

"Maybe I want to feel your tight pussy."

I bite my lip, then nod. "Do you want to taste me as badly as I want to taste you?"

His breathing hitches, roaming down my body until he locks on my chest.

I take his hand, guiding it between my thighs, sliding his fingers along my folds and down to my center.

"Touch me before he comes back," I pant, urging him to penetrate me.

When he does, I tip my head back with a pornstar moan, feigning pleasure and arching my hips into his palm, pulling it closer before acting pained when I push his hand away, pretending to struggle with not being able to take it further.

I groan in exaggerated frustration as I nudge his chair back and rise.

"Thanks," I murmur. "Now I want to fuck you even more."

I stride over to where my dress is still on the floor. Glancing over my shoulder, I watch as he licks his finger clean, then tracks me the entire time as I bend down to pick it up.

The door opens again, and the men return.

Cristiano looks disappointed when he sees me now holding my dress. Maybe he thought I'd still be on my knees. I notice his pupils are blown wide and his eyes are glazed. He's high. Apparently he wasn't just showing them the merchandise. He was sampling it with them.

There's some talking before Cristiano asks the man if they have a deal.

When he doesn't answer right away, Cristiano adds, "If you'd like another twenty minutes to discuss it with Rainey, we can step out. She's very good with her mouth."

The man stands, and my stomach sinks when he says, "No." But as he adjusts his jacket, he adds, "I want the entire night with her."

Cristiano's fury is palpable, his nostrils flaring and jaw locking before his gaze snaps to me. It's the silent tongue-lashing I'd been proud to avoid earlier, and everything in his expression says he's definitely going to beat the shit out of me when I get home… *if I survive the night.*

"Do we have a deal?"

Cristiano glares at me as he exhales, then turns to the man. "Fine."

They shake, a tense stare-off following.

I'm led away without looking back; if I did, his glare alone might kill me.

I'm taken to a hotel, and once inside the room, he shuts the door, the lock clicking into place behind us.

To my surprise, the night is nothing like I expected.

The man is gentle. Tender. He touches me like he actually wants me, not like I'm something to be used and discarded. I feel desired instead of dominated. He takes his time, worshipping every inch of me. He's not great in bed, but the way I sounded, he probably thinks he was god himself.

And when he finishes, we hold each other.

When morning comes, we stand in the middle of the room hugging. His hand slides softly up and down my back, and he smells my hair. When I finally pull away, I grab my dress, but he takes it from me and gets on his knees, holding it open as he looks up at me. I smile, stepping into it, and he slides it up my body.

"You weren't lying," he murmurs against my lips. "I do want to keep you."

His words make my chest tighten, because I played him better than I thought I could.

He leans back slightly, brushing my hair over my shoulder.

"Do you like it there? With Cristiano?"

I meet his eyes, knowing I still need to keep playing him until the deal is done and he's gone.

"I'd like it better with you."

A slow smile curves his mouth. He presses a soft kiss to my shoulder, then lets me go with a reluctant sigh.

I lean against the vanity as I watch him dress, letting him see me take him in. I bite my lip as I look at his unimpressive package, making sure he believes I'd devour him right now if we had the time.

When we arrive home, he takes my hand and I playfully bump into his side.

As we step out onto the patio, Cristiano looks up at us, doing a double take when he sees we're holding hands. His eyes stay fixed on our joined hands the entire way as we reach the table.

My steps falter the moment I see Giulia.

She is sitting stiffly at the table, her entire body bruised and battered. She can hardly move. Her face is swollen, her lip split, and her arms are a canvas of deep black and purple bruises.

I lower my gaze quickly and sit down, not daring to look at her again.

Cristiano sits across from us, casual and composed, as if nothing were out of the ordinary. He stirs his coffee lazily before glancing up.

"So," he says, "how was your night?"

The man I now know is named Leandro smirks. "Very satisfying." He softly reaches over, his palm flattening down the back of my hair in a gentle motion.

I keep my face blank, but my stomach twists.

As Cristiano reaches for his coffee, I see Giulia out of the corner of my eye. She flinches, her entire body recoiling in a quick, involuntary movement.

She had been eager to cozy up to him.

Now she is terrified.

As they begin discussing the deal, Leandro keeps staring at me, his arm resting on the back of my chair as he brushes his fingers through my hair.

I know I am playing with fire here, but fuck Cristiano.

I move my foot next to Leandro's. Crossing my leg, I slowly run it up his shin.

He tugs softly on my hair in acknowledgment.

The conversation seems to be going well until Leandro mentions he wants to make changes to the contract.

Cristiano leans back in his chair, one arm draped lazily over the armrest, his other hand holding his coffee. "I'm open to hearing them."

Leandro glances at me, then turns to Cristiano. "I want her."

The air shifts instantly.

Cristiano doesn't speak at first, but his posture changes. He straightens slightly, his jaw flexing. His fingers curl tighter around his cup.

"No," he says finally, the word hard and cold.

Silence stretches for a beat too long.

"I'm not trying to insult you. But you offered her. I accepted your offer. And I want to keep her."

"She's my girlfriend," he bites out.

Leandro reclines slightly in his chair, the picture of calm. "We do not have a deal if she is not leaving with me."

Cristiano's neck flushes, turning a violent red. The kind of red that means someone's about to die.

The room grows heavy with silence. Then they both speak at once, voices low but sharp, cutting over each other in a language I don't fully understand.

Cristiano slams his hand down on the table. "She's not leaving!"

Leandro stands, buttoning his jacket like he isn't walking out of a war zone. "I will be in touch in a couple of days." He leans down, kissing my cheek.

"I'm coming for you," he whispers, then walks away.

Cristiano stares at me across the table, breathing hard.

"That fucking pussy is going to cause a fucking bloodbath."

I shift in my seat.

"What is the deal? Why don't you make him think you're trading me, and I can get info for you?" I offer.

He scoffs, pure anger flashing across his face.

"You think I want your pussy beat up like this trash?"

He flips his hand toward Giulia without even looking at her.

"I don't need his deal."

"You literally agreed for him to fuck me all night because you wanted the deal," I remind him.

He stands, yelling at the top of his lungs as he grabs his coffee cup and smashes it against the bricks behind him.

Giulia and I both flinch at the sound.

"Get changed and shower. We're leaving."

And just like that, we'll be moved once again.

Chapter

TWENTY-EIGHT

Rainey

Cristiano lets Giulia and me know he better not hear us talk for the entire day. But he doesn't need to worry about that since she won't even look at me. I haven't been able to ask her if she's okay. I know she's not. It's clear she's not. But I can't even comfort her. I want to hug her so badly. Seeing her face swollen and bruised makes me sick to my stomach. But her face is nothing compared to the rest of her body.

He's so mad at me over the deal with Leandro that he's punishing me every second of the day. Currently, I've been standing naked in front of his desk while he works.

Giulia is in the corner, where he graciously lets her lie down, but me—I have to stand. And when his own feelings get in the way, he starts yelling at me. He yells that I have a bad attitude he's ready to beat out of me. That he can't believe I slept with someone else.

That every time he thinks of me letting Leandro stick his penis in me, it makes him want to beat Giulia.

I want to remind him that he already did that, but it would probably just earn her another one.

When my back aches from standing for hours in the same spot, he makes me sit with my legs spread on either side of the chair arms. It's degrading, but I'd rather this than being touched.

When that becomes too distracting, he makes me stand again, facing the opposite wall so he can stare at me from behind.

I focus on the surface in front of me, mentally sketching patterns into the paint, trying to tune out the silence. Then the office door opens and someone enters.

He looks to be in his mid-seventies, thin, with glasses perched low on his nose and a tape measure draped around his neck like a stethoscope. He doesn't introduce himself, but Cristiano must have been expecting him. He rises from his chair and walks around the desk to shake the man's hand.

They speak quietly at first, Cristiano gesturing to his own arms, then dragging his fingers from his collarbones down the center of his chest as if outlining something low-cut. The man glances at me, then back, who answers with a single nod.

Stepping toward me, he pulls a notepad from his coat pocket and unzips a leather case.

"What is this?" I ask Cristiano.

He doesn't answer, only crosses his arms and watches as the man begins taking measurements.

Shoulders. Waist. Hips. He wraps the tape around my bust, notes something on the pad, and moves on. He doesn't leer or react to me at all, just works with calm, efficient focus.

For part of it, I watch Giulia, silently begging her to look at me. I know she understands Russian; maybe she could tell me what's going on. But she doesn't open her eyes. I might think she was asleep if not for the slow movement of her pointer finger picking at her cuticle.

When the man finishes, he and Cristiano exchange a few quiet words before he slips out the door.

"What was that for?" I ask.

"You'll see."

I wrinkle my nose. "No. Tell me what that was."

"No," he says flatly, already striding to his desk.

THE BLANKETS ARE RIPPED OFF ME, AND I JOLT UPRIGHT, MY HEART slamming in my chest.

For a second, I'm completely disoriented. Cristiano usually keeps the covers on us during morning sex. This isn't that.

I blink hard, trying to make sense of what I'm seeing.

A woman I don't recognize is standing at the side of the bed. Her voice coming out clipped. "Get up."

My head snaps toward the door. Cristiano is standing there, casually speaking with two more women.

"What's happening?" I ask.

Cristiano looks at me then returns his attention back to the women.

I'm pulled from the bed and guided to the bathroom. My feet stumble across the floor, my mind still catching up.

The women don't talk. They just work. One starts curling my hair while the other applies makeup like I'm a doll. I try asking again, but all I get are soft murmurs in a language I don't understand.

My hair is left down in soft waves, and small white flowers are pinned throughout. They dust my cheeks with blush and line my lips with something soft and pink. I barely recognize myself in the mirror.

Before I can ask again what's going on, the man from two days ago walks in.

The tailor.

He carries a garment bag over his arm and unzips it slowly. Like this isn't about to upend my entire life.

And then I see the white dress.

My blood runs cold.

I was being measured for a wedding dress.

I'm getting married today.

To Cristiano.

Chapter

TWENTY-NINE

Damiano

I've been hammering the bag for hours. My fists don't sting anymore. The skin's too raw for that.

The floor beneath me is soaked, a mixture of sweat and blood pooling at my feet. I wrapped my knuckles today, for once, just so I wouldn't split them open again before I could land the next punch. My shirt was gone twenty minutes in, drenched and useless. Now it lies crumpled in the corner like the rest of my sanity.

Punch. Punch. Swing.

I don't even register the strikes anymore. My arms move on instinct, my mind somewhere else. Somewhere darker. Somewhere I can't climb out of.

Discus cross, elbow in, rotate, hit.

Again.

And again.

And again.

Every hit lands with a thud that doesn't do a damn thing to quiet the thoughts in my head. Rainey is gone. My girlfriend was kidnapped. I picture what he's doing to her, spliced between images of what I'll do to him when I get my hands on him.

The door opens behind me. I feel the shift in the air but don't stop.

Whoever it is doesn't speak. They just stand there, watching.

"I'll give you five free punches if you want to come over here and take me on," I mutter without looking. My voice is hoarse, scraped raw from disuse and too many silent screams.

I turn, breath ragged to stare at the person who is brave enough to come down here.

Dante.

He stands in the doorway, looking like the world's already ended. Eyes bloodshot. Shoulders slumped.

"Come."

Just one word. But it punches harder than anything I've thrown all day.

I know that tone. It's not a death notice. Not exactly. But it's close.

It's about Rainey.

Because that's the only reason anyone would interrupt me.

That look on his face—whatever Cristiano's doing, it's bad.

And suddenly I'm not tired anymore. I'm wide awake. And one second away from completely losing what's left of my mind.

We head to the meeting room where my brothers are already gathered around Pa. Everyone looks tense, their eyes fixed on the large TV screen mounted on the wall.

I step forward and they move aside, letting me take my place in front of it. My stomach twists at the look on their faces.

"It's being livestreamed," Dante says quietly. "The link was sent directly to me. No one else."

"What is it?" I ask, annoyed. I don't understand why they pulled me in for this.

But then the video feed begins to move.

A camera follows the groom as he steps out.

Cristiano.

I blink, then take a step closer to the screen. Dante places a hand on my shoulder, steadying me or maybe steadying himself.

When the camera shifts, I see her. My beautiful girl—my Rainey.

She's in a wedding dress. It's terrible, overdone, and puffy. She looks like a cake topper. Yet, she's still the most beautiful thing I've ever seen. And the tattoo I gave her is still visible on her neck, which brings me a sliver of relief.

The camera moves in, and she glares straight into the lens.

"Get that phone out of my face or I'll shove it up your ass."

That's my girl.

"Walk," someone orders from off-screen.

"Take that gun and swallow a bullet," she spits.

She stumbles forward and, for the briefest second, the camera catches the barrel of a gun pressing into her back.

And then I watch my entire world walk down the aisle… toward another man.

I'm not sure whether she wants this. Maybe she fell for him in the months she's been gone.

The officiant begins to speak, his voice flat and hollow against the roar building in my ears.

"You're a piece of shit," she says to Cristiano, her head barely turned toward him. "You're disgusting. And all your disgusting friends just sit here, watching you force a kidnapped woman into marrying you."

"Think real hard about what comes out of your mouth next," he says, low and venomous.

Neither of them speaks again as the officiant continues. I'm watching my worst nightmare take place, and I'm unable to do anything about it.

When Cristiano says he takes Rainey to be his wife, I nearly lose it.

I think I'm going to puke when it's her turn.

Seconds stretch into unbearable silence as she stands there staring at him. Then she winces in pain. He's squeezing her small hands so hard.

When her lips part, I stop breathing.

"I, Rainey Lane…" My knees buckle. I'm going to pass out. "Take you… Damiano Volkov… to be my husband."

My name hangs in the air. Even Cristiano freezes, as if his mind is struggling to process what she just said.

Then he backhands her.

She folds sideways but somehow stays upright. When she lifts her head, blood pours from her nose and mouth—yet she laughs. A small, broken laugh that quickly turns hysterical.

He grabs her arm, but her head tips back as the laughter intensifies, manic and untamed.

He reaches out, seizing her by the throat as she chokes on her own breath. He brings his face to hers, and I can't hear what's being said, but he whispers to her, her face turning red. Then he releases her and squeezes the back of her neck so hard she whimpers from the pressure.

"Finish it," Cristiano orders.

The officiant begins speaking again, and when he tells them to kiss, he crushes his mouth to hers. She pushes at his chest, trying to pull away, but he holds her there.

"Technically, I think that makes her married to you." Gio mutters.

"I'm going to kill him."

Rainey is dragged down the aisle, stumbling behind him. Then the camera shifts.

A woman's face comes into the frame, grinning sinisterly. "Don't go anywhere. We'll be back soon." Then she leans in, kissing the lens before the screen goes dark.

When the feed returns, it's at a reception.

"Mr. and Mrs. Fierro," the announcer calls, and when they step into the room, the air leaves my lungs.

Rainey's face is barely recognizable. Swollen flesh, deepening bruises, and shades of red and purple bloom across the limited skin still exposed. I can't even begin to imagine what the rest of her looks like beneath that dress.

They sit at the front table, and I stare at her feet. A trail of dried blood runs down the inside of her leg, disappearing into her left shoe. The white heel is stained deep red on the inside, the blood soaked through.

Dante sees it too. His palms scrape against his stubble as he rocks side to side.

She doesn't blink. Her eyes are glassy and unfocused, like she's looking through everything instead of at it. Her movements are sluggish, and when Cristiano lifts her hand to place a kiss on it, she doesn't resist. She lets him. Just sits there, limp and pliant.

"She's drugged," Gio notes.

"With what?" I ask without taking my eyes off her.

He watches her for a second. "Could be ketamine. Or benzos. Something heavy enough to keep her quiet, but not knock her out completely."

As if on cue, someone leans toward Cristiano and says something with a low laugh.

Cristiano grins, straightening his tie. "Already consummated," he replies with a smirk.

The man claps him on the shoulder and laughs. "Lucky bastard."

Cristiano reaches out, grabbing Rainey by the shoulder and pulling her into him as the camera zooms in. He stares directly into the lens like he's speaking only to me.

"The things I'm going to do to her will make even Carmella roll in her grave. Eat your heart out," he says, unbuttoning his pants. He grabs Rainey's neck and forces her down on him. The moment I hear her gag, he leans back, lacing his fingers behind his head while she moves up and down.

Dante bends over, puking on the floor. And me, I explode.

I roar as I pummel the TV, smashing my fists into the screen until it shatters. I rip it from the wall and throw it, then turn and start destroying everything in reach. Gio must have anticipated this might happen. He's ready. His hands are already wrapped, and he clocks me hard across the face.

And we go at it.

If anyone can take me, it's him. I've never beaten him before. I'm not sure I ever will. We fight like animals, each of us fueled by rage and desperation. He lands brutal hits, and I return every one. By the end of it, we're both slumped on the floor, battered, bloodied, and breathless.

My head tips back, and that's when I hear Ma pounding on the door.

Pa's back is pressed against it, making sure she can't get in.

"Find that son of a bitch and bring my daughter-in-law home," he growls at Andrei, who hasn't stopped typing on his computer.

Chapter

THIRTY

Rainey

’ve been married for two weeks. The worst two weeks of my life. Cristiano called it a honeymoon, but it was nothing more than him having sex with me nonstop. We've been back home for four days now, and it's the first time I've seen Giulia since I was measured for my wedding dress. She's healing. Slowly. But she still won't look at me.

The first day, I wanted to cry.

The second, I got angry.

The third, I nearly begged her to talk to me.

And today? Today I'm just in a shitty mood.

I woke up feeling like this is the end. And somehow, I'm at peace with that.

Everything and everyone is getting on my nerves.

When one of the workers leans over and asks if I'm finished with my lunch, offering to take my plate, I snap without thinking.

"If I was finished, I wouldn't still be eating, would I?" I stab my fork into another bite.

Cristiano pauses mid-typing, his attention shifting to me.

"Sorry," the woman mumbles, quickly lowering her eyes to Giulia's plate in her hands as she hurries out of the room.

Later, when Cristiano has important calls to make, we're sent to one of the seating rooms he confines us to whenever he wants us out of the way. It's a decent enough space, stocked with books, a TV, board games, and puzzles. Giulia and I started an animal puzzle a while back. The pieces are still scattered across the low coffee table in a half-finished mess. But then we were moved to other locations and never got to finish it.

It's the first time I've seen it in months. With the mood I'm in, I don't dare touch it. I'd probably end up flipping the entire table.

I scroll through the channels, one after another, the images blurring together as I jab at the remote. Nothing holds my attention.

The door swings open, and I glance up. My thumb hovers over the remote as Cristiano strides into the room. Giulia straightens in her seat at the puzzle table, waiting quietly for his instructions.

His gaze lands on me, and he snaps, motioning for me to get up. "We need to get ready for dinner tonight."

I scowl and lean my head back against the couch, turning my attention back to the TV. "I don't want to go."

"I didn't ask if you wanted to go," he retorts. "You are going."

I roll my eyes and toss the remote onto the cushion beside me. "I said no."

His eyes narrow. "You can either shape up and have a nice dinner, or stay home with my guards."

"Oh, so now you're going to let other men fuck your wife? What a man you are. Bring it on. Who do I get to sleep with while you're gone?"

He turns to one of the maids. "Has her dress arrived?"

The woman nods quickly.

"Good," he says, cutting his eyes back to me. "Start getting her ready."

As the woman approaches, I lift my chin, my irritation sparking again. "Is Giulia coming?"

"No."

"Why not?" I press, though I'm not even sure why I'm pushing this. She won't talk to me. She's hated me ever since she got beat. Still, I dread the thought of being apart from her.

"Stop complaining," he snaps.

"Stop complaining," I echo under my breath.

He hears it but doesn't say a word as I brush past him.

I'm led to a bedroom designated to getting me ready. It's usually the same girl. After months of this routine, I've gotten her to talk a little.

Her name is Myra. She started working for Cristiano when he got married the first time. She once told me she really liked his wife. But over time, the woman started to lose her mind. Which checks out if her journals were any indication of her mental state.

I want to ask if she knows anything about Damiano, if she's ever heard his name said among the staff, but I push the thought aside. I don't need to hurt my own feelings tonight.

As always, she curls my hair. I still remember the one time she tried an elegant updo. Cristiano tore it apart the second he saw it, yanking through my hair as he growled that it should never be pulled up. He said he didn't need the whole world seeing the trash on my neck.

When she finishes my makeup, she helps me into a long black dress. It fits tightly, clinging to every curve of my body. This dress is definitely going to get me fucked and not in a good way.

Cristiano is already dressed in a black tux, seated in the living room when I enter. He taps idly against the arm of his chair, his expression distant and bored.

His head lifts and he glances in my direction, then does a double take. His lips part slightly as his eyes move slowly over me, from my feet to my chest, then settle on my face.

He rises, locked on me as he crosses the room. Reaching me, he takes my chin, brushing a thumb across my cheek before pressing his lips to mine.

I want to scoff, to recoil, but I keep my face blank.

He steps behind me, his arms circling around to fasten a diamond necklace at the base of my throat. Then he kisses my neck.

For the entire drive to the restaurant, I can feel him watching me.

I roll my eyes, getting annoyed. "Why do you keep staring?"

He chuckles, softly grazing my bare shoulder. "Because you're so beautiful. And I get to call you wife."

I scoff, turning to look out my window at the passing streetlights.

When we arrive, the restaurant is exactly what I expected. High-end. The lights are low, the atmosphere filled with quiet conversation and the soft clinking of crystal glasses. We're led through the busy dining room to a private section in the back, where a round table is already surrounded by men in tailored suits.

Cristiano pulls out my chair, his palm pressing lightly against the small of my back as I sit.

He circles the table, exchanging greetings with the others.

I rest my hands in my lap, letting my gaze drift over the faces until it stops on the man directly across from me. His eyes hold mine, a faint smirk starting to form.

Another trashy man Cristiano keeps company with, openly hitting on a "married" woman. Unlike him, I don't bother hiding my amusement. I give him a smile and add a playful wink.

This might make dinner more interesting.

A waiter appears with a bottle of red wine cradled in his arm and works his way around the table, filling each glass. I keep my focus on the man opposite me as I lift mine, brushing my lips against the rim before taking a slow sip. His stare doesn't waver, curiosity flickering faintly in his eyes.

Cristiano's grip settles on my thigh, tightening on the sensitive spot just above my knee. I take another drink, my mouth curling into the barest hint of a smile as I set the glass down and choose to ignore him.

Anytime the man speaks, I pay extra close attention and laugh at all his jokes, telling him how funny he is, making sure to be over the top with my flirtation.

Cristiano's thumb digs in harder, his hold turning painful. If anything, the pressure only fuels my defiance. He continues talking to the men as he discusses shipment dates, but his grip never eases.

I lean back, toying with the thin strap of my dress as I meet the stranger's eyes again. This time, I bite my bottom lip to convey my interest. The man raises his glass to me, a subtle but unmistakable sign that he's noticed, and I find it comical the way Cristiano's fingers dig in even harder.

I'm pushing him deliberately, and I know I'll pay for it later, but also, fuck him. I don't really care at this point. He's going to hurt me after this regardless.

The man I've been flirting with stands, excusing himself to the restroom along with one of the others. As they leave, the guy seated beside me pushes back his chair, taking the opportunity to slide into a now-vacant spot further down the table, striking up a quiet conversation with his new neighbor. It leaves the chair beside me empty, and I know exactly who will fill it when he returns.

When the man walks back, a small, appreciative grin spreads across his lips as he slides into the open seat beside me. I wink at him, letting my gaze linger on his face before slowly trailing down to his shoulders and back up again. His grin widens, his confidence growing with each second I stare.

I don't need to look to know Cristiano is watching. I can feel the heat of his gaze, his silent rage radiating off him beside me, and it only fuels my need to push him further.

The man leans in. "What do you think? Should I cut my hair, or is it good like this?"

I turn in my chair, then tilt my head as if contemplating, already reaching up to thread through his dark, slightly overgrown strands before curling them into a gentle fist. Then I slowly shake my head.

"It's the perfect length."

I let my gaze drop, deliberately dragging down to the hard line pressing against his slacks. I bite my lip again and inhale, making my chest rise as if the sight of him has left me breathless.

I meet his stare for a beat longer before turning back to my seat, flicking a glance at Cristiano. His nostrils flare, tension winding through his posture. His grip clamps around my thigh with enough force to make me almost whimper, though I still find it amusing.

As dinner winds down and the quiet hum of conversation fades, I push my chair back and stand, only to find myself face to face with the man I've been teasing all evening.

We're close enough to feel the heat radiating between us. His attention drops briefly to my mouth, then lower, lingering on my boobs.

"They're better outside the dress."

He smiles. "I have no doubt."

"Too bad the night's ending," I murmur, letting the words drip with suggestion. "You seem like a good time."

His tongue sweeps across his lower lip. "I could tell instantly you're a good time."

"Maybe we'll be lucky enough to meet again." My palm slides over the front of his pants as I move past him, feeling the hardness beneath the fabric. "Definitely would be a good time," I whisper before I turn away.

The drive home is silent and Cristiano's face remains disturbingly calm. It's the kind of calm that sets my pulse racing, the kind that makes my skin prickle, because this calm always comes right before he unleashes his fury on me.

When we arrive home, I follow him inside, each step feeling like a countdown to my death.

Inside the bedroom, he closes the door and turns to face me. It's when we make eye contact that I see the darkness simmering, but his expression stays perfectly composed.

"Undress."

He watches me for a moment, unmoving, then his lips curl into a slow, cruel smile. He turns to the dresser, pulls open a drawer, and reaches inside. When he turns back to me, a length of thick, braided rope hangs from his hand. My pulse stutters, but I keep my face blank.

He crosses the room, grabs my wrists, and pulls them together. The rope winds around so tightly I have to fight back a hiss, keeping my expression calm as the coarse fibers bite into my skin. My hands begin to turn purple, the pressure pulling at the flesh as he knots it tightly.

He drags me to the bed and ties the rest of the rope to the heavy wooden post at the corner, yanking it until my arms strain. I'm forced onto my toes, chest pressed to it.

I know how this goes. I've felt the cold, detached brutality of his punishments before. But something about his silence puts me on edge. This is going to be worse.

He steps back, his gaze moving down my body, taking in the way the dress clings to my curves.

Then, without warning, he reaches into his pocket and pulls out a small blade. My pulse quickens as he steps forward, grabs the back of my dress, and slices through the fabric with a single, fluid motion. He tugs it down until it's nothing but a pool at my feet, leaving me bare and exposed.

I grit my teeth, staring straight ahead, refusing to give him the satisfaction of a reaction.

But he's unbothered. He leans against the post beside me, crossing his arms, his head tilted slightly as he watches.

"You thought you were really fucking cute at the restaurant, didn't you?" he says, his tone light, almost conversational.

I smile, locking onto him even though I know it will only cost me. "The obvious boner I gave the man next to me would confirm I was pretty cute."

His jaw hardens as he straightens. Without breaking focus, he unthreads his belt, the leather sliding free with a slow hiss. I let out an exaggerated sigh, roll my eyes for emphasis, then tip my head back. My mouth parts in a lazy yawn, making it clear how little his threats rattle me.

The first strike lands without warning against my bare ass, so vicious my knees nearly buckle. The ropes dig into my wrists as I lurch forward. Heat explodes across my skin, sharp enough to steal my breath, the sound tearing from my throat raw and ragged.

This isn't the punishment I expected. Usually, he wraps the belt around my neck and chokes me while he fucks me. I've never admitted it, but I like the choking.

My eyes water, and I want to tell him he's a piece of shit and to go to hell, but before I can find my footing, the belt whips against my flesh again, my scream ripping through the room.

He says nothing, offers no taunt, just keeps swinging. Each blow heavier, each crack ricocheting off the walls. The relentless force drives me to the brink of passing out. My throat burns from the constant cries, my skin blazing as if it's splitting apart.

When the belt finally drops to the floor, the trickle of blood down my thighs is unmistakable. My head droops, my body sagging against the restraints. Nausea claws up my throat, and I vomit onto the floor, shuddering uncontrollably.

He moves behind me, gripping my hips as he hauls me off the post and throws me onto the mattress. I land facedown, cheek pressed to the cool sheets, arms still bound above me, every muscle too spent to resist.

He spreads my cheeks, spitting before shoving something thick inside. The intrusion rips another cry from me, the stretch searing. It's as painful as the lashes, a deep burn that makes every nerve scream. I know exactly what it is—I saw the dildo on the bed earlier, the same one he made Giulia use on him last night. It hasn't been cleaned. Now it's inside me.

He lifts my hips higher, pushing it in until my body gives under the pressure. Another cry escapes, my head lolling to the side. My mind drifts in and out as he lines himself up and slams into me, the impact brutal, my voice muffled against the mattress.

Each snap of his hips forces the dildo deeper. I tighten instinctively, trying to block its path, but he drives forward without pause. The motion is relentless and punishing.

His fingers knot in my hair, wrenching my head back until my spine strains. A stinging slap catches my cheek, followed by another hard thrust. My cry earns a second slap, the rhythm becoming deliberate. His other hand seizes my nipple, twisting until white-hot pain bursts behind my eyes. It's clear now—he's not stopping until I've learned my lesson.

When he removes the dildo, relief floods me, but it's short-lived. Something larger, shaped differently, is jammed into place. I recognize the blunt weight of a butt plug.

I scream for him to remove it, but he just grabs another toy and shoves it inside my vagina, the brutal pace resuming. A harsh grunt escapes me with every forceful push.

When he pulls it out, he tosses it onto the mattress beside me, blood smearing across the gold sheets.

Before I can lower my head, the belt lashes down, igniting fresh agony across my already split skin. The strikes just keep coming. When I try to shift away, he climbs onto the bed, straddling my shoulders, and continues whipping my thighs and ass.

Air feels impossible to draw. I'm certain this will kill me.

It stops only when the belt coils around my neck. He jerks it tight, hauling my head back. He uses it like reins as he shoves his dick into me again. Each time his pelvis slams into my raw flesh, I try to cry out.

I can't scream. My oxygen is cut off, and my vision begins to tunnel.

This is it. This is what I knew was coming today.

The bedroom doors burst open with a loud thud.

"We're under attack!" the man shouts, breathless.

Gunfire explodes outside. Shouting. Screams.

"Nine vehicles. The gates have been breached!"

More gunfire, and then the man is yelling, "We gotta go now!"

Cristiano lets the belt go as he rips himself out of me. My stomach cramps so badly when he's gone that I gasp for air.

He leaves the bed only briefly before returning, hacking at the ropes. He has pants on now and a button-up shirt, though it still hangs open. He grunts, his movements growing more frantic as the bindings prove too tight to cut completely.

When he finally manages to slice through the middle of the rope and my wrists fall apart, he doesn't worry about trying to cut the rest of it away, he grabs my leg and drags me across the bed, throwing me over his shoulder as he runs from the room.

The guard leads us through a back hallway, waiting at the stairs for Cristiano to go first, then following close behind.

Gunfire echoes from every direction, and I have no idea what's happening.

The guard keeps glancing back, firing wildly as bullets shred the walls around us.

When we reach the bottom of the stairs, Cristiano reaches into the kitchen, grabbing a knife off the counter as we pass.

"Leandro?" He confirms as he shoves open a hidden door, setting me down before pulling me into the cold night air.

"I believe so," the guard pants.

The grass is slick beneath my bare feet, wet with dew. I'm glad he had time to get dressed, but he didn't even have the decency to grab me a robe or blanket, or to remove this fucking butt plug. I must be quite the sight, my makeup likely smeared down my face, blood running down my legs from my ass cheeks and vagina. I'm sure my butt is bleeding too, but the plug is keeping it in. My wrists burn where the rope ripped the skin raw, and now the salt of his fingers presses against the wound as he drags me toward the edge of the property, where a boat is already running and waiting, a man yelling for us to hurry.

Gunfire cracks again, so loud it's deafening.

The guard running beside us jerks and drops to the ground with a gasp.

"We're almost to the boat," Cristiano snarls, yanking me harder.

"Rainey!"

Every nerve in my body lights up, my mind refusing to believe the voice is who I think it is. I falter, glancing over my shoulder, only for Cristiano to jerk me harder toward the boat.

"Rainey!" the voice calls again, more desperate this time.

I twist my head, my breath catching. My whole body seems to lock up and come alive at the same time.

There, standing on an upstairs balcony, pained and frantic eyes lock onto mine.

Nikolai.

Chapter

THIRTY-ONE

Rainey

Everything inside me screams that I need to get to him.

I pull against Cristiano's grip, but he clamps down tighter.

"Over my dead body," he snarls.

"Gladly."

I don't think.

I just move.

My hand shoots out, snatching the knife from his grasp, and I drive it straight into his stomach.

Shock flashes across his face as the blade sinks deep. I wrench my arm free, stumbling back as his knees buckle. He crumples into the grass, blood pooling thick and dark across his abdomen. One hand clamps around the handle of the knife, the other reaching weakly for me.

"Rainey," he rasps.

The man on the boat shouts, his footsteps pounding against the dock as he races toward us.

I turn and run.

I run faster than I ever have, my lungs burning as I sprint back toward the house.

Gunshots crack behind me, splintering the air, but I don't stop. I can't stop. I have to get to Nikolai.

I barrel through the back door, my breath ragged, my heart pounding so hard it might break through my chest bone.

Inside, the chaos is worse. More gunshots echo off the walls. Bodies litter the floor, guards slumped in pools of blood.

The rest of the staff has been forced into the living room, herded onto their knees with terrified expressions and trembling arms raised in surrender. One by one, guards are dragged in. Their weapons are stripped away and kicked across the floor toward the feet of the men barking orders, each gun clattering against the tile with a finality that silences any thought of resistance.

At the front of the chaos, the man shouting commands stands tall. It's Giovanni.

I freeze in the doorway as I take him in. He's healed and still just as beautiful. The last time I saw him, he was injured, barely clinging to life. Now he looks fully recovered.

He resembles Damiano so much it makes my heart flutter.

His mouth is moving, expression fierce, flicking toward me for a split second, his voice rising above the noise.

I think he's saying, "In here."

More men pour into the room—Marko, Silvano, Ricco— their rifles raised, aimed at anything that might still be a threat as they fan out.

The chaos dissolves into a distant, muffled roar.

"Where is she?" someone yells.

My mind stutters, struggling to piece it together. The reality of my situation pushes against the fog. My entire life, everything I had known, was over. I was going to die tonight. Damiano wasn't coming for me.

I had accepted that. I had forced myself to believe it.

But right here, in this moment, everything around me slows to a crawl. The buzzing in my ears grows louder, the pulse of my heartbeat drowning out the commotion. Because a shadowed figure rounds the corner, so massive he looks like he barely fits inside this enormous house… and as the light reveals his face, I'm staring at the most beautiful man I've ever seen. *My man. My Damiano.*

He's in full bulletproof gear, his rifle trained forward as he storms in.

The air catches in my lungs as his gaze sweeps the room, frantic and searching, his body coiled like a predator ready for a fight.

When our eyes finally meet, his rifle lowers an inch. His head tilts slightly, and his mouth parts in disbelief.

A single, broken sound slips from his throat, his shoulders collapsing with a ragged exhale.

He's huge. Bigger than before. Muscles on top of muscles strain against his shirt, biceps nearly too thick for the sleeves. Sweat trails down his temple, his jaw locked so hard the veins in his neck stand out.

My body sways as we stare at each other. The world around us is forgotten, and the distance between us stretches impossibly wide.

I don't know if I'm dreaming, if I was shot outside and this is heaven, or if this is real life.

This can't be real life.

This can't be real.

As men move throughout the room, their shouts echoing off the walls, I know this isn't a dream. This isn't some cruel trick of my mind.

They're here.

He's here.

The realization slams into me, and a strangled cry tears free. My legs refuse to move. I'm drained, trembling with exhaustion, using the last of my strength to keep upright as I reach for him.

The shouting and gunfire fade into the distance. My entire world narrows to the man coming toward me.

Time fractures. Everything feels like it's moving in slow motion and all at once.

And then he's here.

His arms wrap around my waist, pulling me into his chest, and the force knocks the air from my lungs. He holds me so tightly I feel my ribs compress.

I cling to him, my fingers threading through his hair—the same soft waves I've memorized, the ones I've run my hands through a hundred times in my mind.

My body shakes as I hold him, heart splintering and stitching itself back together with every breath, every brush of his warmth against me.

I never want to let go.

I inhale the crook of his neck, and the dam inside me finally breaks as every ounce of fear, pain, and longing I've held in for so long comes rushing to the surface.

I go limp, and he holds me tighter, burying his face in my hair, whispering "I've got you" over and over, like he's telling himself it's true.

It's only when he drops to his knees and I sink into his lap that I realize he's crying too.

The man who feels nothing—is feeling.

I refuse to open my eyes. Because when I do, I know he won't really be here. And I can't survive that truth again. Not after getting to feel him once more, even if it isn't real.

He pulls back slightly, his nose grazing mine. "Look at me."

It's his voice.

I shake my head.

"Baby, look at me," his tone is rough and choked with emotion.

"No." My voice wobbles.

"Please."

Another shake.

"Why won't you look at me?"

"If I open them and you're not really here… I can't—" The words crack. "I can't survive any longer without you."

"I'm real," he breathes, resting his forehead against mine. "I'm right here. Look at me."

My eyes flutter open, tears streaming down my face as I lock onto those beautiful, fierce eyes I thought I'd never see again.

A fresh wave of sobs erupts from me, my grip on him tightening as he presses his mouth to mine.

I kiss him back so hard I feel like I might push his teeth out, my entire body leaning into him, trying to fuse us together, trying to erase the distance, the pain, and the time we've lost.

"I'm so sorry," he murmurs against my lips. "I love you so much. You're so strong. You were so strong. You did so good. Nobody is ever going to hurt you again, I promise. You're safe now."

But I wasn't strong.

I didn't do good.

Cristiano broke me. I became someone else's possession, someone else's whore, and I don't know how to tell him that. Or even that another man was having sex with me daily. That other men touched me.

I shake my head, not wanting him to keep talking because his words aren't true. Because I'm filthy. I sit on his lap while another man's semen leaks out of me onto his legs.

"You were. You were strong, and you survived."

"He was just having sex with me."

"You're okay, baby." His hands come up to cradle my face, his thumbs brushing away my tears. "We'll get you cleaned up, okay? You're safe now. I've got you."

I crush myself against him again, wrapping my arms even tighter around his neck.

When I open my eyes, my heartbeat stutters. Dante is standing in the doorway, his broad shoulders shaking as he stares at me.

I reach for him, and he comes, crossing the room and sinking to his knees beside us. His arms wrap around me, surrounding me in their strength, their warmth, their unwavering loyalty. He presses a kiss to the side of my head. For a long moment, the three of us remain like that, huddled together on the floor.

"You brave, brave girl." The words are quiet, full of pride. "I'm so fucking proud of you."

His grip loosens, and he pulls back, taking me in, stopping on the dark streaks smeared across my skin.

"Is this your blood?"

I lift my arm, taking in all the red. "No. I… I stabbed him."

Damiano softly brushes a hand down my cheek, turning my head back toward him. "Where did you stab?"

I swallow hard, my mind flashing back to the split second when I drove the blade into Cristiano's body. My fingers move to my own stomach, pressing against the spot where I felt the knife sink into him.

"Here." I point just below my ribs.

Dom nods. "How big was the knife?"

"It was a butcher knife. He pulled it from the kitchen."

They look at each other, the unspoken question passing between them.

"Fatal?" Dante asks.

"Doubt it." He turns his focus back to me. "Did he say where he was planning to take you?"

I shake my head. "No. He had me… spend the night with a client, and after that… the client wanted me. He said he would kill Cristiano and everyone here to get me. He threatened he was coming back for me. The guard said that's who was here."

"Who was the client?"

I shrug. "All I know is his first name is Leandro. He was nice to me. Gentle, even," I say shamefully, letting my head fall.

Dom lifts my chin. "You did nothing wrong."

I feel like I need to defend myself or explain why I did it, even though I know I don't. "Cristiano was going to beat Giulia if I couldn't get him the deal."

"Baby," he shushes me, "you did nothing wrong."

"So many men have touched me." My lip quivers.

His head tilts to the side in a shrug. "Most of them are dead."

My brows pinch together, unsure how he would even know who any of them are.

"We should get going," he murmurs, leaning in to kiss me.

As he pulls back, I glance down at the ring glinting on my finger. Fresh tears blur my vision. It's one fucking thing after another. He's probably really regretting coming now, seeing the mess that is me.

"Dom… I'm married to him," I confess.

He follows my gaze down to the ring. For a heartbeat, he just stares at it, his expression hardening. Then yanks it off and hurls it across the room.

"I'll get you a better ring, baby."

He stands with me in his arms and gently sets me on my feet.

"Come on. Let's get you dressed and get out of here."

Chapter

THIRTY-TWO

Damiano

I slide my hand into hers and she squeezes gently, leading us out. As we're guided through the house, Dante's eyes drop to her backside. When he catches me watching, he tilts his head slightly, nodding toward her rear.

I take in the damage. She's a mess of swollen, broken skin. Deep red welts crisscross her cheeks and run down her legs, some split open with blood smeared across her flesh. Thin trails trickle from between her thighs, and I have to force myself to keep moving, to not stop and assess the extent of her injuries right here in the hallway. The fact that she's still on her feet is staggering, but I know it's adrenaline carrying her.

She takes us into a bedroom, the double doors still thrown wide open. We must have arrived in the middle of him abusing her.

She mumbles something about washing her makeup off and slips into the adjoining bathroom.

I step farther into the room, immediately noticing the bloodied belt lying discarded on the floor near the end of the bed. As I approach, I spot a darker stain beside it. Puke. She must have thrown up while he was whipping her.

Dante moves to the edge of the bed, catching sight of the bloody dildo still lying on the mattress, the sheets stained beneath it.

I reach out and press on one of the darker spots. When I pull back, my fingertip is crimson. I hold it up to show him. "It's fresh."

"Fucking piece of shit," he hisses, covering his mouth.

Sudden, muffled sobs echo from the bathroom. Dante and I exchange a glance, and then we cross the room, my heart racing as I knock on the door.

"Baby?" I call, already reaching for the handle.

I push the door open and find her standing in front of the sink, a wad of bloodied tissue clutched between her legs, her shoulders shaking as tears stream down her now makeup-free face.

"Where's it coming from?" I ask, stepping inside, my heart sinking as I take in her pale, trembling frame.

She doesn't answer, just looks up at me, her lips quivering.

"Turn around."

She hesitates. "I can't get it out."

My brows furrow as I step closer. She turns slowly, moving the tissue, and I see the jewel on her anus before she covers it again.

Dante stands frozen in the doorway, watching me reach for the tissue, gently pulling it away.

She's so swollen and raw, I do my best not to touch the worst of it as I part her cheeks.

"I'm gonna pull it out, okay?"

She nods and bends over, bracing herself against the counter.

As I grip it, she whimpers. "Dante."

He rushes over, kneeling in front of her.

She clenches when I tug, and I'm met with resistance, but I pull harder and it comes free.

Blood trickles out with it, dripping onto the floor. I press the tissue back, trying to soak up as much as I can.

There's a tear along the rim of her anus. When I dab at it again, more blood wells up, darker and flowing from deeper inside.

"Wet a towel for me," I tell Dante. He moves quickly, then hands it over.

As I kneel behind her, he drops back to his knees in front, letting her hold onto his shoulders while I work to clean her up.

He rests his forehead against hers. "I know you gave him hell."

She gives a weak, broken smile. "I tried."

I press the damp cloth between her legs, trying to clean away the remnants of semen still leaking out while checking for any visible injuries to her vagina. Her body tenses at the first touch, but I move cautiously, watching for any other hidden abrasions.

Thankfully, there don't appear to be any, so I lift the towel higher, carefully pressing it to her butt. I hold it in place for a moment before pulling back, relieved to see the bleeding has started to slow. He must have shoved the dildo into her with alarming force to cause this kind of damage.

I search through cupboards and drawers until I find a tube of ointment. I dab a small amount onto my finger and gently apply it to the tear. She flinches, but then her body begins to relax.

I repeat the process over the deep lashes carved into her butt cheeks. She hisses in pain, lurching forward to wrap her arms around Dante's neck. He steadies her, his fingertips gliding softly over her shoulders.

"How do you vanish for seven months and come back even sexier?" he asks rhetorically.

She lifts her head, their eyes locking briefly, then she winces, her grip tightening as I move to the other cheek, being even more careful because this side is more severe.

When I finish, she straightens and turns. "How bad is it?"

I shrug. "My cock has done worse."

She smiles, and I pull her into my arms, pressing a kiss to the top of her head.

Dante steps out to grab clothes, giving us our first moment alone. She tilts her face up, and I lean down, brushing my lips against hers.

"It also looks just as delicious as the last time I ate it," I murmur with a teasing wink.

A weak, choked laugh escapes her, and we kiss again.

When Dante returns, he hands me a tank top, then crouches in front of her, holding out a pair of panties. She steps in carefully, and he gently pulls them up, repeating the process with a pair of leggings while I ease the tank over her head and down her body.

He slides socks onto her feet and helps her into her sneakers, then rises, his hand resting gently on her arm.

"We need to move," he says quietly.

She nods, and I step past them.

"Watch her back."

He doesn't hesitate, slipping his hand into hers and positioning her between us.

I push the door open, barrel leading the way.

We move as a single unit, my rifle sweeping side to side as I lead them through the twisting corridors.

I follow the sound of gunshots echoing from the main hall, the intermittent cracks of final executions.

"Wait!" she yells, breaking free from Dante and rushing ahead, arms raised. "Let them go. They've been held here too."

She points to the other workers huddled together near the guards.

Gio stares at her, his eyes flicking between her and the terrified faces around them. Then, with a sharp nod, he signals to our men, and the rifles lower.

Rainey locks onto a girl about her age, walking straight to her.

"I know you probably hate me. I didn't mean for that to happen. I hate that we're not talking. I'm sorry. I'm so sorry. Come home with me. I'll fix it. I'll fix us. Please, Giulia." Her voice breaks. "I'll protect you. Always. Just come with me."

Tears spill down the girl's cheeks. She pushes to her feet and stumbles into Rainey's arms.

"I'm sorry too. I'll go anywhere with you," she whispers, clinging even tighter.

From somewhere in the crowd, an older woman steps forward. "Take me with you too," she pleads. "I will serve you always, Rainey. I just want to see Anya."

Silvano's eyes darken at the mention of his girlfriend's name.

Rainey reaches out, takes the woman's hand, and gives it a firm squeeze as she steps closer to him.

"Fedora, I'd like you to meet Silvano Volkov. He's the one I was telling you about, the one who's been taking care of Anya. Silvano, this is Fedora. She looked after Anya while she was here. She's the one who helped her escape."

His face loses its color as the name sinks in. Anya told us everything about Fedora—how she risked her life to help her, how she was the only friend Anya had in this place, and how she believed Fedora would protect Rainey too.

Silvano closes the distance between them, pulling Fedora into his arms as he whispers something too quiet for the rest of us to hear.

She clings to him, her body shaking as she cries.

When they finally pull apart, she grabs his face and kisses both of his cheeks.

Dante steps forward and addresses the group of staff still trembling with fear.

"You're all free. We can get you rides out of here and take you wherever you need to go. We'll also make sure you have funds to help you get by or disappear, whatever you choose."

He pauses, scanning the battered, exhausted faces in front of him. "If you want to come with us, you're welcome to. Just understand that at our home, you'll work too."

Two women step forward, their hands clasped tightly. One of them speaks with quiet determination. "We'll come with you." A man beside them nods, adding his agreement.

Slowly, others begin to rise. Soft murmurs ripple through the group as some exchange hesitant glances, then move toward the exits, choosing to find their own way home.

A few of the men who came with us tonight are local. Others traveled from neighboring countries. They move forward, offering steady arms and calm words as they guide the remaining staff to waiting vehicles. Each person will be taken wherever they need to go, their pockets filled with enough cash to survive, to start again.

The entire ride to the plane, Rainey and Giulia remain huddled together, arms wrapped around each other, their heads pressed close.

Once we board, I guide Rainey to a leather seat near the back, settling beside her as Dante takes one across from us. Giulia sits on Rainey's other side, reaching over and taking her hand.

"There's a shower in the back and a bed." I rest my hand on Rainey's knee. "Once we're airborne, you can clean up and then get some sleep, okay? We've got about eleven hours in the air."

She nods, eyes dropping to her lap as she leans her head against my shoulder.

As soon as the plane levels and the seatbelt sign clicks off, I unbuckle and stand. "Let's go get you cleaned up."

She hesitates, then looks at Giulia, who immediately rises.

Dante presses his lips into a thin line, his gaze shifting between the two of them before he gives me a nod.

I lead them to the back, opening the door to the luxuriously appointed bathroom. Reaching into the shower, I twist the knobs until warm steam begins to fill the space.

As I step aside, they move past me. I lean against the counter, my eyes falling to the floor as they begin to undress.

I catch a glimpse of them in the reflection of the glass shower door as Giulia steps in first, gently guiding Rainey under the stream of hot water.

Rainey lets out a sharp hiss.

"Shit. I didn't know it was this bad," Giulia mutters, trying to adjust the spray away from her.

"It's fine. He was worse to you."

Giulia's mouth falls open. "You know that's not true."

"You've treated me like shit."

"We weren't allowed to talk," Giulia utters quietly. "He got jealous and wanted to drive a wedge between us."

"Well, he did," she snaps.

"Tip your head back," Giulia sighs, reaching for the shampoo. She works the soap through Raineys hair, rubbing careful circles.

When she finishes, she turns to wash her own, the two of them moving around each other in quiet rhythm. Giulia grabs a washcloth, squeezes body wash onto it, and turns back to Rainey, softly scrubbing the blood and dirt from her skin.

"Sorry," she whispers as Rainey flinches when the cloth drags across a welt on her back.

"Tell me you stabbed that bastard in the dick," Giulia murmurs. "He's going to be pissed come morning."

My attention shifts toward the shower, caught off guard by the comment.

"His dick is still intact," Rainey replies dryly. "He'll survive."

"Not without you for his morning delight."

They turn to each other, both wrinkling their noses before bursting into laughter.

When the water shuts off, they each grab a towel, wrapping themselves up as steam rises around them.

I clear my throat, feeling like I'm intruding. "I brought you some clothes, babe. Or an extra pair of mine if that's more comfortable." I glance between them. "Giulia, you look close to Rainey's size. You can wear something of hers."

Giulia nods and they both remain still.

"Do you need anything else?" she asks, shifting her attention from me to Rainey and then back again.

The message is clear. She wants me out. Maybe it's about privacy. Maybe she doesn't want me seeing her naked. Not that I would look. And after what she's likely endured, modesty seems like a strange priority. If she thinks she's going to come between me and Rainey, she's mistaken.

As I reach for the clothes, Giulia steps forward and grabs them instead.

"I've got it," she says quietly, brushing past me with a soft, "Thank you."

I piece together the unspoken dynamic between them. Giulia probably wasn't just a friend. She likely cared for Rainey in every way. She touches her with a careful, familiar tenderness, telling me there was some sort of sexual nature to their relationship.

Through everything they've endured, they've become each other's anchor.

Much like Dante and me.

When it's clear they won't get dressed with me still in the room, I exhale, straighten, and quietly step out. I lower myself to the edge of the bed, forearms resting on my knees, fingertips pressed together.

I was prepared for this to be hard. I was warned she might not be fully herself.

What I wasn't ready for was the closeness she now shares with someone else.

The door opens and Rainey pauses, her eyes locking onto mine. I rise to my feet and move to the side of the bed, pulling the covers back for her.

"Come get some rest."

She slips under the blankets with Giulia beside her.

I retreat to the bathroom, the adrenaline of the night still thrumming through my veins as I peel off my clothes and step into the shower, letting the hot water pound over me as I scrub away the grime and blood.

Then I just stand there, staring at the tile.

It's not their fault. They've been through hell.

They found comfort in each other when there was nothing else.

But all I want is to hold her longer.

I wrap a towel around my waist, water still clinging to my skin as I step back into the room.

Whatever they were talking about dies instantly. Both of them turn to look at me.

Rainey's gaze trails over my chest, pausing on my shoulders before drifting lower, taking in the sharp lines of my abs.

"Did you do anything besides lift weights the whole time I was gone?"

I toss my clothes into a pile. "Killed a lot of people."

"So… you worked out and killed. Did you do anything else?"

Her expression falls slightly. She's wondering if I took anyone else to bed.

I let out a low, amused chuckle, crossing the room, leaning over bracing my knuckles beside her head. She shifts partially onto her back, eyes locking with mine.

"Not even my fist," I murmur against her lips before I kiss her.

Sex never crossed my mind while she was gone. If anyone had dared suggest otherwise, I would have ended them on the spot.

When I pull away, tears are already sliding toward her hairline.

I sit on the edge of the bed, my thumb brushing gently against her cheek. "Just sleep, baby."

I stand and walk toward my duffle bag, reaching for the handle when her voice stops me.

"Dress in here."

I peer over my shoulder and find her still watching me.

I set the bag at the foot of the bed and move to the knot of the towel around my waist, letting it fall.

"God," Giulia breathes, her head lifting off the pillow as she takes me in.

"Yeah," Rainey agrees, her lips parting as her gaze drops lower.

I shake my head and yank on a pair of boxers, then step into my joggers, my muscles tightening with each movement. I pull a tank top on and not once have they looked away, their expressions dazed.

Crossing to Rainey's side of the bed, I sit beside her and brush my fingers through her hair.

"Do you need something to eat?"

She shakes her head.

"K, I'm gonna head back out and let you get some sleep." I kiss her again and go to stand, but she reaches for me, curling around my wrist.

"Stay," she whispers. "Please. Just until I fall asleep."

Warmth spreads through my chest as I settle back onto the mattress, pulling the covers up over the three of us.

"I half felt like I needed to brace myself for the bed to break," she teases.

"Wait until you see me fight now." I wink.

"Well, I see your knuckles are wrecked. You must have had lots of time to improve."

"Do you notice anything else about my hands?" I hold them up.

She smiles and trails her fingertip along my trimmed nails and clean cuticles. "You did good. I'm impressed."

"Thanks."

"I also notice you're wearing my favorite tank top." She lifts a brow.

I packed it on purpose, knowing it's her favorite. Every time I wear it, she digs it out of the hamper and puts it on.

"Pretty sure that was under my pillow."

I smile. "It was indeed."

"Then why is it on this plane with us and not sleeping under my pillow still?"

"I used your pillow and found it. I can't believe you were hiding my shirt."

"I wrapped it around my head when I touched myself." She grins. "Is that the only one you found?"

I lift onto my forearm, my mouth falling open. "There are more?"

She shrugs. "I guess not, if you haven't found them."

She watches me for a moment, then traces the scar along my hairline. She combs through my hair, pushing it back before gliding over the scar again.

"Don't worry, I won't get you flowers," I say with a smile.

"The flowers weren't offensive. You not talking to me for five days and then just waltzing into my room like nothing happened was offensive."

I nod. "Adding to the escalation of events from that night, when I came, I blacked out from blood loss."

Her eyes widen. "Like actually?"

"Why do you think you had to take over? I was going to pass out. Figured at least if you were on top you could get yourself off."

"I kicked you out afterward because I felt so guilty. And it was so disgusting. The blood just kept coming, and when I came down from the high of finishing, I thought I was going to puke when I saw it."

I'd wondered why she went from riding me to kicking me out. I hadn't even considered that she might be squeamish.

"What about now?" I lift my brows a couple times, knowing it makes the scar shift.

"Now, it looks good. Sexy even."

"Good." I lean down and kiss her.

"Good is a good word." She smirks.

"I love you so much."

"I love you too. So much."

"Now, as you like to say, shut your damn eyes and go to sleep." I swipe my fingers over her eyelids.

She laughs and pushes my hand away. I catch hers, kiss her knuckles, then lie down and wrap my arm around her, snuggling my face into her back.

Chapter

THIRTY-THREE

Rainey falls asleep fast, her body curled toward Giulia.

I can't stop pressing my lips to her shoulder and neck, like I'm trying to convince myself she's really here. That I'm not just clinging to a ghost.

With every kiss against her skin, my heart clenches a little tighter. I have my girl back.

"She talked about you all the time," Giulia whispers. "Some nights, after he was really rough with her and she lay there bleeding, broken, and zoning out, the only way I could bring her back was to ask her questions about you."

She's quiet for a moment before exhaling a long, shaky breath. "She didn't think you were coming for her. She saved me. And I couldn't do anything to save her. She—" Her voice catches, and she has to stop, breathing through it before trying again. "She tried to…"

Her hand lifts to her mouth like she can force the words back.

"She tried to kill herself. She tried to jump off the back of the boat. Into shark-infested waters. I saw it in her eyes. She had given up. And the moment she looked at the water, I knew what she was about to do. I barely caught her in time. She ran straight for it, and I've never been more scared in my life."

I can't imagine the helplessness she must have felt. I'm immediately more grateful for Giulia.

"Thank you for saving her."

"Thank you for coming for her."

She lets out a long sigh, as if getting those words out eased something inside her and she could finally sleep.

For a long while I breathe Rainey in, my nose brushing the curve of her shoulder, the faint scent of her still clinging to her skin despite everything she's been through.

She's so beautiful. Her long lashes curl away from her cheeks, her full lips slightly parted as she softly mumbles my name.

Then I hone in on her round butt pressed to my crotch.

She lets out a quiet moan and I know there's no way this erection is going anywhere.

I force myself to pull back, slowly untangling my limbs from hers.

I step into the bathroom and splash cold water on my face, gripping the counter as I meet my own reflection. *Pull it together. You haven't even had her back for two hours.*

I rub my temples, fighting to clear my mind. When my erection finally fades, I head out to the main cabin.

My brothers are seated together, deep in conversation. Marko stands as I approach so I can take his spot.

"That went better than we anticipated," Gio says, his expression thoughtful.

"Yeah," I agree.

"Can't believe she was there," Nikolai mutters. "He almost got away with her again. They were just about to the docks. He was still reaching for her as his men dragged him away. Guarantee if he's not dead, her being gone makes him wish he was."

"He needs to survive," I say flatly. "I need to be the one to end him."

Nikolai's eyes meet mine, a flicker of understanding passing between us.

"What's the deal with the girl?" Silvano tilts his head toward the back.

I exhale slowly, dragging a hand down my face. "Another of Cristiano's victims, I presume."

"Where do we think he's going?" Nikolai asks.

I shake my head. "No clue. Rainey wasn't sure either."

Gio glances toward the closed bedroom door. "Should we have medical on standby when we land? She looked… pretty rough."

I nod, the image of the welts and torn skin on her backside flashing through my mind. "Yeah. We'll have them check her out if she's okay with it. If not, I'll keep an eye on her."

Rainey sleeps for nine hours straight.

I check on her every hour, just to be sure. But she doesn't move. For nine hours, she stays in the exact same position.

When the bedroom door opens, she steps out rubbing her eyes, her movements slow and groggy. She pauses, scanning the cabin until she spots me, then lifts her hand in a small wave, making her way over.

I uncross my leg and she eases into my lap carefully, wincing as she settles, then curls against my chest, resting her head in the crook of my neck.

"We'll land in a couple hours," I murmur.

She nods, then nestles closer.

Dante slips his hands under her legs and pulls them into his lap. She watches as he begins to massage her feet and smiles.

I know the moment she drifts off again when her breathing evens out. I'm unsure if it's from the abuse she endured tonight or lack of sleep in general, but she's overly exhausted.

Each of my brothers wears the same look of relief mixed with fatigue as their attention stays fixed on her.

"Has anyone told Niki we got her?" I ask softly, careful not to wake her.

Simultaneously, they all shake their heads.

Niki completely fell apart after she was released and Rainey wasn't. She spiraled fast, breaking down in a way none of us were prepared for. For months, Ma found her screaming in the middle of the night, trying everything to keep her from slipping too far mentally. But it wasn't enough. Eventually, she had to be committed to a treatment center.

Ma thought she was better after two weeks, and she was allowed to come home. That night, she tried to take her own life. The grief swallowed her whole. She sobbed that she couldn't live with what she'd seen Cristiano do to Rainey. She was recommitted for a month. She's only been home for two weeks, but she's not the same.

Ma is barely holding on herself. Watching her children fall apart has left her shattered. I haven't spoken to her since the last time we argued. The last thing I said to her was, *"She wasn't allowed to leave the property and you sent her to pick up your dress. If I find out you played a role in this… I'll let you figure out the rest."*

She just stood there, staring at me, speechless, as I walked away.

It never made sense why she would ask Rainey, of all people, to pick something up for her. She has hundreds of staff. She never wanted us doing anything to save Rainey but suddenly changed her mind when she found out Niki was with her. Something about it still feels wrong. I didn't have the mental space to sort through it before. But now that Rainey's safe, I will figure out what happened. And when I find out who was involved, I'll kill every single one of them.

Pa's been trying to be present more, holding the family together the best he can. I've heard him late at night, talking on the phone, chasing down every lead he could to bring Rainey back.

He swore that when we found her, he would finally retire if the stress didn't kill him first. Said he couldn't keep doing this much longer.

I study Rainey, not knowing what kind of treatments she'll need, what kind of demons she'll have to face in the coming weeks. I don't even know how she's doing. What scars Cristiano carved into her mind. What ghosts will follow her when we're finally home.

The bedroom door opens again, and a panicked Giulia steps out.

"She's okay," I reassure her.

Her eyes land on Rainey and her shoulders drop with relief as she comes our way.

Silvano rises and gestures for her to take his chair, and he moves to the empty seat beside Dante.

Nobody seems to know how to bring up the question we're all circling. Who she is.

I glance at Dante. If I push too hard, he'll step in. But for now, he just watches the girl in front of us, while she stays locked on Rainey. Her attention shifts to Dante's hands still cradling Rainey's feet, and her brows pull together, like it bothers her.

"How long were you with Cristiano?"

Her eyes lift from Dante's hands to me. For a moment, I see fear.

"I don't know the time frame. It all blurred together."

"Before or after Rainey arrived?"

"After." Her throat moves as she swallows. "I was brought to deals for… sex."

I wait for her to continue but she doesn't.

"And then?"

She hesitates, picking at the skin around her nails.

"And then Cristiano arrived, and the meeting went really bad. Really bad for me. I noticed the girl with him kept staring at me. I thought she was amused or something, but when I looked at her… she just seemed empty. Just like me. Worse, even. Her arms were in casts, bruises covered her skin, and she was barely holding on.

"I wondered if maybe she was going to be raped along with me. They all wanted a turn with her and only one man was brave enough to say he wanted to take her to the bed. Cristiano told them she's his and his alone."

She draws a shaky breath.

"When the meeting ended and everyone was leaving, she told him she wanted me to come with them. He told her that if I did, she would have to service him that night. She agreed."

Tears well in her eyes and she blinks rapidly to keep them from falling.

"And did she?"

She shakes her head. "She fought him. He beat her so bad."

She wipes at the tears trailing down her cheeks.

"Was it just him who hurt her that you saw?"

Another shake.

"She doesn't like to listen to him. She talked back a lot, like she didn't care when he hurt her. Like it didn't matter anymore. And since he couldn't get a reaction out of her… he made *me* hurt her."

I knew it. There was something deeper between them. Something that connected them beyond survival.

"He would tie her up and make me use toys on her. And if we really got in trouble, he would make us have sex with each other while he watched. Then he would have sex with her himself, hitting her for letting someone else touch her. Even though he forced us to do it."

"Where were you tonight?" I ask. "If you two were always together, why weren't you there when we got to them. Why weren't you leaving with them?"

"They went to a dinner. I don't know what happened there, but when they got back, he was calm. And that's not a good thing. His calm is followed by something terrible.

"I was outside the door when I heard the sound of him whipping her. He said something about her thinking she was cute at the restaurant. And she said something like, she must have been if she gave a man a boner.

"One of the guards told me to go downstairs. As we walked away, a group of them stood outside the door. They were touching themselves. Listening to her scream and getting off on it."

"Did he seem to care for her? Or was it more about punishment?"

She shrugs. "Both. He seemed obsessed with her. Like really obsessed. He liked to stare at her while he worked. She had to stand there naked in front of his desk, and if she got too tired, he would let her sit… in a specific way."

She doesn't continue, and I don't care to know. But Dante does.

"He made her sit how?"

She chews the inside of her cheek. "With her legs spread over the arms of the chair."

That revelation knocks the questions out of each of our mouths, and we let silence carry us the rest of the way.

The plane jostles as the wheels touch down an hour later.

Rainey shoots upright, her body tensing.

"It's okay, babe." I tighten my hold. "We landed."

She blinks, trying to make sense of where she is. Her gaze shifts to the window, taking in the stationary plane, and her body slowly begins to relax.

The cabin door opens, a rush of fresh air pouring in as the steps are lowered.

When we finally step out, the bright, warm sunlight hits her face, and she squints, lifting a hand to shield her eyes.

At the bottom of the stairs, she stops and looks around. She's trying to process that she's back. Everyone pauses, letting her take it all in. Out of my periphery, I don't miss the movement of her wiping away tears.

Her fingers lace between mine and I look down at her.

"Thank you for coming for me."

I pull her into me, wrapping my arms around her as she starts to cry.

"You never had to doubt I'd come for you. I'm just sorry it took so long."

"He kept moving us."

"I know." I hold her tighter.

She rests her chin against my chest as she gazes up at me.

I press my lips to hers and she kisses back, just as hard. When I pull away, she shakes her head, releases one hand, and wraps it around the back of my neck, pulling me in again.

THE DRIVE BACK IS QUIET.

She stays curled against my side, head resting on my shoulder, and fingers loosely twined with mine. I feel the shift as we get closer to the property. Her grip tightens and she tenses.

I give her hand a gentle squeeze, brushing my thumb over her knuckles, silently asking what's wrong.

Her lips part like she might speak, but the words don't come. She just turns, focusing out the window as the long, winding driveway comes into view.

When we finally pull up to the front steps, the car idles while Silvano shifts into park. I stay where I am, watching her as she stares at the house, completely frozen.

Chapter
THIRTY-FOUR

Rainey

As we near the main house, flashbacks hit me in rapid succession.

Valentina wanting me to pick up her dress. Her telling me I can't tell Damiano. Her saying it will be our little secret.

She set me up.

She knew exactly what she was doing.

She sent me out knowing I wouldn't come back. She didn't just hand me over to Damiano's enemy, she handed me a death sentence and smiled while doing it.

I try to swallow, but my throat feels tight, my chest constricting as the realization settles over me.

She did it for her son. That much I know. She thought she was protecting him. But how am I supposed to look at her now? How do I walk into that house and pretend I wasn't betrayed by her.

That house… where everything good and bad has happened to me. The house where Niki left with me. The same house where her body was probably delivered back to.

I was so dazed by the shock of Dom coming for me that I didn't even consider the consequences of returning here.

Valentina wanted me dead.

Now, not only am I not dead—her daughter is. And Cristiano is still alive, no doubt wanting both her son and me dead.

Dom's thumb brushes over my knuckles, silently asking what's wrong.

But I can't look at him. I can't say anything.

Nikolai hasn't even tried to speak to me. Other than the moment he called my name, he hasn't said a word. Maybe it's for the best. Every time I think about trying to apologize, the tears well up, my throat closes, and I feel like I'm going to choke.

For a brief, terrifying moment, I wonder if I'm being brought here to be executed.

I force the thought down, my eyes flicking to Giulia beside me. If they killed me, what would happen to her? She's beautiful. They'd probably see if she wanted to work for them.

"Come on," Dom says, pushing his door open and stepping out. His hand extends toward me, his eyes gentle but concerned.

I stare at his outstretched hand, my pulse thundering in my ears. I shouldn't be here. I shouldn't be anywhere near this place. He should have just taken me back to our house.

"Can we go home?" I whisper. "Please."

He leans into the door, resting his forehead against the top of the frame, searching my face. "What's going on, babe?"

I shake my head, the walls of my mind beginning to close in. "I just… I just don't want to go in."

His brow furrows, his mouth starting to open, but a scream rips through the air.

"Rainey!"

I heard that exact scream moments before the final gunshot. I heard my name for the last time and I mourned the voice saying it. I mourned the person it belonged to. But I'm hearing it again right now.

My head snaps up, my heart slamming against my ribs as I look around Damiano and lock onto the front steps.

Niki is barreling down the stairs, her body swallowed by a baggy gray sweatshirt and sweatpants, her hair piled in a messy, tangled bun.

I can't breathe.

She's alive.

She's… alive.

I shove past him, throwing myself out of the car, my feet barely touching the ground as I race toward her, my arms outstretched as I close the distance between us.

We collide, our bodies crashing together, arms wrapping around each other so tightly.

I don't even know if the wail I hear is hers or mine. I cling to her, breathing in her scent. It's a scent I thought I'd never smell again.

"He told me he killed you." The words spill out in a broken, frantic rush. "I heard the gunshot. You were dead."

She shakes her head. "They shot a gopher."

I pull back, struggling to process her words.

"They shot a gopher?" I repeat, framing her face, brushing the wet, tangled, strands that have fallen away from her cheeks.

It's really her. She's really alive.

That son of a bitch.

"I couldn't help you. He raped you and then all those other men... I heard your bones breaking, and I couldn't do anything." She fists my shirt, crumbling with grief and rage. "I wanted you to let them rape me. You're so stubborn. Why did you protect me? You should have let them rape me!"

I grip her shoulders, my heart breaking.

"I'd never sit by and let someone hurt you!"

Her mouth hangs open like I've insulted her.

"I was drugged. I couldn't freakin' move!"

"Niki. I know that. He didn't let them assault me with anything other than their hands and toys. They would have used a lot more than that on you."

She shakes her head. "I don't care. I would have rather they do it to me than what happened to you. I had to watch. I've never felt so useless and trapped in my own worthless skin."

"I'm here now. Your brothers saved me."

"Is he dead? Cristiano."

She says his name like I would need to be reminded who he is.

"No. But I stabbed him."

"You what?" She looks flabbergasted by the admission.

"I stabbed Cristiano… the man who was holding me captive." I remind her that he's the bad guy.

"Oh yeah, right," she nods. "Good."

I pinch my brows together, confused by her reaction.

A gentle touch on my shoulder makes me turn, and it takes a moment for my mind to catch up. To recognize the familiar man in front of me. The older version of Damiano. Lorenzo Volkov.

He still looks so young, though he's definitely added a few more gray hairs since I last saw him. He's a blend of all his sons, with eyes so tired he looks like he's been carrying more stress than I was.

He opens his arms, pulling both Niki and me into a hug, letting out a long sigh into my hair as he clings to us.

"I underestimated you. I thought he would break you. But you're a strong woman. I guess that confirms you'll be able to handle that son of mine."

He pulls back, a small, proud smile on his lips as he flicks his gaze from me to Dom.

I manage a weak, shaky smile, my heart swelling. "I can definitely handle him."

"I have no doubt." He reaches out and pats Dom on the shoulder.

I'm still caught in the fog of everything that just unfolded, not fully believing I'm standing here, when the front door flies open and Anya comes rushing out. She stops briefly to kiss Silvano and tell him she loves him, and then she's crossing the distance between us.

She stops just short of me, her eyes wide and locked on mine.

"I'm sorry for everything. Please forgive me. I never want to fight ever again."

I nod, my arms wrapping around her as I pull her into a tight hug. "Never again."

She shouldn't even be the one apologizing. I was the one who was out of line the last time we spoke. She was trying to help me, trying to be a good friend, and I made a jab about going after Silvano since she wanted me with one of the *nice brothers*.

I brush away a falling tear from her cheek. "I brought you a surprise," I say, smiling.

Her brows furrow in confusion.

I gesture to the open door of a nearby sedan where Fedora waits, trembling as she locks on Anya.

"Mama Fedora," she whispers, her body going rigid for a heartbeat before she suddenly bolts toward her, throwing herself into the older woman's arms.

They cling to each other, years of fear and pain melt away in an instant.

"Are you hungry, dear? We can get you anything you want. Anything at all." Lorenzo says.

I hesitate, turning back toward the vehicle we were in to see if Giulia has a preference. She's standing there looking uncomfortable, but offers her best reassuring nod. "Anything you like."

That strict diet Cristiano had me on ends now.

"Who's this?" Niki asks, taking in Giulia's pale, exhausted face.

"This is Giulia." I hold my hand out for her to come to me. She steps forward, slipping her fingers into mine. "She kept me sane while I was gone. She took care of me."

Niki's eyes soften and she pulls her into a hug.

Giulia stiffens, her free arm hovering uncertainly in the air.

"This is the sister Cristiano said he killed," I explain.

She looks confused.

"He obviously lied."

It takes her a moment to process the information before she slowly lets her arm wrap around her.

The next person to come out the front door has my blood running cold.

Valentina strides out, her head held high, her tears shimmering in the sunlight, her arms already outstretched as she makes her way toward me.

My skin prickles, and I instinctively take a step away, bumping into Dom's chest.

"Hi, sweetheart." Her voice is choked up with emotion as she reaches for me.

I flinch taking another step back, pressing harder into him.

Giulia subtly steps in front of me as a protective barrier.

"I know everyone is excited to see her," Dom says, his arm slipping protectively around my waist, "but we need to get her to medical."

Valentina's composure falters, her eyes flicking between the two of us.

"Are you injured?" she asks with what appears to be genuine concern.

I let out a short, bitter laugh as I glare at her. "I was with Cristiano. Of course I'm injured."

For a moment, I think I see something like guilt flash across her features. It almost looks like she knows I know she's the one who put me in that hellhole.

"Come on, babe," Dom murmurs, tightening his grip on my waist as he starts to guide me away. "Let's get you checked out."

How dare she try to talk to me. To pretend she's not a snake.

The entire walk to the medical room, I'm vibrating with anger. I open and close my hands, shaking them just to let some of the jitters out.

Giulia keeps staring at me, and I know she wants to ask if that was the Valentina who stabbed me in the back, but I don't want Dom knowing anything.

I look at her and mouth, *shhh*.

Her gaze flicks from me to Dom, who is watching, then she gives an almost imperceptible nod.

The medical room is already prepared for me. A gown is waiting, and the doctor tells me to change before stepping out to give me privacy.

I glance toward the metal tray beside the bed. Neatly packaged supplies are lined up for the exam, and I don't think I've ever felt more like a victim. Forcing my gaze away, I move closer to Giulia. I don't need to say anything; she just knows. I kick off my shoes, and she grips the waistband at the back while I hook my thumbs in front. Together, we ease my leggings down, her pulling them outward so they don't scrape against my raw skin.

I lift my arms, and she slips my shirt off before helping me into the gown. I feel utterly exposed, wishing the doctor would hurry so I can leave.

When she returns and asks me to open the gown, I shrug it off. She can start with my butt. I still don't know what it looks like, and I'm not ready to find out. I can tell just from how painful it is to sit that it's not good. She works her way over me, noting every detail on her tablet, documenting each injury and bruise.

When she goes to draw blood, my body starts to tremble from nerves. My arm is extended, my breathing shallow as I try to calm myself.

Dom steps to the other side of the table, sliding in front of Giulia. He bends down and kisses me, catching me completely off guard. When he smirks and playfully nips at my lip, pulling away, my head instinctively follows.

He leans back in, parting his mouth for me. This is the kissing I'm used to, not the drug-induced hallucinations where the Cristiano version of Dom was a terrible kisser. Dom's mouth is soft, moving exactly how I need him to at the perfect pace. He tastes exactly as I remember and smells even better.

I pray the moan I might have let slip was only in my head, but as we keep kissing, I stop caring if anyone heard it.

When he finally pulls away, reality settles in. The doctor stands beside the bed, waiting patiently. My blood has already been drawn, and a strip of pink tape is wrapped neatly around my elbow.

Glad I didn't feel any of that happening. I probably would have puked, then passed out. The passing out portion I was already well on my way.

"She doesn't like needles," he explains, resting his hand lightly on my ankle.

"Not many people do," she says with understanding. "You have a small tear inside your anus. It should heal on its own, but I would advise against any anal penetration until then."

My eyes go wide, my face heating instantly with embarrassment as her words sink in. I chance a quick peek at Damiano, my pulse thundering in my ears, but he just gives my ankle a reassuring squeeze, his expression calm.

I quickly look away, my fingers twisting in the thin paper sheet covering the exam table as I try to suppress the sudden, overwhelming urge to hide under the paper.

The doctor leaves the room and I try to focus on anything other than her telling us we can't have butt sex until my anal tear heals.

I feel like anal is one of those things everyone enjoys but no one wants to admit out loud. The idea of someone else knowing we do it is mortifying. And now the doctor knows I had stuff shoved in my ass—as well as my boyfriend, who wasn't even the one to shove said items in there.

I don't know why I'm suddenly shy in front of him. He's fucked my ass more than Cristiano ever did, because he knows how much I love it. But right now, I just know my cheeks are crimson.

When she returns, she's holding a small stack of papers.

"I ran a full panel." She passes the results to Damiano. "All the tests came back negative."

I blink, letting her words sink in.

It hadn't even crossed my mind that I might have an STD.

Damiano's grip tightens slightly as he scans the papers.

I lean over, my heart racing as I lock onto the word pregnancy. My brain instantly jumps to the conclusion that I'm pregnant and begins painting a future with that monster's child.

I quickly follow the line across the page until I find the word attached to it: *negative.*

That means I'm not pregnant. He never succeeded in getting me pregnant, despite trying so hard to make it happen.

I didn't think I'd ever experience a greater sense of happiness and relief than when Damiano rescued me, but knowing I don't have Satan's spawn growing inside me really amps it up.

"How accurate is this result?" I point to the small, printed line.

The doctor glances at it. "Pretty accurate. Do you have additional concerns you might be in the early stages of pregnancy?"

I shrug. "I don't know," I answer honestly. "He was actively monitoring my periods and when I ovulate."

"How often were you sexually active?"

I feel my throat tighten, my teeth sinking into the inside of my cheek as I force myself to answer. "At least twice a day," I whisper as my lip begins to tremble. "Sometimes… upwards of ten times."

A flicker of sympathy crosses her face. "How often were condoms used?"

I shake my head. "Never."

"How often was semen left inside your vagina?"

I stare at Giulia, words refusing to form.

"Every time," she answers.

Her pen taps lightly against the edge of her tablet and then she makes another note. "When was the last time?"

The first tear slips free and I quickly swipe it away.

"She was being assaulted when we got there," Damiano answers for me, standing and leaning over the table to wrap his arms around me.

She gives a small nod of understanding.

I drop my head, folding into his chest, clutching his shirt as I begin to cry. One hand comes up to cradle the back of my neck as he presses a kiss to the top of my head, whispering how much he loves me.

"We'll test again in a week or so, unless you have any pregnancy symptoms before then. We can also give you a preventative medication that will terminate a pregnancy, especially in the early stages, if you'd like to take extra precaution."

"Thanks," he says, dismissing her.

She offers a tight-lipped smile before slipping out of the room.

Chapter

THIRTY-FIVE

Rainey

As we step outside, the warmth of the afternoon sun hits me, and I pause, tilting my face toward the sky, soaking it in. I'm really here. I made it out of there. But I also stabbed Cristiano, and somehow, I know it wasn't fatal. He's still alive. I can feel it. And the worst part is, I'm relieved. I should punch myself in the nose for even thinking that.

Damiano's truck is parked on the side of the house, just like always. He moves ahead of us, opening the passenger door for me to climb in first.

I try to avoid his gaze, but I risk a glance his way. The second our eyes meet, he blows me a kiss.

I'm not sure why the simple gesture of his lips puckering like that has me weak in the knees and butterflies swarming in my stomach, but it does, and I'm extra thankful my grip holds firm on the grab bar, keeping me from falling flat on my back at his feet.

The familiar scent of leather and cedarwood wraps around me, and my body reacts inappropriately given the circumstances. My nipples pebble and moisture pools between my legs, so I squeeze them together, willing my body to stop.

Giulia climbs in after me, eyes wide as she takes in the interior.

Damiano rounds the front, and I track him the entire way, still unable to believe he actually came for me. As he slips behind the wheel, I try to act unaffected by our closeness. He's so devastatingly sexy I can hardly stand it, and that ripped body of his—swoon.

My knee begins to bounce at the mere idea he might be able to hear my thoughts, but now that seems suspicious.

"How long ago did you guys leave?"

He looks at me, at my lips, then up to my eyes. For a second, I think he's going to kiss me, but he doesn't, and I'm immediately disappointed.

"We got word yesterday of your whereabouts. We were on the plane within an hour."

"What if I wasn't there?"

"Wasn't the first time we went to a location after getting tips it's where he had you."

My mouth falls open as I wonder how many times we were moved just in time to avoid Dom finding me.

"Was Cristiano being tipped off you were coming?"

"Yeah. Months back we arrived minutes after you left. The bed was still warm."

I know exactly which night he means. We got woken up and I was taken from the house wrapped in a blanket, Cristiano in a robe, and Giulia wearing his discarded shirt. It was the same night I'd returned to the bedroom after being sick, when Giulia crawled into bed with Cristiano, and then they both proceeded to have sex with me.

I'm not mad at her for participating. I'm mad that she seemed pleased by his praises afterward, knowing I didn't want it.

We drive in silence the rest of the way, the familiar landscape rolling by, the trees casting flickering shadows across the windshield as we wind our way home.

When we finally pull into the driveway, Giulia's mouth falls open as the massive house comes into view.

"This is where you live?"

"Yeah," I reach over to take her hand. "You do too."

Her eyes flick to me, then back. She might find it impressive for the first couple of weeks, but after months of never getting to go anywhere, she'll find it just as suffocating, maybe only slightly less than the mansions Cristiano kept us in.

"I assume we still aren't allowed to leave the property?" I ask, my tone more resigned than questioning.

He pulls into the garage, shoves the gearshift into park, then shuts the truck off. "We will do whatever we want. You want to go somewhere, I'll take you."

"Let me think on that. I'm sure I can come up with a million places I'd like to go."

"Wherever, whenever."

As we walk toward the door, he scoops me up bridal style.

I laugh as I kick my feet. "What are you doing?"

"Carrying you inside."

"Okay," I shrug, letting it be what it is.

He strides down the large corridor, stopping in the living room entryway and setting me down.

Nikolai stands from the couch, his jaw going slack as he takes me in. This is the first time he and I have been able to acknowledge each other without commotion all around.

Cue the waterworks.

My lower lip trembles as I take a shaky step toward him.

"He told me he killed her," I choke out. "I heard the gunshot before I was drugged."

Nikolai's eyes squeeze shut for a brief, agonizing moment before he crosses the space between us, his long strides eating up the distance.

He wraps his arms tightly around me, lifting me off my feet.

"Even if that were true, I would have never blamed you."

I cling to him, burying my face in his shoulder. I avoided him because I didn't know how to tell him I heard his twin get shot. I didn't want him to yell at me or say he wished I'd been the one killed instead. He was the first Volkov—Dom included—who truly talked to me like I was a person and not a *"worker,"* or so I thought at the time. Granted, he was on babysitting duty, but he made me feel better. I've always felt at ease with him. He just has that way with people. Even now, I feel safe.

"I have a bone to pick with you," he chokes out in a small, breathless laugh. "I've never cried so much in my entire life with you being gone, and I'm not ashamed to admit it."

I manage a weak smile as I pull away.

"Well," I whisper, glancing over my shoulder at Damiano, lingering on the massive, muscle-bound frame leaning casually against the wall, his thick arms crossed over his chest, "it seems your brother has never worked out so much in his entire life."

Nikolai smirks, his grip on me tightening before he sets me down.

"Yeah," he agrees. "He opted out of sleeping and instead pumped weights."

Dom doesn't seem amused by our bantering, especially since he was apparently so upset about me being gone that he spent the entire time working out. But I don't understand him being bothered when he refused Cristiano's trade.

"You probably want to get settled in. I'll be in the game room if you want to shoot some shit," Nikolai offers.

Giulia looks at me confused, and I fight back a grin. "He's meaning on a video game."

Dom takes us upstairs to Giulia's room, a massive suite directly across the hall from Nikolai's. It's beautiful, but I can see her unease as she steps inside. I feel it too, the instinctive discomfort of being separated from her again. We just went weeks apart without talking. Her and I have a lot of relationship mending to do, and being separated like this will only delay that process.

Once we've adjusted and fallen into a new routine, we can learn to be apart, but right now is not the time.

As I get ready for bed, she joins me in the bathroom. I stand at the counter, legs crossed, my bladder uncomfortably full as I grip the cool marble edge bowing my head. I chew on the inside of my cheek, the pressure building in my lower abdomen—a twisted, self-imposed torture.

"Maybe you can just go?" Her voice is cautious as she keeps glancing nervously to the closed door.

I know I can. I know Damiano would let me. That's not the issue. The issue is I want to feel the euphoric release of having the pee sucked out of me along with the orgasm I always received, one last time.

I keep drinking, opening another bottle of water as Giulia watches with concern.

"Rainey, you don't have to—"

"I don't care," I snap, growing more irritable as the pressure rises to an unbearable point.

She wasn't the one forced to do the things I was. She wasn't the one who felt the shame and embarrassment. And she doesn't understand how the pain is worth the pleasure.

She shifts beside me. "Are you gonna ask him to—"

I cut her off. "God, no."

She hesitates. "Then what are you doing?"

"I don't know," I admit. Because the truth is, if I had a way to contact Cristiano right now, I would. I'm desperate to feel his mouth between my legs.

Damiano walks in, stopping when he sees us. I meet his gaze in the mirror and just stare.

"Everything okay?"

"Yes. You can close the door on your way out," I dismiss him.

His brows furrow, and he takes a step toward me.

"I said get the fuck out!" I scream, chucking an empty water bottle at him. It misses by a foot, not that I was actually trying to hit him.

His chin jerks back at the outburst. After a moment, he bends down, grabs it and walks out, closing the door behind him.

"Lock it," I tell her as I begin frantically undressing.

She hurries across the room, flicking the lock into place, and I'm already moving to the shower, stepping inside and sitting on the floor. I immediately rub my clit as I shove the other hand between my legs, sinking two fingers deep into my channel. I tip my head back, picturing Cristiano beneath me, his tongue lapping at me as I grind against his face.

The familiar tingle of an approaching orgasm courses through my body, and I move my hips faster, letting out the first moan as the pressure builds. I quicken my pace, my breaths coming in desperate gasps, and the orgasm rips through me. My chest heaves as I finally release the pee I've been holding, my body trembling as the warmth flows out.

As soon as the high fades, I slump against the shower wall. The disgust hits me like a punch to the gut, the realization of what I just did crashing down on me. I can't believe I thought about Cristiano while I made myself come.

I hate him so much.

I stand, turning the shower on and quickly rinsing off, washing away the shame along with the evidence of my desperation. Then

I spray around to rinse away the traces of my betrayal. I'm not proud of what I just did, but I do feel better.

"I can help you with that," she offers.

And I know she can. We got good at getting each other off—she knows exactly what I like. But now that we're no longer with Cristiano, there's no reason for it anymore.

"Thanks," I say awkwardly, embarrassed that I just snapped at her. "Sorry. I shouldn't have been rude."

"Apology accepted."

She follows me to my closet where I pull out pajamas for each of us and we dress in silence.

When we leave the bathroom, Damiano is sitting at the end of the bed on the bench, waiting. He stands as soon as we walk out, his dark eyes locking onto mine.

For a split second, panic surges, thinking he might have heard me. I shove the thought aside quickly. If he didn't, I don't want him asking questions, and if he did, I definitely don't want to explain myself.

"Hey," I say softly.

"Hey," he responds, his gaze shifting to Giulia, hovering beside me. "Giulia, I need to talk to Rainey. Nikolai is in the living room watching TV, and my sister will be here soon," he adds, politely dismissing her.

She looks to me for what to do. I can see the muscle in Damiano's jaw ticking.

"This is me attempting to be decent," he says, his patience wearing thin. "I need you to get out so I can talk to my girlfriend."

Giulia's eyes dart between us, and I force a reassuring smile, mouthing, "It's okay."

She sighs, her shoulders sagging as she slips past him. He strides behind her, shutting the door firmly and flicking the lock into place.

As he turns to me, I cross my arms, wanting to appear annoyed by this interaction but also to shield myself.

"I don't know what's going on." A hint of frustration bleeds into his tone. "I'm trying to be here for you, but you can't keep shutting me out. I don't know how to help if you won't talk to me."

I force a casual shrug. "I'm fine."

He jerks his chin toward the bathroom. "What just happened in there?"

I follow his gaze, my stomach twisting as I try to keep my expression neutral. "Nothing."

His nostrils flare as he takes slow, measured breaths, fighting for control.

"Babe."

"Nothing happened," I say, my tone firmer this time.

"What's with all the water?"

My mind races for an excuse, a plausible lie that won't make him question me further. Maybe I can tell him the truth. But I can't bring myself to do it. I don't want to. He has no right to judge me.

"I'm trying to stay hydrated."

He shoves his hands into his pockets, the muscles in his neck popping out as he stares, wrestling with whatever he's about to say.

"What?" I snap, my defenses instantly flaring.

He tilts his head, lips pressing into a thin line. "I think this is about more than just wanting to stay hydrated."

A flash of anger tries to take hold. "Dom." I try to keep my voice steady. "I mean this in the most respectful way possible, but you don't know me. A lot has changed in the months I was gone. I mean, we're literally arguing over me drinking water."

I huff out a bitter, humorless laugh, my head shaking to show just how crazy I find this conversation.

"It's not about the water." His tone is clipped. "I know it's not just you drinking water. But we aren't getting anywhere with your attempts to gaslight me."

I scoff at his absolutely correct accusation. "Okay, great," I snap. "Am I free to go?"

He looks to the door, then back at me. "Of course you are, babe. You're not a prisoner here."

I force a sarcastic smile, not really trying to hide my anger.

Not a prisoner.

Right.

I stride away, but before I can grab the handle, his voice cuts in.

"I'll say this once, and I'm not going to say it again."

I glance over my shoulder, waiting for him to continue.

"When I tell Giulia we need a private conversation, she will excuse herself immediately. If she ever questions me again or refuses to leave, neither of you will like the outcome."

I hold his stare for a long, tense moment, wanting to tell him to fuck off. But I settle on rolling my eyes and striding out.

Chapter

THIRTY-SIX

Damiano

Rainey has been home for a week, and she's struggling more than I expected.

She and Giulia are more attached than I thought they'd be, practically glued at the hip. I didn't realize neither of them would be willing to do anything without the other. They're so intertwined that even the smallest separation sends them spiraling.

Rainey refuses to go to the main house, and I still haven't figured out why. I have my suspicions, and they're only reinforced when Ma stopped by to check in and Rainey locked herself in the bathroom for three hours, claiming she's too sick to come out. Now, anytime the doorbell rings, she gets frantic, demanding to know who it is. She's been fine with all other visitors, especially Dante.

Every night, she falls asleep in the bedroom with me, but every morning when I wake, she's gone. The bed is cold and empty, and I find her and Giulia curled up together on the couch.

Something is going on with her and the way she drinks water nonstop.

I can't figure it out. She locks herself in the bathroom with Giulia for long stretches in the evening, and every time, I hear muffled moans. I don't want to blow the roof off the house, but if I find her and Giulia having sex, I'll send Giulia right back to where she came from.

I've tried to ignore it. Tried to brush it off as them just comforting each other and recovering however they can.

But tonight, when she disappears into the bathroom again after chugging more water than should physically fit in her small body, I wait.

I press my ear to the door. When I hear that soft, shaky sound, like the tail end of a moan followed by a low, shuddering breath, I walk in, scanning the room.

Rainey is in the shower, naked, her head tipped back as she touches herself and… pees.

I freeze, struggling to process what I'm seeing.

This is what the water is about? Needing to pee in the shower?

I'm so confused.

"Uh, Rainey," Giulia says as she slowly stands from the edge of the tub. She stares at me with a mix of shock and guilt.

Rainey whips around, her wild, panicked gaze locking onto mine.

Then her face twists into a mask of fury as she shoves off the wall, her finger stabbing in my direction.

"Get the fuck out!"

I stand my ground.

"I'm not going anywhere."

She vibrates with rage as she reaches for the shower handle, twisting it on and grabbing the detachable sprayer.

"You're a fucking voyeur now? You fucking creep."

She rinses off quickly, scrubbing at her skin.

When she shuts it off, Giulia hurries to her with a towel.

She snatches it, wrapping it around herself, her eyes still locked on mine as she steps out, then storms past me to the closet.

I follow, watching her rifle through her clothes.

"You're mad at me?" I can't seem to connect what I did to make her this upset.

"Yes!" she shouts. "The door was locked. Meaning I didn't want you coming in!"

"I'll remove every lock in this house if you think you can start trying to keep me out."

She lets out a bitter laugh, allowing her towel to fall to the floor before yanking her shirt over her head.

"Maybe I wanted to pleasure myself without you being around."

I'm struggling to process what she just said and why she's so hostile toward me.

"Why?"

"Because, Dom! I went from being fucked over and over all day long to not being touched at all. You haven't touched me once. Not one time. You haven't even tried to have sex with me. Am I disgusting to you? You can't stand me? Why did you bring me back then, huh?"

I open my mouth, but the words stick in my throat.

I have made a colossal mistake.

Because I do want her. I want her more than I can put into words. The thought of her skin against mine, her body tangled beneath me, sinking my cock into her warm, wet pussy—it's all I've thought about since I got her back.

But I assumed she wouldn't want that right now.

I don't know everything she went through. I don't know the full extent of what she was forced to endure on a daily basis, the horrors she had to survive. But I know the man she was with. Things wouldn't have been easy.

I thought we'd have a conversation about sex when she was ready.

I thought she'd come to me when the time was right, when she felt safe enough to tell me what we could do, what we couldn't, what felt good, and what brought back nightmares.

I wanted to make sure she was comfortable, that I didn't cross a line or push her into something she wasn't ready for.

But now, seeing the hurt in her eyes, I realize the error in my thinking.

Chapter

THIRTY-SEVEN

Rainey

It's harder being back than I thought. Way harder.

I don't like the attention. I hate when people keep asking the same question.

How are you doing?

What do they expect me to say?

Oh, you know. Your brother murdered a man's pregnant wife, and then your mother handed me over as a peace offering. I was beaten and raped every single day. And now I'm back on the same property with the woman who arranged it.

There's no guidebook for this.

I'm thankful to be home, but guilt eats at me. Dom has only ever been with me, and I've been with… well, I don't know.

I feel disgusting.

He deserves more than this. More than what I can offer him, which is absolutely nothing except my used vagina.

I keep thinking about Cristiano. About how likely it is he'll come for me. It's not a matter of if. It's when. Which makes running away with Giulia pointless.

And pretending things are fine feels impossible.

I don't want to be near Dom, not because I don't love him, but because I can't stand myself.

I can't take the way he looks at me like I'm still the most precious thing he's ever beheld. I hate the way he touches me like I'm still clean. He runs his fingers over my hair, along my arm and back in unspoken affection. He kisses me constantly, like his mouth needs to stay connected to me, always in soft, nonsexual ways.

He's perfection. And all I do is stain it.

I'm in the bathroom, my usual routine playing out, with Giulia beside me at the counter, her eyes downcast as I force myself to chug another bottle of water. She gave up on trying to talk me out of this. My mind is set. She can either stand with me in support, or go away when I'm in here. She chose to stay.

My stomach is already bloated, the fullness mounting, my legs crossed as I try to hold it in, to recreate that feeling, that rush, that twisted need I can't seem to shake.

Locking the door was the last thing on my mind when I got in here. Not that a locked door would actually keep Dom out, since he blew through it a week ago and caught me red-handed, mid-orgasm, peeing all over his shower as I fingered myself.

Beads of sweat gather at my hairline as I pinch my eyes shut, holding out until the last possible second to undress. I have to push myself to that place of absolute desperation, the edge of sanity where Cristiano exists, just to be able to come picturing his mouth on me.

Déjà vu hits when Dom storms in, his body radiating barely contained fury.

"Giulia, out!" His voice is one notch below shouting. The sharpness of it makes her recoil.

She slips past him without a word. He stares at me for a beat, then strides out, the bedroom door slamming shut seconds later.

The silence doesn't last long. I hear his footsteps again, heavier this time, before he storms in and grabs the empty bottles.

"We're done with this."

"Okay?" The sarcasm in my tone is unmistakable. "I already drank those."

"What is going on?" he snaps.

"Nothing!"

"This isn't nothing!" he jabs a finger at my tightly clenched thighs as I begin to lose the battle of holding my bladder.

"I don't want to talk about it."

"Why?!" he drags his fingers through his hair, gripping the strands so tight it looks like he's trying to pull the answer out of himself.

"Because!" My voice wavers. "Because there are things you can't help me with. There are things that…" I trail off, feeling foolish over this and not wanting to vocalize what I've been doing.

"Things that what?!"

"Things that I do that I'm ashamed of! Things that I feel that I'm ashamed of! Because right now, all I want is Cristiano."

He looks at me like I punched a puppy.

I wait with bated breath for him to tell me to get out. Honestly, I wouldn't blame him if he did. I'm sick in the head.

"What does that mean?"

I shift, the pressure in my bladder reaching a breaking point.

"What is this?" he shouts, gesturing to my legs.

I look down, my cheeks burning as the words claw their way up my throat.

"He made me drink water all day. I had to hold it until it hurt so bad I wanted to cry. Until it felt like I was going to explode. And then…" I force the disgusting, vile words out. "And then he had me pee in his mouth while he… while he pleasured me. I hated it. I was humiliated. But it felt so fucking good. I crave it. It's all I think about."

For a long, agonizing moment, the room is silent.

"So this," he sweeps his hand up and down my body, "this is all over a kink he had for you urinating in his mouth?"

"Yes," I choke out.

He studies me, taking in all of me, before returning to my face.

"You want to piss in my mouth?" he asks. "I'll let you. If that will fix whatever this is, tell me what you want. Want me in the shower? Want me to lay down right here? What?"

I shake my head, horrified, like somehow he's a monster now too, just for trying to help me.

"No."

"Yes," he counters, stepping toward me.

"No," I say, backing away. "You're not part of this. I don't want you involved."

"I'm already involved." He closes the distance, his body towering over mine.

Panic surges through me, and I bolt past him, rushing toward the bedroom.

He catches me by the waist, pulling me to him. His chest presses against my back before I'm twisted around to face him.

My palm flies up, connecting with his cheek hard enough to turn his head to the side. The sound registers the same time my jaw drops—immediately scolding myself: *What did you do?!*

For a split second, his eyes flare with anger. Then his lips crash against mine, hard and desperate. He threads through my hair pulling me closer, his tongue rubbing against mine.

I'm lifted off the ground, my legs gripping him while I mold into his body. We frantically tug at each other's clothes, barely making it to the bed in our rush to be closer.

Our shirts fall away, and I fumble at the button of his jeans before pushing them down over his hips. They land at his ankles, and he kicks them aside. Then he shoves me onto the bed, grabs the waistband of my shorts and panties, pulls them off, and tosses them over his shoulder.

His palms slide along my inner thighs, nudging them open. His gaze drops, dark and heavy-lidded, lingering on the slick warmth.

A hungry groan escapes him as he leans forward, brushing a kiss to the tender spot just above my center. His tongue drags from back to front, sucking on my clit, and I nearly black out from the blinding pleasure. When he pulls away, I want to protest, but then he climbs onto the bed, kneeling between my spread legs.

The shift of the bed under his weight jostles my body in just the wrong way, sending a sudden, urgent pressure to my bladder.

"I have to pee," I gasp.

He smirks, teeth grazing the curve of my neck. "We're past that." His tongue flicks over my pulse point before he bites down.

"I can't hold it," I pant, as he shifts his hips, the thick head of his length pressing against my entrance.

"Don't," he murmurs, pushing forward. The first inch of him sends a ripple of euphoria through my body from the stretch.

"Oh." My head falls back, nails digging into his shoulders as he withdraws. Each thrust meets resistance; my body isn't used to his size as he works himself in deeper. His pace builds, breaths come faster, each one a rough exhale.

Every ounce of anger fades away as I lose myself in the man I love and in being intimate with him again.

He doesn't slow, his strokes growing deeper and faster, my body tightening around him as I clench my core in my best attempt to hold everything in.

"I can't—" I choke out, my body seizing up and quivering. There's no chance of holding it in any longer.

He sits on his heels, keeping himself buried deep as he begins to push down and pull up on my hips. It started slow, but he's moving me so fast now, I cry out in pure bliss.

"Holy shit." I arch fully off the bed, clawing at the sheets as I lose the battle. My body convulses. The release tears through me as wetness rushes out between us, and I have no ability to contain the sounds coming from my mouth.

He rolls onto his back, still gripping my hips as I settle on top of him. My thighs frame his waist, and I plant my palms on his knees as I take over.

I move on instinct as I ride him, head tilting toward the ceiling as our moans blend together.

His fingers trail up my chest, curling around my throat, squeezing as he watches me move above him.

I lean forward into his hold, craving it tighter. A strangled whimper slips out as my orgasm crashes over me. I grind down, my body shuddering with each roll.

Suddenly, the door bursts open, and Giulia charges in, looking frantic, yelling, "Stop!"

Her steps falter as she takes in the scene, her expression shifting to one of stunned confusion when she sees he isn't hurting me. I'm the one in control.

Nikolai barrels in right behind her. I'm guessing, by her reaction, she had him thinking something bad was happening.

He wasn't trapped with Cristiano. He wasn't forced to watch or listen to me being raped constantly, his own trauma etched into his memory. But he can see it in her: the way her body tenses, the wild, panicked look in her eyes. Her mind is flashing back to the things that happened, struggling to separate my past from the present, where I have a choice.

His hand falls away, and I suck fresh air into my lungs, my palms still pressed against his chest.

She's frozen in place, staring in disbelief, and I'm struggling to tell her everything is more than okay, because I'm too out of breath to get the words out.

Nikolai's mouth pulls back in an awkward, silent apology. "Let's step out here." He reaches out gently, touching her arm. His tone is calm as he adds, "I'll make you some tea."

I can see it in her face—realization that Dom and I were having consensual sex, even while it must have sounded like something crazy was happening.

"Rainey," she whispers.

"I'm okay." I swallow hard.

"You were being hurt. I could hear you screaming." Her gaze flicks from me to Damiano.

"I'm sorry." I sniffle, wiping the sweat from under my nose. "It was a good scream, I promise."

I motion to Dom, who is completely drenched—and not with sweat—hoping she'll understand I found a different solution to my *problem*.

Her brows draw together.

"Did he hurt you?"

"No." I shake my head.

She stands there, unwilling to leave.

"I'll come out in just a second. I can't get up yet," I say, my walls clenching around him.

He lets out a moan, his eyes rolling back. "Don't do that."

Whether it finally clicks or just pisses her off, I don't know, but she scoffs and briskly walks away.

Dom grabs my hips, thrusting up, and my lashes flutter closed as I smile.

"Carry on," Nikolai waves, closing the door behind him.

"I think I'm in trouble," I whisper, slowly sliding off him. We both watch as he slips free, his erect cock still standing straight up, slick with both of our fluids.

I roll off him, staring up at the ceiling. He turns his head toward me but stays silent.

"He said you were offered a trade and you didn't take it." I turn to meet his gaze.

He doesn't speak for a long moment. "You can only trade what belongs to you. He tried to bargain with something that wasn't his. I would never trade anything when it comes to you because you are mine. Accepting a trade would mean I'm okay with what he did. It would mean I'm admitting defeat. That I don't have any other way to get you back. But I would have burned the entire world down just to find you. I told him I would never agree to a trade because I'm going to kill him, and I will get you back myself."

"Were you that confident he wouldn't kill me?"

"Knowing how much you meant to me, he wouldn't have just to spite me. Knowing who you are as a person and your undeniable beauty, I knew he wouldn't because, as much as he'd try to fight it, he'd want you for himself."

"Did you think he would force himself on me?" I hold my breath as soon as the words leave my mouth.

He doesn't even hesitate when he responds, "Yes."

"And you were okay letting it happen?"

He shakes his head. "No. Even if I had agreed to a trade, he wouldn't have let you go. I'd be dead, and you'd still be with him. If we'd shown up too soon, he wouldn't have hesitated to kill you just to make sure I never got you back—because for him, it was always about causing me the most grief. But the longer you were with him, the more his feelings for you grew, and that made killing you impossible. Instead, he had to find a way to keep you and keep me from ever finding you. I think those feelings grew a lot faster than he expected."

I'm not mad he didn't trade himself, and I never considered what he just said as a possibility. I guess I truly know nothing about this world.

I chew on the inside of my cheek, remembering when Cristiano said *the man you cry for doesn't want you*. That stung so bad, and I believed it. But now, hearing this, I don't know what to believe. "So you still wanted me?"

He rolls onto his side, pulling on my waist until we're face to face.

"There's not a single thing that could ever make me not want you."

My stomach sinks and I look away. He lifts my chin again, forcing me to meet his eyes.

"Stop. Your brain needs to stop."

I shake my head. "I was helpless. And I had sex with him sometimes… willingly, because it felt… good."

He leans in, kissing me softly.

"Sex does feel good. You don't need to feel bad about that."

"How do I not gross you out? Do you not just see all the other men that have forced themselves inside of me?"

He shakes his head.

"Not even once. I see myself inside you."

"Would you feel like we were even if you got a free pass to sleep with whoever you want for one night?"

He bites his lip and nods.

The gut punch I feel is swallowed by a kiss.

"I choose tonight, and I choose you. Only ever you, baby."

I wrap my arms around his shoulders as I kiss him, hoping my tears aren't dripping all over him. When I pull back, I see they have.

"Sorry," I say, wiping them from his cheeks and then my own.

"Are you apologizing for the blue balls I'm getting lying here?"

I look down, and he's still straining hard.

I let out a choked laugh and roll onto my stomach, wiggling my ass.

"I sure hope a sexy, muscular, tattooed man doesn't—"

My words are cut off by him straddling my legs and pressing inside me, my sentence dissolving into a moan.

I DIDN'T MEAN FOR US TO HAVE SEX FOR AS LONG AS WE DID. I GUESS we had some catching up to do.

We come out of the closet still damp from the shower, and I spot the clock. Four a.m. My eyes widen, and I gesture toward it in disbelief.

"Yeah, we can sleep in tomorrow," he says, yawning.

I make a beeline for the door, yank it open, and walk quickly down the hall toward the living room. Giulia, Nikolai, Niki, Anya, and Silvano are scattered across the furniture, all fast asleep.

I spot the empty cup of tea on the coffee table by Giulia and walk over to it, lifting it and sniffing.

I arch a brow at Damiano, tapping my tattoo. It's the same tea Nikolai gave me that night.

He winks, holding his hand out to me.

Chapter
THIRTY-EIGHT

Rainey

I wake to darkness, the room still cloaked in silence. I lower my hand over the edge of the bed, expecting Giulia to take it like she always does when Cristiano uses me. But her fingers never find mine—and even as I lie on my stomach, he doesn't penetrate me.

I kick the blankets off, hoping he'll hurry so we can go eat. Still, nothing.

I scoot my foot across the bed, pushing against his leg until I hear him mumble.

"Can we do it so we can eat?" I spread my legs wider for him, trying to hurry this along.

"You still horny, baby?"

My mind draws a blank. Why is he asking if I'm horny? He's the one who needs morning sex.

The mattress dips as he scoots closer. He grabs my thighs and presses them together before settling against my back and brushing a kiss to my jaw.

"Good morning, beautiful." A playful bite to my cheek has me smiling. Damiano used to do that to me every morning.

"Let's go eat," he murmurs.

What? I'm slightly disappointed he doesn't want sex. My vagina apparently woke up craving it.

As the curtains begin to open automatically, I rapidly blink away the light filtering in. It's daylight? We never sleep in this late. I spot the patio chairs and stare, disoriented. When I turn to look around, Damiano is getting out of bed. I sit up fast, trying to understand where I am.

"What's wrong?" he asks, hurrying to my side of the bed.

I tried to sleep with him, fully convinced it was Cristiano. *What the fuck is wrong with me?*

"I'm so sorry."

"Stop. You didn't do anything."

Though he knows exactly what just happened.

"Where's Giulia?" I'm already rushing to the door, pulling it open and full-blown tripping over her as she lies sleeping at the bedroom door. She wakes up with a startled squeal, and then Niki and Silvano are rushing toward the bedroom to see what's going on.

I lie naked on the floor. Damiano is naked in the bedroom with a full erection, and Giulia is scrambling to her feet.

"My knee," I groan.

"Jesus Christ, Dom, put that away," Niki says, holding up a hand to block it from her view as she hurries over to me just as he does.

He scoops me into his arms and carries me to the kitchen, where he grabs an ice pack and gently presses it to my knee.

"I'm sorry," Giulia says, sitting in the chair next to me, lifting my feet and placing them in her lap. "The door was locked."

"Well, typically if a door is locked, that's a good indicator you're not expected nor wanted in that room." Dom says dryly.

"Says you." I hit his shoulder as I gape at his rudeness.

"What? It's the truth."

"Doesn't mean you have to be a dick. Plus, funny coming from you when you also don't know the meaning of a locked door." I give him a pointed look.

"Speaking of dicks, you one thousand percent need to put yours away," Niki says, wrinkling her nose.

"Why are you in my house?"

She plops a grape in her mouth, then throws one at him. He catches it, snapping it right back at her so fast I almost miss it. I would have, had it not been for the grunt she let out when it nailed her. "Ass." She laughs as she turns and walks back to the living room. "I'm hanging out with my best friend. My annoying brother just also happens to live here too."

The front door opens and Giovanni walks in. He comes straight to the kitchen and leans on the counter. He doesn't even try to hide the way he takes in my entire body with lust-blown eyes.

"Up here." I swipe my first two fingers, forcing his attention off my boobs.

He does and winks. "Still just as sexy." Then he jerks his chin toward my knee. "What happened?" He doesn't wait for an answer, just turns to Dom. "You injure her in here?" he pats the surface of the counter.

"*I* didn't injure her."

"Why are you both in here naked?"

Dom scoffs. "Is everyone forgetting this is mine and Rainey's house? We're allowed to be naked."

"Your nakedness is offensive to my eyes," Niki calls from the couch.

"It's gonna get a lot more offensive when I bend her over this counter."

"No," I groan. "My knee hurts. Take me on the couch."

His arms wind around me from behind. "Who's coming to make breakfast?" He asks Giovanni.

"Ma is having Cleo make breakfast. I was coming to round you all up."

My face falls flat, and I stare at Giulia. She reaches over, taking my hand and giving it a squeeze.

"I specifically said someone needs to come out here." Dom bites out.

Giovanni shrugs. "Ma wants everyone having breakfast at the house."

Dom lets out a frustrated sigh, straightening. He goes to the fridge and scans the contents.

"It's fine, babe."

He looks over his shoulder, trying to figure out if I really mean it. After a long pause, he eases the door shut and stays there, leaning back against it with his arms still behind him. His gaze lingers on me for a moment before he exhales.

"Wanna go have breakfast in the city?"

That question shouldn't terrify me, but it does. Anything beyond this property means danger. The last time I left, I was taken. I don't even need to answer; he can read me like a book.

He comes over, twists my chair, and scoops me up. "C'mon, let's get dressed."

"I'd hate for something to happen. Why don't I step in and carry her for you?" Giovanni calls after us.

I laugh as I flip him off.

"Gladly," he calls.

I'm carried to the closet and set down on the velvet pink chaise lounge. He steps back, leaning against the island dresser with one ankle crossed over the other, fingers tapping a slow rhythm as his gaze drags over every part of me.

"Dress, shorts, or pants?"

I raise an eyebrow. "You're picking my outfit?"

"Yes."

My legs stretch out, one elbow supporting me as I try to be provocative. "Then you pick."

He draws in a breath through his teeth, then pushes off the dresser, moving toward the racks as he starts browsing.

Giulia walks in and looks at him, then at me.

"He's dressing me," I explain.

She nods in approval and goes to select her own outfit.

She glances at Dom as he lifts a soft-colored dress from the rack, then turns to grab something else, likely a backup.

Once she's finished, she comes and sits next to me. We both watch him with admiration. It's funny, seeing a massive, tattooed man walk around naked in a white and pink closet, yet somehow, it only makes him seem more manly.

When he comes to me holding the items I sit up, staring directly into his eyes as I lift his now-limp dick, licking from the bottom of his balls up the underside of his length. I take it fully into my mouth, then pull off, dragging my tongue across every inch before standing and taking the clothes.

"Thanks," I say, brushing past him.

His mouth falls open and Giulia laughs.

"Rude," he teases, spanking my butt, then leaving.

After we get ready, we linger in the space between the closets. She sits on the bench while I look at my reflection. He picked a taupe cardigan that hangs open over a white satin camisole, partially tucked into distressed denim shorts, then sandals with rhinestones on the straps. This is probably one of my favorite outfits, just for the fact that he picked every piece of it.

He's bent over in the chair near the entrance to his closet, tying his shoelace. I pause in the doorway, crossing my arms. "What do you have planned today?"

"Nothing. What's up?"

"Just wondering if you had to work or anything."

"Not that I'm aware of."

I rub my palms up and down my arms, avoiding his gaze.

"What's on your mind?" He steps in front of me while I press myself against the wall.

"Did you… check up on my mom while I was gone?"

He nods. "Yeah." Offering nothing else.

"And?"

"And Ricardo went to jail for six months for a domestic distur-bance. Darla got a new man. Ricardo was released and Darla took him back. Nothing will change."

I pick at the skin around my nail, hating that I asked.

"We can pull her out and clean her up, if that's what you want. But babe, she's been this way your entire life. It's who she is."

I know she won't change. After everything I went through, part of me still hoped she might have felt a fraction of my pain and reached out to see if I was okay. Maybe that *motherly bond* had kicked in and she knew what was happening to her daughter… her only child.

Instead, while I was being sexually assaulted day after day, she had moved on with a new man. Of course she didn't care. This is the same woman who handed me over to be a sex worker just to save herself from her own debts. For a while, I tried convincing myself she knew all along Dom wanted me to be his girlfriend, that I wasn't really going to be used in all the disgusting ways she signed me up for. But the truth is, as much as I wish it weren't, my mom is a piece of shit.

"I'm hungry," I murmur, pushing off the wall, standing chest to chest with him.

"Then let's eat." He bends down and kisses me.

As we pull up to the house, Dom parks in his regular spot along the side, while Giovanni cruises straight to the front. I always found it funny that he does that because he says he hates having to walk from where Dom parks, so he just helps himself to front-and-center parking.

I slide across the seat to Dom's side, and he lifts me out, placing me on my feet before closing the door.

"Hey." He grabs my waist and pulls me to him. "If you don't want to be here, we can go home."

I give him a small, appreciative smile. "Thanks."

"Do you want to talk about what you're worried about?" he jerks his chin toward the house.

"I'm fine." I lie.

He knows I'm not telling the truth, but he doesn't push it. He sighs and smiles back. "Lets go eat."

Chapter

THIRTY-NINE

Rainey

Throughout breakfast, I keep glancing at Dante, and each time he's already staring at me. I haven't seen him in days. He was checking on me consistently, and then it stopped. I know how busy he is, so I'm not even bothered by it. He's also incredibly perceptive, and I'm guessing he knew I couldn't stand the way people looked at me, with sad eyes that made me feel like a victim all over again.

I just want to be treated the way I was before I was taken. The guards who once gave me dirty looks, handcuffed me, and dragged me to the *Fun House* now regard me with pity. Most of them avert their eyes immediately if I head in their direction, but I can still feel them lingering. I catch the silent exchanges between them when they think I'm not paying attention.

I focus on eating, avoiding that end of the table, yet I can still sense every gaze. Giovanni has apparently left all shame at home; if we make eye contact, he either grins or winks. He's a flirt, and I actually prefer this side of him to the version I saw previously. Back then, he always seemed like a jerk, though most of the time I saw him he was injured. I guess that would make sense, he was probably in a lot of pain or high on medications.

Valentina seems happy I'm back, and it's bothering her I'm steering clear of her. Really bothering her. She calls and texts Dom all day every day, then works her way through the rest of the kids, trying to find a good time to come see me. But it has to be for show. She literally orchestrated the kidnapping, and there's no way she could possibly believe Cristiano wouldn't tell me. Yet, here she is, spending her breakfast honed in on me.

There's random banter going on around the table, and all I want to do is leave. I don't even have an appetite anymore. I'm under a microscope and I hate it.

I turn toward Dom and hug his bicep, squeezing the solid muscle. It's quite literally bigger than my thigh. Cute aggression takes hold, and I bite his arm, waiting for him to tell me when it hurts, but he doesn't say a word. When I finally unclench, I admire my teeth marks on his tattooed skin, then rub my cheek over it like a cat.

"How long will we be here?"

"Why? Wanna sneak upstairs for a quickie?"

"No. But I'd be agreeable if you're ready to go."

Before I was taken, if he had asked me if I wanted to sneak off for sex I would have already been out of my chair. But prolonging my time here isn't something I'm trying to do.

"If you're finished eating we can head out."

"Where's Tess?" I'm just now noticing I haven't seen her once. And Marko was with a new girl. I'm assuming they had a falling out. Maybe she finally decided not to renew her contract. It sucks that being gone meant I didn't get to say goodbye.

The banter dies down, and the room goes silent.

Dom stares at Dante, and when I glance around, the rest of them flick between us. I straighten, scanning the room. "What?"

Facing Dom again, he lifts his brows, draws in a deep breath, and rubs his hands down his thighs.

The air feels heavy as everyone waits. I can already tell this isn't going to be good.

When three men stride in, the tension breaks, and the focus shifts from us to them.

I recognize two of them; they're undercover workers. Their presence never means anything good, and I'm willing to bet Dom is, in fact, about to be working.

One of the men nods to Lorenzo, then to Dante, and begins speaking without needing to be asked.

"It was the club off Ninth. We've been watching it under Gio's orders. He suspected three regulars. Said the numbers weren't adding up and money was bleeding out. Thought someone on the inside was skimming. They kept their wins relatively small. One would distract the dealer, the second would swap cards, and the third was feeding signals to the guy at the table. It took time to catch the pattern, but once we did, we reviewed the camera angles and dealer rotation. Everything lined up. They've been cheating for months. We estimate the loss at around two million."

Giovanni gives a single nod at the recap.

"We informed Gio last night," the second man adds. "He said to bring them in." Then he looks straight at Dom. "They're downstairs."

I exhale loudly and release his arm.

"I'll be back as soon as I can." He kisses me, then turns and walks off with Dante, Lorenzo, and the others.

Giulia stares after them. "What was that all about?"

I shrug. "Dom's gonna be working for who knows how long."

"Working doing what?"

Nikolai rises and playfully pulls on our hair, distracting her from me having to answer that question.

"Feel like shooting some shit?"

Niki laughs. "Can we play a game that doesn't involve weapons?"

"Where's the fun in that?" he counters.

"I'll try," Giulia says. "It sounds fun."

We follow them into the living room, and they all take their places on the couch. I hear a faint whistle and turn to find Dante nodding for me to come to him.

I round the couch and stroll into the kitchen, grabbing a bottle of water from the fridge, then lean against the island counter. He stands next to me, his hip resting against the same surface.

"How are you? *I'm fine.'* Good. Now, how are you really?"

I stifle a laugh at the way he played out both sides of the conversation.

"Talk to me," he murmurs, hooking his finger in my belt loop, tugging gently.

"I have nightmares sometimes. And sometimes I wake up and forget that I'm in bed with Dom. I expect morning to be the same as they were… with *him*." I pick at the bottle label, then look up.

"Have you talked to Dom about it?"

I shake my head. "No, but he knows."

He nods. "He doesn't miss anything."

"The day you guys rescued me, I planned on dying." I pause, the words heavier than I expected. "I purposely pushed him, hoping he'd snap and just end it. I woke up that morning convinced it was over for me. And when we were running to the boat… all I could think about was getting far enough out that I could jump overboard and swim toward the bottom, hoping that by the time my brain kicked into survival mode, I'd be so far down I'd drown before I ever made it back up.

"When I heard Nikolai's voice, I thought I'd been shot. I thought I was dead. I thought that was him welcoming me into whatever came next, telling me it was going to be okay."

I blink back tears. "By the time I was running toward the house, all I could think about was getting to him, because if I truly died running into gunfire, being with someone safe… it was worth being riddled with bullets. And when I saw Dom… after everything—every second of being terrified, every beating, every time I was assaulted—my entire world was in front of me, and all the pain and suffering slipped away."

I lift my eyes to him. "And you… you being there too…" My throat tightens. "I don't think you'll ever understand what that meant to me. I don't even know how to say it right, because Dom was what I needed, and then you were there and only then did I feel like I truly had everything I needed. So… just—thank you."

He reaches out and squeezes my hand, eyes welling with tears. "I haven't been able to release how relieved I feel that you're home and safe. I want to hold you more than I can vocalize."

I nod, and a silent understanding passes between us.

He pushes off the counter, and I follow him through the house to his office. Inside, I go to the couch, slip off my sandals, and climb on, lying on my back and holding my arms open to him.

He does the same, leaving his shoes beside the couch before settling half on top of me, his arms slipping beneath me as we hold each other. We lie there in silence, both quietly crying. All the what-ifs of what could have been linger between us, heavy and unspoken. But beneath that is the relief. Relief that he came for me. That they all did. Dom, Nikolai, even Giovanni. And Dante. The man who never takes time for himself, who drowns himself in work, stepped away from it all on the chance the tip was real.

On the chance I was there. On the slim chance that was the place they'd finally find me.

"Tell me about you guys coming for me."

He gulps and after a long moment he finally speaks.

"We got word on your location and headed out immediately. When we landed, my contact confirmed you were still on the property and said we'd be able to get to you, but warned us he might try to kill you first. All Dom knew was that it was your last known location and that a man and a woman had just left. He was already thinking you might have been taken somewhere else.

"We were told there were seventeen guards outside and at least twice that inside, plus given a partial layout of the house and the spot they believed you were being kept. With that much protection, we had to move carefully. Dom's our best shot, so we let him believe we might find clues about where he'd taken you if we could get inside. He and Gio cleared the guards outside while we sent in the first wave of our men to deal with the initial line inside. Then we split into groups. Nikolai and I went to the spot they told us you'd be, while Dom swept the main floor.

"I was in the room next to Nikolai when I heard him call your name. I knew he'd spotted you. But when I got there, you were gone and a boat was speeding away. I thought you were on it, and all the hope I had just… slipped away. Nikolai started firing and I assumed he was trying to stop the boat.

"As I headed downstairs, Dom, Marko, and Silvano were coming toward me, saying there was nothing in that direction. Gunfire was everywhere, smoke filling the halls. Then I heard Gio shout, *'In here!'* right as bullets came our way. Dom didn't even pause—he went straight toward them.

"When I got into the room and saw him holding you, I've never felt relief like that. I didn't think I deserved to feel that much happiness. Then we locked eyes, and I wanted to drop to my knees and thank whatever god had brought you back. But when I saw the state of your body, I felt sick. I held it in for as long as possible but puked before we got on the plane."

I hug him tighter, sniffling. "Thank you. Thank you so much Dante. For being there."

"Thank you for being so brave and strong."

I JOLT AWAKE AT THE SOUND OF A LOUD HUFF, FOLLOWED BY DOM dropping into the chair at the end of the couch, his head flopping back as his fingers rake through his damp hair.

"Sorry. Didn't mean to wake you," he whispers.

Dante is still asleep on me, our legs tangled together. My eyes widen, and I try to sit up, my heart pounding at the possibility of Dom now knowing what Dante and I have done in the past.

He holds up his hands to stop me. "I just need to sit for a bit. Go back to sleep."

He looks exhausted as he leans into the chair.

When I glance at the clock, it's already past seven.

"Where's Giulia?"

He doesn't even open his eyes. "In Niki's room."

I let out a quiet sigh of relief knowing she's safe.

When I blink awake, Dante and I are now in reverse positions. He's leaned back against the arm of the couch, and I'm curled against his torso. He talks with Dom about whatever information they got from the men in the basement. Their voices blend until I focus on Dom in the same chair.

"Hi, sleepyhead," he says, reaching over to wiggle my toes.

I give a lazy wave, then run my palm back and forth over Dante's chest before sitting up and climbing over him. I stretch my arms above my head and yawn, then slip my sandals back on.

"Do you guys still need to talk?"

"We can head home, babe," Dom says, going to get up.

"I was gonna go check on Giulia."

"Yeah, okay. Just come get me when you're finished."

"Okay." I turn to Dante, and he stands as I approach. "Thank you, Dante." I step into his embrace and hold him.

"Thank you." He kisses the top of my hair.

I brush a quick kiss against Dom's lips as I pass, then make my way toward Niki's room. I stop in the hallway, just outside the doors, staring at them blankly.

The last time I was at these doors, I was dolled up for a party, thinking the only man who would touch me that night was my own. None of us knew I was walking toward my rape.

It feels like the air is knocked from my lungs all over again. I take a step back, then another, and another, until I'm pressed against the opposite wall. My vision blurs as I try to focus on the double doors, shifting into a distorted image of lines. My legs start to give out, and I slide down the wall until I'm sitting.

And still, I remain fixed ahead.

Flashes of the dress Niki let me borrow, and then the dress being torn. The heels Dom brought me, dangling from his fingers as he handed them to me, and then the strap being undone and a penis rubbing against my foot. Niki doing my hair, and then it being pulled and messed up.

I close my eyes, letting out a shaky breath, folding my knees to my chest as my mind begins to spin and spin and spin.

Damiano left me after I was raped. I slept with his brother. He didn't leave me. He was getting revenge for me. He still wanted me. I was dirty and tainted, and he still wanted me. My nipples were bitten and sucked on, and he cut theirs off.

I gasp and clutch my chest. It feels like my ribs are folding in. My vision warps, and I start to panic. I rock slightly, trying to fight it off, but the memories come harder now.

Cristiano. The way he smiled before, during, and after hurting me. The softness in his voice while he tore me apart from the inside. I was never locked in a cage, but I lived like I was. Trapped by his control. Owned and conditioned.

My own mother never even cared to see me. She never knew what I went through.

Tears burn my cheeks. I press my hands to my face, trying to squeeze it all away, but the images just keep flashing.

My body forced open.

Damiano.

My breasts bruised and bitten.

Damiano.

The slap across my face.

Damiano.

The pressure of a penis being shoved in my mouth.

Damiano.

The pain of a cock being shoved inside my butt, splitting me apart.

Damiano.

The horrified stares at the Volkov party when we reentered.

Damiano.

Every ugly moment. Every cracked part of my mind. Every piece that starts to float loose, unhinged and jagged. He appears, pulling the pieces back in, sealing them together.

Each fracture closes around his image. Each broken part fuses with the memory of him looking at me like I'm the most precious thing to ever walk this earth.

I don't know how long I've been sitting here, crumbling apart and putting myself back together all at once.

But when I finally focus on the doors, I don't see the girl walking out of the room with her boyfriend and best friend straight to her rape.

I see *him.*

My everything.

The love of my life.

The new him. The one that's still mine and different. He's bigger. So much bigger. He seems hardened yet, still soft. He still looks at me with the same loving expression, only it's deepened. Damiano loves me. Damiano truly loves me.

On trembling legs, I stand and suck in a deep breath, then let it out before taking my first step toward Niki's door.

"Rainey?"

I turn to see Andrei standing at the end of the hall just outside his bedroom, two of the girls peering out from inside the room.

"Are you okay?"

"Yeah," I offer my best smile. "I'm coming to see Niki and Giulia."

"Should I get Dom?" His brows are drawn together with concern.

I shake my head. "No. I'm fine. Have a nice night." I wave and open the door.

Once I step inside, the only light comes from a small lamp in the corner. I walk further in, hoping the room layout hasn't changed. To my relief, it hasn't.

When I reach the bed, I find them curled up the same way Giulia and I do, sound asleep. My heart tightens at the sight. I want to get in and squeeze them both. The two women who were beside me at various times of my kidnapping, the two who had to witness the terrible things he did to me. And now here we all are, together.

"You being a creep or planning on climbing in?" Niki teases.

Giulia's eyes open, startled and wide, and she looks over quickly to see who Niki's speaking to. The second she sees me, her whole body softens.

"I just wanted to check on you." I fold over the side of the bed and wrap her hand in mine, kissing her knuckles.

"I'm okay. How are you?" Her voice is hoarse.

I hold her hand to my cheek. "I'm okay too. I think Dom and I are gonna head home. You gonna come or…?"

She turns to Niki.

"Why don't you hop on in here with us, and we can have a sleepover?" Niki leans over Giulia and pats the other side of the mattress.

"I mean, if she's staying with you, I'm gonna take full advantage of an empty house and go have filthy sex with your brother."

"Yep, yuck. Giulia will be fine here." She waves for me to go.

I crawl on the bed and peck Giulia, then climb off. "Love you both."

Back in Dante's office, Giovanni has now joined them. The conversation doesn't sound as tense as what I woke up to.

I lean against the side of Dom's chair and comb my fingers through his hair. "Giulia is gonna stay here tonight. Wanna go home?"

He looks up, and I pinch my lips together in silent invitation.

He stands so fast. "Yep. Later," he calls over his shoulder, holding up a peace sign. Then wraps his arm around my neck and pulls me to him, striding out of the room.

Chapter

FORTY

Rainey

Every time Dom and I have a night like last night, I let myself believe I'm not broken. That maybe I'm still capable of love, of being loved. We rode each other for hours, giving and taking, licking and sucking like worshippers at an altar. I tasted every inch of him. He devoured me in return. It felt perfect. Whole. Like nothing outside the room existed. None of the pain, the past traumas, mattered while we were tangled together.

But now the sun is up, and all of that heat has cooled.

And I hate myself again.

The moment the high fades, all I'm left with is the crash. The reminder that I'm not worthy of him. That he deserves someone clean. Someone untouched by the filth I've been dragged through. Not someone who used to belong to Cristiano. Not someone who doesn't even know where home is anymore.

Because I don't have one. Not really.

I don't belong here. And I damn sure don't belong with Cristiano. The only thing in this world I feel tethered to is Giulia.

I've been sitting on the porch swing since the sun started to rise, numb and weightless. My head is propped against the chain it's hung from as I rock back and forth, not because it's soothing, but because I need something, anything, to keep me moving when I feel like I'm sinking. If I sit still too long, I'll disappear.

"How are you, sweetheart?"

My entire body goes still, and the swing comes to a stop.

"Please don't go." Valentina reaches out a hand as I start to rise. She walks toward me slowly, keeping to the railing, careful not to come too close.

"I can't begin to imagine everything you've been through," she says quietly. "Our family was falling apart without you."

I huff a dry laugh. "Funny. I thought things were supposed to be better."

The way her expression falters tells me she wasn't expecting that. Now she's watching me closely, trying to gauge how much I know.

She leans against the railing, eyes fixed on mine. "I'm so happy you're back."

I glare at her. At her audacity to say that to my face right now.

"How long have you been out here?" she asks, softer now.

I inhale deep, hold it in, then let it out slow. "Not long enough."

"What's on your mind?"

I don't look at her. I just keep staring ahead. "Where I'll go when I leave."

"Leave?" she echoes, shifting slightly like she wants to come closer but knows better than to try. "You're thinking about leaving?"

"Not thinking about it. I am leaving. It's obvious he broke me. I can't be with Damiano anymore. And I don't care to wind up back with Cristiano. If he finds me, I'm dead anyway. I just want somewhere I can go to start over."

"Sweetheart, anything broken can be fixed," she starts.

"I don't want to be fixed." I glare at her. "I want away from your family. I want to live somewhere safe."

"This is the safest place you could be."

I push my tongue into my cheek, biting back a condescending smile. "For you, maybe. For your family, absolutely. But for someone you don't even want here? It's nothing but fear."

"Rainey, *we* are your family."

That actually makes me laugh. A bitter, humorless sound as I shoot to my feet.

"No. You're not. None of you are. I wish your family had just left me the fuck alone. Every single nightmare I have comes from your goddamn family."

"What's going on?" Dom asks as he steps out in just his boxers, hair messy, eyes still heavy with sleep.

"Nothing," I snap.

Dom looks to Valentina, waiting for an explanation.

I turn to him instead. "You said you'd take me anywhere I wanted to go."

"Yeah," he says, nodding slowly.

"I'm gonna go get Giulia. Can you take us to the bus station?"

He looks between his mom and me, confusion written all over his face. "Babe, what's going on?"

"For starters, I'm not your babe. Secondly, I want the fuck away from this entire freak show."

"What did you say to her?" he snaps at Valentina.

She looks stunned. "Nothing. I didn't say anything."

"She just got here."

Dom turns back to me, eyes narrowing. "Then what changed?"

"What changed?" I let out a bitter laugh. "Oh, I don't know, maybe the fact that I was kidnapped, beaten, and raped every single day."

"…I meant what changed since last night."

I snap my head toward him. "I came to my senses. And I can't stand another second around any of you."

I spin on my heel and storm across the wraparound porch.

His footsteps pound behind me.

I break into a run, shove the front door open, and try to slam it shut, hoping it latches before he catches up. But he's right there, stopping it with his foot.

I sprint down the hall and reach the bedroom, fumbling to shut him out. He forces his way in easily.

"Don't!" I scream, throwing my hands up between us like that's enough to keep him back. "Don't touch me. Don't even look at me."

He stops mid-step, arms dropping to his sides like he doesn't know what else to do with them.

"Rainey, talk to me."

"I don't want to talk!"

He doesn't move. Just stands there, taking up all the air in the room. The walls feel like they're shrinking. I suck in a breath, but it catches in my throat.

"I just want to leave. I need to get out of here. Away from you."

"You're not leaving. I'm not letting you go through this alone."

"Stay away from me! You need to stay away, Dom. I can't even breathe when you're near me."

"I'm not going anywhere." This time, there's no softness in his voice at all.

A broken laugh escapes, ugly and bitter. "Of course you're not. You never do. That's the problem, isn't it? You're the problem. It's your fault. All of this, everything that's happened to me, it's because of you. Because you just decided you wanted some random girl who was having dinner. A little fucking charity case you could try to fix. Well, guess what? All you've done is fuck me up more.

"I'm broken. Cristiano broke me. I was handed over to him, and he broke me. And it's your fault, because you forced me to be here."

He just stands there, looking at me like he's willing to take it. Like he's willing to let me vent, and he won't judge me.

I press my hands into my eyes, trying to hold it all in, but the dam breaks anyway. A sob tears through me.

"How can you even stand to look at me? To touch me?"

I scrub at my face uselessly, blinking through tears that won't stop. "I'm disgusting."

He grabs my wrists, not rough, but firm enough that I can't pull free. I thrash against him anyway, but he doesn't let go.

"Because I love you," he says with certainty. "And there is nothing, nothing that could ever make me not want you. I will kill him for what he did to you. I will hunt him down and kill him. If you want to be the one to do it, I'll let you. But he's going to die. That's a fact.

"And you will never have to suffer alone. Your pain is my pain. And I'm here for you."

I squeeze my eyes shut, trying to block it out, trying not to feel the way my heart aches at his words.

But I do.

I feel all of it.

"You don't even know the half of what he made me do."

He pulls me to his chest, locking his arms around me in a hug so tight I almost can't breathe.

"I don't know everything that happened." He shakes his head. "But you can tell me. Tell me everything."

Everything?

How the hell am I supposed to say it out loud?

"Want to swap stories? I've done things that would make you sick. The kind of sick where you'd hurl right where you're standing. We've all done things that cause nightmares. Do you really think I'd judge you? I've done worse, so much worse than you could ever imagine. If anything, that should tell you we're perfect for each other."

"But you don't have feelings," I shoot back.

We stare at each other, the silence stretching for a long, tense moment.

Then, suddenly, we both start laughing.

I lean back against the wall, my head tipping until it rests against it, eyes still on him.

"Talk to me," he whispers, pressing his forehead to mine. "Did Ma do something to upset you?"

I close my eyes and slowly shake my head.

He lets out a sigh, then puckers his lips, pressing the faintest kiss to my mouth. It's so light I wonder if I imagined it.

When it ends, we stay close, foreheads pressed together, breathing the same air.

I slide down the wall until I'm sitting, wrists resting on my knees. He follows and settles beside me, our shoulders brushing as we lean into each other like we did on the bus.

He stretches his legs out in front of him and crosses his ankles. I keep my knees tucked in, and his hand reaches for me. His fingers press between my legs, resting gently on my thigh.

"I think I was being conditioned to hate your name," I whisper, my eyes fixed on his thumb as it moves slowly back and forth. "Every time you were brought up, he'd hit me. Sometimes just remembering that we were together was enough to set him off. And when it did... he'd hit me so hard."

His grip tightens around my thigh, not out of anger, but to show he's here, that he's listening.

"I knew it wasn't your fault," I go on. "But eventually, my body stopped waiting for logic. Hearing your name just meant pain. I started to feel it before it even came. I saw the signs, I knew where the conversation was going, and I tried to brace myself. But it never helped."

I slide my hand over his, lacing our fingers together, and give a small squeeze.

"Giulia was like my angel. After he'd beat me and assault me, I'd lie there numb. And she would start asking me questions about you. Like she was trying to take your name—this thing that had been used to hurt me—and give it back. Like she was helping me remember you in a way that didn't hurt. Helping me remember us.

"He was distant one day, and I don't know why, but I felt the need to ask. He told me it was his anniversary. I thought he was married and cheating on his wife. But then he told me about you, about Carmella, and the baby.

"When I mentioned the potential age gap, and how it would make her an abuser, he dragged me into his office and made me read her diaries. At first, it just seemed like a woman with a crush. Then she fell in love. But after that… the entries became hysterical ramblings. Like her mind was slipping from reality and into a delusional fantasy.

"According to her journal, Cristiano was out of town for weeks when she conceived. She hinted that it was your baby, but later claimed you never slept with her.

"So if it wasn't your baby, and it wasn't Cristiano's…"

His head tips back against the wall and he squeezes my fingers.

"It was Dante's."

My mouth drops open. I whip my head toward him, searching his face for the joke. But there's no humor in his expression, just pain.

"How?" My voice comes out shaky, and I don't care.

"She assaulted me. I was drugged and tied to a chair. Couldn't move. Dante walked in and saw it happening. She pulled a gun on him and said she'd tell everyone I raped her if he didn't do what she said. So he did.

"She tied him up too. And then she raped him. His body responded the way a man's does, even when it shouldn't. And that one time… she got pregnant.

"She announced it to everyone, smiling. But Dante and I knew immediately who the father was. I begged her to get rid of it. I threatened her. She didn't care. She said she only would if I slept with her."

"Why didn't you?"

He shakes his head staring up at the ceiling. "It's not a matter of just doing it, the issue was I couldn't get hard. I felt nothing. My body just felt nothing. It never had that reaction to anybody. Even if I wanted to, my dick wouldn't get hard.

"I demanded she terminate the pregnancy. And she looked me dead in the eye and said the Volkov genes run strong. She couldn't wait for her baby to be born just so Cristiano could slit its throat the second it took its first breath.

"That's when I knew. She had no love for that child. She was using it to destroy us.

"She destroyed me. She destroyed Dante. He didn't want the baby. He was already talking to Dr. Winn about it, already trying to cope. And then she said she knew the baby was going to be killed. She had white powder on her nose, and in that moment, I knew—she didn't care. Not about the baby. Not about anything.

"I just… I couldn't stand it. The baby was dead whether I killed her or Cristiano killed it because she was right. Every one of us came out looking just like my dad. That baby would have looked just like Dante. Just like me.

"It wouldn't have survived a day.

"So I slit her throat."

We are quiet for a long moment.

"You know about me and Dante, don't you?"

His head turns toward me. "Yes."

I meet his gaze and don't see anger. "You didn't kill him." It's a statement not a question.

He shrugs. "He messed his hand up pretty bad."

"That wasn't the only time he and I…"

"I know."

"I feel like what I'm supposed to do right now is apologize to you," I say quietly. "But an apology only means something if the person saying it actually means it. And the truth is… I'm not sorry I slept with him. Not any of the times. I want to feel bad. I know I should feel bad. But I don't."

We sit in silence for a long moment.

"I don't want Dante," I finally add. "I want you. But I don't regret my time with him, and I do love him. It's just a different kind of love. Not like the all-consuming love I have for you. That love burns through me."

"After everything Dante and I went through, Dr. Winn said we were trauma bonded. For a while, I thought that's why it didn't bother me that he slept with you. But that's not it. I realized it didn't bother me because you wanted it. I knew he did. But you did too. And that made it different."

I search his face. "How long have you known?"

"I went to the *Round Room* the day after. I saw the blood on the wall and asked who had been chained up there. When they said it was you, I knew. I knew exactly what happened. He gave in to his feelings, and afterward, he realized what he had done."

He turns his head toward me.

"I'm not innocent in this. After your rape, I didn't know how to handle your emotional trauma. Honestly, I didn't want to. Dante is better at that. He always has been.

"I had him take care of you while I was working. I thought if he could help you heal, I could have you back without all the pain. That's why I made sure you stayed with him. Because I was self-ish. I didn't want to deal with it myself. I just wanted you back… fixed."

I stare at him, the memory of the text on Dante's phone flash-ing through my mind. The one that said if Dante didn't want to deal with me, to get Nikolai. Dom knew. He had known I was with Dante. He had planned it that way.

"I didn't have sex with him the other day when we were sleep-ing on his couch. We really were just sleeping."

"I know," he replies with a faint smile.

"Would you have cared?"

He shrugs. "I don't love the idea of you going out of your way to screw my brother when I'm readily available for you anytime, but I wouldn't have been mad at either of you."

"I just want you to know… I'll never sleep with him again."

"While you were gone, Niki had to be committed to a mental institution."

My mouth falls open, and I blink, stunned.

"She couldn't handle what happened to you. What she saw happen. She started raiding the med center for drugs. She wasn't eating, wasn't sleeping. She just cried. Constantly.

"Nikolai was the same, minus the drugs. And Dante—he was falling apart. I was checking on him myself. He quit eating. Pa quit eating. Everyone started to unravel.

"And Ma… she was beside herself watching her family crumble."

It's devastating. Every word. And yet, I start to laugh. Soft at first, but then it turns into uncontrollable, hysterical laughter. I must look like a lunatic.

I swipe at the tears running down my cheeks, shaking my head as I try to catch my breath.

"Sorry," I manage between shallow laughs. "It's just kind of funny that everyone quit eating and all you did was eat."

He grins, unfazed. "Had to make sure I was irresistible when you saw me again."

"You are," I murmur, biting my lip as I stare at him. My eyes trail down the sculpted lines of his chest, then lower to his crotch. "I find you so irresistible, I want to eat all the flesh off your body."

His brows lift in surprise, but only for a moment. He turns, grabs my face, and pulls me into a kiss, his tongue plunging deep into my mouth.

I giggle, wrapping my arms around his neck and kissing him back, matching his intensity.

"I want to eat all your skin off too, baby," he says with a grin before pressing his mouth to mine again.

"Whyyy?" Niki groans from the doorway. "Why does your tongue have to live in my best friend's throat?"

I turn and see Giulia and Niki standing in the doorway, both of them smiling.

"Because she's a good kisser," Dom says, smacking my butt.

"Why are you guys sitting against the wall like that?" Niki asks, pointing to where we barely made it inside the door before he pinned me.

"Rough morning," I answer.

"Did something happen with Ma?" she asks, gesturing behind her with her thumb.

"Nothing happened with Ma," he lies.

"Oh. Did you see her yet? She's sitting in the driveway crying. She said her contact was bothering her."

"She should probably get new contacts then," he replies flatly.

"I'd ask if you had the filthy sex you mentioned last night, but you freaks left your toys on the floor." Niki lazily points to where our discarded toys are strewn about.

"Yep. It was amazing," I say with a grin, wrapping my arm around his shoulder as I comb my fingers through his hair.

"I'd fish for all the details if the sexual partner weren't my brother. But I really don't need to know anything about what he does with his—" she waves her hand in a circle toward his crotch, her face wrinkled in mock disgust.

Chapter

FORTY-ONE

Damiano

As the girls head off for their spa day, my brothers and I settle into the living room, the TV playing in the background while we chat about everything from business deals to the latest fights we've watched.

Ricco strolls in, his expression sour as he stares directly at Gio. "Been busy lately?"

Gio reclines back, one arm stretched out over the couch, his fingers tapping idly. "I'm always busy."

"Yeah, only I'm not talking about business. I'm talking about the pussy you've been picking up at the clubs."

Gio's brows lift in mild interest. "What about it?"

Ricco sighs. "You've got some psycho broad at the front gate, refusing to leave until she talks to you."

Gio rests his head against the couch, eyes closing. "Tell her to go away."

Ricco presses his lips into a thin line. "You think I'm in here because I hadn't thought of that? I told her to leave. She refused."

The corner of Dante's mouth lifts. He loves making Gio confront his actions. "Send her in."

We all glance at him, our smiles spreading. He woke up today and chose violence.

"No," Gio growls, sitting up slightly. "Don't send her in here."

A few minutes pass before a blonde woman is escorted in. Her entrance is bold to say the least, her head held high, but the confidence wavers when she takes in all the Volkov brothers studying her with thinly veiled amusement.

Her feet stall at the front of the room as she locks on Gio, stretched out, appearing bored to death.

"You looking for a job? We're not hiring," he says flatly.

Her mouth opens, then closes. Then opens again, her attitude returning in full force.

"I'm not here for a job. I'm here because you aren't answering my calls."

"And you are?"

Her jaw drops, one hand flying to her hip. "Seriously? We slept together last Saturday."

His brows lift, unimpressed. "And you decided it would be a good idea to show up at my house?"

All that swagger drains from her expression as she scans the room, suddenly realizing the gravity of her mistake in showing up here unannounced and uninvited. Her attention returns to Gio, clinging to any shred of hope.

"Can we talk somewhere private?"

"You can get out of my house."

I laugh under my breath, staring at how pathetic she looks, begging for him.

"He's not interested. Why embarrass yourself trying to convince him otherwise?"

Her face twists in irritation as she shoots me a glare, before shifting her focus to Gio.

"Doesn't want me? I'd say he wanted me just fine while he was eating my pussy. And he definitely wanted me when he was fucking me for hours, telling me he was going to make me squirt more than I ever have in my entire life."

We all turn to Gio, who doesn't so much as blink.

"Well?" Silvano smirks.

Gio shrugs. "I make every woman squirt."

Her mouth drops open, a mix of shock and fury flashing in her eyes. "Is that so?" she snaps, popping her hip out.

"Yeah. It doesn't make you special. You all do it."

"And do they all finger your ass?" she retorts.

"Only those desperately trying to stand out. It's never worked yet."

Her bottom lip trembles. "You're a bastard."

He flicks his fingers in a dismissive wave. "Get her out of here."

He turns to Dante, still looking bored. "Are we done here?"

Dante's grin stretches wider. "Yeah." He glances at Ricco. "She can leave now."

Ricco nods, grabbing the woman by the elbow and attempting to guide her out.

"Get your hands off me asshole," she yells, wrenching her arm from his hold.

He reaches for her again, and she tries the same move, but this time he's ready. This chick throws herself onto the floor in a dramatic attempt to stay put, but Ricco grabs her by the ankle and starts dragging her across the marble as she kicks and screams. The door closes behind them, and we all glance at each other before breaking into laughter.

"Always some kind of drama," Dante mutters, shaking his head.

Gio just rolls his eyes and turns back to the TV.

That chick's been gone twenty minutes now, and I still don't get it. One-night stands always end in chaos, yet Gio keeps diving headfirst into the crazy. Every week, it's a new episode.

Rainey walks in, and for a second, my heart forgets how to beat. Her hair is lighter at the ends, just like Ma had it colored when she first got here, and it falls in soft, fresh curls. Her nails are painted a deep crimson, matching her toes, and when she excitedly wiggles her fingers at me, something tightens in my chest.

"You look stunning, Rainey." Dante's eyes travel the length of her legs, up the curve of her waist, across her chest, and finally land on her face.

"Thanks," she smiles, then turns to me. "Well?" She motions to her hair, spinning in a slow twirl.

"Breathtaking" is all I manage as I sit up straighter and hold my arms open. She walks over and settles into my lap, nipping my ear. My hand travels beneath her dress, desperate to feel her, and she bites her lip when I flex my erection.

"I feel that."

I groan low enough only she can hear. "Do something with it."

She begins to respond, but Silvano, the cock block, decides to be impatient.

"What's taking the rest of the girls so long?"

"I didn't want my makeup done." She leans in closer, fingers absentmindedly toying with the hair at the nape of my neck.

He nods, glancing once more toward the spa, even though no one's coming.

Ricco reenters the room, looking more irritated than before. "Now she's throwing shit at the house."

"Who?" Rainey asks.

"One of Gio's one-night stands."

Rainey glances over her shoulder, raising a brow at him. He just smirks and gives her a lazy wink.

"Your one-night stand is here throwing stuff at the house?" she laughs.

He shrugs, unbothered. "I guess."

Once again, Dante chimes in, "Send her back in."

She returns with fire in her steps, storming straight to the same spot, immediately locking onto Gio.

It looks like she's ready to take him on, until she notices Rainey. Her whole demeanor changes in an instant.

"Who the fuck are you?"

Rainey holds her gaze. "Gio's girlfriend. Who are you?"

The girl's eyes flare, and then she's charging across the room, her hands curled into claws, rage twisting her features.

I drop Rainey onto Gio's lap, and she lets out a surprised yelp, but he wraps his arms around her protectively. I catch the girl mid-stride, seizing her by the throat, lifting her clean off the ground, and slamming her down onto the ottoman. Her eyes go wide as I press my palm tighter against her windpipe, keeping her pinned.

"Get off our property and never come back," I growl, my face inches from hers. "If you do, I'll kill you. You're not welcome here. Do you understand?"

She gurgles, mouth opening and closing as she claws at my wrist, desperate for air.

When she still doesn't answer, I press harder. Her face turns blotchy red before she finally nods.

I let go, and she gasps, sucking in a lungful of air and pushing herself upright. Ricco and Marko move in, grabbing her by the arms. At first, she goes quietly, then the screaming and kicking start up again.

Rainey is now straddling Gio's lap, her face buried in his neck. It's the only thing the girl sees as she's dragged out of the room, making her screams turn into belligerent curses and threats.

When they are out of sight, Rainey and Gio look at each other and then both start cackling.

I pull Rainey off his lap, settling into my previous spot with her leaning against my shoulder. She presses her foot against Gio's leg, nudging it playfully.

"Was she that feisty in bed?"

He shrugs. "I vaguely remember fucking her."

Niki and Anya stroll in, pausing to glance toward the source of all the screaming. Niki's eyes go wide with delight.

"Did we just walk in on Dom choking some chick out in the middle of the living room?"

"That was one of Gio's one-night stands," Rainey quips.

Anya arches a brow, giving Gio a slow, teasing once-over. "You sure know how to pick 'em."

Gio raises his hands in surrender, his eyes wide with exaggerated innocence. "I didn't invite her here. I never even told her my name or where I live. That's some straight-up stalker shit."

"Hey, now." Rainey smacks his arm. "Stalking can be sweet sometimes."

I wink at her, enjoying that my baby actually likes my stalking tendencies.

"Besides, it gives you adequate time to learn everything about someone, and if you decide you don't want them, they never have to know."

I press a kiss to her cheek. "You were never getting away," I murmur, tightening my hold around her waist.

"I mean, I could've if I tried hard enough."

"Not a snowball's chance in hell."

She looks to Niki for support. Niki shakes her head no while drawling out, "Yeah."

Rainey's mouth drops open. "I could have."

"My dearest, my brother was obsessed. And not in a cutesy, he likes you kinda way. You weren't going anywhere. Actually, remember when you came to my apartment after Ricardo got handsy? Dom was on the phone, beating the hell out of the guy who tried to steal your purse. He told me I better keep you there until he found out exactly what Ricardo did to hurt you."

Rainey looks from me to Niki. "Is that who you were on the phone with?!"

"Yeah. That's why it took me a second to open the door. I was telling him you were there."

"Aww, babe, you're so precious." She leans in and kisses me. "Where's my purse?"

"At home."

She pulls back, staring. "You kept it? Why?"

"Because it was yours. Plus, you said I could have the forty that was in it."

"And did you?"

"Take the forty? No."

"Did you take anything from it?" She lifts a brow.

I smile.

"What'd you take?"

"Your ID. And the tracker I slipped inside."

She smacks my shoulder. "You did not."

Then she pauses. Slowly, it clicks, and her mouth falls open.

I grin. "Which part are you denying?"

"The tracker. But now that I think about it, you probably absolutely did." She narrows her eyes. "But why would you have my ID? What'd you do with it?"

I sit up, pull my wallet from my pocket, and slide it out from behind mine. I separate the cards and hold them up so she can see.

She snatches them from my hand and stares at her own. "Why do you have this?"

"You look hot."

"I concur," Andrei adds casually from across the room.

He's the one who pulled a copy when he was running her info. Even then, he couldn't stop talking about how pretty she was.

Before she can respond, a couple of the girls step into the room, pausing just inside the doorway like they're not sure whether to come in or turn around.

One of them is Andrei's favorite. The other is newer, still a little unsure of the dynamic here.

Andrei perks up instantly. "What are you ladies doing right now?"

"You, if you play your cards right," Nikolai teases out the side of his mouth.

Rainey lets out a soft chuckle and gives the girls a casual wave.

"Nothing. Wanna play?" Andrei's favorite asks, flashing him a flirty smile.

"Fuck yeah," Andrei says, jumping up from the couch. "And good luck with your psycho, G." He claps Gio on the shoulder as he passes.

Gio leans his head back, drapes an arm over his eyes, and slowly shakes his head.

Rainey pats his leg, smirking. "It's okay. She probably matches your brother's level of crazy. How exciting for you."

He groans, leaning over and resting his head in her lap. "Rub my scalp. I'm stressed."

"Rub my toes, then," she shoots back, kicking off her sandals and propping her feet in front of him.

With a sigh, he grabs her toes and starts rubbing.

"Damn, that worked out better than I planned. Who's gonna rub my shoulders?"

Nikolai and Dante both open their mouths at the same time, then pause, glancing at each other. Dante grabs the remote and unmutes the TV, while Nikolai taps his thumb on his knee.

The room settles into a low hum, the movie playing softly in the background. That's when the idea hits me. It's a little risky, but it might actually work. Rainey's been frustrated lately, still feeling like she has to chug water and hold her pee for as long as possible. We've tried different things to help, but it makes such a mess, and she gets impatient and annoyed with the cleanup.

I've been researching how to make her squirt, experimenting and practicing multiple times. So far, no luck.

When Gio gets up and heads to the kitchen, I follow him.

"You busy tonight?" I lean against the counter as he scoops nugget ice into a cup.

"No, what do you need?" He glances over at me.

"I need you to show me how to make Rainey squirt."

He pauses and turns to face me, beaming.

"Sure. What time?"

"Come by around ten."

"Ten it is. Does she know?"

"That you're gonna make her squirt? Nah. She'll find out when you get there."

"Oh fuck, I get to do it?" His eyebrows lift in surprise, then he grins so wide it looks like his lips might fall off his face.

"Better hope you're as good as you claim."

Chapter

FORTY-TWO

Rainey

I towel off quickly after my shower, focused on one thing and one thing only—seducing Dom. Every inch of me is already buzzing.

I tried to go down on him during the drive back, but he wouldn't let me. Kept saying I should *save my energy*. Well, it's saved, and now it's fully charged. He better be ready, because we're skipping foreplay. I want fast and hard.

I come to a dead stop the second I step into the bedroom.

Dom and Giovanni stand mid-conversation, both going quiet the second they see me.

Giovanni leans against the bedpost, hands in his pockets, one foot casually crossed over the other. Dom stands beside him, feet planted wide, arms folded across his chest. Whatever they were talking about, it ended the moment I walked in.

"I'm so sorry," I blurt, hands flying up to cover my chest. "I didn't realize anyone was coming over."

My entire body feels like it's turning red.

Dom's lips curve into a slow, wicked grin as he roams over me. "No need to cover up. You need to be naked anyway."

I pause, flicking between the two of them. "Why?"

"Gio's gonna make you squirt."

I just blink as I try to process his words. "And why is Giovanni making me squirt?"

"Because I want to know how to do it," Dom says casually.

"Maybe I can't," I counter. "Pretty sure not everyone can."

"He's fairly confident he can make it happen."

"Fairly confident?" I raise a brow, mildly amused now.

"I can," he chimes in with a wink.

I look over, noting that annoyingly perfect smile before locking eyes with him. "And if you can't?"

"I can," he says again. "But even if you don't, you'll still get an orgasm out of it." His smile grows wider.

I glance at Dom. "But I'll probably get turned on." My gaze shifts back to Giovanni, then again to Dom.

Giovanni tips his head to the side like it's obvious. "I'm gonna be fingering you. Getting turned on is kind of the point. We won't get very far if you're not."

I swallow. He's being so nonchalant about this. My sexy boyfriend is standing here telling me his sexy, big-ass brother is going to finger me for learning purposes, and neither of them seems to be struggling with the anxiety I'm feeling just from thinking about it.

"And you're okay with this?" I ask, searching his face for any hint of discomfort.

"Fuck yeah." Giovanni smirks.

"And you are?" I ask Dom.

He points at his brother as if his response was perfect for both of them.

"Are you like… gonna watch?" I ask Dom.

"I'm not going anywhere."

"Okay." I relax. "What do I do?"

My heart is hammering in my chest, and I'm pretty sure my fingers are noticeably trembling.

Dom looks at Giovanni, who straightens and points to the bed. "Lie down and spread your legs."

Well, damn. Any chance I had of trying not to get turned on just went down the toilet at his dominance.

"Should we, like… put down a towel or something?" I ask, my cheeks flushing.

He shrugs. "Sure."

Dom grabs a throw blanket and spreads it out, then steps back, gesturing for me to climb on up.

I drop my hands, locking eyes with Giovanni as I walk toward him. At least now that hungry look is justified as he takes me in.

I settle onto the bed and prop my feet on the bench at the end.

Dom bends over the mattress, stretches out on his stomach beside me on his forearms, giving me a playful wink.

So much for staying calm. I'm already worked up more than I was just thinking about this big, sexy beast getting me off in front of my boyfriend and then I get a wink and I'm butter.

I lay back and turn to look at Dom, giving him one last chance to speak up if he's not okay with this. Maybe the idea sounded fine in theory, but now that it's actually happening, he might feel differently.

He just smiles and leans in, biting my side gently.

Giovanni pulls off his shirt, and my mouth practically waters at the sight of his broad chest and sculpted abs. Every muscle flexes as he tosses the shirt onto the chair. He hooks his thumbs into his waistband, shoving his pants down his thick legs and kicking them off before straightening to his full height.

"Are we having sex?" I ask, lifting up onto my elbows, my gaze bouncing between him and Dom.

"No." Giovanni's deep, gravelly voice sends a fresh wave of heat through my body as he steps toward me.

"Then why are you naked?"

I swallow hard, locked on his big-ass penis swinging at eye level as he gets closer.

"You're going to squirt… a lot." He grins, eyes dark and hungry as he kneels on the bench. His strong hands grab my knees, spreading my legs wide. "Those were the only clothes I brought."

He doesn't waste a second. His head dips between my thighs, tongue dragging up my slit.

Good lord. Yes, please.

I try to watch, mouth parting in a silent *O* as I take in the sight of him buried between my legs, lips wrapped around my clit, tongue swirling in slow circles before sucking hard.

My head falls back, eyes fluttering shut as euphoria takes hold. My hips lift off the mattress, hands threading into his hair, anchoring him there.

Without warning, two thick fingers thrust into me, moving in erratic, teasing patterns. I cry out, back arching, legs quivering as he works me over.

I'm in heaven.

I can't think. I can't breathe. My body's caught in this strange, disorienting limbo—torn between the urge to draw this out and the desperate need to come.

I don't realize I'm grinding against his mouth and hand until he groans. For a second, I forgot anyone else is even in the room. I'm lost in this euphoric haze, fully aware now that I'm absolutely using his face to get myself off.

"Think she can?" Dom asks.

Giovanni pulls back, eyes hooded, lips glistening. "Easily."

I want to whimper at the loss of contact, my hips instinctively lifting, chasing his mouth.

"You savoring the taste?" Dom teases.

"Absa-fucking-lutely," he says, sitting back on his heels.

This man shoves his fingers so deep into my core, his palm flattening against my clit, and whatever he does next causes stars to explode in my vision. My entire body reacts in ways I can't control. I'm pretty sure I levitate off the bed.

My vision goes white, and I claw at the sheets as I scream, liquid bursting from me in a violent, uncontrollable rush.

I collapse onto the blanket, completely disoriented, my body shaking, and I'm not even sure if I'm still a person.

When I finally lift my head, I gape at him. His broad chest is heaving as he wipes his mouth with the back of his hand, completely unfazed by the fact that he's soaked.

"What the actual fuck," I pant.

I love sex. I love when someone goes down on me. I thought I loved peeing in Cristiano's mouth. But this… this was something else entirely.

Whatever that was, it was more euphoric than all of it combined.

"Can you do that during sex?" If it's possible, I can't imagine anything better.

"Yes," he answers without hesitation.

Now I understand why he's so confident. He has every reason to be. No wonder that girl was begging for him. Right now, I'm desperate for him to do it again.

I turn to Dom, practically vibrating with need, silently pleading for him to let Giovanni show me.

Dom sits up, shifting on the bed and motioning with a small wave of his hand for me to go ahead.

Giovanni is already moving, crawling up onto the mattress, his arms wrapping around my waist as he lifts me. He settles into a seated position where I just was, with his feet propped on the bench, lowering me onto his lap.

He lifts me again by my butt, telling me to bend my knees against his sides. I do, gripping his neck for support.

One hand slips between us, guiding his thick length toward my center, the broad head pressing against my entrance.

"Lean back and sit on it at an angle," he directs. "You'll squirt again."

I'll do whatever he tells me to. He's proven he knows exactly what he's doing. Especially after I'd convinced myself it wasn't possible. Then he had me on the brink of blissful death in under two seconds.

Reaching back, I grip his knee for balance, and he holds his cock in place as I start to lower myself, his thick length stretching me open, inch by delicious inch.

Both of our mouths part as we watch his cock disappear inside me. His hands tighten around my ass as I slowly work him in.

He was right. This angle is incredible.

Once I'm fully seated, I roll my hips, my body already tightening. That same spot that shot me straight to heaven with my ejaculation is being pushed on over and over, my skin prickling. When he leans forward and suctions his mouth to my nipple, my body freezes up, and my walls clamp down on him.

He lays back, letting out a guttural groan as he grips my waist, his hips snapping upward, thrusts deep and fast, his eyes locked on me, tracking every flicker of pleasure that crosses my face.

My body seizes up entirely as I scream and writhe on him. Another intense wave crashes over me, liquid gushing out, splashing against his abs as he withdraws his cock.

He slaps it against my clit. My head falls back as he thrusts in and withdraws again, another violent burst of liquid exploding from me while screams I've never heard before rip free.

My muscles spasm as he wraps his powerful arms around my waist, flipping me onto my back as I gasp for air.

"One more." I frantically open and close my hands at him.

He presses my thighs wider, positioning himself between them, then lays on top of me as he drives in again. I wrap myself around him, holding on so tight I don't even want him to withdraw a centimeter as the tingles take over again.

As he keeps moving, I revel in the way my skin prickles, every nerve alive and sparking. I grip his ass, pulling him deeper while rising to meet each thrust. A loud moan escapes as it happens again. Liquid rushes from me, and he slams back in, drawing out even more.

A deep hum lingers through me as the high fades, and I finally sink into the bed, struggling to steady my breathing.

I can hear them talking, their voices low and muffled, but the words don't land. All I can register are thick fingers slipping back inside me, hitting that same spot rapidly. My hips jerk off the mattress, hands clawing at the sheets as I scream. My entire body convulses as another wave crashes through me, more liquid gushing out.

It happens again, and again, and again, locked in a cycle of intense, uncontrollable release.

I squeeze my legs together, unsure if I can survive another one. I half expect that when I look down at Giovanni, his big ass will be crawling toward me, but as I stare, I realize it's Dom's hand buried between my thighs.

"Found the spot," he says.

"Fuck yeah," I sigh, dropping my head against the mattress as he withdraws, my arms draping over my eyes. "If either of you touches my pussy right now, I'll kick your teeth in," I threaten.

My body can't take another orgasm. Even the thought of them looking at me is too much for my overstimulated nerves.

"You did good," Giovanni praises, squeezing my foot as he climbs off.

"How do you feel?" I ask, peeking at Dom from under my arm.

"Pretty confident for bed tonight." He grins, his weight pressing me into the mattress as he leans down to kiss me.

"Do I get a kiss now too?" Giovanni teases, pulling his shirt on.

"Sure." Dom turns his head. "If you want me to knock your teeth down your throat."

"Sex only, it is," he laughs.

I let out a soft chuckle, finally moving my arm from my eyes as I glance over at Giovanni. "You know, we've never officially met."

He raises a brow, confused.

"I mean, we've obviously been around each other, but we've never actually been introduced," I clarify.

He steps up to the side of the bed, holding out his hand, his lips pulling into that same cocky grin. "Giovanni. I'm the man who just made you squirt."

I burst into laughter as I reach up, taking it and giving it a firm shake. "Rainey. I'm the girl you just made squirt in front of my boyfriend… who also happens to be your brother."

"I like you, Rainey. You get my stamp of approval."

"I mean, I just let you put your dick inside me. You should probably like me if you'd agree to that."

"Fair point."

I proceed to watch him as he scoops his pants off the floor, pulls them up, and adjusts his thick shaft into the waistband of his jeans.

"Why do you still have a boner?"

He flicks his gaze up, then looks down, carefully zipping up. "Because you're sexy."

"Oh yeah? So you're just… ready to go again?"

"Anytime for you, doll."

"What about both of you… at the same time?"

Giovanni perks up instantly. "Right now?"

"Absolutely not. I'm overstimulated and my nerves are shot."

"Damn. I'm free anytime." He gives Dom a thumbs up.

Once my limbs start cooperating again, I slip on a pair of shorts and a tank top, pull my sweaty hair into a messy bun, and stare down at the soaked bed. "Well, shit."

"You look hot with your hair like that," Giovanni compliments.

"I'm literally drenched in sweat." I wrinkle my nose.

"But it was worth it, no?"

"It was alright." I smirk, brushing past him as I head for the door.

He laughs, looping an arm around my neck and yanking me into him. "Ever had a noogie?"

"Ever had your dick punched into your chest?" I blink up at him sweetly, elbowing him until he lets me go, still laughing.

I turn and walk backward, facing Dom as I move.

He smiles. "I'll have someone come change the bedding."

"Maybe we need to do that in the shower next time."

"Probably not very safe," Giovanni says, running a hand through his damp hair.

"Pretty sure the way you had my body contorting wasn't very safe either."

"You're like a pretzel. You were fine."

"I am hungry," I say, suddenly realizing how good a pretzel sounds right now. "What are you gonna feed me?"

"A sandwich, since you seem to think I'm your bitch now," he shoots back.

As we step into the living room, I'm caught off guard to find everyone already there, sprawled across the furniture, their attention shifting toward us when we enter. Niki, Giulia, and Nikolai had said they'd be back later, but apparently later came quicker than I thought.

Niki is the first to speak, her nose scrunching as she stares at us.

"Uhh, did you all just come from back there?" She points over her shoulder toward the bedroom.

"Yeah," I say, trying to act casual.

"Why are you all wet?" she asks Giovanni.

His hair's soaked, and there are damp spots on his shirt because he didn't even bother to towel off.

Please be wet from sweat.

He doesn't say anything, and her eyes flick back to me, then to him.

"Yuck." She shakes her head as she grabs a pillow, props it on her lap, and leans into it.

"What?" Giulia asks, confused.

We flop onto the couch, and Niki stares again before shaking her head. "Yuck, yuck, yuck. Nope." She positions her hand to block her view of us.

"What?" Giulia's brows pull together as she glances between us, trying to piece together what she's missing.

Nikolai stares for a beat, quickly catching on to what Niki's complaining about, then turns back to the TV, focused on whatever game he's playing.

"One of my brothers is a pervert for watching people have sex, and the other is a pervert for making someone who's not his girlfriend come like that," Niki explains, refusing to look our way.

Giulia still looks confused.

"Use your eyes, Giulia. Rainey and Gio are soaking wet, while Dom is dry."

She still hasn't caught on.

"For fuck's sake. That applause we heard, the skin slapping and Rainey screaming, that was Gio having sex with her while that other little pervert probably watched." She pretends to dramatically gag.

Giulia's head whips in our direction, her gaze flicking between me and Giovanni. He just smiles, sinking deeper into the couch and throwing one foot up on the coffee table, interlocking his fingers behind his head.

Giulia's brow furrows. "How does that even happen?"

"Well," he says sarcastically, "a man takes his penis and sticks it inside a woman's vagina."

"I know how sex works!" Giulia bites out. "Why was *your* penis in her?"

"For learning purposes," Dom chimes in, his arm snaking around my neck as he pulls me into his side, his lips brushing my temple.

"La la la," Niki sings loudly, covering her ears and shaking her head like that'll erase the mental image.

I whip the pillow from my lap and hit her with it. She cackles, tossing it back.

"Why would you have sex with him?" Giulia's voice rises, laced with disbelief as she glares at me.

"It's not really anyone's business," I retort, suddenly feeling defensive from her clear disgust.

"You made it everyone's business when anyone within a mile radius could hear you."

"Good, then they know how good it felt," I retort.

Her jaw locks as she bolts upright. "I honestly don't know what's worse—you for doing it, you for letting it happen, or you for thinking it was okay to screw her when she's dating your brother." With that, she fires her judgment at each of us and storms out.

We all exchange confused glances, then Dom and Giovanni burst into laughter.

"This is all your fault," I tease as I stand, whacking him with the pillow.

His mouth falls open, arms spreading wide in a mock gesture of innocence. "What did I do?"

"You have an offensive penis." I chuck the pillow at him.

He catches it easily. "You didn't find it offensive ten minutes ago," he calls after me.

Chapter

FORTY-THREE

Rainey

I push open Giulia's door, finding her sitting on the floor on the other side of the bed, her arms wrapped tightly around her knees, her head bowed as she cries.

"Hey," I murmur, kneeling in front of her. I rest my forehead gently against the crown of her head for a beat before pulling away. "Talk to me. What's going on?"

Her head snaps up. Her eyes are red and puffy, but it's not just sadness swimming in them—it's fury.

"How could you do that?" she chokes out.

"You're blowing this way out of proportion."

"You just… you just fucked Damiano's brother. In our house."

I blink at her, not understanding why she's so pissed about it. "Why are you so angry?"

"You're just so… you're so—" She struggles for words.

"I'm so what?" I press, my own frustration building.

She stands abruptly, stepping away from me. "You're so different. Ever since we got here."

I slowly rise to my feet. "What did you expect? I was taken from here. This is my home. This is my life. My boyfriend. I'm not a prisoner with him. We're not prisoners here. We don't have to be meek, broken little puppets anymore."

She flicks over me in disgust. "I can't even stand to look at you. You literally look like you just got fucked."

The second she says it, I bristle. Because it's true. I should've showered. But what happened with Giovanni is the first thing that ever outdid the euphoric feeling I got when I would pleasure myself in the shower. And now she's looking at me like I'm something dirty. Her disappointment stings. Her judgment? That pisses me off.

"You would know best, huh?" I bite out. "You watched me get fucked every day."

Her mouth falls open, shock freezing her in place.

"I don't even know why I came with you." Her voice drops to a whisper, her eyes welling with tears. "We're from totally different worlds."

"Don't say that." I step toward her, my heart clenching. "Why would you say that?"

"Because it's the truth," she chokes out. "I don't want to live here anymore."

My heart cracks open. The thought of her leaving is a punch to my gut, a sudden ache I can't shake.

"Because I slept with Giovanni?"

"Quit saying that! I'm so done being here."

"No," I say firmly, my voice trembling. "You're not going anywhere."

She lets out a bitter, broken laugh. "So now I'm your prisoner?"

"If it means not letting you leave, then yes," I snap, my voice rising. "I'm not letting you leave me."

"Why?" she shouts. "You don't need me! You have all the Volkovs falling all over you. Nikolai will probably cry himself to sleep tonight over you sleeping with Giovanni. Dante never stops drooling over you whenever you're near. Damiano is so obsessed with you it's scary and unhinged, and you walk around hurting the people who actually love you!"

"What are you talking about? None of that is even true."

She scoffs, shaking her head in disbelief. "Either you're willfully ignorant or just cruel."

"This is quite a leap in your mood over sex."

"Dom made you sleep with another man… his brother, of all people—in front of him."

"Every decision I make, I make with Dom."

"No," she hisses, her eyes blazing. "He controls you."

"Did you forget what my life was like with Cristiano? I want to forget all of that."

"Of course I didn't forget!" she snaps. "I lived it right alongside you. I'm the one who got you help when you needed stitches. I'm the one who cleaned you up after the shit he did. But that doesn't explain why you let other men touch you now!"

"Does it make sense that I finger myself and pee in the shower just to feel something good? That I have to picture Cristiano licking my pussy just to get off? It's fucking disgusting. I feel disgusting. I'm messed up, and I'm trying to move forward, but it's not easy. So I'm sorry I disappointed you, but I'm not sorry I did it. It was incredible."

She lets out a harsh huff. "Well, you're well on your way to fucking all the Volkovs. Might as well not even be exclusive with Damiano when you sleep with whichever one of them is convenient."

I grit my teeth as I force myself to stay calm. "Seriously, Giulia. Take a nap. We'll talk when you wake up."

I don't wait for her response. I turn and walk out, leaving her to fester in her own shitty attitude.

I flop back down on the couch between Dom and Giovanni with a huff. Dom immediately drapes his arm around my neck, tugging me into his side, kissing me.

"You okay?"

"Yeah." I lean into him, exhaling. "She's never been this emotional before. And we literally just finished our periods, so I don't know what the hell's going on with her."

Nobody has a chance to say anything before she comes stomping back into the room, stopping at the side of the couch looking furious.

"You know what? I'm not done talking," she snaps, jabbing a trembling finger at me. "I don't appreciate you telling me to take a nap like I'm a toddler and then just walking out. We need to talk about this, Rainey!"

I sit up, my patience thinning fast. "Look at how you're acting. This is childlike behavior. You want to talk? Fine. Let's talk. But don't stand there and call me a slut and expect me to nod along like I deserve it."

Her eyes narrow. "You clearly got your wires crossed while you were gone. I would've thought getting out of that hellhole might've taught you something. Given you a little class. But no. You're still acting like a whore. There's another brother"—she points at Nikolai—"you gonna go crawl in his bed next?"

My mouth falls open, my blood running cold as the room falls silent for a split second. Then it explodes into a cacophony of voices, each one louder than the last, all shouting at once.

Dom is instantly on his feet, his voice a deep, commanding growl. "Get back to your room and calm down. That's the last time you ever disrespect her or my family."

Giovanni, too, is on his feet. "Shut your fucking mouth."

"You're completely out of line," Niki snaps.

"I thought you were better than that," Nikolai says tightly, barely raising his voice but looking disappointed nonetheless.

Giulia laughs incredulously, tears streaking down her cheeks. "Everyone always comes to Rainey's defense," she snarls, her voice breaking. "She had all the guards in a chokehold. Cristiano by the scruff of his neck. And all of you by your balls."

She turns to march off, but I've had enough. I jump to my feet, stomping after her. "What the fuck is your problem?" I shout, grabbing her by the elbow.

She whirls around, ripping her arm from my grasp. "Don't fucking touch me with your filthy, disgusting hands," she screams, stepping away as if my touch burned her.

"You never thought they were filthy or disgusting when I was fingering you with them," I retort.

"And I'd give anything to go back to that. Because I truly loved you then."

Damiano steps up beside me, his shadow stretching over both of us, his presence a towering wall of rage.

Giulia shakes her head, her tears falling faster. "Now I get why you wanted to come back so bad. You shit gold and have everyone in a puppy-love trance. I'm getting the fuck out of here."

"You're not leaving!"

"Try and stop me." She stomps off down the hall toward the stairs.

I turn to Dom, then glance at Niki, my chest heaving from how mad I am.

Everyone looks so angry that I have to inhale and exhale slowly just to calm my own breathing. When I look at Gio I smirk. "God, your penis really is offensive."

He lets out a laugh, his eyes widening. "No shit. She has me stressed out and that's only the second time I've ever been around her. I'm willing to take you back to the bedroom and go for round two." He jerks his thumb over his shoulder. "I think we all need to blow off some steam after that."

I shake my head. "Yeah, she has me all stressed out too. Maybe I *do* need sex."

Chapter

FORTY-FOUR

Rainey

It's been four days since Niki took Giulia to Nikolai's house so she could "calm down." I hate her being gone. Niki has stopped by twice to give me updates. She said Giulia's eating, resting, doing okay, but she's still not ready to talk.

Dom got a call about an hour ago saying he needs to work, so we get ready and come to the main house. He disappears downstairs, and I stay behind in the kitchen, standing at the counter, my focus stuck on the salt shaker.

It glides smoothly across the granite with the lightest push. When it reaches my left hand, I wrap my fingers around it and give it a firm squeeze before sliding it back to the right. I do the same thing again: grip, release, slide. Back and forth. Over and over, just trying to make sense of my emotions.

My feet move before my brain catches up. I know what I'm doing, and I know it's wrong, yet it doesn't stop me. I made sure Dom would be gone for a while so I can ensure I'm not caught.

I don't know what my problem is, but even as I sneak down the hall, there's no talking myself out of the colossal mistake I'm about to make.

I watched Dante leave a few minutes ago and waited until he pulled away before making my way to his office and slipping inside, locking the door behind me.

I hurry to his desk, pulling back the leather chair, scrambling to open the top drawer. I saw a burner phone in there when he opened it to grab the lube.

As soon as I retrieve it, I fall to my knees, crawling under the desk. I pull the chair in, my back pressing against the polished wood.

My fingers tremble as I power it on, the small screen flickering to life, the soft glow casting faint shadows across my face as I stare down at it.

I don't know why I'm doing this.

I don't know what I expect.

But I do it anyway.

I dial the number I memorized, the one I saw on the front screen of the dash during one of those long, silent drives. It's a number I never should have bothered to remember, but for some reason, as the driver called one of the guards and spoke to him through his headset, I kept reading it over and over.

The phone rings once.

Then a gruff voice growls from the other end, "Who's this?"

My throat tightens, and I squeeze the phone tighter, my instincts screaming for me to just hang up.

"Hello?" he grunts.

"Rainey," I whisper. "I need to talk to Cristiano."

The line goes dead.

I pull the phone away from my ear, my eyes wide. I stare down at the darkened screen, tears spilling over, sliding down my cheeks and dripping onto my bare thighs as I sit there.

I quickly erase the call from the history, trying to remove all traces that I was ever on it.

I push back the chair, rolling to my knees to get up, but before I make it to my feet, the screen lights up once again.

An unknown number.

I freeze, my heart stuttering as I stare at the flickering screen. I know it's him.

"Cristiano," I choke out as tears spill faster.

Silence.

I glance at the phone, wondering if the call disconnected again, but he's still there. I hover over the video icon and tap it. The screen flickers as the call connects, the small camera window sliding into place, my tear-streaked face appearing in the corner.

The main screen stays dark, nothing but blackness, but I know he's there. I can feel him on the other side.

"Are you okay?" I whisper, my hand trembling as I wait for a response.

Nothing.

I squeeze my eyes shut as more tears slip down my face. I force myself to speak again, my voice barely audible.

"I'm sorry."

Still nothing.

As I stare at the screen, I try to keep my lip from quivering.

"Can I see you?" The words come out small.

No response. He makes no attempt to turn on his camera. No indication that he's even there.

My heart sinks, the last of my nerves unraveling.

I'm such an idiot.

I end the call. My arm drops to my knees, the phone dangling from my fingers as I press my free hand to my face. My body curls inward, sobs muffled against my palm as the weight of my mistake crashes over me.

The phone vibrates. The screen lights up. UNKNOWN CALLER flashes across it.

I squeeze my eyes shut and hit the red decline button.

It immediately rings again, the same UNKNOWN CALLER flashing on the screen.

"What?" I bite out, roughly brushing the tears from my cheek. "I shouldn't have called."

"Where are you?" he asks, voice low.

"Hiding in Dante's office."

"Scan the phone around the room."

I stare at the darkened screen, unsure why he wants that, but I do as he says. Crawling out from under the desk, I rise to my knees and lift the phone, slowly panning it around the office before retreating back beneath the desk.

The camera flickers on, the small screen filling with his face. His blue eyes lock onto mine, his expression hard and unforgiving.

We stare at each other for a long, agonizing moment.

"What do you want, Rainey?" His voice is flat, and he looks at me like I'm the last person on earth he wants to hear from.

"I'm sorry," I whisper, my heart sinking as his expression remains unchanged.

"You already said that." His eyes narrow. "Why did you call?"

"I want to come home."

He scoffs, his lips twisting into a bitter, mocking smirk.

"You are home, right?" he says coldly.

I shake my head, hoping he can see the regret in my eyes. "I want my husband."

His jaw tightens, nostrils flaring.

"Do you still love me?"

He presses his tongue against the inside of his cheek, then his lips curl into a small, cruel smirk.

"I never loved you, Rainey. You were a means to get back at Damiano."

I stare at him, knowing he can see the look of my heart shattering all over my face. "You don't mean that."

Before he can respond, a hand slides into frame, long, polished nails curling over his shoulder.

"Who is that?"

He turns the camera slightly, the frame shifting. A gorgeous brunette with dark red lipstick and smoky eyes leans into view. Her lips curl into a seductive smile as she wags her fingers at the camera. Her hand glides up his chest, and her head tilts as she licks his exposed neck.

"Your replacement for the night."

Her tongue traces his jaw as she glances at the camera.

"Sorry," I whisper, my voice breaking as tears fall faster. "I shouldn't have called. I won't call again. Sorry."

I hang up, dropping the phone into my lap. My head falls back against the desk as I squeeze my eyes shut, trying to take a steadying breath.

I power the phone off and tuck it into the side of my bra, carefully putting everything back exactly as I found it.

From the main part of the house, I hear Nikolai's deep laughter echoing through the walls. A part of me wants to go ask him how Giulia is. But she obviously still hates me. She hasn't tried to speak to me or come home even once.

I make my way downstairs and step into the large cement underground space. One man sits at the computer monitors while a few others stand at various points, their gear strapped on, weapons across their chests.

In the center, a man is tied to a chair, his face so swollen his eyes don't open. Blood pools beneath him, dripping from deep cuts. The room falls quiet, all eyes flicking toward the door when I walk in. Dom wipes a knife clean on a rag, and I give a small wave, walking toward him. He meets me halfway.

My hands lift to his cheeks as I pull him in for a quick kiss. "I'm gonna go lie down in your office," I say, pointing over my shoulder.

"Okay, baby." He presses another kiss to my lips. "Did you find Dante?"

I shake my head, forcing a small, tight-lipped smile. "No. I guess he stepped out. I'll try to catch him later."

He nods, accepting the answer, kissing me once more before heading back toward the work.

"Go shut my office cameras off," he tells one of the guards. The man heads inside before me, cutting the feed so I won't have to see anything.

I settle onto the couch, hugging a pillow that smells like him, and let myself drift to sleep.

We came home hours ago. When we passed Nikolai's house, Giulia and Niki were sitting outside. The second they looked toward us, I looked away. It felt as childish as I hope she's felt acting the way she has.

At least I managed to use it to my advantage the rest of the night. Dom noticed I'd been off, and I let him assume it was because of her.

But my mood has nothing to do with Giulia. It was all about Cristiano.

I keep up that façade for five days. And for five days, Dom does his best to cheer me up. He succeeds every time, but the moment my mind wanders back to Cristiano, I get grumpy all over again.

I've been watching Dom sleep for the last three hours. I had to pretend to sleep for at least one of those, letting him think I was out while he watched me. But now, I sit here restless, hoping he isn't actually asleep. Because if he is, I already know what I'm going to do.

The longer I stay in bed, the more anxious I get. My heart races, my body tense as I try to talk myself out of what I'm ready to do. But I can't just lie here anymore, trapped in my own head.

I push the covers back and quietly climb out of bed. My steps are slow as I make my way to the closet. I slip down the far aisle to the very end and drop to my knees, digging behind a stack of folded blankets until my fingers close around the burner phone I hid there.

I power it on and wait for the screen to flicker to life. Maybe I shouldn't do this. It's been five days since I called. He made it abundantly clear how he feels, especially with that other woman joining the call.

As the phone finishes powering on, notifications flood the screen, one after another, showing ninety-seven missed calls. Every single one from the same unknown number.

A smile tugs at my lips. I've gotten under his skin. He's not as unbothered as he wants me to believe.

The phone is still flooding with notifications when the screen lights up again. The tiny video icon appears, the same unknown number flashing across the display.

I want to laugh at the fact that he must have been tracking the phone somehow, knowing the second it powered back on and calling immediately.

I take a deep breath, forcing down the smile and putting on my best frown as I press the green button. The screen shifts, the small camera window sliding into place. I expect darkness, maybe another demand to pan the room for listening ears. But we must have moved past that.

Because he's there.

He's dressed, his shirt perfectly pressed, dark hair neatly combed, jaw clean-shaven. His blue eyes are sharp and piercing as he leans back in a chair, the bright afternoon light casting a soft glow over his face.

Wherever he is, it's warm. He sits on a patio, his favored spot for his meals.

"I called," he says casually.

"I saw."

I saw all ninety-seven times.

He watches me, and the way his eyes bore into mine makes it easier to stay sad, to let him see I'm falling apart without him. The slight twitch at the corners of his mouth gives him away. He's enjoying this.

"I'm sorry," I choke out. "I shouldn't have called. It was a moment of weakness."

"Oh?" His brow lifts slightly.

I prop my phone on the shelf in front of me, worried my hands might be shaking, then wipe them on my shorts.

"I won't bother you anymore."

He shifts to one side, resting his chin on his fist, his finger pressing against his cheek as he studies me, eyes still locked on mine.

I want to tell him to go fuck himself. Or better yet, let that woman from the other night do it for him. But instead of starting a fight, I drop my gaze to my lap.

"Did I… when I… did you have to have surg…" I can't even get the words out. I don't know why I'm bringing up stabbing him.

"I survived, obviously. After you tried to kill me," he says flatly.

I look up at him, lips pinched between my teeth. I reach for the phone to hang up, but he cuts in before I can. He knows exactly what I'm doing.

"Are you drinking your water?"

"Yes…"

"And?" He presses.

His smugness makes me want to slap him. He knows he fucked me up with that shit, and it was fucking disgusting. I'm so lucky Dom didn't barf even hearing what I was doing.

"It's not the same," I admit.

His smirk widens, his head tilting slightly as he watches me, finger tapping lightly against his cheek.

"How are you managing?" His tone dripping with smug satisfaction.

"Not very gracefully."

"Well, that's too bad." He sighs, sitting up straighter.

"Baby?" Damiano's voice suddenly calls from the bathroom.

My eyes widen as I stare at the phone.

"I'll call you tomorrow," I whisper, quickly ending the call and shoving the phone back into its hiding spot, my heart still racing as I stand.

I round the corner of the closet just as Damiano steps through the doorway.

"You okay?"

"Yeah," I say quickly, forcing a smile. "I had a nightmare. Needed to change. I was sweaty."

His expression softens, arms opening as he takes a small step toward me.

"Sorry, baby. I didn't hear."

"It's fine." I close the distance between us, wrapping my arms around his waist, pressing my face into his chest, praying he isn't suspicious.

Chapter

FORTY-FIVE

Rainey

Dom, Silvano, Giovanni, and Nikolai sprawl across the couches in the game room, focused on their screens as gunfire and explosions crackle through the speakers.

I rise slowly, telling Dom I'll be back, pressing a quick kiss to his cheek before slipping out. I've put the shower situation to rest. Ever since Giovanni showed him how to make me squirt, that has been more than enough to satisfy me. But tonight, I have been quietly sneaking water because I need it if I'm going to call Cristiano.

I slip into the bathroom, adrenaline pumping as I twist the lock, then hurry to the closet, fumbling for the phone. The screen flickers to life as notifications immediately begin to pop up.

I wait to see what comes through, but it starts ringing again as soon as it loads. He's definitely alerted every time it powers on.

For a heartbeat, I hesitate, then swipe to answer. My pulse roars in my ears as his face fills the screen, morning light softening his features.

Neither of us speaks at first. We just stare at each other.

He's the one to break.

"Why did it take you two days to turn the phone back on?"

I bite the inside of my cheek.

"Because I can tell you don't even want to talk to me."

The smugness fades away and his expression hardens.

"There is a list of things I don't want, and of those things, not talking to you isn't one of them."

HA! So he does still want me.

"Did you have company again last night?"

He inhales and lets it out slow.

"I did."

I nod, mulling over his words.

"As I am sure you were in his bed."

Another nod. I was, and the sex was incredible.

His jaw tightens, then his face smooths out.

"Have you had your water today?"

"Yes." I shift, hoping he notices how uncomfortable I'm getting with how badly I need to go.

"Do you need to relieve yourself?" he asks, head tilting slightly as he studies me.

"Yes."

"Hold it," he commands, his voice firm. Then he watches me, waiting for my response.

"Okay," I whisper, forcing myself to hold his stare.

I know what it feels like to need to go so badly I could die. I remember how my body reacted, how I would adjust positions just to ease the pressure. I don't think I'd ever let myself get to that point again, but I can mimic it well enough for him to believe I'm there. So I continue to fidget uncomfortably, knowing it's convincing with how pleased he looks every time I move.

"Undress."

I swallow, stand, prop my phone on a shelf, and step back until I'm far enough for him to see me. I reach for the hem of my hoodie, slowly pulling it over my head, bare skin prickling in the cool air. His breath hitches at my exposed boobs, and I know exactly how much he likes my body from how often he's said it.

As I slip my thumbs inside my shorts, he tells me to turn around. I do, pushing them down my hips, bending as I slide them past my legs to my ankles. I straighten, step out, and face him again, fully nude.

He studies me for a long moment, jaw tightening as he takes me in.

"Your breasts are bigger," he remarks.

I glance down, not noticing a difference.

"Cup them."

I lift my hands, curling around the soft, sensitive flesh. His lips part involuntarily while he watches my movements.

"Squeeze them."

I do as he says, kneading them the way I know he likes, his features morphing to pure arousal. I keep shifting every so often, pressing my thighs tighter together so he knows I'm still fighting the need to relieve myself.

"When it gets to be too much, what do you do next?"

He's trying to fight his arousal, and I know I have him exactly where I want him.

"I… I finger myself in the shower," I admit. "Until I come… so I can pee."

He smirks at that. "Go to the shower."

I step forward, grabbing my phone as I follow his order. I prop it on the small shelf built into the shower wall, angling it so the camera captures my whole body. Then I turn back to him.

"Sit."

I do, lowering myself to the cold tile.

"Spread your legs."

I bend my knees, opening my thighs. I pray Dom's sperm isn't leaking out of me. I don't know why that didn't cross my mind to check before I turned the phone on, but here we are. If anything decides to seep out and make an appearance, then he will really know what a good time I was having.

"Part your lips."

I reach between my legs, parting my soft, sensitive folds. I act embarrassed, but with the number of times I've been humiliated and abused by this man, I can't seem to find any real embarrassment left in me.

"Rub your clit," he commands.

I press my fingers against the small, swollen bud, slowly circling it. This is something I can't fake—the incredible sensation that sparks the instant I touch myself there.

"Finger yourself."

I do, slowly pumping in and out.

"Describe to me what you envision."

I hesitate, moving faster as my hips lift and fall, chasing the high.

"Sitting on your face," I whisper, pushing in deeper.

His lips curl in satisfaction. My head falls back, the pressure building as I rock harder.

"Hold it." His voice is firm.

I whimper with the need to finish. "Please," I choke out. My eyes squeeze shut as I struggle to stay on the edge.

"Hold it," he growls, leaning closer to the camera.

My teeth sink into my lip as my fingers move faster.

"Please," I whisper, the words coming out in a desperate plea.

"Come," he orders, his voice low and absolute.

I used to think this was the epitome of pleasure, but my views have changed since Giovanni showed me what true pleasure is. So that's what I focus on. I no longer need to think of Cristiano. I concentrate on that special spot inside, the one I can't seem to find but Dom can now, and let my body coil tight the way it did, until my orgasm surges through me. Heat pours out while I shake and gasp, lost in the force of release.

As the rush fades, I slump back against the wall, meeting his satisfied gaze.

"How was it?"

I let the final shockwaves of pleasure ebb away before I turn my head lazily back and forth. "It's just not the same."

He leans back, observing me with open curiosity.

My whole body itches with regret, shame clinging to every inch of me. I push to my feet, switch on the shower head, and scrub myself clean. Afterward, I towel off, grab the phone, and retreat into the closet to dress.

"What's this mood?" he questions.

"Nothing. I want to go to bed."

"Who said we were done talking?"

I stop what I'm doing, whipping toward the phone. "When can you come get me?"

His smirk deepens. "I can't. You made this choice."

My teeth grind as I level him with a glare. "Fine," I snap. "Then I'm done calling you."

Now it's his face that contorts with anger. "You better knock that attitude off."

I roll my eyes, knowing there's not a damn thing he can do to me. "Either agree to come get me, or I'm not going to talk to you anymore."

His nostrils flare at my words, and he presses his lips into a thin line. "Keep this up, and I'll come for you just to punish you."

"Whatever," I mutter.

"Don't push me, Rainey."

I roll my eyes again and reach out, retrieving the phone, pressing the red button to end the call.

It immediately lights up again.

I hesitate for a split second, then press the green button, his sharp blue eyes filling the frame. "Don't ever hang up on me again."

"You know what? Fuck you. I snuck into Dante's office just to retrieve a burner phone to call you. I could have gotten caught. Every time we talk, I run the risk of getting caught. I just fingered myself for your pleasure, and you're still being a jackass. I'm done. Like you said, you never loved me. You have someone new and don't need me. Enjoy her, and I'll leave you the fuck alone."

"You stabbed me. Should we talk about that?!"

I've way struck a nerve.

"Yeah, let's do that. Because you were whipping me. And I was found with a butt plug lodged in my asshole, and I couldn't even get it out. It was humiliating. You treat me like garbage—"

"And yet here you are, like vermin trying to come back."

My mouth falls open, and I gape at him.

"In the most disrespectful way possible—fuck you." I end the call.

I glare at the phone as missed call after missed call comes through, until I'm filled with momentary gratification, knowing he's seething on the other end. Then I shut it off, giving my final screw-you to him, since he'll have no other way to contact me.

I WAKE UP STILL ANGRY. MY USUAL MORNING HABIT OF LYING HERE, watching Dom while he sleeps, doesn't help. I'm just as annoyed. Fuck Cristiano.

I shower, thinking that will help my mood, but it doesn't. Even as I dress, I keep glancing toward the last aisle in my closet, debating whether to wake his ass up just to tell him to have nightmares, but I know him, and my silence will bother him more than me cussing him out. I sit at the kitchen counter, sipping my coffee, picturing how mad he must be right now. The thought gives me a little satisfaction.

"Hi," a soft voice says from behind.

I startle and whip around to see Giulia standing there.

Neither of us moves at first, our gazes locked, until she finally crosses the distance and collapses into me, her body shaking as she begins to cry.

"What happened?"

She pulls me back in, hugging even tighter.

"Giulia, what happened?"

"I don't like fighting. I hate being away from you. I hate not talking."

"Then let's stop fighting."

We stay there, embracing each other. I note her boobs are noticeably bigger against mine. I know her body intimately, and this is different.

When we pull apart, I guide her to the living room, the whole time focusing on her chest. Yep. Definitely bigger.

Trying to lighten the mood, while simultaneously fishing, I crack a smile. "We must have both been PMSing. That's probably why we were at each other's throats."

She gives a weak laugh and shakes her head. "I haven't had a period recently."

I start mentally calculating all her sexual encounters and how recent the last time was. Well, unprotected sex, because Cristiano always used a condom with her. The last time was when he had those two guards assault her. Or maybe she snuck off with Niko again. Either way, if my calculations are correct... *fuck.*

She's likely three months pregnant.

We sit together in the living room, talking through all of our frustrations. The weight of everything that's happened recently lifts as we work through our emotions. It's easy between us once again. No tension. No anger. Just the two of us finding our way back to each other. She leans into me as she shares small stories, and I let her ramble, happy to hear anything she wants to tell me.

Before long, Niki wanders in, dropping down between us in the practically nonexistent space, both of us having to move our legs to make room. "Mind if I join?"

Giulia hesitates, then nods. "Sure."

Niki settles in, adding to the conversation with easy jokes and commentary. But I see Giulia isn't as relaxed as she was.

Finally, she snaps.

"I want to be alone with you for a while," she blurts, her voice cracking with frustration as she looks at me.

I blink, taken aback. "Giulia… we were alone all morning."

Her lip trembles. "That's not what I mean. I don't want people around. I want it like it used to be. Just us."

Niki seems to already know this is how Giulia is feeling. Maybe it's a conversation they've had. Seemingly unfazed, she stands. "I'll head back home and see what everyone is up to. I'll catch up with you guys later."

The second she's gone, Giulia's tears spill over. She pulls her knees up to her chest, hugging them, her shoulders shaking as she cries.

I slide closer, wrapping my arms around her. "Hey… hey, it's okay. I'm here. I'm always here."

She doesn't answer, just lets it out until exhaustion takes over. Eventually, she curls up on the couch, head resting against me as she drifts off to sleep.

By the time she wakes, it's like the storm never happened. Her eyes are clearer, her smile easy again. She stretches, letting out a yawn as she sits up.

"Sorry," she mumbles.

I brush her hair back from her face. "Don't be. You're allowed to need me just as much as I need you."

And just like that, we feel right again.

Chapter

FORTY-SIX

Damiano

Nikolai, Gio, and I are in the game room, locked on the four wall-mounted monitors as we push through another round of the first-person shooter Gio downloaded last week.

Rainey comes in, rounding the couch and stepping over Gio's leg propped up on the coffee table. Just as her foot passes over, he lifts his leg, trying to trip her.

She swats his shin with the back of her hand. "Dick." She laughs, shaking her head as he grins and drops his leg back down.

She sinks into the cushion next to me, stretching her legs across my lap, looping her arm around my neck to pull me in for a quick kiss on the cheek.

"Hi, baby." I press a real kiss to her lips before snapping my attention back to the screen, mashing the controller buttons.

Her teeth graze along my jaw before her finger traces the same path, finally drifting across my bottom lip.

"You're so sexy it makes my teeth hurt," she whispers.

I glance at her, catching the mischievous glint in her eye, and give a quick wink. She moves in closer, breathing me in as her nose glides along my neck.

"You look so good I forgot what I came in here for," she murmurs.

"Keep doing that." I shift to bring her closer.

She drags her tongue across my skin before nipping behind my ear. Then she pulls back abruptly, the reason she came in re-surfacing.

"Giulia's pregnant."

I hit the pause button without thinking. The screen freezes, the echo of gunfire cutting off abruptly. Gio and Nikolai both turn their heads, the room suddenly charged with a different kind of energy.

"What makes you say that?"

My mind is already racing. How far along is she? Does she know? Who's the father? Is she sleeping with someone here? Is she planning to keep it?

Rainey sighs. "She's been moody. Her boobs are huge. Our periods synced when we were together, and I just had mine. She hasn't had one since we got back. I guess it could be something about being here throwing her off, but I just feel it. She's pregnant."

I nod, considering what we'll do next. "Do we know who the father is?"

"Depends on the time frame. If it's who I think it is, two of the guards assaulted her when she refused to assault me."

I drag a hand down my face. "Do you think she wants to keep it?"

She shrugs. "Maybe? I don't know. But I think we should tell her."

I hold my hands up. "I think that's a conversation meant for the two of you."

I want no part in letting anyone know they are unknowingly pregnant from a potential assault that happened while they were being held captive.

Her mouth falls open. "You're not actually trying to make me do that myself, are you?"

I look to Gio for backup because this seems like something she is better equipped to handle on her own, especially given their history. But his eyes widen and he shakes his head, making it clear he doesn't want to be involved either.

She smacks my chest. "Stop it. You're there as my emotional support person."

"Babe, are you forgetting who you're talking to? I hurt feelings. I'm not sure how useful I'd be in that situation."

"Well, actively try not to hurt her feelings," she says. "Or I won't have sex with you for like a week… maybe longer."

Gio laughs, leaning back into the cushion and interlocking his fingers behind his head.

"Settle down, Chump. Doesn't mean she'll be sleeping with you," I quip.

"That is prematurely stated." She fixes me with a look that suggests it might be a possibility. And if I didn't know how much she loved sex, I might think she was bluffing, but she'd absolutely hold out on me and probably sleep with Gio in front of me.

"Soooo," she drawls.

Hormonal women and I don't mix well. I manage with Rainey because she's mine, but with anyone else, I can think of a hundred things I'd rather do. Cutting off my own finger would rank near the top.

I sigh. "Is she gonna bite our heads off?"

"Probably. But I'd be terrified too."

Chapter

FORTY-SEVEN

Rainey

Giulia asked if she could come home. The question felt silly. She's always welcome here. My home will always be hers.

I impatiently wait at the window, leaning against the frame for Niki to bring her back. When they finally pull up, excitement surges through me. I'm ready to meet them at the door, eager to see her, but I pause, watching as Giulia rounds the front of the car.

Niki stops, opening her arms, and Giulia walks straight into them. They wrap around each other and then kiss. Not a quick peck. A real kiss. A really deep kiss.

My mouth falls open, and for a second, I just stare, trying to process what I'm seeing. It's clear their time alone didn't just bring them closer as friends. It's more than that.

I often wondered if the things that happened to Giulia would make it harder for her to be in a relationship one day. I guess it would definitely be easier to be with a woman since it was men who hurt her.

I rush away from the window, moving quickly down the hallway toward my bedroom. I peer over my shoulder to make sure they haven't reached the door yet, only to slam right into Dom.

"Whatcha doin', babe?" He smirks.

"Nothing. Where are you headed?"

I notice he's dressed, shoes on like he's about to leave.

"I thought you went outside. I was coming to see what you were up to." Before I can reply, he leans down and kisses me. "Why are your lips so juicy?" He drawls, pulling me back in.

Oh, I don't know, maybe because I just accidentally caught my best friends making out in the driveway. And the "juicy" you're referring to is my upper lip sweating from said accidental sighting.

The front door opens and voices carry inside, so I drag him closer, our tongues entwining in a frantic, heated kiss.

"Do you guys do anything besides suck on each other's faces?" Niki teases.

I want to crack a joke about her and Giulia doing the same in the driveway, but I hold back. Instead, I turn toward them with a smile and step forward, wrapping Giulia in a hug.

"Hi. Welcome home."

"Thanks. I'm glad to be home."

"Nikolai is bringing dinner over now," Niki tells us as we head to the porch.

The weather is beautiful, making it the perfect evening to eat outside. Giulia and Niki sink into the couch bench, lost in quiet conversation. Dom and I settle onto the porch swing, rocking gently while I take in the view of the tidy flower beds and manicured yard.

Nikolai drives up in his truck, head banging to music so loud I'm surprised he's not deaf. He parks and jumps out with two large bags packed with food containers.

"Yummy, what'd Cleo make?" Niki asks, meeting him at the stairs to help.

They set them on the table and start taking out the boxes. The smell is rich and mouthwatering. She hands me a container, then Dom. Inside is lemon herb chicken with crisp, golden skin, roasted potatoes coated in olive oil and garlic, and green beans tossed with butter and a hint of sea salt.

We barely get a few bites in before Giulia jumps up, covering her mouth, racing toward the front door.

Dom and I look at each other. We know exactly what this is. Niki and Nikolai, though, are confused and concerned.

Nikolai peeks down at Giulia's barely touched plate. "Do you think it's the food?"

"Nah. It'll pass in a couple weeks or months." Dom states casually.

They both stare at us.

I sigh and stand, waiting for him to get up. "Shall we?"

"What's going on?" Niki studies me, then Dom.

"She's pregnant."

I gape at him. How do men not have the brain capacity to differentiate when something is meant to be discreet? "Really? You're just going to blurt it out like that?"

"What?" He shrugs.

"She's what?!" Nikolai nearly shouts.

"Shhh," Niki and I hush in unison.

"You don't have to be so loud," Niki adds in a sharp whisper.

"We'll be back," I tell them as Dom and I head inside.

"Wait. Does she not know?" Niki calls after us.

I shake my head. "I don't think so."

I make my way upstairs to her room with Dom trailing reluctantly behind. He makes a last-ditch attempt to escape, swiping at nonexistent dust on the banister and mumbling something about needing a towel. I grab his belt loop and drag him the rest of the way, telling him he's not getting out of this.

The bed is untouched, which tells me she went straight to the bathroom. My stomach knots when I find her slumped beside the toilet, sweat-damp hair clinging to her face, eyes half-shut as she rests against the wall.

"Hey, babe, you okay?" I kneel beside her, brushing her hair back.

She rolls her head to the side. "Don't touch me," she croaks. "I might be contagious."

I check the contents in the toilet, then lower my gaze to her stomach. It's mostly flat, but there's a small swell low on her belly. I don't know how she hasn't figured out what's going on.

"I'm not worried about catching what you have." I scoot in closer. "You wanna shower? Or maybe come downstairs and watch a movie with me?" I offer, keeping my tone light.

She lets out a weak, almost pitiful whine. "Will you hold me?"

I nod, my heart clenching. "Of course I will."

I get up and extend my hands, helping her to her feet. She wobbles but holds on, leaning against me as we exit the bathroom.

Downstairs, she goes to the living room, and I stop at the fridge to get her a water.

I brace myself against the counter, crossing my arms as I catch Dom's attention. He pauses, placing a coffee mug in the dishwasher—a task he never does.

"We need to tell her," I mouth, motioning toward Giulia.

He wrinkles his nose, then glances at where she's curled up on the couch. When he turns back to me, I widen my eyes at him for emphasis that his attempts of being too busy won't work. He exhales, and I grab his hand, pulling him along.

I pass her the water bottle and settle beside her, Dom sitting on the coffee table directly in front of us.

"Giulia," I start, trying to ease into it. "Did you have sex with anyone else after that night Cristiano had those two guards… the night you were punished for refusing to touch me?"

Confusion flickers across her face. "Like, have I had sex since then?"

"Yeah."

Her gaze shifts from me to Dom, then back again. "Rainey… we had…" She gestures between us.

I smile, softening my voice. "I mean besides you and me. Did you have sex with any other men?"

She stares at me for a long moment, uncomfortable by my question.

"I'm not judging you," I reassure her, resting my hand on her lap.

"I just don't get why we're talking about what happened to us?"

"There's a reason, I promise."

Her brows pinch together and she shakes her head. "No. There was no one else."

I rub her arm, knowing how uneasy this topic makes her. "Was the last time you had sex the night Leandro and I spent together?"

"I was with Cristiano?" Her tone makes it seem like that's explanation enough.

I nod. "I know."

"Cristiano didn't have sex with me. He just punished me."

I blink, trying to process her words.

"He didn't," she insists. "He beat me, shoved things inside me, whatever he could to hurt me… but he never had sex with me. He was too angry, thinking about you spending the night with someone else."

Guilt crashes over me. I thought they had rough sex, his way of punishing me for being with Leandro, but it was something even more brutal. I wondered why she was so mad at me. She enjoyed having sex with him and getting his attention. I didn't realize he was just awful to her without her getting the part she actually liked.

"Did anyone else in that house assault you?"

"No." Her tone hardens. "Why are you asking me this?"

"Because, Giulia… you're pregnant."

Her mouth opens, a disbelieving laugh slipping out, but when she sees the seriousness in my expression, her face falls. "What?"

"You're pregnant," I repeat. "You're throwing up, your belly's starting to round, your boobs are swollen, and your mood swings have been all over the place."

She's ready to deny it.

"If you'd like confirmation." Dom holds out a pregnancy test, still sealed in its foil packaging.

She glances at it, then at me. Without a word, she snatches it and storms off to the bathroom.

He exhales, long and slow. "Zero out of ten, would not recommend."

I smack his bicep, then rub my palms over my temples.

She's only in the bathroom a few minutes before a burst of sobs echoes down the hall.

"Welp, I guess we have our answer." I sigh, pushing off the couch and heading for her.

When I open the door, she's sitting on the closed toilet lid, her face buried in her hands, her shoulders shaking. The test stick lies discarded on the floor, the second pink line much darker than the control line.

"Giulia?" I step inside and kneel in front of her.

"It was Niko," she chokes out.

"What was Niko?"

"The father. The one I was sleeping with."

My eyes widen. I knew they did on the yacht, I didn't think it happened more than that. Maybe I'm not thinking of the right guy.

"The chef?" I ask for confirmation.

She nods, fresh tears spilling down her cheeks.

"Damn." I lean back on my heels. "I mean… hell yeah. He was hot."

She lets out a small, broken laugh before dissolving into more tears.

"How long were you sleeping with him?"

"I don't know. Since the first time we were on a boat. We were both lonely, I guess."

"When was the last time?"

"The day before Leandro."

Okay, so she might be farther along than I originally thought.

Dom steps in, squatting beside me, his forearms resting on his thighs. "Giulia, are you wanting to keep it?"

She glances between us, then down at her belly. For a long moment she stays quiet, and then she gives the smallest nod.

"Good," I say gently, squeezing her hand.

"Do you want him to know?" Dom asks. "We can try to find him if that's what you want."

She hesitates. "I should… it would be wrong not to."

He shrugs. "You don't have to do anything you're not ready for. The circumstances weren't exactly ideal."

"Do I have to decide right now?" she whispers.

"Of course not," I reassure her.

She blinks hard sucking in a shaky breath. "What do I do now? Do you think Niki will hate me?"

I smile. "I think she'll be thrilled."

"It doesn't matter what she thinks."

I look at Dom, silently telling him he's not helping. Giulia's lip trembles, her voice barely holding steady. "Rainey…"

I shake my head, letting her know she doesn't have to explain anything she isn't ready to share.

She stares for a beat, then throws her arms around me, crying into my shoulder. I hold her, rubbing slow circles on her back.

"I'm so sorry. I love you, Rainey. I didn't mean for it to happen. I didn't think I'd fall for her… but I did."

I pull away enough to see her face. "Niki's hot. You're hot. Neither of you needs to explain anything to me."

Dom glances between us, confused. "Uhh…"

I can't help but smile as I tuck her hair behind her ears. "Come on. Let's get you downstairs so you can stretch out on the couch."

Dom rises first. "I'll call our doctor, see what we need to do next and how soon they can see you."

"Thanks," she whispers as she pushes to her feet.

I lace my fingers in hers and lead her out. Downstairs, Nikolai appears to be eating everyone's food on the porch, while Niki is pacing near the window. The moment she spots us, she stops, locking onto Giulia.

Giulia's grip tightens as she stares at Niki.

"I'm so sorry, Niki." Her voice trembles. "I'm pregnant."

Niki's features soften. She crosses the room and cups Giulia's face. "Are you keeping it?"

Giulia nods, tears brimming in her eyes.

"Then we'll keep it." Niki smiles, pressing a light kiss to Giulia's lips.

"Whaaaat?" Dom drags out the word.

"I wouldn't have known either if I didn't accidentally catch them making out in the driveway."

"I wanted to talk to you about it," Giulia says. "It just kinda happened."

I hug them both. "My two best friends. I couldn't ask for a better match."

Nikolai comes in, and the look on his face tells me he already knew. Of course he did.

"Want to go up to your room and talk? We'll work everything out together," Niki promises. Giulia agrees, and they head upstairs.

Dom drops onto the couch next to me, resting his arm along the back. "Wow. I wasn't expecting that."

"It's kinda perfect though, right?"

He thinks it over. "Yeah. Actually, it is."

We sit in the quiet for a moment before I tilt my head toward him. "Speaking of relationships, did Tess and Marko break up?"

Nikolai's eyebrows rise, and he gets to his feet. "I gotta get back. Out of here. At home." His words trip over each other as he hurries out the door.

I focus on his retreating figure, suspicion creeping in. "Dom."

"Yeah, baby."

"Where is Tess?"

My unease builds, and it's in this moment I know where she is—or where she no longer is.

He's quiet, and I sit forward, turning toward him, my eyes welling with tears. "Say it."

He exhales, slow and heavy.

"Say it," I demand.

"I killed her."

The words hit harder than I was anticipating. I want to lash out, to scream that I hate him. But I don't. I need to make sense of it. I wait for him to speak, but he just stares.

"Explain."

"The first day I met you, I was at the diner for Cristiano's new girl, Contessa. I thought you were her. She was supposed to meet with the cartel. I didn't realize I had the wrong target until the bartender called you Rainey. I missed the meeting completely because I was focused on you.

"After that, we hired a new girl. I didn't know who. I didn't care. We hire all the time for other houses, other businesses. None of it mattered. It wasn't part of my job.

"Someone was feeding Cristiano information. When we learned it was a woman, I knew it had to be a female who worked in the house. I checked the diner footage and realized Contessa is Tess. She was the one feeding him information. She admitted she was sent to get the job so she could pass info to him.

"Though we originally thought she was his girlfriend, she said she never was. She just worked for him and was loyal. She gave the location where you were most likely to be found. It was the location we got you from. She was never tortured. She willingly gave the info."

Tears spill down my cheeks. "How'd you do it?"

"A bullet."

The tears fall faster. I think of her in that van, how she held my hand. The first friend I had here.

"You need to understand. The info she gave him was information he could use to try to kill me."

I wipe at my face. "It still hurts."

He looks at me like he truly doesn't get it.

"Friends do shitty things. But part of having feelings is being sad over something like this." His expression remains blank. I sigh. "If I fed Cristiano information on you, would you kill me?"

His chin jerks back. "Of course not."

"Why?"

"Because you're mine."

"Okay, what you're *feeling*, that flare of emotion, I have that for everything. Even things that are insignificant to you."

He huffs. "I don't know what you want. I don't care about her."

I shoot to my feet. "But I did." My voice shudders with anger.

"Rainey… I believe she played a significant role in your kidnapping."

My jaw practically hits the floor. "Is that why she died?"

"I told you why I killed her."

My nostrils flare. "Would you have killed her if you hadn't thought she had anything to do with me being taken?"

"Probably," he deadpans.

"Take me to Dante. Now!"

Without waiting for him to answer, I stride toward the garage.

We reach the main house, and I head straight for Dante's office, Dom on my heels. I shove the door open, and inside, Dante and Giovanni stop mid-sentence, both turning their attention to me.

I pace, shaking my hands out, trying to breathe, trying to think.

"It was Valentina." The words burst out of me. I stop and turn toward Dom.

"What was?" Dante asks.

Dom stares at me, his chest rising and falling hard, eyes flicking between mine.

"Tess had nothing to do with my kidnapping. It was Valentina. Your mom set it up."

His entire body tenses.

"What are you talking about?" Dante comes out from behind his desk. Giovanni rises too, easing back from the chair, watching Dom like he might have to intervene if something goes down.

"Cristiano told me. He said Valentina set me up. That's why she sent me to pick up her dress. She told me not to tell you, Dom. She said my ride was waiting. But when I went outside, Niki was just getting home and insisted she come with me. The lady at the shop said it was supposed to be just me. Cristiano said he didn't know how Niki got caught in it. I believe Niki came home at the wrong time. She wasn't meant to be there. I think maybe Valentina found out we had sex, Dante. I don't know. I thought she liked me, but she had to know what Cristiano would do to me." My voice wavers.

Giovanni lunges before I can process what's happening, and in an instant he and Damiano are locked in a brawl. A sound tears from Dom's chest, more beast than man, a raw, guttural roar that rattles through the room. I've never heard anything like it, never witnessed him consumed by such unrestrained rage, his anguish breaking loose in a way that makes my blood run cold.

Dante wraps his arms around me, dragging me backward out of the way. I can only watch, horrified, as they tear into each other. Furniture crashes. Papers scatter. Everything in Dante's office is being destroyed.

"Stop!" I scream as tears stream down my face.

The door flies open and Andrei comes inside, stunned by the chaos.

"Call Silvano, Niki, and Nikolai. Now!" Dante bellows over the noise.

Andrei moves instantly, retrieving his phone. But Dom and Giovanni don't stop. They keep going, fists landing, blood spilling, the room in ruins. Dante holds me tight, murmuring that it's okay, that it'll be fine, but I'm clawing at him, desperate to break free.

Everyone else enters, but none of them seem as disturbed by what's going on as me.

When Dom and Giovanni finally start to tire, I break free and rush between them. Dom's hands are bloodied, his face battered, and Giovanni looks just as bad. I throw my arms around Dom, and he catches me, sinking onto the couch with me in his lap.

"Pull any calls or messages from Ma's phone leading up to Rainey's kidnapping," Dante orders Andrei.

The room is silent except for the sound of Dom and Giovanni trying to catch their breath. Andrei goes to Dante's desk, getting to work.

"What? You think Ma participated in our kidnapping? She would never," Niki denies any likelihood that her own mother could do that to her.

Andrei freezes, fingers suspended over the keys. He shakes his head side to side as shock sets in. "What the fuck?"

Giovanni is ready to snap. "Was it her?"

Andrei nods. His mouth parts, but nothing follows.

Dante steps behind him, pointing at something on the monitor. "What is that?"

Andrei types, pulling up more files. Then a video appears.

It's me.

The room falls into an agonizing silence as the footage begins. My first rape by Cristiano. I stand on shaky legs as it all plays out from this angle, as if I'm seeing my own nightmare through someone else's eyes. When my wails for Damiano echo through the speakers, I know he's about to break. I turn into him, locking my arms around his waist. He shakes with fury, and I clutch him harder.

When the sounds of my assault fade, I finally gather the strength to look back at the monitor. All that's left is a shattered version of me, crumpled on the floor, crying.

"Why does Ma have that?" Nikolai asks, his voice hollow.

A text pops up, the one linked to the video. The words burn into me.

Thank you for this. She's tighter than I could have ever dreamed.

And then I'm no longer holding Dom. He's smashing through the screen, glass and plastic shattering to pieces.

My body locks up. I can't breathe. I claw at my throat as I try to inhale, panic rising fast as the room begins to spin and everything blurs around me.

"Rainey!" Niki shouts, racing toward me.

Dom's face fills my vision. His hands cup my cheeks, his voice urgent. "Baby, look at me. Breathe. Please, you have to breathe." His eyes search mine, but I can't focus. The sound of frantic voices tunnels, distant and muffled. Then I'm on the floor, my skin turning cold.

I don't know what's happening anymore. I no longer feel attached to any one place, suspended in limbo between life and death, and death's pull is stronger. Suddenly, it's as if air is forced into my lungs and I suck in a breath so hard it feels like it tears through me. My body jerks, and I gasp, desperate for more.

Dom tugs me close, holding me like he's trying to keep me safe from it all. My head rests on his shoulder, my eyes unfocused, seeing nothing. Medical staff clean and bandage his knuckles and tend to Giovanni's cuts, but not once does his grip on me loosen.

The voices around me blend into one another, something about Pa, then more muffled talking, and then something about Ma. It's Giovanni's voice that finally cuts through clearly. "I'm with Rainey and Dom. Whatever they decide."

The others all follow his lead, simultaneously pledging their support.

The conversation turns to what happens now, but I can't keep up. My mind gives out, and my thoughts are swallowed by darkness.

When I open my eyes again, I'm in bed. The room is completely dark. I blink, trying to gauge the time based on the amount of light from outside, but the blackout curtains are drawn. I try to move and can't. I try again, slower this time, and feel the weight holding me in place. Dom's arms. Still wrapped around me, still keeping me close.

I glance over my shoulder and find his face close to mine. We're both still fully dressed, which tells me he must have carried me in and laid down beside me just like this. In the faint light, I see a tear pooled at the corner of his eye.

I reach up and gently wipe it away.

He flinches at the touch, his eyes snapping open. When they meet mine, they soften despite the exhaustion.

"Hi," I whisper, then press a gentle kiss to his lips. I mean for it to stay soft, but he leans in, guiding me onto my back as the kiss deepens.

Chapter

FORTY-EIGHT

Damiano

We're all still reeling from what we learned three days ago. Everyone keeps commenting on how well Rainey seems to be handling it, like she was holding it together better than the rest of us. But Giulia told us Rainey had already fallen apart when she found out. She had a full meltdown, spiraled into a deep depression, and spent weeks trying to crawl her way out. While we were blindsided, she's already had time to process it.

Now it all makes sense. I knew Rainey picking something up for Ma didn't add up. The fear she carried when she returned, the way she welcomed everyone's hugs and hellos, everyone except Ma. How she avoided the house entirely, keeping her distance as if even being near Ma physically hurt. It wasn't just about needing time to readjust.

Niki is over the moon about Giulia being pregnant. She said she didn't think she'd want kids, especially not yet, but she's committed to raising the baby with Giulia if that's what she wants. Niki has spent all of her time attached to her upstairs, catering to and pampering her. She's still pretty sick, but a specialist is coming in a couple of days to check on her and the baby.

Gio and Nikolai have been camped out in the living room, keeping close watch on Rainey since the other day. Normally, that kind of hovering would drive her crazy, but with those two she doesn't seem to mind.

She's been in the shower for half an hour. She got waxed earlier and kept complaining it felt like there was still residue on her skin.

I'm in the kitchen pulling bottles of alcohol from the cabinet, determined to make everyone relax tonight. I'm not spending another evening watching movies while the room silently monitors her every breath.

When she walks in, she leans against me, eyeing the growing lineup. "Are we getting drunk?"

"Yeah," I reply casually.

"Yay! What's the occasion?" She raises her arms toward me.

I lift her by the waist, setting her on the counter, and she swings her legs playfully.

Gio strolls in resting next to her, gently bumping her as he grins. "Threesome."

Nikolai's head whips toward him with a glare.

"Foursome," Gio amends, holding his hands up in mock surrender.

She wags her brows. "Exciting." Reaching over, she pinches my chin, turning my face toward hers, brushing a soft kiss across my lips before smiling and leaning in for another.

"Grab those." I nod toward two bottles, while Gio, Nikolai, and I get the rest. Turning, I bend down so she can get on my back.

"I like this view of your backpack, Dom," Gio remarks.

Carried like this, I'm sure Rainey's booty shorts are giving her entire butt a spotlight.

When we reach the bar in the game room, I set her on the counter. Nikolai and I start mixing drinks for everyone. We clink shot glasses and down them in one go, then pour another round and do it again.

"Wanna play darts?" Nikolai asks Rainey.

She eagerly agrees and hops down, following him over, then proceeds to wipe the floor with all of us.

"I worked at a bar," she laughs, sinking another bullseye without seeming to try.

As the night goes on, we keep the drinks coming, letting her laughter fill the room.

Eventually, we settle onto the couches. Rainey crawls into my lap, straddling me as she pulls her shirt off and tosses it aside, shoving her tongue into my mouth. I kiss her back just as deeply until she fumbles with my belt.

"Later," I tell her, tilting my head back as she follows my mouth.

She smiles and leans in again, pressing her bare chest against me. "Don't be a prude. You already had sex with me in front of both of them."

"That was to make a statement."

"So? Do it again."

I shake my head.

She pouts, resting her palms on my knees and wiggling her boobs at me. "You don't want this?"

"He has whiskey dick," Gio jests.

She turns. "Do you?"

He smirks and shifts, showing he, in fact, doesn't.

She climbs out of my lap and goes straight to him, straddling his, grabbing his shirt, and pulling him in for a kiss.

"Rainey," I growl, but she ignores me, sliding her hands under his shirt and up his chest.

He doesn't stop her. He presses right into it, gripping her hips, and drawing her closer.

"You two drunk together is the worst," I mutter as I catch Rainey at the waist and guide her away. She clings to his neck, but I manage to peel her away and set her on her feet.

She immediately goes for the bulge straining against his jeans. "Take off your pants," she purrs, eyes hazy with lust.

We've been matching her shot for shot, but she's a foot shorter and a hundred pounds lighter than any of us. She's done for, probably can't even tell the difference between me and him right now.

I draw her down onto the couch, wrapping an arm around her. She goes straight for my throat, sucking and biting until it's guaranteed to leave a mark. Apparently, that's all it takes for my dick to wake up.

When she finally pulls back, I stand and sling her over my shoulder.

She giggles, landing a playful smack on my butt. "Where are we going?"

"You win. We're headed to the bedroom."

She squeals, kicking her feet.

"Can we come?" Gio calls out from behind us.

She lifts her head, curls a finger at him, and grins. "Please."

"Fuck yeah," he says, trailing us down the hall.

Chapter

FORTY-NINE

Rainey

I wake up sore. Like, really sore. The kind of sore that makes your muscles ache in a satisfying way. A reminder of the snippets I can recall from last night, tangled up with Dom and Giovanni.

Nikolai had been invited to join, and for a split second, it looked like he might actually cave. But then he shook his head, muttering something about not wanting to ruin his relationship with me.

"You probably won't even remember it," Giovanni teased.

"That makes it worse," he shot back, and then the video game started ending all further talk of him joining.

After that, it was just the three of us—and they didn't hold back. Not even a little.

I've had men take me at the same time, and I hated every second. It was nothing but pain and humiliation. But this… this was different. Maybe because I'm madly in love with Dom, and I knew I was completely safe.

They were rough and gentle all at once, each of them seeming to know exactly when I needed to be handled with care, and when I needed to be dominated.

I was fucked and choked, spanked and bitten. Their hands roamed every inch of my body, their mouths exploring every sensitive spot. They went down on me until I was writhing, gasping for air, then had me on my knees, returning the favor until their groans filled the room.

I vaguely remember Dom struggling with a new bottle of lube at one point. He got so frustrated he said he was about to rip it in half. When I suggested using the one we'd already opened, he insisted it was all gone. Then he added, you love anal so much we go through it fast.

I was already slowly riding Giovanni, but the longer he took, the more impatient we both became. By the time he joined us, he was irritated with the bottle, raging with desire, and completely wrecked me. I knew, just from the way he grunted climbing onto the bed, that my ass was about to get brutalized, and it was absolutely delicious. Intense. Overwhelming in the best possible way.

I wish I hadn't been as drunk as I was, though. I think I might have blacked out a few times, my body too impaired and exhausted to keep up with their relentless pace.

But I remember enough to know that I want it again. Sober this time.

As my eyes flutter open, the morning light filters through the small gap in the curtains, casting a soft glow across the room. I stretch, my arms extending above my head, and my elbow bumps into something solid.

I turn and find Giovanni beside me, his face angled toward mine, features relaxed in deep sleep. He looks so different like this—peaceful, almost boyish.

Rolling the other way, Dom is sprawled on his back, one arm draped over his eyes, the other resting on his toned abdomen. Heat curls in my belly at the impressive bulge beneath the sheets.

Sliding down, I slip under the covers, warmth enveloping me as I settle between his legs. One knee is bent, the other stretched straight, giving just enough room to move.

I'm I gently cup his balls, lifting as I lean in to lick a slow, wet stripe over his taint. A faint groan rumbles from his chest, and I smirk, moving lower. I know exactly where he likes my tongue.

When his hips shift, I trail back up, licking along his length, pausing at the swollen head. I flick over the sensitive underside, swirling around the tip before wrapping my lips around him, hollowing my cheeks, and slowly bobbing.

I moan, letting the vibrations travel through him, and his hips jerk in response.

It doesn't take long before he's fully awake, thrusting up as I take him deeper, dragging along the vein beneath his shaft.

His thighs flex as he starts to fuck my mouth, fisting my hair to keep me where he wants me until he's coming.

And I love every second of it.

As I emerge, his lips curve into a lazy, satisfied smile.

"Oh good, you're awake," I quip, crawling up his body until I'm straddling his waist, my hands splaying over his chest.

Movement catches my eye, and I glance to the side, finding Giovanni rolling onto his stomach, grabbing my pillow and bunching it in his arms.

"Wanna join?" I tease as I rock my hips, rubbing myself against Dom's hard length.

"No," he groans, burying his face in the pillow. "I want sleep. You're a horn dog."

"Suit yourself," I return my focus to Dom as I reach down, guiding him to my entrance, my body more than ready.

W̲HEN̲ I̲ WALK INTO THE KITCHEN, G̲IULIA AND N̲IKI ARE PERCHED AT the counter eating breakfast.

"Good morning, sleeping beauty," Niki greets, and her eyes go wide. Giulia glances over, and her expression is the same.

"Fun night?" Niki asks.

"Yeah, it was fine."

"Looks a little more than fine." She raises her brows. "Also, you're welcome for cleaning up the alcohol mess you guys left. Definitely looked like a good time."

"It was." I move to the coffee pot and pour myself a cup, stirring in creamer when a hand smacks my butt, followed by a kiss on my forehead.

"Morning, beautiful," Giovanni says, grabbing a mug to pour his own coffee.

I turn, leaning back against the counter as I take a sip. Giulia and Niki are grinning, and Niki nods. "A really good night."

Giovanni looks at them, then down at me, doing a double take. He lifts my chin, his lips pulling back. "Shit, sorry."

"Okay, what is going on?" I ask.

I set my mug down and walk to the bathroom. When I flip on the light, I freeze.

There's a bite mark on my jaw. My neck is covered in so many hickeys I can't tell where one ends and another begins. Even in my tank top, I can see dark marks trailing down to my chest.

Flashes of last night hit me, Giovanni's mouth on my boobs, his teeth sinking in, Dom's lips on my neck, sucking hard.

Now I'm wondering what else they did to me.

Chapter

FIFTY

Dante

As I push open the door to Andrei's room, I immediately regret it. He's on the couch, completely naked, with two of the girls kneeling in front of him, their heads bobbing.

I knock on the wall to get the girl's attention, growing more impatient by the second. Andrei lets out an irritated sigh, signaling for them to get out. They grab their clothes, avoiding eye contact as they pass.

He gets up, pulling on his pants, and stares at me.

We're all coping however we can. Ma isn't supposed to return for another week, but she called to say she was coming home early. I tried to get her to stay with Pa for the full amount of time, but she said she wants her *babies*. I spoke with Pa afterward to tell him he needs to come home with her, but he said he's dealing with shit he can't leave right now.

We know Dom told the guards to notify him as soon as she arrives, and they will remain loyal. I knew it was pointless to tell them to keep it a secret. Everyone either wants to impress him or is too scared to go against what he says. They said they wouldn't tell him, but I'm positive we will have about a ten-minute window to talk to her before Dom comes in, and I don't know how he will react. I'm not sure how much talking will actually get done.

I'm still struggling to wrap my head around the fact that Ma could do something like that, especially to Dom. I want to ask her what the fuck she was thinking, if she really thought she would get away with it, and why, out of all of us, she chose to fuck with him. She had to have considered that outcome, too.

"How are you holding up?" Andrei asks.

"Like shit. Did you find more?"

His mouth presses into a thin line, and he nods. "How much are you wanting to see?"

"Everything."

He points to his chair, and I sit as he pulls up a folder, then steps back. "Messages, phone calls, and any other communications they've sent back and forth."

It's organized with dates, each corresponding to any communication between the two of them. I work through every single file, feeling like Ma sealed her own fate when she did this, even when she had remorse and tried to get Rainey back. But the phone calls where she was putting the deal in place make me so sick I'm glad she isn't here, because I would kill her with my own bare hands.

The first messages sent back and forth show Ma panicking that Niki was accidentally taken too. She doesn't even seem fazed when she's sent a single text with a photo attached. It's a picture of Rainey, swollen and bruised and the message below reads: "Hats off to you. Her pussy is divine."

Ma brushed past the fact that Rainey had just been raped. All she cared about was getting Niki back safely.

I press my fingers into my temples, feeling the pressure building behind my eyes. My mother bargained one life for another. She was willing to let Rainey be tortured, raped, and likely killed as long as Niki was spared.

Days after Niki was released, Ma still received texts and videos. Her only response back is: "I don't need to see what you're doing to her anymore. Do whatever you want. Just let me know when it's done."

But the final nail in the coffin comes when video after video floods in of Cristiano brutalizing Rainey, each one showing even more ways she had to endure his torture.

I hang my head, my elbows resting on my knees. I knew it was bad. I just didn't realize it was *this* bad.

"I'm so sorry, Dante." Andrei squeezes my shoulder. "Let me know what else you want me to do. Anything at all. I've got you."

I nod, my throat too tight to respond, and stand, leaving his room. The house feels colder and empty as I move through it.

"Have you heard anything from Dom?" I ask Marko as he steps back inside, wiping his hands on a rag.

He shakes his head. "Gio just talked to him. He's headed to their house."

"Thanks."

My chest feels like it can't take any more pain. As I pull down Dom's drive, Gio, Dom, Nikolai, Rainey, Giulia, and Niki are all on the porch talking. They all look in my direction, and the moment I step out and lock eyes with Rainey, my composure crumbles. The amount this beautiful, flawless woman had to endure because of my own mother. Because of *me*. Because of Dom.

Her mouth is moving and then she's striding toward me. The second she reaches me, my legs give out, the weight of what I just discovered crashing down on me. I drop to my knees, a choked sob tearing from my throat.

She sinks into my lap, wrapping her arms around me, her body molding to mine as she holds me close. My fingers dig into her back as I bury my face in her hair, the familiar scent of her calming and devastating all at once.

"I guess you must have found more?" she whispers.

My head presses into her shoulder, unable to find the words. I can't tell her the worst part. I can't tell her that Ma not only betrayed her sons, but also that she watched the horrible things being done.

"I'm so sorry," I choke out.

"It's not your fault," she whispers, her fingers threading through my hair. "None of this is your fault."

Dom's presence registers before he speaks, squeezing my shoulder, making this all hurt so much more.

"Baby, why don't you take Dante inside so you can talk privately."

"We don't need to talk privately," Rainey tells him.

But I can't let her go. Not for a second, not when I feel like I'm drowning in the truth. I tighten around her, and manage a weak, "Please."

Dom's hand moves from my shoulder to Rainey's back. "Come on," he says gently. "Let's get you inside."

He helps Rainey to her feet, then claps me on the back, a silent reassurance. I force myself to stand, my legs unsteady, and follow them back into the house.

Once we reach their room, Rainey helps me out of my suit jacket, tossing it onto the nearby chair. She climbs onto the bed, holding her arms out to me, her eyes full of the kind of understanding that shatters me all over again.

I collapse beside her, half laying on top of her as the sobs return, shaking my entire body. Her fingers thread through my hair again, her other arm wrapped around my back, holding me close as I fall apart.

Dom leans over, pressing a kiss to her forehead, his gaze lingering on me for a moment. "I love you," he tells her before he turns and leaves the room.

She holds me, her fingers moving through my hair, her lips brushing against the top of my head every so often. I slowly calm, my breathing evening out as the warmth of her body seeps into mine. She lets out a shaky breath, her arms tightening around me.

"Was it pretty bad?" she whispers, her voice small, almost afraid to ask.

I nod as the memories flash behind my eyes. I can't bring myself to say it out loud. I can't tell her just how bad it really was.

"Do we know why she hates me?"

I shake my head, my throat tightening all over again.

She goes quiet and then her voice cracks. "She is the only mom I've ever really had. She played me so good. I truly thought she cared about me."

I pull back, my forehead pressing against hers, my hands cupping her cheeks, brushing the tears away. "I'll never let anyone hurt you again. Not ever," I promise.

I'd rather die myself than let anything happen to her.

"I just don't understand why," she cries harder, her entire body trembling against mine. "She wanted me dead."

I have no words for her. I can't comfort her, because I don't know why either. I can't explain why Ma would do something so cruel, so unforgivable.

"What do I do?" she asks, her fingers gripping my shirt. "The saddest part, is I don't want her dead. I just want her to love me."

"I know, mi amore. I'm so sorry. But we all love you. And we will all protect you."

RAINEY AND I MUST HAVE PASSED OUT HARD. I'M STILL WRAPPED around her, face buried in her hair, and for a moment I forget everything that's happened, letting myself pretend this was our happily ever after.

She tilts her head back, bringing her hand up to flick my bottom lip down.

"Good morning."

"Morning." I manage a smile back.

"How are you feeling?"

I let out a sigh, pulling her closer. "I don't know how to feel. I can't wrap my head around the fact that Ma could do something like that."

"I get it. I didn't believe it at first either. When Cristiano told me, I swore he was lying. Afterward, I kept denying it. But then I remembered the day she sent me to get her dress. That's when I knew it had to be true."

"You're scared of her." It's been obvious since she came back.

"Yeah," she agrees. "She wanted me gone so badly she handed me over to the enemy. And now that I'm back, every second I'm here, I'm terrifieed she's going to kill me. Or have someone else do it."

She doesn't hide the fear that grips her. "I'll protect you."

"I know you will."

"Growing up, we had money. More money than we knew what to do with. But Ma refused to hire a nanny. Said she didn't want anyone else raising her kids. She was the best mother, no question. I've never seen a woman love her children the way she did.

"When Dom was hurt, she wouldn't leave the hospital. Not once. She sat by his bed, reading to him, singing to him. When he came home, she kept singing, every night, until he fell asleep. It became the only way he could sleep. I think that's when she bonded with him in a way none of us could touch. That's why we all joke she only loves him.

"When Dom killed Carmella, Ma said she wished she could bring her back just to kill her again for what she did to him. I know she blames herself for what happened to Dom, since it was her best friend who abused him. She's got demons, more than most, and I guess growing up in this world, it makes sense she lost her mind."

"Haven't we all."

"Yeah. Maybe."

The door opens, and Dom leans against the doorframe, crossing his arms. "You guys missed dinner. Hungry?"

"Starving." I yawn and stretch my arms over my head.

He steps closer, holding his hands out to her. "Come on. Let's get some breakfast."

She reaches up, letting him help her out of the bed.

I watch them for a moment, knowing that should have been me. The ache that follows is sharp and I don't like it. I look away, pushing myself off the mattress and walking to the bathroom. I strip down, turn on the shower, and let the scalding water wash over me. My mind drifts to Ma, to the betrayal, the messages, the videos. I press my forehead against the tiles, rocking my face back and forth, my attempt to clear the painful thoughts away.

Chapter

FIFTY-ONE

Damiano

Dante is the most level-headed out of all of us. Cool, calm, and collected. He's always been that way. Had he not been the oldest, he still would have been the one picked to take over because of his controlled nature.

The way he fell apart a few days ago, clinging to Rainey, tells me he learned more about what happened to her. I don't understand why he would go digging for more details when what he already knew was bad enough, especially if it tore him up like that. I've never seen him cry like he did. None of us had. Gio said whatever it was must've been really bad to break him.

Rainey never mentioned if he told her anything, but they talked for a while before both of them passed out from emotional exhaustion. Yesterday, she and Giulia spent the whole day together.

Niki left them alone, saying she thought Rainey needed it because she kept crying. She must know Dante found out more.

"Babe," she calls from the bedroom.

"Yeah?"

"Your phone keeps going off."

I walk in and tap the screen, seeing seven missed calls from Davis, the front gate guard over the last twenty minutes. I go to call him back, but my phone starts ringing again.

"Yeah?" I answer.

"Mr. Volkov, your mother just returned."

She's so predictable. Always comes home days early because she can't stand being away from her kids for too long. She probably figured something was up, too, since I didn't answer any of her calls or texts. She always starts with me, then calls Dante, working her way down the list until someone finally tells me to call her back. It used to be worse before Rainey. Constant. She's eased up some, but she's still relentless when she wants a response.

"Thanks."

I check for any messages from my brothers, but there's nothing. I'm positive Dante would have known she was coming home today. He must have wanted to warn her.

"Let's go," I tell Rainey as I head to the closet. I grab my gun, check the clip, slide it back into place, and tuck it into the back of my waistband.

She watches me, her eyes widening and then she follows me out. "What's happening?"

"Ma is home."

Rainey chews on her thumbnail the entire drive. I park in my usual spot on the side of the house, walk around to her side, open the door, and help her out. We walk hand in hand around back, winding our way to the doors.

The moment I step inside, the room goes silent. Andrei isn't here, but the rest of my brothers and Niki are, all standing with

Ma. Maybe Andrei, being the youngest, can't bring himself to watch his mother die.

Rainey steps in behind me, her face tight with anger as she stares ahead. I shut the door and walk toward Ma, stopping a foot away, looking down at her.

She takes a deep breath and meets my gaze, her lip trembling. "Should we talk downstairs?"

I guess she was informed on what this meant for her.

Niki covers her mouth, trying not to cry.

"Why?" Rainey steps forward. "Why did you hand me over to be raped and tortured? All I ever did was love your son."

Ma looks at her, eyes full of pain. "Sweetheart, I'm so sorry your mother never cared for you the way she should have. I wish you had always known what it felt like to be loved by a mother. A mother should do anything to protect her children and keep them safe. I just wanted to protect mine."

"With me? How? Did you think that would end the feud?" Rainey's voice shakes with anger.

"Ma, Dom knows." Dante's voice is hard as he grabs her shoulders and shakes her. Not hard enough to hurt, but enough that I can see him fighting to keep control.

Ma looks confused as she stares at him.

"Dom knows I slept with Rainey." Dante's words come out flat, his hands dropping to his sides. "That's what this was, wasn't it? You thought Dom would find out and kill me."

The tears Ma's been holding back finally fall as she looks from Dante to me.

"Were you having me followed? How did you know we slept together?" Rainey demands.

Ma sniffles. "After you were assaulted, I went to the meeting room to check on things. I asked the boys where Dante was, and they said he was with you. When he came back, his collar was flipped up, and there was a mark on his neck. I fixed it and could smell you on him."

"So you decided I should die? Because I had sex with him? I wanted to marry him."

Ma's head hangs in shame. "I know, sweetheart."

"No, you don't. You think you know everything, but you don't. You knew exactly what was happening to me. You watched it, up close, on video. For someone who was kidnapped, tortured, and raped yourself, it's disgusting you'd do that to someone else. Especially to the woman two of your sons love."

"Three," Gio says.

We all look at him.

"This isn't really the time," Rainey snaps.

Dante's brow tightens as he glances from Gio to Rainey to me.

"Four," Niki adds. "Except I'm the only one who hasn't slept with her. Not for lack of wanting to."

"You slept with Rainey?" Dante bellows, pointing at Gio.

"Yes!" Rainey chimes in, furiously. "Both of your brothers, at the same time."

"You're fucking kidding me," Dante roars at Gio, his face turning red.

"You asked Em to move in with you," Gio shoots back.

"So that means you should go fuck Rainey?"

"It means you knew every one of us wanted to have sex with her. And if I got the chance, I was going to take it. I don't regret it. Not for a second."

Before Dante can move, Rainey slaps him hard across the face.

"Don't you fucking dare. You did this. You gave me up. You lost every right to me when you chose your role here over me as your partner and wife. So fuck you, Dante. And how fucking dare you get mad when you're with Em now."

"You think I could ever fully give myself to someone else? You were it for me, Rainey."

"Get over yourself," she scoffs. "You'd have a long ass list of men to fight if you think you need to put your fists on every single man that has touched me. Or do you only care when it's men I actually wanted? Because there are three people I've wanted to sleep with, and all three of them are in this room."

"Rainey—"

"No." She steps back when he reaches for her. "Fuck you. You got me into this shit. You broke my heart so badly I spent months moping around the city, hiding out in diners like some pathetic lovesick idiot. You're the reason everything in my life went to shit. What the hell is wrong with this family? I want to go home, Dom. Now."

Home it is.

I retrieve my gun, and the room goes still.

Ma's legs give out, and she sinks back into the couch, staring down at her lap.

Andrei storms in, his expression dark. "This has gone far enough."

Ma lifts her hands, trying to calm him. "Son, enough."

"Tell them everything." His voice is sharp as he points at her.

She lowers her gaze, shaking her head.

His anger snaps toward Rainey. "You must think you're the luckiest person alive. Or maybe you're just naïve enough to believe almost killing someone ends with you getting a slap on the wrist and paid for doing community service."

Rainey's brows pull together in confusion.

He turns on Dante next. "Ma went to bat for you with Pa for months over the *poor girl her son wanted to marry*."

Then he cuts back to Rainey. "You broke the senator's daughter's jaw and put her in a coma. She legally died twice. You think you just got lucky? That you walked away without charges?"

Her mouth falls open in shock. "Those records were sealed."

Andrei scoffs. "Who do you think is powerful enough to make that happen? Who do you think met with the judge after your sentencing?"

He holds up a piece of paper, thrusting it forward, Ma's signature at the bottom.

"Bet you never thought the woman you cut a deal for to stay out of prison would be the one to get you killed," he spits.

"Son, that's enough."

"I'm just getting started. Anyone here want to tell me since when court-appointed community service comes with a paycheck? Because it doesn't. But Rainey served two hundred hours and got paid for every single one. Even more interesting, the exact amount she was paid? Ma paid that to the court two days before."

Dante turns to Ma. "Is this true?"

"I just wanted her taken care of."

"Why?" he asks, stepping toward her.

Ma lifts her chin, her voice trembling. "Because you wanted her to be part of this family. I had to take care of my daughter-in-law."

Rainey's mouth falls open as her eyes meet Ma's, tears rising to match the ones slipping down Ma's cheeks.

"Her dad called me a mafia whore. Right after I got released. I didn't understand. I didn't have ties to the mafia. I never questioned it."

Ma gives a soft shrug. "Back then, you didn't know that one day you'd be proud to wear that title."

Rainey steps closer, moving to sit beside her.

"Why? Just… why?"

Ma's sweeps the room, landing on Dante, then me, before returning to Rainey. "My son wanted you, and my husband refused to accept you. But I accepted you the day Dante said he loved you. I just wanted to protect you until my husband came to his senses. Then my son could take over as your protector."

Rainey still looks confused. "So you knew who I was when I was brought here?"

Ma nods.

"Why protect me, only to have me kidnapped once I was accepted for Damiano to marry?"

Ma's shoulders drop. "I couldn't bear the thought of one of my sons killing another. I panicked, thinking I could fix everything, but it only made it worse. I knew you had Damiano, Dante, and Niki's loyalty, but I didn't realize how fast my family would fall apart without you."

She swipes at her tears.

"I didn't know who to tell in order to get you back, how to admit what I'd done. When months passed and you were still gone, I started to believe maybe we could get you back, especially seeing how tirelessly the boys searched for you. And when I heard you'd been rescued, I hadn't even known tips had come in. I fell to my knees and prayed in thanks."

"It's sick that you pretended to be happy I was back."

"I wasn't pretending, sweetheart. I was so happy you were home."

"You handed me over to die. Every second I've been back, I've been terrified you'd have someone finish the job."

Ma's eyes widen and it's like she's just realizing how scared Rainey has been. "I'm so sorry."

"You're the only person who's ever treated me the way a mother should," Rainey whispers. "And I hate how betrayed I feel."

"May I hold your hand?"

Rainey lowers her chin in agreement, and Ma turns toward her, taking them into her lap and squeezing them tightly.

"I've made terrible mistakes in my life. I've admittedly been a lousy wife, a lousy friend, and a lousy mother at times. But what I did to you is my biggest regret. I'm sure if it had been anyone else, they wouldn't have survived. There's something so incredibly special about you, and I hope one day you see yourself the way the rest of us do."

She leans in until their foreheads almost touch.

"For the time I had the honor of knowing you, you brought me so much happiness. In the way you love my son, and the way you bring out a side of him we've never experienced. You better keep taking good care of my baby boy. And if he ever disrespects you, slip beans into his food. He can't stand them."

Tears streak Rainey's cheeks as she pulls Ma into a hug, the two of them crying in each other's arms.

When they pull apart, a quiet sort of peace hangs between them.

"Sweetheart, I'm so sorry for what I did. For what you endured. I'm so incredibly sorry."

"I forgive you. I forgive you because I don't think I would have done anything different if I were in your shoes."

Ma tries to smile, but it looks broken as she swipes the tears from Rainey's face.

"And you will be on diaper-changing duty a lot when Damiano and I have a baby one day."

Ma's eyes widen, and the room eases with the realization that Ma won't be killed.

My teeth grind, nostrils flaring while I shove the gun back into my waistband. The room goes silent, all eyes shifting to me.

"This is the only time I will ever spare a life, and it's only because of Rainey. I want it known, I don't forgive you, and I'd have no regret putting your brains on the wall."

And I turn and stride out, slamming the door behind me.

I know I lack feeling in a lot of areas, but when it comes to Rainey, I feel everything. Deeply.

I've had to watch her wrestle with demons Cristiano put inside her, watch her try to leave me because she didn't feel worthy of love. And now, the one person who orchestrated all of it won't face a single consequence.

I climb into my truck, slamming the door hard enough to shake the frame.

Hurried footsteps reach me, and in the rearview mirror, I spot Rainey racing toward the truck.

"Baby!" She yanks open the driver's door, stepping up, breathless. "Don't make me exercise like that."

She straddles my lap, her mouth crashing into mine as her arms wrap around my neck. I grip her thighs, sliding my hands under her dress, squeezing her butt as I press her into the bulge straining against my jeans.

She reaches between us, undoing my pants, her fingers slipping inside, freeing my cock. Biting her lip, she stares into my eyes while sliding the tip along her slit, teasing her clit.

"She's the only mother I've ever really had," she whispers, moaning softly as she circles my head at her entrance. "I need you to forgive her."

I groan, trying to thrust up into her, but she grips my length, stopping me with a shake of her head.

"You need to forgive her," she repeats, her voice firmer now.

She pulls the top of her dress down, letting her breasts spill free. Her eyes stay locked on mine as she circles her hips again, dragging my tip through her folds.

"Sit. Down."

She smirks and licks a slow line across my lips.

"Tell me you'll forgive her," she purrs, dragging my cock down her slit again.

When I don't answer, she starts to lift off me.

I grip her tight, holding her in place. "Don't," I warn. "Let me put it in."

She raises her brows, then reaches between us, guiding me back to her entrance. She sinks down just an inch, and my eyes roll back.

"Is there something you want to say?"

I nod, desperate. "Sit. Now."

She shakes her head and slides down a little more, then pulls off entirely.

"Please," I whimper. Actually whimper.

"Not until you agree."

"Okay," I rasp, my voice strained. "I'll work on it. I'll try to forgive her."

She sinks down on me fully, both of us groaning as her heat swallows me whole. Our breaths mix, lips hovering but not touching, as she rolls her hips against mine.

"Plus," she breathes, "I'm planning on demanding free childcare once we have a baby."

My head falls back against the seat. All I can see now is Rainey and a rounded belly with my child. "A baby," I repeat.

"Yeah. Maybe seven," she smirks, "just so we know what it felt like raising all you hellions."

"Whatever you want."

Chapter

FIFTY-TWO

Damiano

As we drive into the city, Rainey and Niki chatter animatedly as Rainey squeezes my thigh unknowingly every time she speaks about something that has her excited. Gio leans against his door in the backseat, already looking bored, but he stays focused on Rainey the entire time. He made it abundantly clear he's uncomfortable with her being out in the city again, since the last time she was here, she was kidnapped.

He *volun-told* me he was going to personally take charge of her safety.

Niki knows the real reason we're here. She's supposed to be distracting Rainey so I can pick up what I came for. When I first mentioned heading into the city, Rainey flat-out refused to let me go without her, insisting on tagging along. Realizing I had no choice but to bring her, I roped Niki, Gio, Silvano, and Nikolai into coming with us.

As I pull up in front of the mall, Niki leans over, grabbing Rainey's hand, practically bouncing in her seat. "Come on, let's go baby shopping."

Rainey slips out after her, without acknowledging me, but hurries back to the truck, slides in, kisses me quickly, then hops right back out. "Love you," she calls as she slams the door behind her.

"Don't let her out of your sight," I tell Gio as he climbs out.

He gives a thumbs up and strides after them.

As they disappear into the glass doors, I pull back into traffic. We head for the reason I'm here: the jewelry store where Rainey's engagement ring is finally ready.

The older gentleman behind the counter straightens, his eyes lighting up when he spots me.

"Mr. Volkov." He rises, buttoning his suit jacket. "I'm so glad you're here."

He should be. I likely paid his rent on this store for the next ten years with her ring alone.

He disappears into the back room, returning a moment later with a small, crimson velvet box. He presents it to me with a slight bow.

I look to my brothers, wondering if they found that odd too, and they both look like they're trying not to laugh.

I take the box, my pulse spiking as I crack it open. Inside rests the most beautiful ring I've ever seen.

A massive crimson diamond, the color deep and rich, sits at the center, its perfectly cut facets catching the light and scattering it into a thousand different shades of red. Smaller diamonds encircle the center stone, wrapping around the band in an unbroken line.

For a moment, I just stare at it, my mind racing with thoughts of Rainey. My Rainey. The woman I'm going to spend forever with. The only person who is, has ever been, and will always be my entire world.

I can picture it on her finger, that crimson glowing like blood against her soft skin, a symbol of the love that's consumed me, that's torn me apart and put me back together again.

I'm the luckiest man alive.

As night falls, things quickly take a turn for the worse. It starts when a bird craps on the pot of flower seeds Rainey planted on the porch. She had just finished watering them, standing back to admire her work, when the bird swooped down and ruined it. She gaped at the mess, then grabbed the entire glass pot and threw it off the porch. It shattered on the sidewalk below and judging by her reaction, that wasn't what she was expecting it to do.

When she comes inside to wash her hands, she notices the towel that's usually under the sink is missing. Her head whips around and she locks onto me.

"Where's the towel?" she snaps, her wet hands dripping into the sink.

"I don't know. I didn't touch it."

I don't dare tell her she used it to clean up her coffee mess this morning.

She glares, slamming the cabinet door shut, then swinging her hands around wildly, splashing droplets everywhere before grabbing a fresh towel from the drawer, muttering under her breath as she storms out of the kitchen.

By the time we're in the bedroom getting ready for bed, she's on a full rampage. She grabs the throw pillows, chucking them across the room one by one, each one hitting the wall with a dull thud before dropping to the floor.

I know this is going to escalate quickly, but I've already made up my mind. I planned on giving her the engagement ring tonight.

While she's in the bathroom brushing her teeth, I slip the ring out of its box, sliding it onto my pinky to hold it. It only fits just below the second knuckle, but it won't be there long.

She still looks pissed when she finally comes out. She climbs into bed, yanking the covers over herself and rolling onto her side to face away from me. I stare at her for a second, already bracing for the next thing she'll snap at me about.

"Turn off your damn light," she hisses.

I let out a long sigh, propping one arm behind my head as I keep my eyes on her. "Come suck my dick," I say, half because it feels as disrespectful as she's been treating me, and half because she's incredible at it, and I'd love to come in her mouth.

She doesn't respond, but I can practically hear her eye roll.

I reach over and flick my light off, then scoot to her side of the bed, wrapping my arm around her, waiting for her to tell me to get on my own side, but she pretends to be sleeping. I take her hand, slipping the ring onto her finger, placing the empty box on the sheet in front of her before facing the opposite direction.

She stays frozen for a long moment, her breathing the only sound in the room. Then the click of her lamp breaks the silence, and I glance over my shoulder to see her staring down at it.

"Is this an appropriate time for me to tell you to shut your light off?" I tease.

"Shut the fuck up and kiss me," she says, practically launching herself across the bed, grabbing my face as she presses her lips to mine.

SHE LIKED HER RING. AT LEAST I'LL ASSUME SHE DID, CONSIDERING she rode me until I thought my dick might fall off. And when she was still too horny to stop, she allowed my fingers and mouth to take over, giving my dick a much-needed break.

I was ready to call Gio in to tap me out, but she finally settled.

I half expected to wake up to her riding me again, but when I reach for her side of the bed, it's empty. I scan the room and find her sitting by the glass doors. She looks upset or maybe just lost in thought.

As I sit up, I notice the ring is off her finger, back in its box as she stares down at it. I guess this is what it feels like for people when they say their stomach sinks. I climb out of bed, moving toward her, bending down to kiss the top of her head.

"Morning, baby."

She closes the lid and clutches the small velvet square.

"How'd you sleep?" I drop onto the edge of the table in front of her, moving her feet into my lap.

"Fine. You?"

I study her, trying to read her expression, but it's just blank.

"Wondering why your ring is in the box and not on your finger," I admit.

She lets out a sigh, leaning her head back against the chair, her gaze fixed on the ceiling.

"I'm already married."

I shake my head, rubbing her ankle. "No. You're not."

And it's true. The papers were never filed. Well, they were submitted, but Andrei deleted them before they became official.

"Okay. Well, I went through a wedding ceremony, and I didn't like it. I don't want to do it again. I'm sorry."

I stare at her, that sinking feeling I previously felt turning to irritation.

I want to be supportive of her feelings, I really do. But quite frankly, I don't care if she wants to marry me or not—she's marrying me. If I have to coddle her to get her down the aisle, I will. But one way or another, this ends with her being my wife, whether she likes it or not.

This is just one more thing Cristiano has taken from me. He stole my girlfriend, shattered the woman she once was, and left me with an empty shell of the person I fell in love with. And now she doesn't want to marry me, when that was always the plan. She was brought here because she was going to be my wife.

I reach out to take the ring box. She resists for a second, tightening around it, but I stand, slipping it from her grasp.

"Where are you going?" she bites out as she glares at me.

"To return it."

Before I can take a single step, she's out of her chair, grabbing my arm.

"You fucking asshole. You're not returning my ring."

I raise a brow, feigning surprise. "You just said you didn't want it."

Her eyes flare with anger, and she lunges for the box. I lift it higher, holding it just out of reach. She jumps for it again, and I let it slip from my hand, watching as it bounces once on the carpet before disappearing under the bed.

"Seriously, Dom?" she hisses.

I let out a dramatic sigh, dropping to the floor to reach under the bed. I grab the box, kneeling on one knee, the other foot flat out in front of me as if I were going to stand, only I remain there. I flip it open, holding it out in front of her.

"Rainey Lane, I love you. I love you when you ride me for so long you make my dick hurt. I love you when you're in a bad mood and want nothing to do with me. I love you when you love me back with everything that you are, broken and all. Our broken pieces complete each other, and there is no other broken person in any universe, in any galaxy, in any form of reality, that I would ever want to walk through life with. Please, make me whole and marry me."

I wait for her to answer, maybe tell me no, or make me sweat it out. But she moves so fast, snatching it and sliding it back onto her finger before I even process what just happened. I tilt the box, staring at the empty slot where the ring sat a second ago, then look up to find her already admiring it.

I let out a breathless laugh, shaking my head. "I think I was supposed to put that on. So give it back."

She steps back, clutching her own hand to her chest, her lips curling into a defiant grin. "You can go fuck yourself."

"I'd rather not do that. It sounds painful." I grimace at the thought of touching my own dick right now.

"What if I want to?" she bites her lip suggestively.

I hold up two fingers, then curl them toward me, my meaning clear that these are all she can have right now.

She laughs, swatting my chest before stepping closer, her arms sliding around my waist as she hugs me tightly.

"I know this is going to be hard," I murmur, pressing a kiss to the top of her head. "It's going to feel like we're reopening an old wound, but we can take our time. We can rehearse, work through it together, and if it's ever too much, you just say the word."

She nods, her head tilting up just enough for me to catch the way her eyes glisten before she wipes a stray tear from her cheek.

I tighten my hold on her, pulling her even closer, wishing I could squeeze every ounce of hurt from her body.

"I think… we should go talk to Dante."

That sounds ominous. Perhaps she thinks she needs to explain to him our engagement.

Chapter

FIFTY-THREE

Rainey

It's time to tell Dom the truth.

I don't know how he'll take it, but I can only hope he understands why I kept it to myself, why I needed to see if the plan would work before dragging him into it. Now I'll find out if that was the right call.

We reach Dante's office, and the door is slightly ajar. His deep voice rumbles from inside, cutting off when he sees us waiting. He ends the call and motions us in.

Dom shoots me a look, trying to gauge what's coming.

"We have to tell him," I blurt, guilt clawing at my chest.

Dante arches a brow, a single nod following as he gestures for me to continue.

Dom's gaze flicks between us.

For a split second, I consider easing into this, but what's the point? The plan's already in motion. I've already been working it. No reason to tiptoe around his non-feelings.

"I'm setting Cristiano up." The words tumble out and not very gracefully.

Dom's face twists in confusion, like he's trying to process what I've just dropped on him. This isn't how I pictured it going. In my head, he'd get mad, tell me I was stupid for getting involved, and insist he'd handle it. Instead, he just stares, waiting for me to keep going.

I throw a look Dante's way, hoping for a lifeline, but he doesn't even try to take over the conversation or add his two cents. Considering he's the one who said I need to make Cristiano believe I want to go *"home,"* you'd think he'd back me up instead of leaving me on front street alone.

"I've been calling him," I admit, heat crawling up my neck. "Dante got me a burner."

Dom's silence stretches, and I bite the inside of my cheek. "Do you have any questions?"

His chin jerks back. "Tons."

"Okay, like?"

"Like, start from the beginning. You're dropping me into the last five minutes of a movie and expecting me to pass the final exam."

I glance over at Dante, widening my eyes to let him know it's time for him to say something.

He clears his throat. "We received intel that Cristiano was looking for Rainey. He knew she would most likely be brought back here and has eyes everywhere. The likelihood of him taking her from the property is slim, but I wanted to get ahead of this before anything got out of our control. We discussed having her reach out, pretending she wanted to go back, just to see if he'd take the bait. He did. Now, every Thursday, she has a video call with him—"

"That's what you're doing for hours in the bathroom?" Dom cuts in.

"Yes."

"Just talking?"

"Not exactly."

He exhales loudly. "Not exactly, as in?"

"As in... he has me undress."

"Why tell me now?"

I glance at Dante, seeking some sort of silent reassurance, then force the words out.

"Because it's Thursday… and… you know the thing he had me do? The thing I was doing in the shower?"

His head tilts slightly, a flicker of understanding crossing his face.

"That's what the phone calls are." I wait for an explosion, but one doesn't come, which makes me word-vomit even more. "I have to do it or he'll know something is off. You can watch," I add quickly, "off camera."

A wave of guilt washes over me. Out of everything, this feels like the biggest betrayal, knowing he's aware of what "peeing" really means, and it feels too emotional, almost like cheating.

He sighs. "Just peeing?"

"What do you mean peeing?" Dante asks, looking between us.

"Nothing," Dom and I say in unison.

Then his focus returns to me. He stares for a long moment, rubbing a hand over the scruff on his jaw.

"I will absolutely be there."

My heart nearly gives out as relief crashes over me. This isn't the reaction I expected but hearing him agree lifts some of the weight off my shoulders.

Dante pulls out a folder and hands it to Dom, who sits down and starts flipping through the pages. Dante leans forward, resting his forearms on the desk, and begins explaining the plan—each man listed on those sheets, every known property Cristiano owns, where he was last spotted, even our call logs. I didn't realize Dante was tracking things this closely. I definitely didn't know he was monitoring the length of my calls.

Did he somehow hear them, too?

That would be awkward.

I keep my eyes on Dom, studying every small shift in his expression as he reads. Finally, he sighs and drops the folder back onto the desk.

"I think it'll work."

Both Dante's and my shoulders relax at that.

When we go to leave, Dante walks us to the door, his footsteps slow, almost reluctant.

"It appears a congratulations is in order," he says, pausing as he reaches for the handle.

I blink, confused. Is he saying congrats for the plan working so far?

His chin tips down, and he gestures toward my hand. I follow his gaze to the massive ring on my finger.

"Oh… thanks."

Am I supposed to show him the ring? What do people do in this situation? I feel like he wouldn't even want to see it. But he's moved on with Em, so he wouldn't care. Yet he cared that I slept with Giovanni. This is so weird.

"Congratulations." He holds his hand out to Dom.

Dom takes it firmly, shaking it back, giving a nod. Then he turns to me, moving in for a hug. He squeezes me, inhaling deeply and holding his breath.

When we pull apart, he plasters on his best smile. "Take care of each other."

"Of course," Dom replies, lacing his fingers with mine and leading me away.

Back at the house, I decide I need to clear my head before I have to call Cristiano for our usual video chat. I tug Dom toward the bedroom, biting my lip as I flutter my lashes at him.

He catches my wrists, pulling them away gently.

"No," he shakes his head. "Your pussy can't look beat up right before Cristiano sees it."

"Beat up?" I gape.

"It will be when I'm done with it after what you pulled."

A grin breaks across my face. "Don't make idle promises."

The corner of his mouth curves into a sinister smirk. "Guess we'll find out when you're done."

It hits me now, he's absolutely going to beat the shit out of my pussy after this call. I didn't even think about how this must feel for him, knowing exactly who I'll be on the phone with, doing intimate things.

He brings me a cup of water, and for the next hour I drink steadily. This is the only day each week I do this now, and whatever thrill it once held is gone. However, Cristiano doesn't need to know that.

I keep checking the clock, wishing it would hurry, wanting to get this over with so Dom and I can return to something that feels close to normal for a few days before the next call.

When the time finally comes, I raise my brows and take a deep breath.

"He's… well… Cristiano. The way he talks to me is how he always does. I just don't want you to think I'm not okay. Because I am. And I will be knowing you're with me."

Dom moves closer, cradling my jaw, kissing me firmly. I feel a gentle pull on my finger and look down, realizing the ring is gone. My lips part in shock, but he kisses me again. "You'll get it back after the call."

He follows me into the closet as I move to the spot where the phone is hidden. I pull it out, feeling guilty.

When I look back at him, he's leaning at the end of the aisle, arms crossed, a soft smile on his face.

The phone powers on, the screen lighting up with the incoming call, Cristiano's number appearing.

I turn the screen so Dom can see, and he nods.

I take another breath and let it out.

I press the video button, and the call connects. Cristiano's face fills the screen, his expressionless blue eyes locking on mine.

We stare at each other for a long moment, the silence stretching between us. He's always been the most difficult person to read.

"How are you?" he asks at last. His voice is flat as he tilts his head, tapping lightly against his cheek, studying me.

"Fine."

"What's with the attitude?" He raises a brow.

"I don't have an attitude. I'm uncomfortable." I shift, pressing my thighs together.

The slightest tilt of his lips tells me he's enjoying this. "What have you done this week?"

I fight the urge to smile, thinking about how I got engaged to the man of my dreams.

"Nothing."

He sighs. "Darling, this vague bullshit pisses me off and you know this."

"I'm not being vague. I didn't do anything. I sat at home. Nothing exciting happened."

He huffs a laugh. "Exciting? Nothing exciting?" he mocks.

"Maybe we should just talk next week."

He straightens, glaring. "You think an hour-long call once a week is sufficient enough?"

"It is when you refuse to come get me, and you're being rude for no reason."

His jaw flexes, and for a moment, it looks like he's going to yell. Instead, he swallows it down, closes his eyes, and takes a breath before looking at me again.

"You really know how to press every button I have."

"Why are you always such a dick?" I retort. "You fucking married me. The least you could do is treat me with some respect."

"I would if you ever deserved it."

"I'll hang up if you don't stop."

His jaw tics, and his nostrils flare. "You're lucky this is a phone call."

"Why?" I snap back. "So you can whip me with your belt again? Or assault me with a perfume bottle? Let your disgusting friends stick their fingers in me while you watch?"

A dark look flashes across his face. "You're damn right I would. You think you know pain? You don't. But you will."

"I'll whip you back."

"You'll get the chance to try soon."

I have a retort right on the tip of my tongue, and then I realize what he said. "Am I coming home?"

"If you act right."

"And Giulia? She's coming too."

"No." He looks irritated I even mentioned her. "You don't need her."

"I'm not leaving without her."

"Goddamnit," he snaps, dragging in a sharp breath, trying to calm himself. "Rainey… darling… you are…" He pauses, debating whether to proceed with an insult, but reins in his temper. "Do you need to use the bathroom?"

He completely changes the subject, pulling me back into the role I'm supposed to be playing. I'd almost forgotten I was supposed to be uncomfortable.

"Yes."

I shift again, letting discomfort show on my face as I settle back into the act.

"Undress."

I hesitate, then do as I'm told. I prop my phone on the shelf, step back, and pull my shirt over my head. Cool air hits my skin, my nipples hardening, and I hear him suck in a breath. He loves my boobs. I know how much he loves every part of my body, but my boobs seem to be a favorite of everyone.

I slide my shorts down my hips, letting them drop around my ankles before I kick them away, then hook my fingers into my panties, pulling them down and stepping out of them.

I wait for him to tell me what to do next, but he just looks at me, taking his time before saying anything.

He stands abruptly, the view shaking with his movement. It steadies again when he sets it down in an office.

"Get to the shower. Now," he bites out, but this tone isn't one of anger. He's turned on, really turned on. He unzips his pants and pulls himself free, stroking once as he watches me.

"Now, Rainey."

"I'm going." I groan as I grab the phone and turn, nearly jumping when I see Dom still standing there. I had completely forgotten he was here.

He steps back, moving down the other aisle, staying out of view while I leave the closet. In the shower, I prop my phone on one of the shelves, adjusting the angle so Cristiano can see.

Dom is just outside the glass, arms crossed, watching. He winks, and that's all I needed to get turned on. I won't put on a show for Cristiano, but I will for Dom.

I proceed to do everything I'm told. Touching myself how he wants, fingering myself, working myself closer until I finally finish… when he says I can.

My body slumps against the wall, panting, while he cleans himself up on the other side of the screen.

By the time I tuck the phone back into its hiding spot, my legs are still shaking. When I turn, Dom is right there, slipping my ring back on where it belongs. Then lifts me by the waist, pressing me against the mirrored wall at the end of the aisle, his mouth crashing onto mine.

I lock my legs around his waist, clutching his shoulders as he drives into me. Strong hands anchor at my hips, and his mouth finds the curve of my neck, warm breath brushing over my skin with every ragged exhale.

He fucks me hard, just like he promised, pressing me into the glass. Each thrust sends heat sparking through my veins, keeping me frozen in that sweet, aching bliss.

I come three times before he finishes once, my body trembling so violently from the pleasure that I don't think I could handle another orgasm.

We lay tangled together on our bed, my head resting on his chest. His arm wraps around me, tracing slow, absentminded patterns along my spine.

When I lift my hand, holding it against the air, he brings his up to mine. My fingertips trail slowly up to his knuckles, outlining each calloused fingertip, then back down to his wrist, and I smile.

"What?" He smiles back.

"Just thinking about the naughty way these beautiful fingers were just touching me."

We both continue watching my movements.

"You're good at acting with him."

I shrug. I probably am good at acting with him. It's how I survived.

"It is acting, right?" he adds, his head turning slightly to look down at me.

I pause, my fingers stilling for a brief moment, then I pinch his side playfully.

"Maybe it's not," I tease.

He lets out a quiet laugh, squeezing me tighter, then stares up at the ceiling. "I'm gonna enjoy ending him."

Chapter

FIFTY-FOUR

Rainey

Dom's phone blares so loud I jolt upright.

"Who the fuck is that?" I huff.

His sleepy eyes squint at the screen, the glow lighting up his face.

"Gio." He shows me the screen, then answers the call.

"It's four a.m., Giovanni. We aren't taking booty calls," I call out, flopping back onto the pillow.

"Hey, sorry to wake you both. I have someone here Rainey might want to talk to. One of Cristiano's men."

Dom pulls up the photo Giovanni sent, and the second I see his face, I'm on my feet so fast it makes me dizzy. That's the asshole who laughed when Cristiano made me give him head in the car. He made my life a living hell, always hanging around the house when he wasn't chauffeuring Cristiano around. I never imagined he'd get caught, much less brought to me. But I'm glad he is.

I rush toward the bedroom door, needing to get to the main house ten minutes ago.

"Uh-uh, babe. Clothes."

Fuck.

I spin back, following Dom into the closet, pulling on the first things I can grab. I'm barely dressed by the time I'm in the garage, meeting Niki and Nikolai at Dom's truck.

"You okay, Rainey?" Nikolai asks, rubbing a hand over my shoulder.

"I will be," I mutter, climbing in, "when he's dead."

I step into the basement, my entire body vibrating with hatred as I move past the Volkov brothers waiting down here. Four of them stand in a silent semicircle, eyes locked on the man tied to the metal chair in the center of the room. Dom, Nikolai, and Niki follow me in, closing the distance until they fall into place beside their brothers, forming a wall around him.

I grab a metal chair and drop it with a loud clank in front of him, then sit down, head held high as I meet his glare. He acts like he doesn't know who I am, but he knows damn well.

For a long moment, I let the silence stretch between us. It's taking every ounce of willpower I have not to haul off and beat the ever-loving shit out of him. He shifts in his restraints, struggling to sit up straighter.

"Do you remember the dinner party? Cristiano's birthday dinner?"

His jaw tightens at my question. Of course he remembers the dinner party.

"How you treated me," I continue, crossing one leg over the other as I rest my hands in my lap. "The comments you made under your breath. I was made to walk out into a room full of fifty people, all dressed in suits and beautiful dresses, while I was completely nude. I had to crawl across the dinner table, butt-ass naked, while every single person at that table put desserts on me. Desserts in places that should have never been touched. And when I reached the end of the table, Cristiano feasted on me. I was humiliated, stripped of every shred of dignity, and you sat there and laughed."

I watch as the color drains from his face, his Adam's apple bobbing as he swallows hard.

"You told someone to shove a strawberry in my ass and even offered to eat it out yourself."

His eyes drop to the floor, a pathetic attempt to avoid what he's done. I can only imagine he's trying really hard to think of anything that might get him out of this situation. But he won't leave here alive. Men like him are the worst and will forever be predators.

"And then I had to lie there at the table as Cristiano ate and licked every single thing off me. Then he fucked me in front of all those people. People who yelled for him to do it harder. And when he was finished, you gave him a cucumber. Do you remember what he did with that cucumber? How he made me cut it up when he was finished fucking me with it and forced me to feed it to the guests at the table? And when I was done, still sobbing, you offered to get an eggplant. A fucking eggplant for him to shove in my vagina! And it was his heartless ass who said he didn't want it stretching me out."

My anger boils over, and I reach out, slapping him across the face.

"I'M A FUCKING PERSON! You fucking piece of shit!" I bellow. "I was raped every fucking day. Every fucking day something was shoved inside my vagina. Even when I was raped so hard my insides felt like they might fall out, it didn't matter. He still raped me, and you fucking laughed at me!"

I take a shuddering breath, my chest heaving.

"I remember you watching while I was hurt, smirking like I was pathetic, and I would stare and think about how I wanted to rip off every single one of your fingernails slowly, then dump salt over them. I thought about how I'd want to have every hair on your body tweezed out one at a time, just to be annoying. And maybe see how big I could make your pee hole. Maybe start with something the size of a pen and keep going up until you had an entire cucumber shoved inside of you. So you could feel how it felt. While I watched and laughed at your suffering and misery.

"Well, guess what, motherfucker. The time has come. And I'm going to watch every second of my fiancé torturing you."

His jaw works back and forth, the muscles in his neck straining with the effort to stay silent.

"How was Cristiano when he found out it wasn't Leandro coming to get me, but Damiano?" I tilt my head as I watch his expression tighten.

And yet, he still refuses to respond.

"You know, for months, I was told Damiano didn't want me. Do you know how that felt? To be in a place I didn't recognize, every second fearing for my life, completely trapped with no way to escape? Nobody coming for me, no one even trying. I was trapped with a monster. Even as you sit here, you'll never understand that kind of fear. Because for you, this ends. Your clock is already ticking down. Hours left to live, maybe days. But I had forever. He was trying to get me pregnant. Can you imagine what life for a daughter would have meant?"

His jaw clenches harder, but he still says nothing, his eyes flicking away for a brief moment before snapping back to mine.

"I heard you guys jerking off outside the bedroom while I was being whipped," I add, leaning in closer. "Is that what you like? Helpless girls when they cry? Is that what gets you off?"

I let the words hang in the air, watching the way his knuckles turn white as he grips the arms of the chair.

"What do you think Cristiano would have done if he found out you tried to rape me? That you nearly succeeded, if not for Niko walking in and finding you with your pants around your ankles, tearing at my underwear. How did you explain away the broken nose?"

I smirk remembering the way Niko's fist connected with this piece of shit's face. He dropped to the floor, clutching his bloody nose and screaming that Niko was dead. Niko just shrugged and said, "Sure, let's go tell Mr. Fierro what you were trying to do, and we can let him decide who dies."

"What made you so cruel?" I ask, not really expecting an answer.

I let out a slow breath, glancing over my shoulder at the Volkovs, all of them watching with varying degrees of anger.

Dante steps forward, eyes locked on the man. "It appears you've reached the end of your rope." He turns to Dom and gives a curt nod. "Make it fucking hurt."

And with that, he strides out of the room, the door slamming shut behind him.

"Got tweezers?" Niki asks, looking over at Dom.

Marko steps over to a drawer, pulling out a pair.

"Two, please." Niki holds up her fingers.

Marko grabs another pair and hands them to her. She turns and holds out one of them to me.

She moves a chair right up next to our prisoner. "C'mon," she says to me, before leaning in and plucking an arm hair, then another, then another. When he starts to squirm and spits at her, Dom steps forward and injects him with a paralytic.

I scoot my chair in closer, opposite Niki, watching as my fantasy for this piece of shit comes true right before my eyes. I take my tweezers and grab a patch of his skin, staring into his open eyes as I pinch so hard I make him bleed.

"Oops."

For the next several hours, Niki entertains me with animated stories while we meticulously tweeze his hair. We pluck each eyebrow hair out, then move to his mustache, plucking random hairs wherever until it's a patchy mess, and slowly work our way down his arms again.

When we become too tired to keep going, I lean back and glance at Dom.

"I want him to lose his fingernail." I point to the one he would always shove me with.

Dom pulls a pocket knife from his jeans and flicks it open as he steps forward. He grabs the man's finger, holding it steady while sliding the thin blade beneath the nail, prying it up slowly until blood flows freely. The man's eyes go wide, veins straining in his neck as his silent scream echoes in his mind.

When Dom's done, he bends down, kisses me, and steps back, giving us space again.

Watching him do something so brutal, something so small yet agonizing, has me wound so tight I can barely stand it. I tweeze a couple more hairs but can no longer concentrate.

"You're so fucking hot."

He raises a brow. "Popping a nail off gets you hot and bothered?"

"Apparently."

"He's got nine more." He winks.

I turn to Niki. She has stopped tweezing too.

"My fingers are cramping," she says, answering the question I hadn't asked yet.

For the next twelve hours, I don't look away. Not once. I revel in every sick, twisted, grotesque thing Dom does. Every broken bone, every scream that echoes through the basement, every gurgled plea for mercy. I drink it in, every drop of suffering, because the man in that chair deserves every second of it.

When it's finally over, when the room is quiet, Dom wipes his hands on a rag and turns to me. "Let's go home."

I study what's left of the mangled body. He's nothing but a shattered corpse now, and I search for even a trace of regret. All I find is satisfaction.

Upstairs, everyone wants to pepper me with questions. I knew it was coming with my list of confessions downstairs. However, Dom hasn't asked anything about what I revealed, and I definitely don't want to divulge more to anyone else.

"We need sleep. Sorry, guys," he says, grabbing my hand and steering me toward the back door.

Chapter

FIFTY-FIVE

Rainey

As I pass by Dante's office, I notice Lorenzo's door is open. I peek in and spot Valentina sitting at his desk, her brow furrowed in concentration, papers spread out in front of her.

I pause for a moment, wondering if I should interrupt, but my feet move on their own, carrying me just beyond the threshold.

I tap on the door even though it's already open, because it feels like the polite thing to do. Her head lifts, and when she sees me, her face lights up.

"Hi, sweetheart." She takes her glasses off and sets them down, coming around the desk, wrapping her arms around me. I let myself sink into her hug, allowing the warmth of a mother's embrace to settle over me.

She must feel it too because she doesn't let go, holding on just as tightly until we finally pull back.

She smiles, brushing a hand down my arm. "How are you?"

"Good. I was hoping we could talk, if you're not busy."

"Absolutely, come on in."

She leads me over to the seating area where we settle onto the large couch, turning toward each other. She opens her mouth like she's about to ask what's on my mind, but her eyes drop to my hand, and her mouth falls open as she grabs it, pulling it closer.

"Rainey. It's stunning."

I look down at the ring, unbelieving it's truly mine. "It is."

We both stare down at it for so long that I almost forget why I came here.

I clear my throat. "I know I'm beating a dead horse, but I need to know how the deal with Cristiano came about."

She pats my hand before letting it go, smoothing her palms down the front of her dress as she exhales.

"After I found out about you and Dante, I went through every scenario in my head about what would happen if Damiano found out. I tried to convince myself he never would—that Dante was smarter than to let something like that slip. It ate at me for days, and I ended up going to Dante's room to talk to him. He never sleeps at night, so I knew he'd be awake. But when I went in…" Her voice falters. "You were there, in his bed again. The two of you were so lost in each other, you didn't even hear me come in."

I remember hazy snippets of the nights I was with Dante. He gave me sleeping pills, but I recall thinking him and I had sex… a lot.

"The next day, I went back, and it was the same thing. It felt like such a betrayal on Dante's part. He knew what you'd just been through, and he kept taking advantage of it. I thought about what would happen to this family if Damiano killed him. I thought about everything we'd built, the feud with Cristiano, how Carmella was killed, and how our empire was going to crumble. I just wanted everything to go back to the way it was before. When things were peaceful. When we were happy.

"I started thinking about solutions, and before I knew it, I was calling contacts to get in touch with Cristiano. When he called back, I told him I wanted to end the feud—a life for a life. I thought he'd hang up, but he didn't. He said he was interested. I thought he'd kill you within the first week, and it would be done."

She gulps loudly. "But then the videos started coming in, showing what he was doing to you. That's when I realized he wasn't going to kill you. He was going to keep you alive, to make you suffer. I tried to get you back, but he wouldn't give you up. Then he just stopped contacting me. I was scared to tell anyone what I had done and knew none of my boys would give up searching for you until Damiano had you back."

"Okay." I nod slowly, letting her words settle. It's more straight forward than I expected.

"Okay?" She looks at me, confused, like she's bracing for me to lash out.

"Yeah. Okay. Thank you for being honest."

Her shoulders relax. "You're welcome."

"Thank you for keeping me out of prison."

She smiles, a small, almost tired softness in her eyes. "Well, Emily Abbott and her entire family are insufferable. They're all a bunch of bullies who get away with it because of their power. They just messed with the wrong family when their daughter decided to relentlessly spread rumors about you."

"Do you know what she told everyone?" I pray she doesn't, but her expression confirms she does.

"And you know what I did?"

"You had five girls jumping you. Grabbing a crowbar to protect yourself was nobody's fault but theirs. Her face just happened to be the one in the way."

I press my lips between my teeth, trying not to smile. Because the truth is, she had tormented me since kindergarten. She was awful. And when I found out how bad her injuries were, I was happy. I wished I had killed her. I prayed she would die in the hospital. And she did, but I guess even Satan didn't want her in hell, because he sent her back… twice.

"Andrei said you've done more for me. I'm not sure what else I should thank you for."

"It doesn't matter." She waves a hand dismissively. "We don't keep tabs on who does what for who in this family."

"Do you blame yourself for what happened to Dom when he was younger?"

She looks caught off guard by the question. "Yes and no. Yes, because it was me who brought Carmella around my family. No, because she was sick. I often wonder if she went after Damiano because everyone talked about him being slow or not all there after the injury. But he just hates talking. I believe she targeted him because she thought he wouldn't ever say anything. And she was right. He didn't. He endured years of her abuse because he wouldn't speak up."

She falls quiet, her eyes flicking to the window before returning to me. "I was terrified when nobody could talk him out of the auction. We thought maybe he'd have a hard time... performing or wouldn't know what to do. We begged him to… test that out privately, to make sure everything worked. He refused."

"I think he tried."

Her brows draw together. "How so?"

"When he came to my room after I was brought here, we were headed in that direction. But before we got too far, he told me his full name. It killed all the heat."

Now her eyebrows lift as she lets out a small exhale.

"And then I had a panic attack."

"I remember."

"Are you disappointed? That now two of your sons have chosen me when I'm a nobody. I can't add anything to your family or your family lineage."

She shakes her head. "Absolutely not. You, Rainey, you are enough."

A small huff leaves me, trying to lighten the heaviness pressing down. "I'm kind of a loser. I didn't graduate, I don't know how to do anything useful. I don't have any talents—unless you count my natural talent of being good in bed." A terrible joke, but it's all I have.

She tries to smile, but her eyes stay soft.

"I hate how easy it feels now to sleep with other people. I didn't even question it when Dom wanted Giovanni to bed me. I was excited. And I worry it could go too far, that feelings will get mixed up, and I don't want to keep doing it. Dom probably thinks it's what I want, but once we're married, I never want either of us to be with anyone else."

This time, her smile is real, warm and proud. "You, sweetheart, are wise beyond your years."

We sit in silence for a long while. I wonder if it's hard for her, being around me when I'm just making my way through each of her sons' beds. I disgust myself. I can't even imagine how the mother of those kids is feeling. And it looks even tackier on me when everyone knows Dante and Em's relationship status.

"About the wedding. Do you have a date planned? Any details yet?"

I sigh, leaning back. "I don't know. If I'm being honest, I don't even want a wedding again. I don't want to deal with any of it."

She nods, understanding in her eyes. "If you're up for it, Nikita and I can plan it for you."

"Yes," I blurt before fully processing what she's offering. "Sorry, yes. I'd really appreciate that. I don't want the details, and

I don't want to be part of it. I just want to show up and marry Dom... Is that shitty of me?"

"Not at all."

I look past her when Dom's voice carries in, asking where I am, and Dante answers that I'm in here. A moment later, he walks in. I don't know how he'll react. I know he still won't even acknowledge that she's alive.

"Hey. Your mom is going to take over the wedding planning so you and I can focus on more important things." I wink.

He bends down to kiss me. "We can get married in the bathroom with just the two of us if that's what you want."

"Oh, son, no," she protests.

"Nobody asked for your opinion." He deadpans.

I swat his arm. "Babe, stop."

"I have a meeting with my brothers. I'll be back in a bit unless you want to come."

I wrinkle my nose. "Not necessarily."

"Okay, I'll be back soon." He kisses me again before leaving.

Unaffected by his dismissive tone, she stands and holds her arms out. I rise to meet her, slipping into her embrace.

"I'll talk to Niki," she says, squeezing me. "You don't need to worry about a thing."

"Okay. Thank you."

I leave the office so she can continue working and find myself sitting in the same spot by the window where Tess first told me about the contracts. Tess. Tess is gone now. Tess was working for Cristiano. How did she even know him. How had Anya not known of her. Then again, they were never really near each other. Maybe Tess did know Anya and made sure to avoid being anywhere near her. Nobody has said how Marko is doing. He seems fine. But that doesn't mean that he actually is.

Ever since I've been back, I've tried to stay away from here because I was scared. It feels like I haven't seen Marko or even

Ricco since I've been back. But maybe Dom is trying to make sure everyone gives me space.

I've been such a mess that I didn't even realize how much I've blocked out everyone. I guess it's a good thing Dom doesn't like people anyways so he's more than happy to have nobody around.

"Hey, Rainey." A voice startles me out of my thoughts. "Mind if I sit?"

I whip my head in the direction of the voice and find Em approaching me. My heart practically falls into my butt.

"Sure, of course." I swallow the lump in my throat, straightening in my chair and gesturing to the seat across from me.

Her gaze follows mine out the window. Then she draws a deep breath, her shoulders tightening.

"I'm really sorry for everything you went through," she says.

I start to dismiss it with a reflexive, *"It's fine,"* but she holds up a hand, cutting me off gently.

"Please, let me finish." Her eyes meet mine with an intensity that makes me nervous. "I've been working up the nerve to talk to you for a while, and I finally have the chance."

I pinch my lips between my teeth, hating for both of our sakes that this conversation is even happening.

"Dante was a mess while you were gone," she continues. "I've never seen him like that. I've never seen him cry. He wailed at night for you, Rainey. He told me about your past, who you were to him, but I've known. I tried to be there for him, to hold him together when he was falling apart. But now that you're back, now that you're safe…" She pauses, her hands fidgeting. "Rainey, he's asked me to move in with him. His house is finished, and we want to start our life together… But I need to know… Are you done sleeping with him?"

I knew the words were coming, but hearing them out loud makes me freeze. I wonder how long she's known. If the casual conversations have been a mask. She's always been kind to me, never letting on that she might suspect something.

She leans forward, her gaze locked on mine. "I need to know for me. Because I don't want to share him. And I've never had to question whether I was until you. If you're still seeing him or planning to in the future, that will make my decision to move in with him clear."

I shake my head, finding my voice. "No, I'm not going to sleep with him ever again. And I'm so sorry for any and all pain that my actions have caused you."

She reaches out, taking my hand, her touch unexpectedly warm. "No, I'm sorry for everything you've gone through. I'm sorry you were assaulted mere feet away from Damiano. I'm sorry for whatever you endured while you were with Mr. Fierro. I'm just… I'm so sorry, Rainey, and I want you to know that I think you're an incredibly strong person."

Her words crack something inside me, and I lower my head, tears spilling before I can stop them. She moves to sit beside me, wrapping her arms around my shoulders and holding me as silent sobs wrack my body. The one who was cheated on is trying to console the homewrecker. It's just one more reason she is a better woman than me.

When I finally relax, she pulls back. "I'm madly in love with Dante."

I meet her gaze, the rawness of her confession settling between us. "I know."

She hesitates, her lips parting as if she's weighing whether to say the next words. Then she does. "I'm sorry you were refused. That has to hurt, knowing you were considered unworthy, and then someone like me—a contracted whore—is found to be worthy of him."

My brows pull together. "I don't think that at all. You are worthy of him, Em. And you're not a whore."

She gives a small, sad smile. "Well, I signed on here knowing what I was getting myself into. I also knew the first night I was with Dante that he was wasted out of his mind, rambling on about the woman he loved being from a trailer park, about how his dad wouldn't let him marry her."

A bitter laugh catches in my throat, but I swallow it back. It's not funny. Not really. Especially for Lorenzo's sake. He still ended up with the girl from the trailer park marrying into his family.

"I was so upset," she admits, her eyes shimmering with unshed tears. "I was just trying to comfort him, to make him feel better. We didn't do anything that night. He just complained and went on and on about how she was the most beautiful woman he'd ever seen. And then the next day, he called me into his office, apologized, and said he was out of line. You know how he gets.

"He seemed to move on, and when he started seeing only me, when things began to develop between us, I knew we were moving forward in our relationship. Yet, for some reason, when I saw you and when I heard talk about you being Damiano's and that you were a girl from a trailer park, I knew exactly who you were.

"I saw Dante's face at the auction. I watched how he looked like he was trying to claw his way out of his own skin as he watched Damiano have sex with you, and the way he stared when you were sitting on Damiano's lap. He was… he was shattered to pieces. And day after day, he was all over the place.

"He watched the cameras in the house of you. He accidentally left them up one day when I went to his office. I asked him who you were, and I learned really quickly not to mention your name.

"I could hear Gio and Silvano talking about wanting to have sex with you, and Dante flipped out on them. They assumed it was because of Damiano, but later on, it clicked that it was because of his own feelings. I know he still loves you. I don't think he will ever not love you, but I think he's at a good place mentally to understand and accept that you and Damiano are getting married.

"He was really mad when he found out Giovanni slept with you. I think he was more mad at that than Damiano being the one who gets to marry you."

I don't know what she wants me to say. Dante and Giovanni are different in bed, and at this point in my life, Giovanni is the one I need. Dante is a lover; Giovanni is a fucker. And right now, being fucked is what I crave. But the only one I truly need is Damiano.

"We never intended for anyone to know. And we definitely weren't intentionally trying to hurt Dante. I believe after some time, Dante's feelings will go away and he will realize they were never real."

"I hope you're right." She stares for another moment then stands. "I guess I should start packing. I have a new home to decorate."

I smile and nod. "Yes, you do."

Chapter

FIFTY-SIX

Rainey

I hate this.

I hate every second of this.

I hate that I have to go through another wedding.

Okay, well, this one is pretend.

But still, a wedding again feels impossible. Anytime it's been mentioned in the last two weeks, I completely shut down. Niki and Valentina decided we should do a walk-through to help me adjust and figure out what kind of prep I still need, but this walk-through feels too real.

The full setup.

The aisle.

The vows.

The expectations.

The only part I actually like is Dante walking me down the aisle.

He asked if he could, and I cried.

There's no one else I'd rather have give me away.

He practically already did once.

This is just a practice run.

This.

Is.

Just.

A.

Practice.

Run.

We're outside, in the gardens, near the sprawling pond and waterfall.

It's beautiful. It should be beautiful.

Rows of white chairs with dark crimson bows all neatly placed.

A deep crimson aisle.

White flower petals for Anya to scatter.

Everything perfectly staged.

Except me.

I stand at the end of the aisle with Dante, his arm over my trembling hand.

Dom waits at the other end, his eyes locked on me, Nikolai and Giovanni beside him, Giulia and Niki on the other side, casually holding flowers they picked from the garden.

This should be perfect.

This should feel like a dream come true.

But then the music starts.

And everything cracks.

Dante's arm feels solid, like a lifeline I'm clinging to, but my grip is slipping.

The aisle stretches before me, longer than it should be.

Dom is too far. The air is too thin.

Why is he getting farther away?

I can't breathe.

I can't breathe.

Cristiano is waiting for me.

Not Dom.

Cristiano.

All those eyes.

Those people who knew.

Who watched.

Who didn't stop it.

Who didn't save me.

I can't breathe.

My chest is tightening.

My throat is closing.

I'm clawing at someone's arm, my own neck, but the air won't come.

I can't get enough.

I'm breaking.

Splintering.

Cracking open.

Am I falling?

I'm on the ground.

Everything is muffled, like I'm underwater.

Voices are shouting, but I can't make them out.

I stare up.

The sky is too bright.

Too blue.

The color of Cristiano's eyes.

A bird soars above, a small black dot against endless space.

Then, a voice.

"Baby... baby... I'm right here. I've got you."

Dom.

He's here.

That should mean I'm okay.

That I'm safe.

Dom is here.

The thought is nice, comforting even. Maybe we died? I don't actually know. I'd be okay if I did. I'd be okay if he did to, and he was here with me.

But I don't feel okay.

I don't feel safe.

I don't feel anything at all.

Then, a sharp, sudden prick in my thigh, like a bee sting. My muscles jolt, my lungs expanding as if air has been forced back into them, and I gasp, my mouth opening wide as my body shoots upright. I clutch at my throat, the feeling of suffocation breaking all at once.

I claw at my skin as I choke on my own sobs, eyes wild and unseeing. My pulse thunders in my ears, drowning out the frantic voices all around.

When my vision finally sharpens, I'm met with the terrified faces of the people I love. Dante is behind me, cradling me tightly, while Damiano leans over me from the front.

"Baby." His hands cup my face. "You're okay. I'm here. I've got you."

But I'm not okay. I'm trembling so hard my teeth clatter.

The sob that tears from my throat as Dom scoops me into his arms is raw and guttural, ripping through me with a force that has others around us crying. Everything narrows to the feel of his arms around me as he carries me away.

The world outside blurs past the windows as he drives us home. My head rests against his shoulder, my mind trapped in a swirling haze of grief and panic. I'm only partially aware as he lifts me again before laying me down on our bed. He stretches out behind me, molding his body to mine, holding me close until my tears slowly taper off, leaving me hollow.

I don't know how much time passes before I hear a soft, hesitant knock on the door. Dom kisses my back gently before slipping out of bed, pulling the door halfway closed as he steps into the hall.

Muted voices filter through the crack, their words blending into a distant, buzzing hum at first, before one voice breaks through clearly.

"How is she?" Giovanni asks.

"Maybe an actual wedding is a bad idea." Another voice murmurs.

Their words hit me like a punch to the chest, and my eyes sting with fresh tears. My trauma is going to ruin Dom's chance at a real wedding. Cristiano has ruined me, broken me in ways I can't fix, and now I'm going to ruin Dom's life too.

It's been a week since our last attempt, and this time, everything feels different. Instead of me standing at the end of the aisle with my heart in my throat, the entire wedding party is gathered around me, their voices a comforting mix of laughter and conversation. The officiant stands beside us, her clipboard in hand as she walks us through the rehearsal.

She slowly guides us down the aisle, pointing out that the front row of chairs will be reserved for family, while an additional 150 chairs will be set up for our guests. She gestures toward the side, explaining that a massive tent will be set up with a dance floor for the reception, complete with twinkling lights, dessert tables, and a bar.

As we reach the end of the aisle, the officiant begins walking us through the ceremony, guiding us through the vow exchange. Dom and I agreed to stick to the traditional wording, keeping things simple, with just a repeat-after-her format, followed by the classic "I do."

"And then," Giovanni adds with a grin, "I will assist Dom in consummating the marriage with Rainey."

Dom smacks the back of his head, but even he is smiling, and I find myself relaxing even more.

By the time we turn and start walking back down the aisle, the officiant talking us through the dinner menu and what to expect as we enter the tent, I'm actually feeling okay. Maybe this wedding thing doesn't have to be so terrifying.

On the third walk-through, the very next day, everything feels different. More real. This time, a lot of the chairs are filled with staff watching as we rehearse. It's a small audience, but it still makes my heart race.

Dante leans in to whisper, "Just keep your eyes on Dom, or if it's too much, focus on the aisle. I've got you."

When he offers me his arm, I slip my fingers between his, letting our joined hands rest at our sides. My other hand curls around his bicep, and he reaches up with his free hand, covering mine as he gives me a reassuring smile.

"Does this feel okay to you?" I whisper, my nerves starting to flutter.

He shrugs, his lips twitching with a hint of a smirk. "Meh. I'd rather you guys already be married. Never thought I'd see the day my baby brother actually ties the knot."

I glance up at him, my anxiety easing a little. "So you're happy for us?"

He meets my eyes, his expression softening. "More than you know," he says, giving my hand a gentle squeeze before nodding toward the end of the aisle. "Come on. He's waiting."

As we reach the end, Dom stands there, his eyes locked on mine, and I feel that familiar warmth in my chest. Our officiant steps forward, her voice calm as she starts walking us through the vows once again.

Each time we do a run-through or discuss the wedding, it feels a little more real. We've made adjustments along the way, like moving the ceremony closer to the evening so the celebration can carry into the night. It feels fitting, like we're slowly building up to the real thing.

I've had my hair and makeup done twice now, each time a little closer to what I want for the actual day. Cristiano never let me wear my hair up, so for the wedding I've decided to wear it up. It feels like a final way of reclaiming myself. Yesterday, we all got our nails done, and I'm a creature of habit, so I went with my usual dark crimson gel polish to match the theme.

Today I was warned this would be the closest thing to the actual wedding day. They've brought in *friends and family* to fill the chairs, making it feel more authentic. I won't know a single person sitting there, but Niki insists they're all long-time family friends. I've chalked that up to them belonging to other families who probably dabble in some kind of illegal activity.

When the dress is pulled into place, I turn to the mirror and gape at my reflection. It's stunning. It's form-fitting down to my thighs, where it flares subtly to the floor. The neckline plunges low between my breasts, revealing more than I would have chosen, but I'm guessing this was a Niki touch. The back is completely bare, dipping to just above the curve of my butt. It's bold. Sexy. My boobs look incredible, my waist small, my hips perfectly emphasized. I can't wait for Dom to see me like this.

When Dante steps in, he stops in his tracks, his eyes widening as he takes me in. His mouth opens slightly, and he lets out a slow, appreciative breath.

"Wow, you are… you're stunning, Rainey," he says, his voice rougher than usual.

"Thank you," I smile.

He clears his throat, rubbing the back of his neck as he watches me. "Dom is so incredibly lucky."

The bridal suite is set up right near the ceremony space, close enough that we won't have to worry about crossing the grounds in heels and dresses.

A gentle knock comes at the door before Valentina peeks inside. "Are you ready?" she asks, her smile warm as she steps in a little farther. "You're so beautiful, sweetheart."

"Thanks." I murmur, feeling my nerves starting to bubble up.

"We're ready whenever you are." With a final wave, she slips back out.

Dante turns to me, drawing in a deep breath and slowly letting it go. He does it again until I follow his lead, exhaling with him. "You've got this." Then he offers me his arm.

The music shifts as we step toward the aisle, and a fresh wave of nerves crashes over me. I hadn't realized they planned to fill every chair—not just with the wedding party or a handful of family, but everyone. Row after row of guests dressed to the nines, eyes already fixed on me. Suddenly it all feels too real, and my chest tightens.

I should bolt. I can't walk past all of them. I can't do this.

"Just watch Dom," Dante whispers.

So I do. My gaze finds him instantly. His hands are pressed to his mouth, emotion written all over his face, and Giovanni pats his shoulder.

"Let's get you to your fiancé," Dante says, guiding me into that first step down the aisle.

I move forward toward the man of my dreams. He's so handsome that it steals every ounce of air from my lungs. When I finally reach him, he offers his hands, and I take them, trembling so badly I just know everyone can see.

"We can stop here if you want," he murmurs. "Or we can continue and see how far we can get."

I nod, unable to speak, not even able to look at the crowd.

He smiles. "You're doing amazing." Then his voice drops to a husky whisper in my ear, "I'm going to lift your dress, bend you over, and devour every inch of you."

The words send a rush of butterflies spiraling through me, and I pinch my lips between my teeth.

I spend the rest of the rehearsal thinking of him licking my asshole and wanting to finish so we can get to that part.

I even manage to make it through the vows, and I love when we get to the kissing part. He kisses me hard, then dips me, deepening the kiss.

I keep my gaze on Dom as he scoops me up, carrying me bridal style down the aisle. He holds me until we're back inside the bridal suite. Relief rushes in—a massive weight has finally lifted. I made it through the rehearsal without a single panic attack.

He bends me over the vanity, just as he promised. His tongue traces every inch of me until I'm writhing and grinding against his mouth, desperate for more. When I finally break, pleading for him to stick it in, he does, consummating our pretend marriage right here and now.

When I was gone, I struggled with the bond I feel with him. I have never felt anything like it with anyone else. At first, I thought it might be because he took my virginity, but I knew even before that. I felt it on the bus. I felt it the moment I arrived here. I fell so completely for him, it was as if he alone was the lifeline that kept me breathing. Being with him now, the feeling is even stronger.

More than once, someone slips in to remind us that the guests are waiting in the reception tent. We don't care. Food and dancing couldn't matter less.

As we readjust our clothing I stare at Dom, my heart swelling with happiness.

"I think I'm ready to go through with the actual wedding."

He pauses fastening his belt, as he leans in and bites my lip, then kisses me.

"No need, baby. That was the actual wedding."

Chapter

FIFTY-SEVEN

Rainey

I'm married. I get to say I'm a married woman, to Damiano Volkov of all people. I'm not sure of the logistics of it, but he showed me it's already official and my name is legally changed. I'm officially a Volkov.

Dom seems to be enjoying me being his wife, too, because he has only been referring to me as "my wife." When I asked if I'm a possession now, he said I'm as much his possession as he is mine, and now *"my wife"* has stuck.

I didn't get a honeymoon. I didn't really expect one, not with how important it is for us to keep our routine consistent, but I'd be lying if I said I didn't secretly hope he had something planned. Giovanni offered to take us out dancing at one of their clubs he runs, but with Cristiano still out there, it didn't feel like a good idea. None of the guys would be drinking, and the idea of going out and not being able to truly let loose with my husband just sounded… lame.

So instead, I've been moping around the house all week.

Dom invited Giovanni over, and I knew exactly what that meant. I sat Dom down and told him I took my vows seriously, and I never want to share our bed with anyone else again.

I don't know if he felt relieved or if he was indifferent, but after that conversation, we had the best sex of my life. I told him that from now on, every time he has sex with me, it better be just as good or better. He laughed and pulled me into his arms, holding me so tight all night that I could hardly move—but I didn't mind one bit.

My calls with Cristiano have been unbearable, each one somehow worse than the last. I don't even know why he insists on talking. I can hear the hatred dripping from every word, and when his name lights up the screen, I want to smash the phone.

The last call was the night after the wedding, and I refused to play. I wasn't in the mood to pretend with him or hold my pee like that. He was furious. When he saw the hickies on my neck, it set him off. He called me every name he could think of, screaming that he was going to kill me. His threats pissed me off so badly that I undressed, letting him see every mark Dom had left on me. Every hickey, every bite, even the intimate places where Dom's teeth marked me. Cristiano lost it, smashing everything within reach.

His words got worse. Each threat was more cruel than the last. Dom hovered nearby, inching closer, so close at one point, I wondered if Cristiano could see him on the screen. And when Cristiano's rage spilled over and he became out of his mind, I hung up. I knew I'd "pay for it" during our next call, but I didn't care. He started bringing Giulia into it, and that was my line. She's pregnant, emotional, and it makes me emotional for her. I wasn't going to let him threaten her or talk about her.

I almost slipped up and mentioned the pregnancy, but I caught myself. If he knew, if he threatened her baby, I'd blow our entire plan because I'd never talk to him again.

Now I sit on the porch swing, staring out into the yard, trying not to think about how tonight's call will go. I didn't just hang up on him, I shut my phone off so he couldn't reach me. I can only imagine the rage that evoked, especially after seeing the marks on my body, and knowing exactly how they came to be there. I'm sure he's been fantasizing about all the ways he wants to kill me and Dom.

"It's time, my wife." Dom leans against the porch pillar, crossing his arms, watching me.

I keep swinging, not acknowledging his words.

"Come on." He steps forward holding his hands out.

"I don't have it in me tonight."

He sits beside me instead, draping an arm around my neck. We remain in silence for fifteen minutes, our heads pressed together and my fingers laced with his on my shoulder.

Finally, I let out a sigh and look at him. "Ready."

He nods, taking my hand as we walk back inside together.

I prop the phone on the same shelf I always do, waiting for it to power on while I stare up at the chandelier. The glass catches the light, fracturing it across the walls, giving me something to focus on besides the dread I'm currently experiencing.

When the phone begins to vibrate, I glance down, Cristiano's video call flashing across the screen. I look at Dom, and he winks, giving me the push I need to answer.

I brace for his wrath, but it doesn't come. Instead, he's calm. It completely throws me off. It's fake, that much I know. I can see right through his bullshit façade.

"How are you, darling?"

The words are nice, but they feel like a trap. I let out a slow sigh, rubbing my eyebrows to stave off the tension headache already creeping in.

"What is that?" he asks, his voice tightening.

"What is what?" I sigh, annoyance threading through my words.

Then I see my wedding ring, glinting in the light. I forgot to take it off.

I internally begin to panic. I need Dom to somehow tell me telepathically what to do because I'm drawing a blank. When my eyes drop to the ring, everything else falls away. *Damiano is my husband*. Damiano and Rainey Volkov. I'm a Volkov now. I'm part of this family—officially.

"What has you smiling like that?"

His voice cuts in, snapping me back. I hadn't realized I was. I press my lips together, forcing it away as I look back up at him.

"Well?"

"It's nothing." I lower my hand, covering the ring.

His eyes narrow, the control beginning to slip. "Show me your hand, Rainey." His tone is a thin veneer of calm, barely masking the simmering anger I know too well.

Slowly, I extend my fingers so he can see the ring. His jaw muscle flexes and his breathing shifts.

"What have we here?"

"Nothing."

"Nothing?" he repeats. "As in, you think I can't see the ring on the same finger my wedding ring is supposed to be sitting? The wedding ring I found discarded like trash in our home."

I wonder if he found it himself when he returned to his house where all his men were left slaughtered. I'm sure he enjoyed finding it, especially after I stabbed him then left with his enemy.

I won't deny what this ring means, and I won't lie about Dom being my husband now. Instead, I opt for silence.

He studies the ring for a beat longer, then exhales. "Keep your phone on you for the next couple of days." And the call disconnects.

My eyes widen as I look at Dom. "I think he's having big feelings right now," I tease.

DOM HAD A MEETING WITH DANTE AND SAID I COULDN'T GO. HE never even told me what the meeting was about. I would have protested if I weren't already cuddled up with Giulia on the couch.

"You just gonna keep kicking Auntie's face?" I coo into her rounded belly.

Another kick.

"You're so strong, buddy." I push back gently against his tiny feet.

"He's so active around you," Giulia says with a soft smile.

I let out a contented sigh and rest my cheek against the spot he keeps pushing.

I trace lightly along the side of her bare belly, feeling the rise and fall of her breathing as she drifts off to sleep. I tilt my head to look up at her, and my heart squeezes a little tighter. I still remember the first time I saw her. How she lay there, letting those men use her and then walk away like she was nothing.

But she isn't nothing. She's incredible. Brave, strong, supportive. She kept me alive, kept me sane, when we were stuck in that hell together.

Aside from Dom, I've never let anyone in the way I let her in. She was all I had for so long, and I don't think I'll ever let someone that close again. The fact that she plans to stay, to build a life with Niki, means I get to keep her in my life too.

Dom asked if we should try to find the family she had been taken from, but I selfishly told him not to bring it up because I didn't want to risk her leaving. He still spoke with Niki, and she eventually brought it to her. She said that while she's pregnant, she doesn't want to pursue it, but will consider it once the baby is born.

The garage door slams shut and it startles Giulia, the baby, and me.

Dom strides through, his expression hard, disappearing into the bedroom without a word. I'm guessing his meeting with Dante wasn't good. I don't really want to piss him off further, so I'll just stay put.

Niki sinks down on the couch beside Giulia, lifting her head and gently setting it in her lap, brushing her hair back.

"Why does he seem mad?"

She doesn't get a chance to answer me. Dom reappears with a bag slung over his shoulder.

"Come on." His tone leaves no room for questions as he heads for the garage again.

I scramble to my feet, my pulse spiking.

"Damiano, is everything okay?" Giulia asks, sitting up, her eyes wide.

"Babe. Now."

I lean down, pressing a quick kiss to Giulia's cheek before hurrying after him. He pulls open the driver's door of his truck, then steps back for me to climb in. I barely settle into the seat before he's in beside me, the engine roaring to life, and we're speeding away.

I'm still trying to piece together what's happening when we pull up in front of the main house. He never parks here. Ever. My confusion only deepens when we step inside, and Giovanni, Nikolai, and Silvano are in full tactical gear, their faces grim and focused. Dante stands nearby in a suit, phone in one hand, barking orders while pointing at two bags on the couch.

"Get her hair and makeup done," he calls.

Three girls appear and usher me to a stool at the counter.

"What's going on?" I ask as brushes and palettes are unpacked.

"We have a dinner tonight," Dante says. "I wasn't going to have you come until I knew for certain, but Cristiano was spotted landing an hour ago. Dom mentioned he knows about the ring. I'm guessing he's planning on making a move to get you back. We made sure word got to him about the dinner and our location. He'll be there."

My stomach drops, my heart pounding so hard I can feel it in my throat.

"How do you know?" I manage.

"He wants you back. That's how I know. You're ready, Rainey."

Dante sounds so sure, but I don't think I am. For so long, this has just been a plan, a distant, theoretical conversation about what we would do if we ever got the chance. But now it's real. He's here.

I feel like I might do one of the three P's: puke, poop, or pass out as they finish putting me together. My hair is curled into loose waves down my back, and my makeup is subtle. A black dress is held up, the girl waiting expectantly. I undress right there with everyone watching.

"Bra and panties too," she says, nodding toward the last pieces of fabric on me.

Well, okay then.

I take off my bra, tossing it into the chair I was just in, then slide my panties down my legs, picking them up and tossing them to Dom. "A present for my husband." I wink.

"That's fucked up." Giovanni's mouth falls open as Dom tucks them into his suit pocket.

I'm handed what I think is a black thong, but it's barely more than a few strings sewn together. As I pull them up, Gio calls out, "Dibs on those ones."

I turn to the girl holding the dress, and she bends to help me step into it.

"I can literally feel all of you staring at my ass."

"It's a good ass," Dom says, giving it a slap just as the fabric is pulled up over it.

Heels are slipped onto my feet, and then we're moving.

Outside, there are two vehicles waiting. Giovanni, Silvano, and Nikolai head toward one while Dante strides to the passenger door of the other.

"Why are we splitting up?" I ask, the worry creeping into my voice.

"We're going to dinner. They're lookout," Dante explains, walking back toward me.

I chew on my lower lip, staring at Giovanni.

"Got this to protect me, dollface. I'm good." He taps his bulletproof vest, giving me a reassuring smirk.

I hold his gaze, trying to figure out what will protect his face from a bullet. He walks to me, pulling me to his chest and kissing the top of my head. I squeeze him a moment longer before letting out a sigh. "I'll fucking bring you back to life just to kill you again if anything happens to your big ass."

He laughs, spanking my butt. "Yes, ma'am."

Then I climb into the backseat of the other vehicle.

The entire drive, Dante and Dom go over the plan. Dom has gone through every possible scenario and told me exactly what to do in each one.

"I'm fucking scared," I admit quietly. "What if he gets away with me?"

He cups my face, pulling me close so I have no choice but to look at him. "The only way that happens is if every one of us is dead."

"And if that happens?" I gape at him.

He shrugs. "We'd be dead. Nothing would happen on our end. You'd have to figure it out yourself."

"Dom!" I punch his stomach.

"I'm not dying, my wife." He reassures me.

"Good. Because if you do, I'm gonna fuck your dad."

It was a joke, but the way Marko's eyes widen as he gapes in the rearview mirror, Dante turns around with his nose wrinkled in disgust, and Dom saying "Yuck" at the same time makes me laugh.

"Make sure we all go home in one piece then."

When we arrive at the restaurant, Dante steps out first, adjusting his jacket before heading for the entrance. Dom opens his door and steps out, then turns, holding out his hand. I take it, and as soon as I'm on my feet, he pulls me into him, gripping my waist, his lips crashing against mine.

He pulls back, lingering just a breath away, smiling before coming in for one more quick, possessive kiss. His fingers lace tightly with mine as he guides me inside.

I let out a quiet sigh of relief once we're through the doors, grateful we weren't riddled with bullets on the way in.

At the table, Dante falls easily into conversation with the men around us. It actually sounds like a real meeting, and I can't tell if this plan was woven into a dinner that was already on the schedule or if this entire thing is an act. Either way, I know I'm just meant to sit here.

I peer around the dimly lit restaurant, my heart picking up speed. I don't know why, but I can feel him. *Cristiano is here.*

For an hour I sit rigid, trying to relax but I can't. I can sense the exact moment when his eyes aren't on me anymore, that strange awareness fading like a shadow slipping back into darkness.

I dab at my mouth with my napkin and murmur that I need to use the restroom, easing my chair back.

Each step I take, I have to tell myself to just keep walking. I feel like the entire room knows what we are up to, and I can't get to the bathroom fast enough.

I take a deep breath, hands braced against the cool porcelain of the sink as I glance up at my reflection. My lipstick is still intact, despite Dom's hungry kisses. I check my teeth, making sure I don't have any food still trying to hang out, then smooth my hair back into place.

I turn to the small, frosted window on the far wall, pushing at it to see if it'll budge, but it doesn't move. I just want to peek outside, to see if he's really out there or if I'm just imagining his presence. Maybe he isn't even here.

I linger for a moment longer, trying to calm my racing heart, before turning back toward the door. I push it open, my eyes dropping to my clutch as I make my way down the hall, mentally rehearsing the cool, composed expression I need to have when I return.

A hand clamps over my mouth, cutting off my startled gasp as an arm wraps around my waist, hoisting me off my feet. I kick and thrash, muffled screams tearing from my throat as I'm dragged down the darkened hall and out the back exit.

A blacked-out limo waits in the alley, and I'm dragged toward it. The door swings open as we approach, and I'm shoved inside. I grab the handle and frantically tug, but it's locked from the inside. Panic surges, but then I catch movement out of the corner of my eye and turn.

Blue eyes stare back at me, cold and unblinking as he lazily sips his whiskey.

It's dead silent in here, and he looks pissed. He's on the seat catty-corner from me, just watching.

"You have five seconds to get that fucking ring off your finger before I cut your finger off."

I rip it off so fast, throwing it to the floor on the other side of the limo.

Now it makes sense why Dom swapped it with a fake. I'd never disrespect my actual wedding ring like that.

He downs the rest of his whiskey, then hurls the glass at the partition between us and the driver. I yelp as shards explode across the floor.

He moves, shifting to the seat beside me. I press my back against the door, eyes locked on him as he turns his head toward me.

"Come here, darling." He holds out his hand.

I stare at it, then look up at him.

His slap comes so fast I don't see it, pain exploding across my cheek as stars dance in my vision.

I wipe my lip, tasting blood, and a fistful of my hair is yanked as he pulls me closer.

"You fucking slut," he spits, his whole body vibrating with rage. "You're fucking dead. Do you hear me," he grits out through clenched teeth.

Oh, I hear him. And I will be if I don't snap out of this damsel-in-distress act.

"I missed you," I whimper, reaching for him with trembling fingers.

Another slap comes just as fast, and the world blurs. I might have blacked out for a second on that one, but the pain drags me back.

"Please," I beg, reaching for him again. "Let me kiss you."

He drives his fist into my stomach, knocking the wind out of me. My eyes widen, my mouth falling open as I stare at him in disbelief. I'm still gasping for air when another slap lands. He yanks my face close, and I'm certain he's about to snap my neck.

"I hate everything about you. I can't stand the sight of you. You're disgusting. You sicken me." He shoves me back, and I finally gulp down air as it fills my lungs.

Then his fist crashes into my jaw, sending me sprawling to the floor, the ringing in my ears drowning everything out. I push up onto my hands, glass shards embedded in my arm and shoulder as blood trickles from the cuts.

But this one pisses me off.

"Fuck you!" I scream, hurling myself at him, shoving and clawing as he tears at my dress. The fabric rips, my breasts spilling free as he bites down on my nipple so hard I wail at the blinding pain.

You will die if you don't fight!

In the haze, I twist the top of the ring on my other finger, feeling the tiny needle slide into place. I don't think, I just drive it into his neck as hard as I can.

He releases my nipple and clamps around my throat, squeezing. His grip is crushing, a strength I know is meant to end me, but just as my vision begins to fade, it slowly sharpens again as his hold weakens. His jaw slackens, and I pull back, locking onto him. Confusion flickers across his face as he touches the injection site. The back door swings open and Dom bends down, peering inside.

"I'm going to kill you," Cristiano manages, his words slurring as his body begins to go limp.

I shake my head. "No. *You* won't." I jerk my chin at Dom. "*He* is going to kill *you*."

Dom reaches for me, and I slide off Cristiano's lap, letting him help me out.

Giovanni breaks into a sprint the moment he sees the condition I'm in. Dante rounds the corner, eyes sweeping for threats, and as soon as he spots me, he speeds up.

Marko and Ricco move in, hauling Cristiano's limp body toward a waiting van, his legs dragging across the pavement.

The adrenaline hits all at once, every inch of me shaking violently as the reality of what just happened sinks in. Tears burst free, shoulders heaving, while Dom dabs at my nipple, inspecting the bite.

"Are you okay?" Giovanni asks, gently turning my face toward him, taking in the damage with a frown.

I nod, then suddenly a laugh breaks free. They all exchange wary looks as I throw my head back, unable to contain myself. "What a fucking loser!" I howl.

Dom opens the trunk of the SUV and guides me to sit, pulling out a first aid kit to clean my boob. I wonder what he's feeling right now. After years of hunting Cristiano, after all the pain and planning, he finally has him.

Nikolai uses tweezers to pull shards of glass out of my arm, while Giovanni wipes blood from the corner of my mouth. "I fucking told you we should have moved sooner," he mutters at Dom.

"And I said she could take care of herself."

"Yeah, and he still put his hands on her."

"And he never will again." Dom straightens.

They're nose to nose now, glaring at each other.

"Stop it." I push them apart with my legs. "It's already done. Let it go, Giovanni." I give him a pointed look.

He exhales, nostrils flaring, then cups the back of my head and kisses my forehead. Without another word, he turns and storms back to his SUV, slamming the door so hard the entire vehicle rattles.

Nearby, Dante paces with his phone to his ear, deep in conversation with Lorenzo.

From what I've pieced together from the conversation, Lorenzo and Valentina are on a flight home as we speak and will be back within the next several hours. Dante says we are about to head home now and will wait to do anything until they return.

It feels like those last words were meant for Dom, but he gives no response. Instead, he slips out of his shirt and holds it open for me, then buttons it over my torn dress.

When Dante ends the call, he lets out a long sigh, studying my face. "You okay?"

"Yeah."

He watches me for another moment, then gives a small nod. "Okay. Let's get home."

Chapter
FIFTY-EIGHT

Rainey

Cristiano is handcuffed to a chair in one of the glass rooms. The same room Trixie died in.

I shouldn't enjoy seeing him like this, but I do. He's slumped against the wall, head lolled to the side, still passed out. I've seen that face sleeping so many times before, back when I used to lie awake, imagining all the ways I could kill him while he slept. Now, here he is, so close to death.

He always felt untouchable to me. Now he's nothing. Helpless. It makes everything he did to me feel small in comparison, almost like it never happened.

But it did. He was awful to me.

There's no real plan for what happens next. Lorenzo asked Dom if he was good. He just gave a single nod. This must be emotional for all of them, the past finally colliding with the present, the end they've all been waiting for. All the Volkovs are here, all the men who spent years hunting Cristiano, risking their lives to help bring him down. Everyone gathered to watch how this ends.

I'm alone in here with him. Dom gave me that.

My back is to the crowd, the walls disguised to look normal, though I know they can see everything on the other side of the glass. I sit and watch. And keep watching, until his eyes start to flutter.

He lifts his head, blinking against the light, testing the cuffs before realizing he's trapped.

When his gaze finally finds mine, his eyes are empty.

"Darling."

Darling.

That fucking nickname I always hated, and I'm so close to never hearing it again.

"You and Damiano spent years trying to kill each other, and now you're the one who lost. How does that feel?"

His jaw ticks, a slow exhale leaving him. "Like he's taken the only two women I ever loved."

I scoff. "You never loved me."

"I did. Still do."

"No." I lean forward, letting him see how little fear I have left for him. "You loved knowing you had the only thing Damiano cares about. You don't beat and rape the people you love."

"Were you not raped when you were chained to a dirty mattress and fucked in front of a room full of people? Who took your virginity that night? The one you like to call your boyfriend?"

"Husband, actually," I smirk. "We're married now. Two weeks. Funny, now that I think about it, I said *I do* to the same name at both weddings… you remember, right?" I revel in the way his fingers twitch at my words. "And after Dom and I got married, we fucked and fucked."

I tilt my head. "Well, actually, that's not much different from how we've always been. I used to worry you'd see all his semen on our video calls, but we didn't really care. We'd go at it right up until I had to take your stupid little call, and as soon as I hung up, we'd go at it again."

"Yeah, sluts like to fuck."

"I do. Wanna know the best part about Damiano having so many brothers? They just pass me around. I practically never even leave my bed."

"Shut your fucking mouth." He strains against the cuffs, trying to get to me but going nowhere.

The one thing he could never stand was the thought of me having sex with another man. His hatred for the Volkovs runs deep, and I know exactly how to twist the knife.

"I wonder how an entire family of men managed to get massive cocks."

I've seen three of the brothers naked, and they're all well-endowed. I'm willing to bet it doesn't stop with those three. So technically, I'm not lying—it's just inductive reasoning.

"Fuck you!" he roars. "Fuck you! I treated you like a queen, and this is the bullshit you do!"

"Good thing I played your ass." I gesture to my bruised face. "Look what you did to me. You were going to kill me, remember?"

Rage flashes in his eyes, teeth gritted as he spits out, "I fucking dream about all the ways I want to kill you. You stabbed me and ran back to the same family that gave you to me in the first place!"

"What exactly did you do that would have you think I'd want to stay with you?" You stole me from my boyfriend and expected me to just fall for you? You treated me like trash the entire time, and you're surprised I wanted to go home to the man I love? You faked Niki's death. You watched me mourn for her for months. You're sick."

"Spare me. You're just as twisted," he shoots back.

My chin jerks back. "Me?" I scoff. "That's bold."

"Did you tell Damiano you like pissing in my mouth?"

I lean forward, glaring. "You forced me."

"You begged for it."

Our eyes lock, neither of us backing down.

He lets out a short laugh. "What about when you fingered my ass and sucked on your own fingers? I sure as fuck didn't ask for that."

"You got me high, and I thought you were Damiano. Your dumbass even let me moan his name while I fucked you."

"And fucked me you did, because you're a filthy slut who's into weird shit and fucks like you've been taking dick since you hit puberty. But sure, I'm the one that's mental."

"You say that like I should be ashamed I enjoy sex. An orgasm feels good, no matter who you are. And even though I find you disgusting, I could picture Damiano the entire time just to get through it." I sit back, refusing to let him see he's getting to me.

Even cuffed, he holds himself with infuriating confidence. I have to remind myself he has no power here. He can't touch me.

"I'm dying today, and I'd rather it be by the hands of the one I love. Come fuck me, and I'll let you kill me however you want."

I'd think he was joking, but his face remains serious.

I hold his stare, letting it stretch, then trail down his frame before locking eyes with him once more.

I push up from my chair and move to his side, leaning against the table, fingers curling around the edge. "If I reach in your pants, pull your erection out and ride you, you'll let me choke the life out of you?"

"Yes. If you do it while I'm coming, I can't imagine a better way to go."

My eyes narrow. "And if I kiss you? Are you going to try to bite me?"

"No, darling."

"Okay." I bite my lip seductively. "Do you miss my pussy?"

"Yes." His eyes drop to my mouth, lips parting.

"What about it?"

"How tight it gripped my cock."

I hum low in my throat. "Anything else?"

He nods. "How good you taste."

"Taste where?"

"Between your legs."

I shift my chest subtly side to side. "What about my filthy mouth?"

"I love your filthy mouth."

I lean back on my hands. "Now what?"

He licks his lips. "Spread your legs."

I obey, and he audibly exhales.

I rub my hand over my vagina, spreading my lips. "Do you want this filled?"

"Yes." He's panting now.

"Me too."

The door slams open. Dom storms in, belt already undone, cock out, grabbing my legs and thrusting into me.

My mouth falls open on a gasp as I look down, watching him bury himself inside me.

"Is this filled enough?" Dom growls.

My brain registers Cristiano's wild threats. The chair should be shaking with how hard he's fighting, but it's heavy enough that it doesn't move at all.

He's cursing us, and I can't focus on anything but the way Dom keeps hitting that perfect spot—the one that has my body tensing and shaking as liquid bursts out. My head falls back on a moan, and I writhe against him as he grunts, his tongue pushing into my mouth as we make out while he comes.

When he pulls out, I smirk, watching him zip his pants.

Cristiano's face is red, eyes squeezed shut, chest heaving with rage.

I feel Dom's cum leaking out of me. I look, then scoop it up and step closer, smearing it across Cristiano's mouth. His eyes snap open with fury.

"How's that taste, asshole?"

He loses it, pulling against the restraints, shouting nonsense. "Cunt—dead—"

I stand over him. "Pathetic."

He spits, hitting my chin. I wipe it off, glance at it, then slap him harder than I've ever hit anyone. "Fuck you."

Then I take Dom's hand and walk out.

Chapter

FIFTY-NINE

Rainey

For ten minutes, he doesn't settle. He thrashes against the restraints, cursing and yelling, saliva running down his chin as he fights the cuffs locking him to the chair. His eyes are wild, like he's trying to convince himself he still has control.

Another twenty minutes pass before his movements slow, and the mask of superiority he wears so well slides back into place.

Niki clears her throat and says she wants to talk to him. Dante, Valentina, and Lorenzo all shut it down at the same time, telling her it's not a good idea, especially since he kidnapped her. But she says that's exactly why she needs to. She needs to confront him to find closure.

And with that, she's permitted to go.

She enters the room and walks to the same chair I was in. They stare at each other, locked in a silent battle, and so much passes between them without a single word spoken.

Just when I think neither plans to speak, he does.

"You never tried to be discreet about your feelings," he starts. "I guess that was intentional. Out of your whole family, you were the one I could barely stand. You'd flaunt around half-naked, thinking it made up for your awful personality." He smirks when she doesn't react. "When you ended up in the middle of this, I thought, *of course Nikita would insert herself.* Always needed to be the center of attention. I figured years away would kill that little crush you had on me, but after that first night—when you saw I had been inside Rainey's tight little cunt—you looked pathetically heartbroken."

Niki doesn't so much as move.

"It's one thing to hear about someone fucking, another to watch it. Did you ever tell Rainey you hated her for choosing herself over you, when deep down you thought it meant you'd finally get to fuck me? That while she was getting touched and fucked by all those toys and hands, your pussy was dripping for me?" He pauses, eyes narrowing. "Did you ever tell Rainey, or your family, that you tried to cut a deal? You begged me to let Rainey go, and you'd stay with me forever. Even now, you can't get over your stupid little crush. You're pathetic, Nikita."

His gaze sharpens. "Did Rainey ever tell you how, after months of trying to resist me, she'd initiate sex, begging for it? She's a wild little thing in bed." He sucks in a breath, shaking his head slightly. "And that body—fuck, that body. She makes these little whimpers right before she comes. It's incredible."

Niki still watches him, and I wonder when she plans on talking. *Cut him off. Don't let him spew his useless nonsense.*

Their stare-down drags on before she crosses her legs and clasps her fingers. "You were my first crush. I thought I could give you better. A paper sack could have given you better. Everyone knew your wife was screwing around, but you were too stupid to see it. You thought she was loving and devoted, but she just wanted your money. She'd come home with everyone's semen in her but her own husbands, then pretend to want you, rub all over you, but never actually put out for you. So, yeah, I tried to seduce you like you said. It was hard to get over that crush because I thought I knew you, that we were the same, that I could give you everything you wanted and you'd finally know a loving and devoted partner. When Damiano killed your pathetic excuse of a wife, I fantasized that you and I could fix everything that was broken. But you're a lousy human. You're nothing, and now you'll die as nothing."

Then she pauses. "You're wrong about one thing, though. I wasn't turned on by watching you brutally rape Rainey. I was horrified. What you did to her haunts me. You haunt me. You went from being a dream of what I wanted for my future to the nightmare I can't shake. But after today, you'll be forgotten, because none of us will ever think about you again after tonight."

He shrugs. "Do you think anything you say will bother me?"

She mirrors his shrug. "I know better than to expect real feelings from you."

"Then leave."

I can't see her face, but she doesn't move. When she speaks again, her voice cracks. "Why? Why any of it?"

"Why does anything matter?"

"Because you're not even fifty, and you're dying today. You threw your life away for what? Revenge? It's so Stupid."

A sob slips out, and she bolts, jerking the door open. She glances back once before stepping out, closing it behind her. She doesn't come back right away, and I imagine her still standing on the other side, trying to collect herself.

I glance at Giulia, and she looks back, worried. I pull her into me, and she wraps her arms around my waist.

When Niki returns, there's hurt in her eyes I didn't expect. I had no idea she felt that deeply about Cristiano.

No one says a word, and Giovanni decides it's his turn. I wasn't exactly sure what he would say, but he went in with his metaphorical guns blazing.

"Just wanted to say, I make Rainey squirt, and it's heaven. Her body writhes on my dick, and after that first squirt, she turns into a hellcat. We're gonna celebrate your death by all fucking her. Picture it—her tits pressed against the glass, palms flat, cheek against the window while every one of us fills her with Volkov DNA."

Cristiano looks like he's barely holding it together, his jaw clenching so hard it might crack.

"Who even are you?" he scoffs. "There's so many of you worthless kids, hard to keep track."

"I'm this one." He pulls out his phone and plays the video of me riding him, with Damiano climbing in behind me.

That gets a reaction. A big one. Cristiano hawks a loogie and spits on Giovanni. "Fuck you, fat fuck."

I can't think of a single insult that could hurt Giovanni's self-esteem. He knows he's hot and isn't ashamed of it.

"Only fat thing on me is my cock." He smirks, raising an arm to flex his massively large muscles. "The only fat thing that will be on me is Rainey's ass and that plump pussy choking my cock."

"My men will find you and gut you." Cristiano's face is bright red, veins pulsing on his neck.

"You like watching, huh, pervert. You wanna watch her pussy get pounded again?"

"Get the fuck out!"

"Yeah. I think I will. I don't get off on pervs watching me." He says, patting the back of Cristiano's head really hard.

Others go in and out, offering their final words to the devil in that room. Not all of them are even bitter. Some say they wish things could have ended differently, that everyone might have found some kind of understanding before it came to this. But he let hatred consume him from the inside out, and once it took hold, there was no stopping it. His mind was set.

When Lorenzo finally enters, he appears genuinely sad, like he is saying goodbye to a friend. They talk quietly for a few minutes before Lorenzo steps to Cristiano's side, placing a hand on his shoulder.

"May whatever waits for you on the other side bring you the peace you never found here." He turns and leaves without looking back.

When Valentina enters, Cristiano tells her to "get the fuck out."

She's the only one he immediately talks to, and it's just to get her to go away, but it still throws me off. After a moment of back and forth, I realize he blames her for all of this. For bringing her son around his wife. For sending me to him, where he fell for me. For losing me because her son came for me. And now, for being here, all because of her.

"Rainey was never yours. Carmella was a whore. And you, you're nothing worth remembering. My son, the boy you called retarded, married the love of his life. He will give me beautiful grandbabies with Rainey while you rot in the ground, forgotten."

"Don't forget who put us in this shit in the first place, you two-faced wench."

She steps closer and looks down at him. He glares at her, and she slaps him hard across the face.

"For hurting my daughter-in-law."

Then she strides out.

Dante and Dom stare at each other, and I'm not sure what's passing between them, but something does.

Dante exhales then strides to the room. He doesn't sit. He stands there with his hands stuffed in his pockets.

"I'm sorry." He starts.

Of course level-headed Dante would start like that.

"I'm sorry that you're about to watch proof the baby wasn't yours. It was mine. But I didn't sleep with her in the way you're thinking. There was no secret affair, no devious backstabbing. Carmella was an abuser. I'm not sorry I saved my brother, that I walked in and figured out what she'd been doing to him. She was never able to take his virginity, but she still broke him. She made sure Dom and I knew I was the one who got her pregnant. And I was so angry that she did that to me, to Dom, and to you. You're a victim in this too. At least you were, until you became the terrorizer. Until you hurt Rainey."

Cristiano doesn't seem to care. He lets out a short laugh.

"My god, you too. I never did stand a chance when all of you are in love with Rainey."

Dante doesn't respond.

Cristiano shakes his head, almost amused. "Well, ain't that some shit. And the retard married her."

Dante stares him down.

Cristiano sighs. "She grew up in an abusive home. Of course she ended up right back in the same mess."

"I wish you could have seen past your hatred. Seen the way Damiano and Rainey love each other so deeply. Maybe you would have realized the only other time you've seen that kind of love was with my parents."

Silence stretches between them before Dante pulls his hands from his pocket.

"Brace yourself for what you're about to see. It's rough."

When Dom walks in, we all watch nervously. It's the first time they've seen each other in years, aside from when Dom just boned me in there.

He circles the table and leans against the wall, crossing one ankle over the other. Cristiano notices Dom's wedding ring, and his breathing shifts, his chest rising and falling more heavily.

"You think you know what went on between Carmella and me. But you have no idea. I look forward to enlightening you."

Dom adjusts the monitor while Andrei works at the computer. "Andrei put together a rendition of your wife's behaviors."

The moment the screens on our end mirror what he's seeing, Dom walks out, leaving Cristiano alone.

Chapter

SIXTY

Rainey

The first video has my eyes welling with tears and my hands cupping my mouth and nose. The first time it shows her drugging him and unable to move against her unwanted assault, the tears flow freely.

When I see what happened to Dante and Dom, I begin retching as a sob breaks free. They both rub my back as I fall apart. The entire room watching Dom being abused repeatedly makes me sick. Seeing Dante try to save his brother, only to be raped, makes my soul weep for them.

For a half hour, years of his abuse is played. Some without audio. Most with audio. And we all watch on the other side of the glass as the realization sinks in that it was Carmella that was the perpetrator. Not Dom. Years of him seeking revenge on a man that was victimized by his wife. The amount of years wasted hating the wrong person, when all along he should have hated himself for not seeing the monster he was married to.

The video ends with Dom confronting Carmella. I've seen this footage before, but never with sound. This time, I hear her admit the baby is Dante's, sneering that Cristiano is too stupid to figure it out. She says she can't wait for the child to be born looking just like a Volkov and that she'll revel in seeing it killed. Dom tells her she's sick and needs help, but she threatens that if he refuses to be with her, she'll tell Cristiano he raped her.

I can't tear my eyes from the screen, yet even as I watch the video, I can't help but think how perfectly matched Cristiano and Carmella were. Both vile. Both disgusting. And she was carrying a life inside her… a life that was half Dante. The thought twists in me as I finally look away, my gaze lifting to him, hating that he ever had to experience that.

I can tell by the look on his face that he's still carrying the weight of what happened. I wonder if, in his heart, it ever truly felt like that was his child. I'd never ask, but the truth is an innocent life was lost because of her. Maybe that soul will one day find its way back to Dante and Em—back to two loving parents who could give it the life it deserved.

As the video comes to an end, Dom steps away and heads toward the room. When he enters, the two of them lock eyes while he circles the table slowly before taking a seat.

"Different perspectives." He says flatly.

Cristiano stares at him, unblinking.

Seeing this video should have made him change his attitude, realize everything he's done over the years was aimed at the wrong person. But apparently, years of hatred are hard to let go of.

"You use one's heart in order to get ahead. I'd say you didn't win at anything. This is a cheap shot. Be a real man and fight me," Cristiano challenges.

Dom just shakes his head. "I have nothing to prove to you."

Silvano and Marko enter the room, and Cristiano looks back at them before scoffing. "Fuckin' goons."

"Fucking clown shoes," Silvano fires back as they both work on uncuffing him.

Cristiano tries to squirm out of their hold, but they're both strong. He's only powerful when it comes to women. Against men, he always relied on his own to do the dirty work. He's no match for Silvano and Marko.

His hands are cuffed behind his back, and he's dragged to the middle of the room where we're all gathered, me standing at the front. He's shoved to his knees, staring up at me, the first trace of reality settling across his face.

"I've dreamed of this exact moment for so long, and yet this feels so anticlimactic." I stare down at him as Dom steps up beside me. "Any last words?"

"Your body will age, the elasticity of your pussy will loosen, and you will be replaced by a younger version."

"And you'll never know whether you're right or not, because you'll be six feet in the ground with bugs eating away at what once was a miserable son of a bitch."

Dom steps in front of him and squats. "I've thought of a million ways I'd torture you when I got my hands on you. I settled on peeling your skin off layer by layer. But that's so time-consuming." He looks down at the knife in his hand, then tosses it in the air, catching it by the handle once again. "Now you can go reunite with your atrocious wife in hell."

He looks over his shoulder at me, and I wait for a long moment before I nod.

Giulia and Niki both step up, grabbing my hands and squeezing, as Dom seizes Cristiano Fierro by the hair, holding tight, and drives the knife into his heart.

His mouth falls open on a gurgled choke, his eyes widening, locking onto mine. I step forward as it looks like he's trying to say something.

I put my face close to his, breathing in his last breaths. "I. Fucking. Hate. You."

And when he stops moving, Dom releases his head, and he slumps to the ground, lifeless.

A collective sigh of relief ripples through the room as Dom and I stand over his body. This man brutalized me, tortured me, raped me, held me hostage, lied to me, and wore me down bit by bit until there was nothing left. He can never hurt me again.

Niki was right when she said he wasted his life. He became a monster. Or maybe he always was one. He could have still had so many years left, but he let hurt and vengeance eat him alive.

Everything he built for himself—the drug business, his employees, his properties—he has nobody. Maybe another group will step in and take them over. If I could remember every place I was moved to during the months he had me, I would go to each and every one of them and burn them down. But it was too many. He kept us on the move for so much of our time.

When I look up, Gio and Marko are staring at me. I turn and look around, and everyone else in the room is staring too.

Dom takes my hand and squeezes it. It feels like he's telling me it's over. All the pain either of us endured because of this man lying dead at our feet is over. Dom will go on and never think of this again. But I will. Even when I said I wouldn't, I knew the words were a lie. I wish I could fast-forward to the point in time when all of this is just a part of my life, but no longer hurts me.

I scoot closer to him as men begin to encircle Cristiano, lifting him and carrying him out of the room.

It's surreal, seeing his limp body. Where did his soul end up? Where is he now? He's no longer tethered to the vessel that was rotten to the core. Maybe he'll get a chance to do life over and do better next time. Or maybe the knife piercing his heart instantly shifted him to an alternate dimension where he got away with me.

But in this reality, in this version of life, he didn't get away with me. He didn't win. Dom won.

Dom looks down at me, then nods in the direction they're taking him before guiding me after them. I stare at the blood on the floor as we pass and absentmindedly walk with everyone else.

Cristiano's put in another glass box, similar to the one he was just in. Only this time it's nothing but glass, empty inside.

He's laid on the ground, and the door is sealed shut behind him.

He always wore a hat, and now he's not. I stared at that hair so many nights. Every strand of it is hair I've never touched. He's had enough haircuts by now that the strands I once grabbed while fighting him off would be long gone. Yet the hair looks the same. I know that hair.

His eyes are still wide open, pale enough to look see-through from this angle. I hate how light his eyes are.

Were.

And then there's fire. I stand there and watch as his corpse is burned beyond recognition. We hold hands until we're the only two people left in the room.

"Now what?" I ask, peeling my gaze from the past.

He tugs my arm, pulling me toward the door and draping his arm over my shoulder. "We're going on a honeymoon."